D1551512

Pinkerton Partners

BY

DAVE BROWN

To **Don Carter** and **George Estrada**,
Jim and my long-time friends and part of our "family."

PINKERTON PARTNERS

A Golden Feather Press book / November 2001

This is a work of fiction. The characters, incidents, and dialogues are products of the author's imagination and are not to be construed as real. Any resemblance to actual events or persons, living or dead, is entirely coincidental.

November 2001

Published by: Golden Feather Press
                      PO Box 209
                      Jefferson, CO 80456

PINKERTON PARTNERS copyright © 2001 by Dave Brown

Cover art copyright © 2001 by Judy M. Moya
Cover graphics copyright © by NZ Graphics

All rights reserved. No part of this book may be used or reproduced in any form or by any electronic or mechanical means, including photocopying, recording or by any information storage and retrieval system without the written permission of the Publisher.

First Edition

Library of Congress Number in progress

ISBN 0-9709273-0-4

Printed in the United States of America

www: goldenfeatherpress.com

AUTHOR'S NOTE

They had condoms in the late 1800s, but few used them. They should have. Syphilis, a ghastly killer during that time with no known cure, carried with it insanity and often a violent death.

AIDS is far from over today.

We have many ways to express love for one another. Please don't be careless. Being "blood" brothers may have been safe a hundred years ago, but unprotected sex in the 1800s was still risky. It is again.

So love, but be careful.

Guess I'm like Linus. I need *all* my gay brothers and sisters as a security blanket.

* * *

This book is long overdue. Sorry.

Last year, Jim and I and our two dogs moved to our cabin on the cliff above Chipmunk Rock and spent this year adding on to it amid emergency trips to Milwaukee.

While it may seem romantic to take a bath in a galvanized tub in the middle of the kitchen when it's 30 below zero outside, it's the pits. Plus, our butts froze to the outhouse seat. We needed an indoor bathroom...and more space. Jim and I not only gained space and an indoor bathroom, but also the greatest respect for every human who lived before we got so spoiled.

INTRODUCTION

Wiley scanned the dining room and the Men's Quarters of the riverboat, then rushed outside and continued weaving through the evening strollers on the deck...

"Strollers!" Dave Brown shouted to himself while writing. "Sounds like Wiley's struggling through a bunch of baby carriages! Maybe use...'fog-enchanted strollers.' No! Now the baby carriages glow and move around on their own! What about using 'evening walkers?' Right. Now the deck's clogged with senior citizens!"

Watching Dave sitting at the computer, Jake sighed. "Wiley, this here story'a ours ain't never gonna get told. Why don't Dave just say what you did?"

Wiley smiled and slid his hand over Jake's shoulders. "Dave's a writer. He's torn between perfection and what's real. And many words from the 1800s have different meanings in the second millennium."

Jake nudged Wiley. "Let's go whisper what really happened."

CHAPTER 1

The full-length batwing doors of the Silver Heels Bar in Alma, Colorado were shoved open by two big men who stepped into the room. They stamped snow off their boots, brushed each other's shoulders, and unwrapped themselves from fur-lined, elk skin dusters, scarves and gloves.

Behind the bar, Tubs eyed the men carefully. Strangers often came into the Silver Heels, even in December, and he always sized them up while they took off their coats. He grinned when he recognized the two ruggedly handsome men.

Wiley Deluce, the area's resident Pinkerton and one of the fastest gun-draws alive, looked fearsome with his short black hair and beard, muscles bulging under his rawhide shirt and a small crescent scar on his right cheek. Tantalizing stories drifting from the East told of Wiley, part Indian, using Iroquois torture when riled. Tubs doubted it as he watched Wiley hang his coat on a peg, then help his struggling partner slide his coat down his arms.

Tubs chuckled. Jake Brady's unruly, blond hair stuck out the sides of his hat, and his short, darker beard and rock-hard muscles made him look as formidable as Wiley. He knew Jake cussed at the drop of a hat but didn't have a mean bone in his body. But if anyone did manage to get Jake riled, he'd best leave town. Fast.

"Damn, Wiley," Jake shouted as Wiley pulled on his coat. "My gloves is turnin' backwards in there an' my hands won't go no further. I gotta put my coat back on."

"Hold your arms rigid, and I'll pull it up to your shoulders." Wiley yanked the duster until Jake's gloved hands poked out the sleeve ends.

After Jake removed his gloves and stuffed them into the pockets of his coat, Wiley helped him out of it and hung it beside his own. With hats left on, the six-foot, two-hundred-twenty pound blood brothers headed for the bar.

"You gents're shore a welcome sight fer a fat ol' bartender," Tubs said. He clunked down a bottle and two glasses in front of them. "Whatcha been up to? Ain't seen you gents goin' on two months."

"When it's cold and snowy, it's too far to come clear up to Alma." Wiley poured Jake's drink, then his own. "We've been staying close to home getting ready for a long winter."

Jake grinned at Tubs. "We been choppin' wood an' stuff. Tomorrow we're goin' huntin'." He chugged his drink, set the empty glass on the bar and glanced around the room. "We come up the hill to see Bill an' them. They around?"

Tubs turned to his Seth Thomas balloon clock sitting on the ornately carved mahogany back-bar amid bottles of whiskey and rows of glasses. "You gotcha ten minutes there 'bouts to wait. Ever' Saturday night them four waddle in 'bout six after stuffin' theirselves in the Regal Cafe. They'll look jist like me if they don't watch it."

Tubs grinned, patted his rotund body, then headed for the end of the bar to serve a man who had come in behind Jake and Wiley. Hunched over the bar, the man had left on his leather duster and hat, brim pulled low. He'd tracked snow across the scarred wood floor.

Wiley scanned the room, glad the stove burned cherry-red hot. It must only be ten degrees outside...about the same temperature of last May when he and Jake had met and became blood brothers while sitting next to that stove. During the fight later that week, he'd nearly caused the stove to be knocked over and had gotten his face coated with soot from its dislodged chimney. Thoughts of Billingsly, the foppish lawyer, came to mind, and Winder, Billingsly's hired gun. They had killed Belinda Castille's father and his partner. Wiley shuddered. That murder is why he'd been sent here from Philadelphia, and he'd bungled it. Thank God he'd met Jake, the love of his life. So what about being a Pinkerton. Maybe he'd quit and live quietly with Jake herding cattle.

He shifted his left leg to the floor rail and a twinge of pain shot through it. Winder had shot him in the leg and he'd woken up later in another Time, far into the future. Wiley glanced at Jake's open shirt and sighed when he saw the rawhide bag hanging around his neck. The spirit of Chief Eagle Rising had given Jake that bag and a golden feather and had sent them to nineteen-ninety-three. Wiley knew he'd been saved from bleeding to death, and the transport to the future had kept both of them from being murdered by Winder.

Wiley shuddered when he thought of going to that future Time. Things were so different there, and so many gadgets. And the people seemed so dissipated. He sighed. Jim and Dave, gay partners as they called themselves, had befriended Jake and him and even saved them from criminals. When his leg had healed, they had brought Jim and Dave and a punk named Hank back to eighteen-eighty-six. It was after that, trying to escape being captured, Billingsly had shot Winder in the back, then was shot himself by Sheriff Cline as he galloped down the street. Billingsly's body had been dragged out of town by his horse...not to be seen again.

Later, Dave and Jim had been transported back to their Time, but Hank had decided to stay in Kentucky with Zeke and his mother.

Betty! Wiley cringed when he thought of her. Working with her at the Pinkerton agency in Philadelphia, Betty had become obsessed with him. She'd even traveled to Alma to try and get him to marry her. His lies to Jake about who he really was, then Betty's appearance, had caused Jake to leave and go back to his farm in Kentucky. Then Jake had been captured by the Harrises. Wiley shivered when he recalled how distraught he'd been without Jake at his side. He *never* wanted to see Betty Gringold again, and he would never again lie to Jake.

"You okay, Wiley?" Jake asked, seeing Wiley staring into space.

"Er, I'm fine. I was thinking about the first time I met you in here. It was almost as cold outside as today."

Jake snickered, then remembered the terrifying days that had preceded his meeting Wiley. Seth Harris, his neighbor in Kentucky, and four of his sons had chased him clear up here after falsely accusing him of getting Sara Jean pregnant. Seth, Aaron, Abe, Clem and Zeke had captured him three times, twice even after he'd met Wiley. He'd managed to escape, but not before many deaths. Jake shuddered, then thanked Jesus that Zeke and Hank, the man from Dave and Jim's Time, had fallen in love. Jake sighed, glad Zeke wasn't jealous of Wiley anymore. He wondered if Hank had learned to plant crops.

Jake noticed Wiley scanning the room. He longed to be a Pinkerton like Wiley. Watching Wiley, Jake knew he'd never be as good as Wiley. His father had always called him dummer'n hog shit. Maybe he was? Jake shrugged. He couldn't even read. But even if he wasn't a good Pinkerton, he'd always protect Wiley.

Wiley watched miners at a table suddenly laugh and hoot as one tried to pull his stuck finger out of the neck of his beer bottle. Glaring at his companions, the man smashed the bottle on the floor. Foamy beer and glass splattered everywhere, but he'd freed his finger.

"Don't walk in that!" Tubs yelled, hurrying from behind the bar with a small broom and dustpan. "Don't you take no mind to that, sonny. An' don't bother helpin'. I do this least once a day."

Wiley turned to Jake. "Tubs said the same thing to us the night we became blood brothers."

Jake snickered and poured himself another shot. "Hell, an' that was a near full bottle'a whiskey I knocked off the table. I was laughin' at the story'a your pants fallin' down."

They laughed.

Jake chugged his drink, then glanced around. He saw two poker games in progress in the next room, but the piano player was nowhere to be seen. He looked at three cattlemen near the middle of the bar discussing business and, beyond them, to the man wearing the leather duster.

The man turned and stared at Jake. His bulldog jowls had a growth of stubble, and his brown stringy hair hung below his flat-crowned, leather hat and curled over his collar. Partly shaded by the lowered brim, his eyes seemed cruel and hateful.

Jake shuddered, spun to face the mirror behind the bar, lightly nudged Wiley's arm and whispered, "Wiley, that man at the other end gives me the willies."

Without moving his head, Wiley peered into the large back-bar mirror. He nudged Jake back. "That's Rice Haden."

"Damn," Jake whispered under his breath. "Is he that killer?"

"He is." Wiley looked at Jake. "How did you know?"

Jake sneaked another look into the mirror. "Hell, he come through Wilmore one time an' killed Ol' Man Spencer just cuz he wouldn't trade him a horse."

Looking back into the mirror, Wiley noticed Rice's eyes widen. The man recognized him! Wiley remembered the night in Philadelphia when, during a struggle, he'd killed Cade Bently after Cade had jammed the pipe into his face which had caused the crescent scar on his right cheek. He'd seen Rice Haden escape out the side door of Broad Street Station.

"Jake, Rice just recognized me, and he might draw on me right here in the bar." Wiley shifted his gunbelt slightly to place the holster in a precise spot on his left thigh. He wished he'd worn his right-hand holster since his draw was faster with that hand. Not expecting trouble and needing to practice his left draw, which he'd done during their ride to Alma, he'd taken the chance and worn it. If Rice braced him, would he be fast enough?

"Jake, I want you to wander the room," Wiley whispered. "Keep behind Rice. If he shoots me, knock him out and get Sheriff Cline."

"Shoots you? Wiley, I won't let..."

"Jake, do what I said! I don't want you in the line of fire. And don't let him get away if he's a faster draw than I am."

"But, Wiley..."

"Jake, wander the room! *Now!*"

As Jake left the bar, Rice Haden filled his glass, grabbed it and turned toward Wiley.

One of the cattlemen sensed something happening and motioned to the others. The group hurried into the next room to watch. A miner near the stove jumped to his feet, whispered to his companions and vaguely nodded toward Rice Haden. He made the sign of the cross and blew it toward Wiley, grabbed his coat and rushed out the door.

Holding his drink, Rice started down the bar and stopped three feet from Wiley. He downed the whiskey, slid the glass onto the bar, then raised the brim of his hat a few inches.

Still leaning against the bar, Wiley looked into Rice's cruel eyes. The man outweighed him by twenty pounds, and his muscles bulged out his duster. Wiley had heard Rice was one of the fastest draws that breathed, and being an arm's length away would mean certain death to both of them if there was any gun play. What would happen to Jake if he got killed? God, he *couldn't* get killed, for Jake's sake if nothing else. He asked the spirit of his Iroquois grandfather for courage, then steeled himself.

"Ain't you William Deluce, the gunfighter?" Rice growled. He swept back his duster and held his right hand above the butt of his gun.

Wiley moved away from the bar and faced him. "I'm William Deluce, but I'm not a gunfighter. I'm a Pinkerton."

Jake silently moved behind Rice, drew his gun and pointed it at the outlaw's back.

Patrons gasped.

"Damn if you ain't a gunfighter, Deluce!" Rice shouted. "You killed Cade. He was my pard. Hidin' b'hind that Pinkerton crap makes you yellow. I'm gonna kill me a yellow-bellied, William Deluce *gunfighter*!"

Rice grabbed for his gun.

Rice froze. Wiley's Navy Colt already pointed at his forehead. Wiley cocked it.

"There's a vast difference between a fast-draw and a gunfighter, Rice." Wiley's eyes turned lethal. "If I *were* a gunfighter, you'd be *dead* right now."

Rice gasped and let his half-drawn pistol drop into his holster. He turned toward the bar, grabbed Jake and Wiley's bottle and slugged down a swallow. He clunked the bottle on the bar, glared at Wiley still pointing his gun at him, then turned and headed toward the door.

Wiley swung his Colt toward Rice's back. "Stop right there, Rice. You're under arrest. You're not going anywhere until Sheriff Cline gets here. Put your hands on the top of your head. I might not be a gunfighter, but I will shoot you if you take one more step toward that door."

Rice stopped and spun around. "You ain't got nothin' on me. You out drew me is all."

"You started it!" Jake yelled. "You said you was gonna kill Wiley!"

"That's called attempted murder," Wiley said calmly. His countenance darkened. "I *said*, put your hands on your head!"

Rice glared at Wiley, slowly raised his hands and rested them on the top of his hat.

Keeping his Colt leveled at the outlaw, Wiley slipped a rawhide cord from his pocket. "Jake, get his gun and cover him."

Jake grinned, slid Rice's pistol out of its holster, then shoved the barrel of his own gun into Rice's crotch and cocked it. "You move an' you're gonna be talkin' like a woman."

Holstering his gun, Wiley walked to Rice, yanked the outlaw's arms behind his back and tied his hands Iroquois fashion. The strap would have to be cut to free him, and the more Rice struggled, the tighter the strap would become.

"Someone get Sheriff Cline," Wiley said to the staring patrons.

"Sneed already went to get the sheriff," one of the miners yelled. "Mighty impressive left-handed draw, Wiley," he added.

The right batwing door slammed against the wall as Sheriff Cline burst into the bar. Bundled in a sheepskin coat and pulled-down leather hat, he shoved through a group of onlookers standing just inside and walked over to Wiley. "Who you got there, Wiley?"

"Rice Hayden. Do you have anything on him?"

"I've got three different posters and five wires about him. As I remember, you just earned about five thousand in reward money."

The sheriff grabbed Rice by the arm, yanked him past the four men still standing near the door and shoved him outside.

Everyone in the room clapped and cheered Wiley.

Wiley smiled. He grabbed Jake by the arm. "Jake, I think that may have been the fastest left-handed draw I've ever made. And I owe it to you."

"Me? What'd I do?"

"I couldn't let Rice kill me. You'd be alone."

Bill Chasteen, the town hostler and part of the group Sheriff Cline had shoved through when he'd entered and left the building, started toward the bar. When Bill reached the blood brothers, he grabbed Wiley's arm. "You sure did prove you was a dang good Pinkerton just then by not killin' that no-good scum." Bill grinned. "Even if you *are* a gunfighter."

Wiley raised an eyebrow at Bill. "You can call me a gunfighter. I'll call you *old*."

Bill laughed. "It's good to see you, Wiley." The two men grabbed each other in a brief hug.

Jake and Wiley gave pats on the back to Bill and also to Harry Winslow, Alma's bath-giver and masseur. Matt Conway and Frank

Waters, miners and also partners, crowded toward the blood brothers to exchange half-hugs.

"That was quite a show, Wiley," Matt said. "And with your left hand!" When the tall, handsome and raw-boned man smiled, the slight cleft in his chin disappeared. He still wore his brown hair tied back in a short tail. "We don't see the two of you for months, then you bluster in with the snow and stir up the town." Matt clasped Wiley's shoulder and shook it.

Wiley shrugged. "Sometimes it can't be helped."

Frank waved at Tubs. "Matt an' me want to buy Jake an' Wiley a drink." Shorter than the rest of the men in the group, Frank had the largest muscles. With straight black hair, green eyes and a handsome face, always with an impish countenance, he presented an imposing figure. Noticing one of the miners eyeballing his body, Frank winked at the man and grinned, then raised his eyebrows to Matt.

"I never want to be *your* enemy, Wiley," Harry quipped. He looked Jake up and down and sighed. "Yours either."

Wiley smiled at Harry, then at Bill. The two men looked like brothers. Both in their forties, Harry was a bit taller and leaner than Bill and balding in front rather than the back. Wiley agreed with Jake that they looked fatherly and felt Bill's blunt toughness fit perfectly with Harry's wit.

"You and Bill partners yet?" Jake asked Harry.

"Dang!" Bill yelled. "We ain't seen you gents fer two months an' you hafta go an' bring *that* up?"

Harry glanced at the ceiling and sighed. "We haven't gotten that far, Jake. Some days I think Bill has stopped feeling sorry for himself because of his former partner's death, then he starts all--"

"Well, dang it, I miss Chuck!" Bill yelled. "An' how'd you like it if you saw *your* partner get his neck broke in front'a you?"

Harry folded his arms. "That was five years ago."

"We was partners fer *eleven*!"

"So? Are you going to mope around for another *six*?"

"You outta become blood brothers like Wiley'n me," Jake cut in. "Then you'd be partners even if you didn't want to."

Even the eavesdropping miners laughed.

Jake grabbed the sleeve of Frank's billowy green shirt with a V-neck that failed to mask his huge muscles. He remembered Frank mentioning he was half-Indian from Arizona, but couldn't remember the name of the tribe. He thought it had sounded something like "Yaki."

"Why're you wearin' a shirt, Frank?" Jake asked. "Thought you never got cold."

Frank chuckled. "This is Matt's. Figured it was a mite chilly for just a vest."

The batwing doors banged open and Sheriff Cline stomped back into the bar. He stamped the snow off his feet, then approached the group. His lean, handsome face and dark, handlebar moustache made him look as tough and dangerous as he actually was.

Sheriff Cline nodded to everyone, then singled out Wiley. "You okay?"

"I'm fine, Sheriff."

Jake rested his hand on Wiley's shoulder. "Wiley drew his gun so fast, I didn't even see him do it. An' with his left hand, too."

Not taking his eyes off Wiley's, Sheriff Cline said, "Rice Hayden is behind bars. I'll contact Judge Parker in the morning. With all the charges against him, he might hang." Cline shrugged. "It will take about two weeks to round up your reward money."

"Don't put it in the Alma bank," Matt said. "At least not until the examiners from Denver get through checking out Crain. They've been here a week, and Crain looks more worried every day."

"What're we gonna do with all that money, Wiley?" Jake asked.

Wiley grinned. "Who knows? Maybe we can buy a few hundred acres from Belinda and Jimmy near our cabin and raise some of our own cows like we've talked about." He looked at Sheriff Cline. "Have you found Billingsly's body?"

"Not a trace," Cline said. "Bears or coyotes have taken care of it by now. His horse showed up back at Colonel Bass's ranch where he'd bought it. Bass wasn't one bit pleased. Said it's so ugly he might feed it to his dogs."

After the sheriff left the bar, the blood brothers spent two hours with their friends over a bottle of Tubs' best whiskey, then headed for the Regal Cafe and home to their cabin, built snug against a rock cliff, before the temperature plunged below zero.

CHAPTER 2

A raven landed on the top of a pine high on the southern slope of Bristlecone Peak and watched two riders far below. As Jake and Wiley dismounted and tied their horses to a leafless aspen, the raven swooped down and soared over the men carrying rifles. As the men rounded a large snow bank and crept into an aspen thicket, the bird alit and watched them stop at a rock outcropping that jutted twenty feet into the air, providing a view of the entire area. He often sat up there himself.

"Jake, I'm going to climb these rocks and look around," Wiley said softly. "Keep me in sight. I'll signal if I see any game."

The easy climb up the pinkish granite rocks made Wiley wonder if a giant had stacked them in a huge cairn. A giant? Impossible. But was it? He and Jake had traveled from eighteen eighty-six to nineteen ninety-three and back again.

When Wiley neared the top of the pinnacle, he stopped and removed his hat, then slowly studied the surroundings. Behind him to the north, Bristlecone Peak pointed its rocky summit to the sky far above his own elevated position. He cautiously climbed to the top of the rocks and peered over the top. The aspen-dotted land to the south sloped down between two pine-forested hills to a treeless plain a mile away. Thirty miles distant, he could see shark fin-shaped Black Mountain. Miles farther, the snow-covered, pyramid-top of Crestone Peak poked the turquoise sky.

Wiley noticed movement below.

He spotted a five-point buck elk cautiously picking its way up the slope toward the aspen grove where Jake stood. Farther down the hill, three elk cows grazed in a clearing. He'd often seen elk in this draw and was glad the southwestern breeze concealed his scent.

Wiley slowly ducked behind the top of the rock, caught Jake's eye, put his hands to his head and made antlers with spread-out fingers, then pointed out the direction the bull elk might come.

Jake grinned, crouched behind a thicket of leafless current bushes and raised his rifle.

Wiley heard the elk carefully stepping closer. Moments later, Jake's rifle blast echoed four times, the fifth barely audible and miles away.

"Got 'im, Wiley!" Jake yelled. "Right through the ol' noggin'!"

The blood brothers avoided the deepest snow as they rode back to their cabin, dragging the gutted elk behind Mac on a travois of sturdy spruce poles and cowhide.

Riding next to Jake, out of the corner of his eye, Wiley watched his partner grin in silence, pleased with himself for shooting the elk, and he thought back to yesterday when they'd stopped at the Fairplay telegraph office on their way to Alma. There had been a telegram from Mike McGelvy, the head of the Pinkerton agency. Wiley had read it out loud to Jake.

"'Wiley. Surprised you have a partner. Jake must train in Philadelphia. Wire his arrival time. Mike.'"

Wiley folded the telegram, slipped it into his pocket, and remained silent until Jake figured out what it said.

After a few moments of frowning, Jake shouted, "Damn! Mike said I gotta go to Phil'delphia!"

"We would both go. Training lasts three months."

"Hell! We can't be gone three months! Miss Castille...er, damn, can't never remember! I mean, Mrs. Ratchett an' Jimmy need us here." Jake eyed Wiley crossly. "Thought *you* was gonna train me? You're the best Pinkerton there ever was!"

Wiley expected Jake's reaction to spending three months in Philadelphia, but his last statement took him by surprise. He remembered mentioning he'd train Jake himself since he'd learned so much from his Grandpa Gray Feather and Bristol Campion at Boston University, but Jake hadn't brought it up recently.

Wiley beckoned Benton Riley.

"What can I help you with, Wiley?" The portly telegraph operator adjusted his green visor to hide a grin as he glanced at Jake's pouty face.

"I need to send a response wire."

Benton shoved a pen and a bottle of ink toward Wiley. "Fill out that form, and I'll send it right away."

Absolute silence took command of the office until Wiley finished writing. He held up the paper and read it to Jake. "Mike. I will train Jake here. He already knows more than most. Will be a formidable agent. Wiley."

Wiley looked up from the paper at Jake. "How does that sound?"

Jake's face lit up. "You're really gonna train me? Damn!" He grinned at Benton. "I'm gonna be the best Pinkerton there ever was with Wiley trainin' me!" His face turned contrite. "'Course, I won't never be as good as you, Wiley."

"Don't be too sure."

Benton sighed and shook his head. "I'd hate to be a crook with you two after me. I'd probably give myself up to the nearest lawman just so I wouldn't have to meet up with a pair like you."

Wiley's thoughts of yesterday's happenings vanished when Jake glanced back at the elk on the travois and grinned even broader. "This here's the first elk I ever shot, Wiley, an' the meat'll feed us for a month. We can share it with Soaring Raven, an' she might make us somethin' outta the hide."

"We should make jerky out of most of it. I'll show you how. We can use the currents we dried to make a batch of pemmican."

"What the hell's peckamin?"

"Pem-mi-can. They're small cakes made from jerky, fat and currants. They last a long time and are nourishing for long trips or wintering over." Wiley heard his own words and thanked the Great White Father that his grandfather, an Iroquois brave, had taught him how to survive anywhere, to be self confident and to use a rifle. Raoul, his French-soldier father, had taught him to use a pistol. He wondered what he would be like now if he'd had a hateful father like Jake's.

When the partners arrived at their cabin, they skinned the elk and spent the rest of the day slicing the meat into thin strips which they placed in the sun on aspen-limb drying racks. Before daylight faded,

Jake hoisted the covered racks and the cloth-wrapped rib sections and hind quarters between two tall trees out of reach from coyotes, bears and occasional cougars.

With a hatchet, Wiley cracked the larger leg bones of the elk and later roasted them in the fire as their dinner steaks sizzled.

At the table, Wiley shoved two bones toward Jake. "Scoop out the marrow and eat it."

"What for?"

"Bone marrow is nourishing. You're going to start training tomorrow, and I want you in top shape."

Jake grabbed a bone, twisted it until it splintered and scooped out the marrow with his fingers. He grinned at Wiley. "We gonna practice shootin'?"

"Being a Pinkerton is not only about shooting. You have to learn other types of self-defense and survival. Plus, there are things you need to know about criminals, like what they're most apt to do in a tight situation. When I'm through, you'll even think like a criminal."

Licking his fingers, Jake frowned. "I ain't gonna do no criminal thinkin'!"

Wiley half-smiled. "You have to. Once you can think like a criminal, you'll know how to outsmart him."

After cleaning their few dishes, the partners took separate trips to the outhouse. Wiley added a few dry aspen logs to the rock-shelf fireplace, then stretched and began removing his clothes.

Jake returned from the outhouse, slid the door bolt to keep out bears and walked over to Wiley just as he'd unbuttoned his long johns halfway down. Jake shoved his hands inside Wiley's underwear and over his powerful, hairy chest. He slid his hands to Wiley's shoulders, then down his back, stripping Wiley's long johns from his upper body. At the same time, Jake pinned Wiley's arms to his side, pulled him close and kissed him.

Wiley struggled to free his arms so he could slide them around Jake, but Jake held him too tight.

"Jake, I can't move my arms. I want to hold you, also."

"I know, Wiley," Jake said breathlessly as he slid his face against Wiley's chest, then buried his nose in the crook of Wiley's neck. He continued holding Wiley's arms at his side with an iron grip.

"Jake, this is unfair. I can't move."

"I wanna hold you like this for a spell." Jake pressed his cheek against Wiley's. "My whole life I been called a damn sissy by Pa an' dummer'n-hog-shit Jake by him an' ever'body else. I wanna hold you strong-like." Jake raised his head and looked into Wiley's eyes. "I wanna feel I'm a man like you, Wiley."

Wiley squint-eyed a challenge. He tried as hard as he could to get out of Jake's grasp, astonished at Jake's strength. He finally relaxed his body and lowered his face to Jake's shoulder. "I'm truly in your power, Jake. You have subdued me and you can hold me like this all night if you want." He raised his head. "But I'll tell you something you need to hear. Not only are you a powerful man to pin me, but you've retained the innocence of your boyhood. Not many can say that. It's another reason I love you."

Jake released Wiley and lowered his head. "You let me win, Wiley. Maybe someday I'll be as good an' strong as you."

Wiley shuddered from a surge of loathing for Jake's father who'd caused such feelings of insecurity and worthlessness in Jake. He forced himself to dismiss thoughts of the Iroquois torture he would have inflicted on Jake's father if he'd ever met the man.

"Jake, I didn't let you win. After tonight, don't *ever* say you aren't a man. As strong as I am, I could *not* break your hold." Wiley raised Jake's bowed head and smiled at him. "Your strength truly astounded me, and there has never been a more perfect match between blood brothers than we are." He kissed Jake's flickering grin.

Wiley stripped off his underwear. Naked, he helped Jake undress, then blew out the lamp. They slid into the featherbed and into each other's arms.

Shadows in the room danced the rhythm of the lazy fire as the two men pressed into each other.

Wiley felt Jake's hard cock against his own as they kissed. Nothing on earth smelled better than his and Jake's sweaty bodies together. His head spun. How beautiful they were as partners and blood brothers. Tingles caressed his cock when he thought of Jake's blood mingling with his own. He kissed Jake deeper and their teeth met. The tingles in his cock intensified, and he drove his hips into Jake.

So turned on by the feel of Wiley's body, Jake almost spunked when Wiley kissed him harder. Wiley, the most handsome and strongest man he'd ever known held him and kissed him. Wiley was the perfect gift from Jesus, and he loved smelling Wiley and the way his hairy body tickled him all over. Jake felt Wiley shoving his dick against his own. His body trembled as he shot with Wiley, digging his fingers into Wiley's back.

The two men lay in an embrace long after they had slowed their breathing, then fell asleep amid flickers of golden light.

CHAPTER 3

Single gunshots spaced minutes apart echoed in Horseshoe Canyon. A loud curse and four rapid-fire blasts startled a curious jay in a far-off tree. The bird flew away as bullets whined among the rocks.

"Damn!" Jake yelled. "I can't hit nothin'! I ain't *never* gonna be no Pinkerton!"

Wiley grabbed Jake's wrist and pointed the barrel of Jake's double-action Colt at the ground. He sighed when Jake shoved the gun into his holster.

"Jake, you can't expect to hit that small rock from so far away on the first few tries. It takes practice."

"Hell, I been doin' this for *two hours* an' still can't hit that damn rock!"

Wiley gently pulled Jake close. "Calm down. I've practiced my draw and accuracy for ten years. It's taken that long to perfect it. And I told you, using a pistol is different than a rifle. You don't aim a pistol, you point it."

Wiley encompassed Jake with his strong arms and kissed him. "I let you practice shooting like you asked, and you have to do it every day. But being a Pinkerton also means staying alive. Let's go home. I want to show you a different type of training."

* * *

The two men dismounted at their corral, brushed and fed both horses, then trudged up the hill to their cabin. They had ridden home and taken care of the horses in total silence. Jake still pouted.

As they approached the cabin, Wiley looked straight ahead and said, "Survival is the next lesson."

"Hell, I'll most likely get hit by damn lightnin'."

"There's no lightning in winter."

Out of the corner of his eye, Wiley saw Jake's pout deepen into a frown. He bit his lower lip to keep from smiling.

Jake's foot snagged a snow-hidden aspen branch and lurched forward. He kicked the branch and growled, "I'm so dumb I can't even walk right!"

Wiley stopped, grabbed Jake's arm and jerked him toward himself. "Jake, your father is *dead*! I don't want you keeping him alive by thinking like he did!" He drew Jake closer. "Your father is the only one who ever called you dumb...except *you*." He shook Jake once. "I want you to stop it. Neither of us like your father. Let's forget about him. And that means forgetting about you saying you're dumber than hog shit!"

Jake pulled away. "Hell, I can't even read nothin'."

"I'll teach you to read."

Jake folded his arms and dug a hole in a patch of snow with the toe of his boot, then looked Wiley in the eye. "Promise you won't laugh at me when I'm messin' up while you're teachin' me to read?"

"Jake, I...I can't promise I won't laugh at something you say." Wiley shrugged. "I'm trying not to lie anymore."

Jake's face brightened. "It's okay, Wiley. *You* can laugh at somethin' I say that's dummer'n hog shit."

* * *

"What we gonna be doin' now, Wiley?"

"Survive in the woods."

After a bite to eat, they dressed warmly in layers of clothes, packed supplies in the saddlebags and secured their bedrolls. Carrying canteens of water and rifles, they headed on foot toward Bristlecone Peak, a quarter mile north.

They hiked around the west side of the peak. On their right, they passed the saddle between the double peaks of the mountain. As they climbed the southern slope of an adjoining hill, Wiley stopped and surveyed the area, then headed for a thick stand of ponderosa pine clustered in front of a jumble of large pinnacle-shaped rocks.

Jake hurried after him. "Wiley, I been' wonderin' what survivin' means to a Pinkerton."

Wiley continued walking toward the stand of ponderosa. "Survival has everything to do with being a Pinkerton. Here in Colorado, many men we'll be tracking will know these mountains. We need to know how to keep from starving and freezing to death between towns."

Jake snickered. "Guess you're right. It'd take a big travois an' team'a horses to haul our cabin with us."

Wiley laughed. "It wouldn't do any good if we could. One wall of our cabin is the cliff. It would be missing that wall."

They laughed.

Reaching the trees, Wiley lowered his saddlebags to the ground, propped his rifle against a foot-thick trunk, folded his arms and surveyed the area. The ponderosa and a few wizened spruce grew in a ragged circle in front of pinkish spires of granite. He noticed a gap between two of the rock pillars. Approaching it, Wiley saw the gap was wide enough for a man to squeeze through, which he did with difficulty. Three feet long, the slot opened into a room-sized area completely surrounded by a high wall of crumbling granite spires.

After inching back through the narrow passageway, Wiley announced, "We camp here."

Wide-eyed, Jake glanced around. "Here? Hell, we ain't even gone no-place yet."

"Jake, this is training. We don't have to go far. We can learn to survive in our own area." He pointed to the gap in the rocks. "That room inside is the perfect place to camp." He grabbed a bottle-brush-shaped tuft of needles at the end of a ponderosa branch. "We can make a soft bed out of these branches on the floor of that rock room. If we lay dead aspen logs across the tops of the rocks to make a roof, we'll be almost as snug as we would be at home."

Jake frowned. "Thought we was out here survivin'. Ain't survivin' sleepin' on the ground out in the open an' tryin' to stay warm?"

Wiley pulled the hatchet from his belt. "You can do that if you want. Grandpa Gray Feather taught me to use the things nature provides for the best means of shelter and warmth on a cold night. Caves, rock overhangs, pine trees with their branches touching the ground like a tent make the perfect shelter. Survival means using what's available to stay as warm as you can, especially in winter." He gestured toward the gap in the rocks. "That's a perfect place to camp." He swept his arm at the surrounding forested hills and the sloping valley to the south. "It's beautiful here. If I were traveling cross-country, I'd stay here for several weeks, maybe even a month, provided I could find water and game nearby."

After carefully scraping away the loose rock and padding the floor of the room with pine needles, they made a roof over the top with aspen logs. When Wiley left to gather firewood, Jake shoved away branches at the back of the room and used a rock to scrape a hollow into the crumbly granite floor.

Entering the shelter with a load of wood, Wiley watched Jake for a minute. "What are you doing?"

"Makin' a place for the fire."

"Jake, the fire goes just inside the passageway."

"How am I gonna get out to pee?"

"It'll be a small fire. You'll be able to get by it. The fire's placed there to keep animals out. And the room won't fill up with smoke. It will go out the gap."

"Damn, how d'you know all this stuff, Wiley?"

Wiley grinned. "Grandpa Gray Feather was an Indian...er, Native American." He liked that title from the future. It gave his grandfather's people a distinction different than someone from India. And a distinction of being the first Americans. He scowled. The white race seemed too embedded in conceit, for some unknown reason, to understand the greatness of Native American people.

Jake got to his feet and struggled through the narrow gap. "I gotta pee an' look around some."

Wiley watched Jake squeeze his muscular body through the passageway. It was only the middle of December, but he wished for summer. Riding naked on a horse with Jake was the most pleasurable experience he'd ever known. He especially loved riding behind Jake so he could slide his hands over Jake's hard packed, hairless body and watch the wind caress his collar-length, blond hair.

It was fully dark when Jake returned. Wiley had a small fire going near the inside entrance, and Jake leaped over it, cursing.

"I found us a spring," Jake said proudly as he dropped to his knees next to Wiley and watched him stir potatoes in the skillet with a forked stick. "While I was peein', I saw some deer an' watched 'em drinkin'. When they left, I found the spring. It's a hunnert yards over."

"Good work, Jake. You get an A for this lesson."

They both heard it. A rustling outside, and labored breathing.

Wiley leaped to his feet, grabbed his Winchester and pointed it into the slot between the rocks. Still on his knees, Jake drew his Colt pistol.

They heard a roar. Jake peered into the slot and saw a bear stick its head into the ragged corridor. The animal's body was too broad to enter, and it growled. The bear rose to its hind legs and began clawing its way through.

With the side of his boot, Wiley moved the skillet, then shoved the small fire into the passageway and tossed in a few twigs he'd piled in a neat stack. The dry sticks caught instantly and began popping fiery sparks.

Glowing missiles from the twigs flew in every direction. The bear roared, then backed out of the entrance as a spark singed the fur on his shoulder. Jake forgot about the bear, jumped to his feet and began stomping the glowing-red dots before they caught their pine needle mattress on fire.

Hearing the bear lumber down the slope, Wiley pulled the twigs away from the fire and snuffed them with his boot.

"Damn, Wiley," Jake said as he stomped on a stubborn ember. "What kinda sticks *are* those?"

"Spruce. Tomorrow I'll show you what the trees look like. For sparks in a fire to scare away animals, collect the twigs from the trees with the smallest and sharpest needles. The harder it is to break off the dead twigs, the more they pop in a fire."

"Hell, Wiley, is that why you always go through the kindlin' I bring in at the cabin an' pull out somma them twigs?"

"Yes. I should have told you why I was doing it. We should only burn aspen in the cabin since I've found it pops the least. I pull out the spruce kindling so they don't send sparks into the cabin and burn it down."

Wiley placed the skillet back on the fire and squatted in front of it. "When I was little, my folks would make a big fire on Independence

Day. We would throw in small spruce branches and cheer when they popped loudly." Wiley grinned as he stirred the potatoes. "It was my job to put out the sparks in the clearing. It kept me busy. Grandpa would always help." He looked at Jake. "He would dance and sing in Iroquois at the same time." Wiley's eyes teared and he pretended to inspect the potatoes. "I miss him."

After Wiley finished cooking their meal of elk steaks, potatoes and onions, they ate ravenously.

* * *

Snuggled together in their bedroll, Jake woke up in the middle of the night.

"Damn, Wiley. Let's don't put no more wood on the fire. It's hotter'n hell in here."

"Whatever you say, Jake." Wiley raised up and adjusted the end of a branch so it didn't poke him in the butt.

They nestled closer and went back to sleep.

* * *

Heavy breathing woke Wiley. He heard a scraping sound and listened intently.

More scraping...near the passageway.

Unable to see anything, Wiley felt for Jake. Jake was gone!

Wiley raised up on his elbow. "Jake?"

"Hell, Wiley. I can't get this damn fire goin'. I ain't never been so cold my whole life."

* * *

The morning sun brought little warmth. At Jake's insistence, the partners gathered up their bedroll and saddlebags and headed back to their cabin.

When they arrived, Wiley quickly built a fire on the rock shelf. He knew something was bothering Jake from his silence on the trek home.

"What's wrong, Jake? You haven't said two words all morning."

"I don't like survivin'. We had to sleep with our clothes on, an' I couldn't feel you naked next to me."

Wiley slid his arms around Jake. "Let's remedy that right now."

While Wiley stoked the fire, Jake stripped naked and dived into the feather bed. Wiley quickly undressed and chuckled as he watched Jake thrash his arms and legs to warm the covers. He slid into bed and snuggled next to Jake's warm body.

They kissed.

"What we gonna be doin'?"

"First, I want you next to me." Wiley grinned. "After that, we may not have time to think of anything. Just your body touching mine is all I ever need."

Jake snickered. "Me too, Wiley."

CHAPTER 4

As the blood brothers rode up to the gate of the Castille Ranch house, Wiley glanced at Jake and smiled. Knowing Jake could hardly wait to show Soaring Raven the hind quarters of the bull elk he'd shot two days ago, he'd declined to tell Jake the meat of an elk cow was much more tender. But no one would care. It was Jake's first elk. If Jake didn't notice while eating it, Jimmy or Soaring Raven would give him a subtle hint.

After dismounting, Wiley trudged through ankle-deep, granular snow and tied Buddy to the rail outside the fence. He removed his gloves, draped them over the snow-covered tie-bar, then cupped his hands and blew into them. Buddy nuzzled his back and Wiley turned to the horse, closed his hands over Buddy's ears and held them, knowing his horse loved it. If they stayed for dinner, he'd take both horses to the barn and blanket them.

"Jake, do you need help with the meat?" Wiley asked as he held Buddy's ears.

Already dismounted and busy removing the hind quarters he'd secured behind Mac's saddle, Jake grinned at Wiley as he tossed the end of a rope over the bundle. "I killed it, Wiley. I gotta carry it my ownself."

Wiley chuckled. He let go of Buddy's ears and stroked the horse's neck, grabbed his gloves and pulled them on. As he watched Jake untie the frozen bundle that resembled cement-filled pantaloons, he noticed Jake's blond hair, sticking out beneath his hat, glistened in the sunlight that tinged his beard reddish. Jake's blue eyes danced with delight.

Wiley pulled off his leather hat, raked his short, black hair with gloved fingers, then repositioned it and tugged at the front brim. "I think you're right. You should carry it yourself. I'll open the gate."

Jake hefted the frozen hind quarters off the thick blanket covering Mac's haunches. As he maneuvered the bundle past the horses and through the gate, Jake said, "Damn, Wiley, that elk had him a big butt. This here meat must weigh two-hunnert pounds."

Wiley closed the gate and followed Jake toward the back of the house. "It was a good idea of yours to tie the meat outside and let it freeze. The temperature must have gotten well below zero the last two nights. Soaring Raven won't have to use it until it thaws."

Struggling with the frosty, ungainly bundle, Jake stopped and spun toward Wiley. "I never thought'a that. All the way here, I was hopin' Soaring Raven'd cook us some meat from this here elk. Tonight." He frowned and kicked a pile of snow. The bulky, iced-over bundle slipped from his grasp and hit the ground with a muffled thud.

"Damn!" Jake kicked it.

Wiley hefted the frozen carcass, half-legs up, and placed it into Jake's arms. After Jake had a firm grasp, Wiley dusted off the snow. "We'll be here again. We can ask Soaring Raven to let us know when the meat is thawed enough to slice."

Jake frowned. "Hell, I know that. I wanted to eat somma my own meat that Soaring Raven cooked, *today*."

When Wiley reached the kitchen door, he climbed the two steps, cracked the door open and backed away to give Jake more room.

"Jake, I think the steaks we cooked last night in our camp were just as good as hers."

At the landing, Jake spun toward Wiley. "Don't let Soaring Raven hear you say that."

Jake's rapid motion caused the frozen hind quarters to slip out of his grasp. It narrowly missed Wiley's foot as it banged down each step and slid three feet along the snow-trampled pathway.

"You break steps, you fix.

Soaring Raven stood in the open doorway, arms folded. The huge Ute woman eyed Jake sternly, then peered over his shoulder at the white-wrapped hind quarters in the snow. "What that?"

Jake beamed. "That's elk meat. I shot me my first elk."

"Why it frozen? Me need axe to cut."

"Cuz I left it hangin' in the tree while Wiley'n me was trainin'." Jake ran down the steps, groaned as he lifted the partial carcass into his arms, then started up the stairs.

"No bring in house," Soaring Raven said. "No room." She pointed to the barn. "Put there. It ready in spring." Seeing Jake's crestfallen expression, she gave him one of her rare smiles and waved him inside.

* * *

At the dinner table, for the third time and with much embellishment, Jake told Belinda and Jimmy Ratchett, owners of the Castille Ranch where Jake and Wiley worked, how he'd shot the elk, then began describing the training Wiley had been putting him through.

"That reminds me," Jimmy said, scooting back his chair. He headed toward the desk by the stairwell door. "I went to Fairplay yesterday and ran into Benton Riley. He had two telegrams for you." Jimmy plucked the papers from a wire holder, returned to the table and handed them to Wiley.

"Thanks." Wiley opened the first one and read it, then looked at Jake. "Curtis and Morgan won't be coming to Colorado. Sheriff Tyborn caused Curtis grief, probably because he stayed so long at your farm. Curtis took a position as a Lexington police officer. They moved there."

"Who's Curtis and Morgan?" Jimmy asked.

"Curtis was deputy sheriff in Wilmore, Kentucky," Jake said. "He come out to my farm with Sheriff Tyborn after the shootin' with Sergeant Moss an' his men." Jake shrugged and lowered his head. "Sergeant Moss was my friend once, but he turned to a crook an' come after me." Jake looked at Jimmy. "Curtis an' Morgan're partners like Wiley'n me." He grinned at Wiley. "Curtis must'a got him a job where Morgan sells his wood-made stuff."

"I remember. You told us about them when you got back," Jimmy said.

Wiley shrugged. "I was hoping they'd come here, but I don't think either of them would like working on a ranch."

As Wiley read the second wire from Mike McGelvy, he forced his face to remain impassive.

"Wiley," the telegram stated, "you and Jake be in New Orleans by February 20, 1887. Santivan will be there that day only. Your lodging is arranged." SM-1213862PMT-LM, ended the wire.

Santivan! Wiley sat stunned. The death-crazed assassin was returning to the country. Wiley remembered a year and a half ago when Santivan had been in Philadelphia. Somehow the man had captured the two Pinkerton agents sent to arrest him. Authorities said Santivan had dug out their eyes with his knife and sliced off their privates, presumably while the agents were still alive. Then, he'd decapitated them. Wiley shuddered. He'd been assigned to that case. Alone. But he'd been detained by the Cape Cod police after he'd out-drawn and killed a gunslick who'd braced him outside a pub. He hadn't made it to Philadelphia in time.

Wiley read the telegram again. The code at the end meant Mike would send him a secret message on December 13th at two in the afternoon, Mountain Time. It would be a long message. How could he be alone in the telegraph office for any length of time to receive it?

Unnerved by Wiley's long silence and his stony face that briefly flickered fear, Jake asked, "What does it say, Wiley?"

Wiley peered over the top of the telegram. Everyone stared at him. He folded the paper and looked apologetically at Belinda and Jimmy.

"Jake and I are being sent to New Orleans...on a job. We have to be there before February 20th. I'm not sure how long we'll be gone. I'll hire a few hands to take our places during that time."

"New Orlins!" Jake yelled. "That's where them gators live! An' we can't be gone from here that long!"

Belinda smiled at Jake, then glanced at Jimmy. "It's fine with us if you both go, but why would they send you there? It's such a long way from here."

Not wanting to think about why Mike picked them, Wiley stated flatly, "Mike must want Jake to learn first-hand what being a Pinkerton is about." He shuddered when he thought of Jake's cock and balls being cut off by Santivan. Or his own!

"Can you inquire about hiring ranch hands?" Jimmy asked.

"Certainly. Jake and I will go to Fairplay in two days. That will give us time to check on the cattle by the Horseshoe River."

* * *

That night, snuggled naked against Jake in the featherbed at their cabin, Wiley wondered how he was going to tell Jake the contents of Mike's telegram and that he had to receive the secret message alone. He formulated an elaborate story, then realized it was a lie and remembered the consequences of lies he'd told Jake about who he was when they'd first met. Jake had fled back to Kentucky.

Wiley decided to tell the truth, but thinking of Jake being butchered by Santivan, he shuddered.

Pressed against Wiley's hairy chest, Jake felt Wiley shudder. He scooted closer. "I'll keep you warm, Wiley."

Squeezing Jake, Wiley sighed. "I didn't tell you everything about that message we got from Mike." After a short silence, he said, "Santivan will be in New Orleans." Wiley explained about Santivan and his ruthlessness, and about receiving the secret message at the telegraph office. "If you know how we can get Benton Riley out of his office at two o'clock on the 13th, tell me."

Jake felt their hard dicks touching and buried his face into Wiley's hairy chest. A surge of happiness washed through his being.

"Hell, Wiley, I'll pick him up an' carry him outside on my shoulder."

Wiley laughed, shoved his hand to Jake's crotch and cupped his balls. "We need to be a bit more cagey, Mr. Strong-man. Benton can't know I'm receiving the message."

"I'll think'a somethin', Wiley. But I ain't gonna do no thinkin' now."

CHAPTER 5

Leading a pack horse, Jake and Wiley rode into Fairplay on Monday, December 13th. The temperature of the sunny yet frosty day hovered at fifteen degrees, and the two men felt frozen to their saddles as they walked their horses up the busy street. The townsfolk seemed not to notice the cold as they went about daily chores.

Wiley smiled and nodded to bundled-up Judge Parker, driving his black buggy past them. He'd sentenced Rice Haden to hang, which had been carried out the next day. The white-haired, goateed judge nodded, then smacked his horse's rump with the reins.

Jake noticed a lone cowboy in his mid-thirties riding toward them. The man sat in his saddle hunched over from the cold. He'd pulled his hat brim down to ward off the biting wind, and his much-too-small coat left his wrists and thick forearms as bare and bluish as his hands.

Steering Mac toward him, Jake blocked the man's path.

"You need you a bigger coat," Jake said to him.

Startled at the intrusion, the cowboy snapped his head up and frowned. "I'm down on my luck. What's it to ya?"

Jake stuck out his hand. "I'm Jake Brady. D'you need a job? Wiley'n me work at the Castille Ranch. We're goin' to New Orlins, an' we're gonna be needin' help."

Overhearing, Wiley quickly turned Buddy toward the two men. "Jake, what are you doing?"

"Hell, Wiley, we're goin' to New Orlins. Jimmy said we gotta hire help for when we're gone."

"You're right, Jake."

Wiley scrutinized the disheveled cowboy. His weathered face seemed too lean for the rest of his muscular frame and Wiley detected a fierceness in him, held in check by vast experience with hard times. In any case, Wiley knew the striking man must have been dubbed a lady-killer, and hoped he still was...for his and Jake's sake.

Liking him at once, Wiley looked sternly at the cowboy, who observed them with skepticism. "I'm Wiley Deluce, foreman of the Castille Ranch. I hope you can convince me to hire you."

The cowboy sat straight in his saddle and his eyes twinkled. "If I got work, I work. If I don't, I loaf. You pay the same either way."

Wiley extended his hand. "You're hired. What's your name?"

The cowboy shook Wiley's hand. "Name's Pike. Pike Lacy." After releasing Wiley's hand, Pike patted his horse's neck. "This here's Bucko. I'll be acceptin' that job if the pay's right."

"Forty dollars a month and found," Wiley said.

"Mor'en fair fer winter. When do I start?"

Wiley dug into his pocket, pulled out a gold, double eagle and handed it to Pike. "You start by going to Hyndman General Store and buying a new coat, gloves and a muffler. Buy any other clothes or boots you need. If twenty dollars isn't enough, I'll settle with Hyndman's when we get there. Jake and I have some business to take care of. We'll meet you at the store in an hour."

He pulled out his watch and glanced at it. "Jake, it's one-thirty. We have to get to the telegraph office." Wiley turned Buddy toward the main part of town, then glanced back at Pike. "The twenty dollars I just gave you is not part of your salary."

As the partners rode up the street, Pike stared at the twenty-dollar coin in his hand. Maybe things would be all right after all. He'd liked Jake at once. And Wiley? One tough hombre. The scar on Wiley's cheek made him think of...

Pike jerked Bucko around and watched the two men dismount in front of the telegraph office. Pike's mouth dropped open. "I'll be dammed! That *is* William Deluce!" Not wanting to get on the bad side of that gent, Pike spurred Bucko into a trot toward the general store.

Jake and Wiley looped the reins of the three horses around the tie-bar in front of the telegraph office, a narrow building and the only one in the block that stood by itself. Piles of snow shoveled from the boardwalk discouraged passage of adults through the empty lots on either side, but two red-cheeked faces peered out the entrance of a snow cave dug into the largest pile.

Jake shivered and stamped his feet. "Damn, Wiley. I'm gonna stuff my toes in my cup'a hot coffee."

After nodding to Pike as the man rode by, Wiley scanned the street and breathed in the frigid air. It was good to be in a town like Fairplay...in eighteen-eighty-six. He sighed with relief remembering the closed-in mall he and Jake had visited when they'd been transported to the Time of nineteen-ninety-three. Here, each business had a home-like quality, and every proprietor was genuinely helpful. The problem in this time? Everyone knew everyone else's business. But at least people here knew each other.

Wiley breathed deeply again and watched Jake warming Mac's ears with his hands. "Jake, have you thought of how you're going to get Benton out of the office? We don't have much time."

Jake glanced at Wiley and grinned. "All the way here I been thinkin' about what I'm gonna do. After hearin' Mr. Riley tell about his son gettin' all cut up by that bear last time we was here, I think I know what I'm gonna do."

Wiley grabbed the door latch, then stopped and looked Jake in the eyes. "I trust your judgment. And I'm anxious to see how you'll do it."

Benton Riley, wearing his green visor, looked over the counter into the small waiting room as they entered. "Howdy, gents! Good to see you're not frozen."

"Good to see you, too, Mr. Riley," Jake said. "An' I *am* frozen. My toes most likely look like them little carrots Jim cooked in nineteen..."

Wiley nudged Jake, then winked at him.

After slipping off his heavy coat, Wiley smiled at the operator. "It's nice to see you, Benton. How's your wife and son?" He hung up his long, shaved-beaver-lined elk duster with coyote fur trim that Soaring Raven had made for each of them. He watched Jake hang up his lighter-colored duster.

Both men headed for the stove.

"Clara's fine," Benton said. "Son's in Leadville. He's now foreman at a new Tabor mine." He waved at the partners. "Hold on an' I'll get you gents cups. Just made coffee." Benton turned toward a cupboard with glass doors, opened one and grabbed two white china mugs. As Jake and Wiley warmed themselves, Benton approached the stove, handed each of them a mug and quickly poured their coffee. He clunked the pot down and hurried behind the counter.

Wiley watched to see if Jake really would stick his toes into his cup and half-smiled when Jake didn't make a move for his boots. He turned to Benton. "Do we have any messages today?"

Benton shook his head. "Nope. Not this time. It's been quiet today, but I don't take chances." He raised one bushy eyebrow. "By the way, did you hear they found Billingsly's body? After all this time, the only way they could tell it was him was the rings on the skeleton's fingers."

Holding their cups tightly to warm their fingers, the partners walked to the counter.

"Where'd they find it?" Wiley asked.

"Couple'a prospectors camping beside the Platte came across it near Tit Rock, about two miles north'a here. You gents most likely don't know where that is."

Jake and Wiley winked at each other. Clem Harris, Jake's neighbor from Kentucky, had shot at them from that very rock. Later, they'd laughed and wrestled under a blue spruce overlooking it.

"We know where it is," Wiley said.

Jake looked at the Seth Thomas, drop-octagon wall clock. The schoolhouse in Wilmore, where he'd grown up, had one just like it before it had burnt to the ground. Benton's clock read twenty minutes to two.

Leaning on the counter, Jake grinned at Benton. "I been thinkin' about what you said last time Wiley'n me was here. You talked about your son gettin' all cut up by that bear, an' I been hankerin' to tell you what happened to my friend, Stinky, an' my pa when I was still a boy."

In an especially graphic way, Jake told how Jed Harris had cut off Stinky's thumb, describing every detail of Stinky's capture, Jed's long knife, the one he'd called a Tennessee toothpick, and Stinky's screaming. Jake could still feel Abe's hands gripping his arms, forcing him to watch.

"An' when Jed cut Stinky's thumb off real slow-like, I could hear the bone crack."

While telling of his father's goring by the Harrises' bull, Jake said, "An' I seen this big flap'a skin hangin' down Pa's leg, an' his leg bone was all bloody."

Benton's face had already drained of color, but with that statement, he grabbed the edge of the counter, closed his eyes and wavered.

Jake glanced at the clock. Four minutes until two. He grinned at Wiley, rushed for his duster and slipped it on, then grabbed Benton's coat.

"Wiley, I think Mr. Riley needs some fresh air." He rushed behind the counter, helped Benton into his coat and steadied him as they walked toward the door. Jake turned and said, "Wiley, you guard this here office." He looked down at Benton. "Hell, I'm sorry I made you sick."

As the door shut, Wiley shook his head. He watched his tough, handsome partner gently help the older man to one of the boardwalk chairs. After what he'd just witnessed, Wiley swore if Jake ever called himself "dummer'n hog shit" again, he'd flatten him.

Wiley glanced at the clock, then slipped behind the counter. He slid into Benton's chair, grabbed a pen, dipped it, and then pulled the message pad toward him. At precisely two o'clock, the telegraph started clicking a message in the code the agency used. It was a long message, taking several minutes. The moment he heard Mike's name in code, Wiley ripped the page off the pad, then glanced at the window. He could see Jake but not Benton and assumed the man still had his head between his knees.

After carefully arranging the desk the way it had been before he'd sat down, Wiley walked through the swinging gate and stood at the counter. He grabbed his cup, took a swig of coffee and began decoding the message. He'd nearly finished when the door opened. Wiley quickly folded the paper, slipped it into his shirt pocket and slowly turned around.

"Feeling better?" Wiley asked as he saw Jake helping Benton into the office..

"Much," Benton said weakly. Jake led him behind the counter, helped him out of his coat and into his chair.

"Jake, you're going to have to quit telling those gory stories," Wiley said, fighting to keep his stony expression.

"Hell, I said I was sorry."

"We should be going, Jake." Wiley walked to the wall and grabbed his coat. "We have errands to run."

"I'm gonna stay with Mr. Riley awhile an' make sure he's okay. I'll meet you at the general store when he's better. Besides, my coffee got cold."

"I have to go to the bank first." Wiley said. "I'll meet you and Pike at Hyndman's. Don't be too long."

Outside, Wiley untied two sets of reins, leaped into Buddy's saddle and headed up the street leading the pack horse.

Still in his coat and holding his coffee cup, Jake ambled to the door. He stepped out on the board walk and tossed his cold coffee into the street. When he saw Wiley enter the bank in the next block, he went back into the office and poured a second cup of coffee while muttering to himself, "Drinkin' this damn coffee's gonna make my dick freeze off when I'm peein'."

As he approached the counter, Jake asked, "Are you feelin' good enough to send a message for me?"

Benton looked up at Jake, smiled and nodded.

"I can't write nothin'. Wiley's gonna teach me, but we ain't had time yet. Can I tell you what I wanna say an' you write it?"

"Certainly." Benton rubbed his face with his hands then picked up his pen and dipped it into the ink bottle. "Who's the message to?"

"It's to Bill Chasteen in Alma. He's the hostler up there."

"I know Bill well. What do you want to tell him?"

Jake squinted and scratched his head. "Tell him...tell him Miss Castille...uh, *damn*! I can't *never* remember that. Tell him Mrs. Ratchett...an' Jimmy...an' me're havin' a party for Wiley next Saturday. Wiley's birthday's that same day an' he's gonna be twenty-six. We want Bill an' Harry, an' Matt an' Frank to come. An' Sheriff Cline, too, an' his deputies. An' Doc Coulter an' his wife, if they can." Jake looked at the ceiling trying to remember all the names on the list Belinda had made that he'd forgotten to bring. He shrugged. "An' anybody else that wants to come."

Jake glanced at the window, then back to Benton. "We don't want Wiley to know nothin' about it." He grinned. "I'm real excited about this here surprise party, an' don't want nobody tellin' Wiley."

Benton smiled at Jake. "I know what to say. When is the party, and what time should everyone be there?"

Jake gave him the details, apologized again for making the man sick with his stories, then grabbed his hat. "An' you're invited too, Mr. Riley." He grinned and quickly left the office.

* * *

In the bank, Wiley tossed his duster over the back of a chair. God, it was hot in here! As he approached the teller cage, he noticed the stove glowed red.

Wiley handed an envelope to the man behind the grille. "Could you see that Crain at the bank in Alma gets this for Belinda's mortgage payment? I won't be up there today."

Ted Hoover, a thin, delicate man with a fertile crop of brown hair, smiled at Wiley's chest-hair peeking out the top of his gray, wool shirt, then looked him in the eye. "I certainly can. I'll have the stage driver deliver it this afternoon." Ted leaned closer, glanced briefly around the bank, then riveted his gaze on Wiley's handsome face. "They found Billingsly's skeleton by Tit Rock." Ted rolled his eyes and snickered. "Strange place to find *his* bones."

Wiley smiled. He assumed Ted was "gay," like they would say in nineteen-ninety-three. "Benton Riley told us. Who has his gold and what happened to his Double Dipper mine?"

"Sheriff Cline's got everything locked up. Said he didn't trust Crain with it. A district judge is coming to settle Billingsly's estate. Sheriff Cline wants it divided among his miners, but the judge has the final say."

Wiley hesitated, then asked, "Do you know what happened to the woman recuperating in Doc Coulter's office up in Alma? The one Winder shot?"

Ted leaned even closer to the massive man on the other side of the grille. "Miller, he's the assistant at the Alma Hotel and a good friend of mine." Ted glanced around the empty bank, then looked back at Wiley. "Miller told me a wire came for her while she was still laid up in the doc's office. The telegram was about the woman's parents." Ted grabbed his chin and squinted. "I think the woman's name is Betty Gringold."

"It is," Wiley stated. "Go on."

Ted grinned and tried to memorize Wiley's huge biceps that nearly split the seams of his shirt. "*Well*, it seems Betty's mother and step-father were sailing off Cape Cod when a nor'easter came up and capsized their boat. It sunk to China."

Hoover pulled back, gripped the edge of the counter and rolled his eyes. "From what Miller told me, Betty inherited a fortune, a mansion and half ownership in one of the biggest ship builders in Boston. She went East a month ago."

Wiley thanked Ted for taking care of the mortgage payment and for the news. He nodded and headed for the door, glad Betty was out of the area and his life. He was convinced Betty was mad. She'd been one of the reasons Jake had left him last summer and had gone back to Kentucky. What would Betty become now that she was wealthy? He shuddered.

* * *

When Jake walked into Hyndman Brothers' General Store, Wiley looked up from the candy counter and beckoned him over. He pointed to a glass plate with a few squares of fudge left on a paper doily, then lifted up a small bag.

"I bought you a pound of fudge since you were so clever in the telegraph office. How did you think of that?"

"Hell, when we was in there before an' Mr. Riley was talkin' about his son an' that bear, I saw him gettin' sick when he talked about the blood. I figgered he'd get sick again." Jake lowered his head. "I felt bad doin' it."

Wiley slid his hand over Jake's shoulder. "I know you did, but you did a masterful job." As Wiley handed the bag of fudge to Jake, he pulled him close and said in a low voice, "I got the message. I've decoded most of it. If I have a chance, I'll read it to you on the way home."

Pike Lacy approached them. He'd already snuggled into his new fur-lined, sheepskin coat, rabbit-lined elk hide gloves and wool muffler. He grinned crookedly at Jake. "Much obliged for you stoppin' me in the street." He rubbed the sleeves of his coat. "Never had a coat like this." His countenance flashed remembrance and he pulled off his new gloves, dug into his pants pocket, pulled out a handful of gold dollars and held them out to Wiley. "Much obliged, Mr. Deluce. Here's yer change."

Wiley pushed back Pike's hand. "You're supposed to buy extra clothes with that. Stock up on pants, shirts and boots...whatever you need to do your job. You're a good man, Pike. Jake made an excellent choice in picking you." Just to satisfy his own curiosity that people in eighteen-eighty-six were much more tolerant about "gays" than nineteen-ninety-three, he said, "Just so you know, before you start this job, Jake and I are partners and blood brothers. That means we have a bond closer than marriage. Does that bother you?"

Pike looked at the two handsome men in front of him and remembered the cattle drives he'd ridden in his youth. All the men, even the trail boss, had paired up. Some had remained partners to this day.

"Don't mind," Pike said. "Had a few pards way back, but I hanker on women better." He lowered his head. "Had a wife fer two years, but Constance went back east fer a better life than I could give." He turned abruptly and headed to the clothes section.

After loading their supplies on the pack horse and getting a bite to eat at Martha's Cafe, the three men started the long, frigid ride to the Castille Ranch.

A short distance out of town, with Pike trailing behind and leading the pack horse, Wiley pulled out the telegram from Mike McGelvy. He finished decoding it and said, "Jake, this message is about New Orleans. We're going to be staying in Senator Faubourg's home. Mike already made the arrangements. Also, Mike is sending Jamie Chapman to help us while we're there. Jamie is a top agent. We're to meet him on February 20th at the Levee Pub on Chartres Street. It's only a few blocks from where we'll be staying." Wiley folded the message and slipped it into his pocket. "We won't need our horses in New Orleans. We'll leave them here." He braced for a protest.

"Hell, Wiley!" Jake shouted. "What's Mac gonna do with me gone that long?"

"We were gone almost two months when we went to Jim and Dave's in nineteen..." He broke off and glanced back at Pike, then lowered his voice. "Mac was fine then. This trip shouldn't be that long." Wiley rubbed his jaw and smiled. "Well, maybe it will. I've decided we're going to take a riverboat from St. Louis to New Orleans. That takes about five days there and six days back."

Jake snapped his head toward Wiley. "A *riverboat*?"

Wiley worked at keeping a straight face. "Yes."

"Damn, I ain't never been on a riverboat my whole life! Thinkin' about a riverboat ride's even more excitin' than thinkin' about the surprise birthday party we're plannin' for...."

* * *

Twenty-seven people gathered at the Castille Ranch for Wiley's party. All the people from Alma that Jake had named came. Benton Riley wouldn't have missed it for the world. Miller, the clerk at the Alma Hotel, arrived with Hoover from the Fairplay Bank. Mrs. Mercer, owner of Mercer's General Store in Alma, proudly rode in the buggy next to Sheriff Cline. His two deputies flanked each side on horseback.

Tubs, bartender at Alma's Silver Heels Bar, brought his son Tiny and his wife Hilda, a huge woman with blondish-gray hair so severely pulled into a bun she looked bald. Hilda plopped into a straight-back chair, folded her arms and glared at everyone and everything.

The Harrington family from the ranch to the south and several of their hands arrived. Reverend Becker, Marshal Elliott, his two deputies and several other people from Como also came.

Jake, proud of Wiley for acting so surprised at the gathering, snickered and blushed when each person arrived.

"Is Thunder Joe still in El Paso? Or have you heard?" Wiley asked Jimmy after they had greeted Alma's Doctor Coulter and his wife, Marian. "Jake and I haven't seen him for months."

"The last Soaring Raven heard, he was living in northern Arizona with his Navajo wife."

"Navajo wife? When did this happen?"

"Years ago. He won't talk about it. Soaring Raven said he feels guilty that he travels up here so much and leaves her alone for months at a time."

Wiley folded his arms and scowled. "Well, he *should* feel guilty!"

Guests filled the parlor, stairwell, dining room and kitchen. Reverend Becker said a blessing over Soaring Raven's platters of food. After everyone had eaten, they sang "Happy Birthday" to Wiley as he cut one of Soaring Raven's famous apple pies.

Some of the guests brought Wiley gifts. Bill and Harry went together and got him a leather pouch filled with a twist of expensive tobacco. Matt and Frank gave him a chunk of white quartz with pure gold needles covering one side and bright, reddish-pink rhodochrosite crystals encrusting the other. Mrs. Mercer handed Wiley a gingham bag filled with doughnuts and a package of peppermints. Soaring Raven had made Wiley a pair of elk skin moccasins with cowhide soles. The intricate bead and bone design on the side of each moccasin concealed Wiley's bone-handled knife he could store in a hidden slot sewn into the right one. Wiley instantly knew why Soaring Raven had asked to see the knife a few weeks ago.

Belinda and Jimmy presented him with a fifty-foot length of braided rawhide rope that Jimmy had made. Soaring Raven nodded her approval of it.

Jake squirmed in his chair until Wiley had opened the last gift, then jumped up and handed Wiley his present. He'd wrapped it in the Fairplay Flume newspaper.

Wiley grinned at Jake as he opened the gift, then held up a leather strap with a thick pad attached. He stared at it with a puzzled expression.

Doc and Marian Coulter looked at each other and chuckled.

"What *is* this, Jake?" Wiley asked.

"Hell, Wiley, that boy workin' at the general store in Fairplay said it was a truss." Jake glanced at the guests, blushed and looked at his knees. "He didn't know what it was for, neither, but thought it was somethin' for your nuts."

Everyone laughed. No remembered ever seeing Sheriff Cline laugh until he cried.

CHAPTER 6

A tall, lean man in his late thirties, sporting a Vandyke beard and wearing a heavy black frock coat trimmed with mink, tapped his black lacquered cane on the frozen walkway in exact rhythm with his right foot. He stopped at Walnut Street, turned to his left and looked up into Philadelphia's Rittenhouse Square, a district of stately mansions. His mother had lived in this area when she was a child. This would be his first visit to his mother's old neighborhood. He thought of how horrified she would be at what he did for a living. After a moment, he lifted his head, breathed in the frigid air, stiffened his neck and headed up Walnut.

He walked two blocks and stopped in the middle of the third. Opening his coat, he reached into the breast pocket and pulled out a slip of paper. His precise, script-written address matched the numbers on an imposing three-story structure. Raising an eyebrow at the house, he crumpled the paper and tossed it into the street, then tugged at the brim of his top hat and climbed the four steps to the iron gate. Silently closing the gate, he looked at the virgin snow covering the shrubs and wrought iron bench, all placed with precision in the tiny front yard. After a slight hesitation, he glanced around, then ascended the three steps to the porch and pulled the brass chain. With each pull, he heard a muffled tinkling of small bells.

Shortly, the lock clicked and the huge oak door opened a crack. A gray-headed man with stooped shoulders peered out.

"Yes?"

The tall man on the porch removed his hat and bowed his head slightly. "Lyonel Fainsworth, to see Miss Betty Gringold."

The door opened wide and the man smiled. "Miss Gringold is expecting you." He stepped aside and allowed Fainsworth to enter.

After closing the door, the man said, "I'm Dillard Glaver, Miss Gringold's butler. May I take your hat and coat?"

Fainsworth handed Glaver his hat, upside down, then peeled off his gloves and plopped them inside. He slipped off his coat and draped it over the old man's outstretched arm. When Glaver hesitated and glanced at the black walking stick, Fainsworth held it up and said, "I'll keep this, if you don't mind."

"Very good, sir." Glaver turned and headed toward the coat tree beside the front door.

Fainsworth looked around. The entrance hall, while not large, reminded him of a museum. He immediately noticed two matching oak buffets facing each other from opposite sides of the room. Three brass pressure dials, obviously from a steamboat, had been mounted on mahogany bases and placed along the back of the buffet on his right. Several framed, tintype photographs, all of the same handsome man in a ship captain's uniform, sat near each dial. Browned, curled maps and nautical charts artfully overlapped on all three walls.

The buffet on his left supported grotesque human figures carved from ebony and teak. Wooden masks, some with red protruding eyes and blue lips, covered the walls above and beside it. A chair, made of gazelle horns with a zebra-hide seat and looking extremely fragile and uncomfortable, sat opposite him.

Glaver returned from the coat tree. "This way, sir." He headed past double glass doors that closed off a lavishly decorated parlor, opened a side door and proceeded down a long hallway.

As Fainsworth followed Glaver down the hall, he noticed an open door to his left. When he walked by, he marveled that the large room had been crammed with artifacts from around the world. Floor-to-ceiling bookcases filled with leather-bound books, statues and pottery lined the entire room. Huge urns, wall-mounted animal heads, bizarre lamps and brown leather furniture gave the room an eccentric but comfortable feel. He wished he could relax in there for a day. Maybe three.

Glaver stopped at the next door on the left and knocked. A muffled woman's voice said, "Come in."

The butler opened the door a crack and peered inside. "Madame, Mr. Fainsworth is here."

"Show him in."

Glaver opened the door wide and motioned with his arm. Fainsworth stepped into a large room with rose-patterned wall paper and dark mahogany trim.

Glaver shut the door. His footsteps retreated quickly down the hall.

Fainsworth thought the room resembled a small flat and wondered if the woman lived only in this chamber. Near the door, a rose-covered love seat flanked the stove in the left corner, and two other chairs, also on his left, had been turned awkwardly to face the wall to his right. Wondering about it, he turned and saw a high table that held a candelabra with all nine candles lit, illuminating a gilt-framed portrait of...*William Deluce*, the Pinkerton gunman! He gaped at it.

Betty looked up from her desk, which she'd placed in front of the room's only window, a huge, arched stained-glass depicting the battle between Michael the Archangel and Satan. She raised her eyebrows and smiled when she saw Fainsworth looking at Wiley's portrait.

Betty walked toward Fainsworth across a thick Persian carpet. "Isn't he breathtaking? We're engaged, you know."

This woman was engaged to William Deluce? Why did she want his services? Fainsworth spun toward her, then caught his breath. Betty wore a lavender, puffy-sleeved tea gown, and filled it out quite attractively. He liked the way she'd piled her blond hair high on her head. But there was something about her that concerned him. It was her...crazed expression when she looked at the portrait of William Deluce, the very man he'd spent the last two years trying to avoid. He'd have to be very careful around this woman. Deluce may have put her up to this to trap him.

Betty held out her hand. "Mr. Fainsworth, I'm glad you chose to come."

Fainsworth gently shook her hand. "The payment seemed adequate for such...er, I was intrigued by your offer."

Betty swept her hand toward a rosewood armchair angled toward her desk. "Please, come sit down. Would you like a glass of sherry?"

"Yes, I would. And please, call me Lyonel." Reaching the chair, he slid into it and watched Betty walk to a bar near her desk and pour topaz-amber liquid into tall crystal goblets.

Betty handed Fainsworth his wine, then seated herself in her chair behind the desk. She sipped sherry, placed the goblet close and looked Fainsworth over carefully. He had a long slender nose, a wide mouth and high cheekbones. She thought him handsome the way they all fit together perfectly behind his Vandyke beard. She felt drawn to him in a strange way. Betty suddenly realized he was not muscular and he must be at least ten years older than Wiley. Dearest Wiley! Wiley, my love! Even though she had a guest, Betty stared at the portrait of Wiley and allowed herself to imagine being naked with him.

Seeing Betty's eyes become glassy with a faint smile on her face as she stared at the painting, Fainsworth fidgeted, grabbed at his cravat and loudly cleared his throat. What was he getting into? The woman was obviously mad. He wondered about her statement that she was engaged to Deluce. From what he'd heard about the Pinkerton agent, and seeing Betty's expression, he doubted Deluce even knew the woman.

Betty composed herself, looked at a sheet of paper on her desk and said, "Mr. Fainsworth..."

"Please, call me Lionel."

Betty flashed distaste at being interrupted. "I got your name from the files at the Pinkerton agency...where I worked. I assure you...Lionel...if you accept this job and don't succeed, I will make your life extremely miserable." She smiled sweetly.

Fainsworth leaped to his feet. "Madame, I don't know how you could have gotten my name from the Pinkerton files! I run a respectable business in three cities on this coast and--"

"*And*, you hire yourself out to kill people!" Betty stood, grabbed her goblet, took a sip, then plunked it on the desk. With a sweep of her arm, she said, "Do you see this house? It is now mine. As of three months ago, I am an extremely wealthy woman." Betty walked to Fainsworth and stared into his eyes. "My mother and her third husband, Captain James Jenson, were recently drowned in a boating accident. You may have read about it. This was Captain Jenson's house. He was quite wealthy. Since he had no living heirs, this house, and his entire fortune, are now mine!"

Betty turned toward her desk, picked up her goblet and drained it. Still holding the glass, she turned back to Fainsworth and smiled. "I quit the Pinkerton agency last year, but know someone there who agreed to pass me necessary information. I now have that information and want someone killed. Like I said in my message, I will pay you three thousand dollars, half now, and the other half when I know for certain that Pinkerton agent, Jake Brady is *dead*."

Betty opened a desk drawer and pulled out a bulging envelope. Without speaking, she handed it to Fainsworth.

After counting the bank notes inside, Fainsworth smiled at them. He'd never heard of Jake Brady. Glad he hadn't been hired to kill William Deluce, he raised his eyes to Betty. "I'm at your service, madam, but I assure you, if this is a trap to get William Deluce on my trail, I'll--"

"Wiley knows nothing of this! Besides, he's in Colorado. If he *ever* finds out about this, I will have *you* killed. Do I make myself clear?"

Betty gave Fainsworth Jake's itinerary to New Orleans that Wiley had wired to Mike, then dismissed him. She intentionally omitted Wiley's name, knowing Wiley would kill Fainsworth after he'd murdered Jake. That would save her fifteen hundred dollars and successfully erase her involvement.

Once Fainsworth had left the house, Betty carefully looked around the room. This house, the money, half ownership of a shipyard...none of it meant anything to her.

"All I want is Wiley," She said out loud. "And I'll get him if I have to kill everyone he's ever known."

CHAPTER 7

Pike Lacy fit in at the Castille Ranch as though he'd lived there all his life, and he wished he had. Claiming the bunk house as his own, on warm days he patched the roof, painted the outside light blue with brown trim and fixed the front steps. When finished, he'd whitewashed the picket fence around the yard and mucked the horse shit out of the main barn. After a month, he hunted with Soaring Raven. The two got on famously and razzed each other endlessly. Pike even talked Soaring Raven into eating at the dining room table with everyone else, something Belinda and her late father had never accomplished.

Pike loved South Park's wide open spaces, the smell of cattle and sage while driving strays back from the river, hunting game and playing poker in Fairplay on Saturday nights. Life here brought him close to the bliss he'd experienced in the cattle-drive days of his youth. With a new audience for his stories, he felt so comfortable on the Castille Ranch he vowed never to leave.

* * *

"Wiley, I'd be 'bliged to drive you and Jake t'Como in the wagon," Pike said across the dinner table the night before Jake and Wiley left for New Orleans.

"I ain't ridin' in no wagon!" Jake hollered. "I'm gonna ride Mac. Won't be seein' him for a long time. You can bring him back on a lead rope."

"I feel the same about Buddy," Wiley said.

"Unnerstood," Pike said. "Had a bay geldin' once that could turn on a biscuit an' never break the crust, an' ol' Moss could run faster'n gossip at a church social."

"Why ain't you got him no more?" Jake asked.

"Had ta shoot 'im. Broke his leg durin' a stampede in Oklahomee back'n seventy-nine. Whole herd was comin' full at me an' I like'ta been killed myself. Had ta use Moss's body t'keep the cattle steered 'round me. Couple'a cows jumped over us, an' one cracked me on the noggin' with it's front hoof." Pike pointed to a barely noticeable spot on his forehead just below his hairline. "That cow kicked me right here."

"I've seen a stampede," Jimmy said. "I don't see how you survived even with your dead horse in front of you. A herd of stampeding cows trample everything."

"Er...well, just so happened, most'a the cows turned right and went on by."

Wiley and Jimmy locked eyes for an instant and flickered a smile. Pike caught it and chuckled.

"Damn!" Jake yelled. "You was lucky! My friend Jesus must'a been sittin' on Moss!"

"Don't cuss, *Jack*," Wiley said. He looked at Jake and grinned.

Pike swept his arm towards Jake. "Nothin' wrong with Jake's cussin'. Fer him it ain't cussin'. He don't even know he's doin' it. He'd fit snug with the hands I rode with on drives." He turned to Jimmy. "Tomarra, when I get back from takin' them two t'Como, I'll muck out the smaller barn."

Pike shoved a chunk of rare meat into his mouth, chewed a moment, then raised his fork and tapped it in the air at Soaring Raven, sitting stoically at the table with everyone else. "Shouldn't a shot that antelope with your rifle, Soarin' Raven. Meat's kind'a gamey." Lowering his fork, he grinned at his plate while slicing off another chunk.

Soaring Raven grabbed her fork, rose from the table and walked around it to Pike. Stabbing his steak, she lifted it out of his plate, turned and headed toward the kitchen. A line of bloody drippings traced her path on the floor.

The kitchen door slammed.

"Hey! Gimme me back my meat! That was the last piece!" Pike scooted back his chair, leaped to his feet, frowned at the kitchen door for a moment, then started toward the kitchen.

Finished eating, the others glanced at each other and quickly retreated to the parlor to let Soaring Raven and Pike bicker. Belinda shut the doors of the dining room and the parlor, hoping the wide stairwell would muffle the shouting.

Before Pike could get to the kitchen, Soaring Raven re-entered the dining room, empty handed.

"Where's my meat?" Pike demanded.

"You no like, you no eat."

"Didn't say I didn't like it! I been eatin' gamey meat all my life!"

Soaring Raven began clearing the table. "Me know. You shoot off ears. Follow game for days. Watch it die bleeding, then eat." She raised up and scowled at Pike. "*That* gamey meat!"

The four in the parlor suddenly heard Pike laughing.

"I've never known Soaring Raven to get along with anyone like she does with Pike," Belinda said. "I wish we could have hired him years ago."

"He's been a boon to this ranch, that's for sure," Jimmy said. "Even with his baloney stories." He shook his head. "I've never heard so many 'cowboy sayings' in my life. But Pike knows everything about working cattle and operating a ranch. I guess that's to be expected. He said he grew up in West Texas."

"We have Jake to thank for hiring him," Wiley said. "And personally, I think you should make Pike foreman. He already *is* the foreman. They didn't teach me how to be a ranch foreman in college."

Pike continued to shout in the dining room.

"Damn," Jake said. "Pike sure ain't scared'a Soaring Raven."

Belinda smiled. "I think that's why she likes him so much. I've never seen her in such high spirits. Lately, she's been chanting in Ute while she cooks."

Wiley leaned forward in his chair. "I'm serious about you making Pike foreman. You couldn't do better, and I'd trust him to hire other good men." He smiled at Belinda and Jimmy sitting together on the divan. "Since Jake and I are Pinkertons, we draw a salary from the agency. I would prefer you stop paying us and let us pay rent for living on your ranch. Besides, while we're in New Orleans, I don't want the added responsibility of being foreman here."

"Wiley's right," Jake added. "In New Orlins, he's gotta be the best Pinkerton there is. Like he was before he met me."

Belinda and Jimmy smiled at each other. Belinda put on a boss-like expression, knowing Jimmy still considered this her ranch. "Wiley, you're fired as our foreman. Starting now, you and Jake have to pay us a dollar a month to squat on our land."

"Five dollars a month and it's a deal," Wiley said.

"Hell, that's the best thing you could'a said, Miss Castille...er, damn, uh, Mrs. Ratchett. Wiley'n me ain't gonna be doin' no work while we're gone. We don't want nothin' happenin' to our cabin, neither." Jake turned to Wiley. "Maybe Pike could live there."

"Pike would never live at our cabin, but I'm sure he'll watch over it."

Smiling, Belinda said, "Jake, don't worry about calling me Miss Castille. Jimmy said he likes hearing it from you. So do I. It seems natural to both of us, and it also helps me remember Father and John. They loved each other like you and Wiley."

"I ain't helpin' with them dishes!" they heard Pike shout from the dining room.

"You no work, you no eat!" Soaring Raven bellowed.

"I muck horse shit all day! Don't see *you* doin' that!"

"Me hear horse-shit *stories* all day! That *more* than work!"

The four in the parlor heard Pike's laughter mixed with deep chuckles.

Looking wide-eyed at the others, Belinda asked, "Did we just hear Sa-Ra laughing?"

CHAPTER 8

In St. Louis, Jake stepped onto the crowded gangplank of the Natchez. He tingled with excitement. His first riverboat ride! And all the way to New Orleans...where *alligators* live! Jake stopped in his tracks, touched the butt of his Colt and turned to Wiley.

"Wiley, when I was little, Bobby Rasby told me them gators eat people. Are them gators walkin' around New Orlins?"

Wiley grabbed Jake's arm and ushered him up the slanted walkway at the same pace as everyone else. Near the top they stopped at the end of the line.

"Don't worry about alligators, Jake. They're only in the swamps, and where we'll be staying is a long way from there."

When it was their turn to board, Wiley showed his ticket to the young, scruffy man standing at a podium, barring everyone's way onto the boat. The young man's eyes bulged at the name on the ticket and gasped, "You're William Deluce?" When Wiley glared at him, the head clerk pointed at the double-horseshoe staircase behind him. "Uh, take the stairs and turn right at the top. Cabin eleven."

After scanning Jake from head to toe, then glancing at his ticket, the clerk gestured again toward the promenade deck above and said in his normal loud voice, "Same way up, Mr. Brady. Cabin thirteen."

"Hell, I ain't stayin' in no cabin thirteen! I'm gonna be stayin'...'"

Wiley grabbed Jake's arm and pulled him away from the clerk. He leaned close and whispered, "I had to pay for two cabins. It's Pinkerton regulations when two men travel together." He grinned. "We'll take the room with the largest bed."

Standing in line, a tall lean man dressed in a black frock coat and carrying a black walking stick and traveling bag, heard Jake's name and room number. Fainsworth handed his ticket to the clerk but didn't hear the directions to his cabin. He'd riveted his attention to Jake ascending the staircase.

Jake frowned at the polished wooden steps he climbed. "All them rules makes me feel like I done somethin' wrong cuz I wanna sleep next to you."

Wiley chuckled. "Not everyone is as open-minded as you are." He glanced over the railing at the passengers boarding below and raised an eyebrow when he saw Fainsworth. Wiley heard the man audibly curse when their eyes met. What was Fainsworth doing aboard? Realizing the man was angry he'd been seen, Wiley knew the slippery killer-for-hire would bear watching. Fainsworth had left a trail of bodies up and down the east coast. So far, none of the murders had been pinned on him, and all his alleged victims had been killed by a single knife stab to the heart. Wiley studied the walking stick Fainsworth carried. Could that hold a concealed dagger?

Fainsworth cursed when he saw William Deluce walking with Jake. Drat the luck! Betty Gringold hadn't mentioned that Jake Brady would be traveling with Deluce! He'd have to re-think his strategy. Somehow, he'd have to get Jake alone.

Three young ladies traveling together caught his attention. He took one last glance at Jake Brady as he disappeared from view and casually followed the women up the curved staircase.

When the partners reached cabin eleven, Wiley whipped out his Colt. "Wait here, Jake."

Wiley hesitated, then flung open the door so it banged against the wall. The small cabin seemed packed with furniture. A double-size iron bed took up the entire right side. Against the left wall of the wood-paneled room stood a mahogany wardrobe, double doors wide open. A single armchair seemed squeezed between the wardrobe and a dresser with a tall, oval mirror. A round frosted-glass window on the back wall let in light from the Main Saloon and dining room in the center of the boat.

Wiley holstered his gun and entered. He tossed his bag on the blue-and-brown striped quilt covering the bed, then turned and held out his arms to Jake. "Please, join me in my cabin."

Once inside, Jake kicked the door shut, dropped his bag, threw his arms around Wiley and kissed him. He slid his hands to Wiley's chest, then pushed away and grinned. "I'm not wantin' to see nothin' the whole trip but you naked."

Wiley laughed. "That's a wonderful idea, but we'll have to eat sometime." Wiley's face sobered as he grabbed Jake's shoulders. "Jake, when we were halfway up the stairs, I looked below and spotted a man named Lyonel Fainsworth. He's suspected of being a hired killer. The reason he's on board may mean trouble. He wasn't pleased when we recognized each other."

"What's he look like, so I'll know him?"

"He resembles Billingsly in build. Tall and thin. But he's quite handsome. He's about thirty-five and wears a Vandyke beard."

"What the hell kind'a beard's that?"

"It's a small moustache that curves around his mouth to a pointed beard. He's wearing a black frock coat. But as we get farther south, he won't need it on deck. And he certainly won't wear it in the dining room. He carries a black walking stick. It could hide a pull-out dagger."

Wiley pulled Jake close and kissed him. "Forget about Santivan for now. This boat ride might be our first assignment together. We have to be watchful." He pecked Jake on the nose. "Let's check your cabin to see which one we want."

"Is it gonna be bigger'n this one?"

"No. The Agency doesn't authorize the larger rooms."

After Wiley shut the door to his room, he locked it and dropped the key into his pocket. They found Jake's cabin identical to Wiley's except the bed quilt had a flower print.

Jake shut the door behind him, looked around and grinned. "We're gonna have to flip for which room." He pulled out a quarter and tossed it into the air. When the coin came down, Jake lunged for it but missed. The quarter bounced on the floor and rolled under the bed.

"Damn!" Jake dropped to his knees and peered under the bed. "Hey! Who the hell're you, an' what're you doin' under my bed?" He looked up at Wiley. "There's a man under my bed!"

Gun already drawn, Wiley dropped to his knees and yanked up the quilt. "Get out from there with your hands in sight!"

Slowly, and with a whimper, the man untangled himself from a tight ball and crawled from his hiding place, groaning as he struggled to his feet.

The partners gasped. A boy in his mid-teens!

"Who are you? What are you doing here?" Wiley demanded. For effect, he shoved the barrel of his gun against the boy's chest.

"Don't shoot me," the boy whimpered. "My name's Rodney. Rodney Stern." He looked at the floor as Wiley holstered his gun.

"Are you a stowaway?" Wiley asked, less gruffly.

"Uh...yes, sir." Rodney glanced at both men with terrified eyes. "You *can't* turn me in. I gotta get to N'Awlins. Ma's dyin' and I got no money for a ticket." Unable to meet Wiley's glare, he fixed his gaze at Jake's accepting countenance. "I gotta get there 'fore she dies."

Jake slid his arm over the boy's shoulder. "We won't tell nobody, an' you can have his here room. Wiley an' me ain't gonna be usin' it."

"Jake! We can't let--"

"Hell, Wiley, his ma's *dyin'*. We gotta help him get where he's goin'."

Suspicious that Rodney was a con artist, Wiley folded his arms and frowned at Jake. "You're in charge of him, Jake." He jabbed his finger at Rodney's chest. "If I find out you're lying about your mother, you'll have me to deal with. And I'm not a pushover." He squinted at Jake. "And don't expect Jake to be a pushover!"

Wiley walked toward the door, stopped and turned toward Jake. "I'm going to inspect the deck. Get the truth out of him. And remember, his mother probably doesn't know where he is. I'll meet you in my room in thirty minutes."

Wiley opened the door a crack, peered outside, slipped out to the promenade deck and pulled the door shut.

Alone with Rodney, Jake removed his suit coat and tossed it on the end of the bed. He yanked off his tie, dropped it on the floor and unbuttoned his collar. Rodney would be a handsome man in a few years. His curly brown hair and the few freckles on his upper cheeks made Jake think of Zeke, but he didn't look a bit like Zeke. It must be just his boy-ness.

Stunned by Wiley's words and fierce countenance, Jake wondered if Wiley was right about the boy. Wiley was the best Pinkerton there ever was, and he ought to know. Suddenly realizing that he was now a Pinkerton and Wiley expected him to get to the truth out of Rodney, Jake slid his finger into the front of his shirt and touched the rawhide bag. He felt an instant surge of...something.

"How'd you hear about your ma dyin'?" Jake asked. "An' who was you with?"

"Uh...I was stayin' with Gramma. She got a telegraph message." Rodney lowered his head. "Ma's been in N'Awlins workin'. She's been sendin' money to Gramma to keep me."

Still conscious of Wiley's suspicions, Jake tried to think what Wiley would ask him. "Where's your granma live?"

"Ashburn. It's upriver. I been walkin' two days to get here."

"How'd you get on this here riverboat an' nobody seein' you?" Jake asked.

Rodney frowned. "Why you askin' me all this?"

"Cuz Wiley'n me're Pinkertons. We gotta ask stuff like this."

Rodney's face mirrored shock. "You're Pinkertons?"

"Sure are." Jake reached into his back pocket, pulled out his badge and held it in front of Rodney's face. "I got me this here badge last month, but Wiley got his a long time ago. Wiley's the best Pinkerton there is."

Backing up a step, Rodney gasped. "His name's Wiley? Is he...is he William Deluce the Pinkerton *killer*?"

"Wiley's William Deluce, but he ain't no killer. He can draw his gun faster'n anybody, but he tries not to kill people. Sometimes he don't even kill people tryin' to kill him."

Seeing the terror on Rodney's face, Jake decided to try scaring the truth out of him by talking about Wiley.

"Wiley gets cranky when people lie or steal. I seen him beat up three men at a rodeo in Denver for stealin' my rawhide bag. An' his leg was all shot up, too." Jake pointed to the head of the bed. "You sit there an' tell me what you're doin' on this boat, or like Wiley said, he'll be dealin' with you." Jake shook his head. "An' he's already riled at you bein' in my room."

Rodney shoved the pillows aside, sat at the head of the bed and leaned against the iron grillwork. He studied Jake sitting in the chair beside the dresser. He'd never seen a more handsome man in his life. He hoped he'd look like Jake when he was older. If he lived that long. He'd better watch what he said.

Impatiently, Jake said, "You'd best tell me why you're on this here boat. Wiley'n me're partners an' blood brothers. If I tell him not to tie you up an' send you to the boat sheriff, he won't. But you gotta tell the truth. Are you runnin' away from home?"

"No." Rodney looked mournfully at Jake, then turned away. "I ain't got no home. I was lyin' about Ma dyin'. She died four years ago. Pa died then, too. They was both in a theater in St. Louis an' it caught fire. They couldn't get out." He bowed his head and clasped his hands together.

Jake felt stunned. The boy was all alone! "Where's your granma an' granpa?"

"Ma's folks're dead. Pa's folks live in Mass'chuses. But I won't go there."

"Why?"

"Ma an' Pa'd talk about 'em. They didn't like Ma. Said she was too poor t'be married to Pa." Rodney's eyes filled with tears. "Ma had no schoolin' an' her pa only made shoes, but Pa loved her." He side-glanced Jake to see if this story was working.

Rodney's tears made Jake want to believe every word he said, but remembering Wiley's distrust of the boy, Jake slid his finger into his shirt again and touched the rawhide bag, hoping for more guidance. He also asked Jesus for help.

* * *

Thick, damp fog hugged the river. Wiley stood at the rail and stared into it. Rising tendrils of mist turned the sunset blood red. He hunched his shoulders against the penetrating cold and flipped up his fur collar. One of the two huge paddle wheels, mounted on the side of the boat inside an enclosure, churned incessantly. Rapidly changing to violet, the sky seemed to warn of sinister doings aboard the riverboat.

Gruff voices and the clucking of chickens filtered up from the main cargo deck below. Wiley pushed away from the rail, turned and looked at Jake's cabin door, hoping Jake would get the truth out of Rodney. He smiled, confident Jake would get the job done.

Looking back at the fading sunlight, Wiley wondered what Lionel Fainsworth was doing on board. The man had a right to travel where he wanted, but... Wiley glanced around. The deck was nearly empty. Maybe he was being too suspicious. He and Jake would soon be hunting Santivan in New Orleans, and Jake's safety came first. Should he have allowed Jake to come with him? He'd never forgive himself if Jake got killed by Santivan. Remembering how he'd felt when he thought Jake had been killed in Dodge City, Wiley vowed never again to experience such depth of loss.

He began walking and passed a couple standing at the rail admiring the darkened-purple sunset shrouded in fog. Wiley thought the man extremely handsome and nodded at him. The woman never looked away from the view, but the man nodded back. Elated by the man's hint of a smile, Wiley remembered what Dave had said at the Gay Rodeo in nineteen ninety-three, that when a handsome man smiled at a gay man it made him feel cozy inside. He realized Dave was right. Walking a few steps farther, Wiley looked back. The man still watched him. They smiled broadly at each other. Wiley chuckled as he continued toward the stern. Gay or not, that man felt the same way he did.

He buttoned the top of his duster against the cold as he walked down the narrow gangway between the enclosed paddle wheel and a row of cabin doors. After walking around the boat, Wiley climbed the stairs to the Texas deck. On the top deck, the fog seemed thinner, the sky velvety blue-black. He glanced up at the huge, black smokestacks still belching inky smoke from burning pine knots loaded with pitch. He'd overheard someone say riverboat captains always ordered pine knots burned in major ports, creating black smoke for the benefit of crowds watching arrivals and departures.

A brisk wind tugged at Wiley's coat as he headed for the pilothouse high above him. Climbing the stairs, he pulled open the side door and stepped into the dimly lit room.

"Are either of you the captain?" Wiley asked.

A muscular bearded man with a flattened nose stood at the helm. He briefly took his eyes from the river, squinted at Wiley and motioned with his head to the man standing beside him.

"I'm Captain Finn," the other man said.

Even though the captain was dressed immaculately in his white uniform, Wiley guessed he could be a terror in a dock-side bar. His wide, puffy face, scarred on his right cheek and over his right eyebrow, held a look of confidence. Wiley thought of the prize fighter, Leo Borzoi. He'd seen Leo fight in Boston. Leo had put his foot on the chest of the boxer he'd just knocked out, raised his gloved hand and shouted, "Number twelve!"

"What are you doing up here?" Captain Finn snapped.

Wiley heard "stickler for rules on his boat" in the captain's voice. He smiled, then slowly pulled out his wallet and showed the captain his Pinkerton badge.

Captain Finn grinned. He motioned to the man at the wheel. "This is my pilot, Mort Benchly."

Wiley shook both men's hands. "I'm William Deluce. A known criminal is on your boat. My partner and I will be available until we reach New Orleans."

Captain Finn gasped. "You're William Deluce? The fastest gunney in the world? Welcome! Who's the man?"

"Lyonel Fainsworth. He's a suspected killer for hire. I don't know why he's on board, but he knows I'm here. It angered him when we spotted each other."

Finn squinted. "Fainsworth? Can't say I've heard of him. Where's he from?"

"The East Coast. He's out of his territory."

Eyeing Wiley up and down, Finn said, "I'm surely glad you're not after *me* for anything. If you watch this Fainsworth, your tickets are free."

"Thanks, but no need," Wiley said. "My partner is in training. This will be a good setting for him to learn. *If* anything happens. Fainsworth may only be traveling."

After Wiley left the pilothouse, he walked completely around the Texas Deck. He chuckled at its name. He'd heard that the first man to build a third deck on a riverboat named the rooms after each state, but forgot Texas. He'd named the deck after Texas to make up for his error.

Each door of thirty-eight staterooms had a brass nameplate of its state, its motto and the year of its entry into the union. The Colorado was the last room on the deck. The plaque, glowing from the deck lamps, read, "Centennial State. 1876." Colorado was the most recent state admitted into the union, one hundred years after the United States became a nation, and Wiley suddenly missed South Park and the cabin he and Jake had built.

Wiley descended the stairs to the Promenade Deck and walked around the boat again. A few people, bundled in coats, hats and mufflers, walked outside. Some sat on benches along the railing. Wiley thought it too cold and damp for sitting outside. Passing Jake's cabin, he wondered how Jake was handling Rodney. He'd give them a few more minutes.

At the front of the boat, Wiley watched the boat plow through the water in the inky fog and shuddered at the responsibility of boat pilots, glad Mort Benchly had barely listened to the conversation between the captain and himself. Wiley turned away from the river and entered the Grand Saloon at the Gentlemen's Social Hall.

Taking in the long room, he smiled. This boat was more opulent than any he'd traveled on in the East. He looked up at the ornately ribbed ceiling, brightly lit with eight candle-lit chandeliers, and remembered the trips he'd taken on the Hudson River. Wiley ambled toward the huge silver-gilded stove, nearly four feet in diameter at its base which reminded him of a queen in a chess set. It marked the separation between the Gentlemen's Cabin and the dining area. Two spittoons flanked each side of the stove, and poorly aimed spits had stained the polished oak floor around them dark brown. A mahogany table near the stove held a silver coffee urn and a tray of inverted cups. Men crowded the bar on his right. All three gambling tables were in use. Looking to his left, he noticed no one was reading in the palm-decorated library. Most smoked cigars and conversed in groups or sat in overstuffed leather chairs holding drinks. Wiley watched the various groups a moment, straining to hear their conversation. Money! Always money. Wiley wondered when the white man's love affair with money and possessions began. He shook his head. It would get much worse in nineteen-ninety-three, Dave and Jim's Time.

Wiley looked beyond the stove to the long dining room. Past that, toward the stern and luxuriously carpeted, extended the Ladies Cabin. Wiley hoped all the women chatting in that large area had husbands.

After walking completely around the Grand Saloon and not seeing Fainsworth, Wiley went back outside, instantly missing the warmth and coziness of their cabin in South Park with a fire blazing in their rock-cliff fireplace. Wiley passed the top of the main staircase and made his way to cabin eleven.

Wiley tried the door to his own cabin. Locked. He remembered locking it when he and Jake left to inspect the room next door. He quickly went to Jake's cabin. As he reached for the knob, the door opened and Jake appeared. He shut the door behind him.

"Wiley! I missed you lots an' was comin' to find you."

"I just got back." Wiley grabbed Jake's left elbow and pulled him toward his room. He unlocked the door, struck a match, scanned the interior and looked under the bed. Satisfied no one was there, he walked to the dresser and lit the lamp.

Jake peered behind the door, then closed it. "Did you see that killer, Wiley?"

"Fainsworth? No. I'm sure we'll see him at dinner." Wiley walked to the door, bolted it, then slid his hands around Jake. "I missed you, too, Jake. I don't even want to know about Rodney right now."

Ignoring the cold in the room, they undressed, slid naked between the soft sheets and pulled each other close.

Jake felt Wiley's hairy body against his own and he tingled all over. "Wiley, I love feelin' you next to me, an' havin' your dick touchin' mine. I wanna stay right here 'til we get to New Orlins."

Wiley chuckled and kissed the smooth skin on Jake's massive chest. He stopped at each nipple and gently bit it. When Jake groaned and arched his back, Wiley slid under the covers and slowly kissed Jake's body down to his crotch. Each time, he felt Jake's muscles contract. With the tip of his tongue, Wiley touched the head of Jake's hard cock, then cupped one hand around Jake's balls and gently squeezed. He teased Jake's cock by licking the shaft, the underside of the head and his balls. When Jake's body began to quiver, he slid the full length of Jake's cock into his mouth.

"Oh, damn, Wiley!" Jake yelled. He came instantly and his body jerked for nearly a minute.

When Jake finally relaxed, Wiley scooted forward.

"Hell, Wiley," Jake gasped as Wiley slid into his arms. "I couldn't help spunkin'. Thought I was gonna be squirtin' for an hour with your mouth on my dick."

"I wouldn't have cared," Wiley whispered. "I like making you feel good."

Jake wrestled Wiley onto his back, sat on him and began sliding his fingers through Wiley's chest hair. He reached behind him, grabbed Wiley's hard dick and began stroking it. Jake dipped his head under the covers and twisted his body so he could take Wiley's dick into his mouth.

"You don't have to do that to me," Wiley said.

Jake raised his head and caused a large bump under the blankets, pulling them free from the mattress. "After that first time I done it to you in Dave an' Jim's cabin when we were in their Time, I can't get enough'a your juice."

Under the covers, Jake ran his hands up and down Wiley's powerful legs, felt his tight balls, then slid his hands up to Wiley's rock-hard chest. While squeezing Wiley's nipples with his fingers, Jake slid his mouth down Wiley's dick and held it still.

Wiley groaned, arched his back and slid his hands under the blankets and grabbed Jake's head.

With Wiley's fingers caressing his hair, Jake slowly slid his mouth off Wiley's dick, licked its entire length, then slid his mouth over it and began taking it in and out.

Wiley's body shuddered. He groaned, and his body jerked in powerful spasms as he spunked.

Jake kept Wiley's dick in his mouth until Wiley sighed and relaxed back to the bed. Wiley grabbed Jake and pulled him so they could lay against each other.

"God, I love you," Wiley whispered. "Maybe we *should* stay in bed until we reach New Orleans."

Jake sighed, snuggled closer but said nothing.

After a few minutes of silence, Wiley asked, "Jake, what's wrong?"

Jake jerked, then ran his hand over Wiley's chest. "Ain't nothin' wrong. I ain't never loved nobody like you, an' feelin' you spunk in my mouth is like you becomin' part'a me. Like when we become blood brothers." He kissed Wiley's chest and snuggled closer.

Wiley gently rocked Jake as he held him, but his gut suddenly tightened when he thought of Santivan. Why had he ever suggested that Jake become a Pinkerton?

CHAPTER 9

When the bell announced the evening meal, the blood brothers stirred in each other's arms.

Jake raised his head from Wiley's chest. "Hell, I wanted to stay here the whole time, but your juice didn't fill me up. I gotta eat somethin'."

Wiley chuckled. "I thought you'd say that. We could order room service, but we need to check out the dining room for Fainsworth. I value your down-to-earth observations."

They sponged each other, dressed again in the suits they'd purchased in St. Louis and left their compartment. Wiley locked the door.

As they walked along the deck, Jake stuck his finger in his collar and tried to stretch it. "I ain't never had to wear one'a these damn suits my whole life!"

"I know how you feel. I still dislike wearing one, but being a Pinkerton, they're often necessary."

Jake looked straight at Wiley. "You don't like wearin' suits, neither?"

"No. I'd rather be in Levis." Wiley nudged Jake's arm. "Or naked."

Jake snickered, then grimaced as he pulled at his collar.

As they entered the double doors of the two-hundred-foot long Grand Saloon, Jake stopped and looked around. "Damn! This here's like that pitcher of Jonah sittin' in the belly'a that whale!"

Wiley raised an eyebrow at the ornately ribbed ceiling of the long room and smiled. The Grand Saloon seemed immense even though it was only twenty-five feet wide. He looked beyond the Gentlemen's Social Hall, saw people already seated for dinner and led Jake to an empty table for two in the center of the dining area. He switched the chairs so they could see the length of the room when they looked sideways.

As he sat down, Wiley spotted Fainsworth.

Leaning over the table and nodding his head to his right, Wiley whispered, "There's Fainsworth. He's the one in the black suit, two tables over, with his back to us and sitting with three women."

Jake looked over his left shoulder, watched Fainsworth for a few moments, then jerked his head toward Wiley. "Them ladies're in danger! We gotta warn 'em!" He scooted back his chair and sprang to his feet.

Wiley grabbed Jake's arm. "They're not in danger unless someone paid Fainsworth to kill them." He relaxed his hold as Jake plopped into his chair. "Jake, he may be traveling, and no one on the boat is his target. We can't accuse him of something he hasn't done."

An elderly black man dressed in a white dinner jacket and black trousers, carrying a crystal water pitcher, approached their table. He poured both men water, then bowed. "Evenin', fine sirs. Cocktails? Wine perhaps?"

Jake grinned up at him. "I want me a beer."

"Jake, let's order a bottle of wine. Wine seems to fit this occasion."

"Hell, I don't want me no sweet wine. Sweet wine makes my head stomp around in the mornin'."

The waiter produced a wine card, and Wiley studied it a moment, then handed it back. He smiled at the man. "We'll have a bottle of burgundy. Your choice."

The waiter bowed. "Yes, sir!" He smiled broadly at both men, then whisked toward the side door.

Halfway through his rack of lamb with mint sauce, boiled new potatoes, steamed collard greens with bacon bits and eggplant soufflé, Wiley noticed Fainsworth pull out his pocket watch, turn and scan the dining room. His eyes locked with Wiley's for an instant. He glanced at Jake, then quickly turned back to the women at his table.

"Jake, Fainsworth is looking for someone in this room," Wiley said in a low voice. "Maybe he isn't just traveling."

Peering over his left shoulder at Fainsworth, Jake shuddered. There was something about the man that filled him with dread, and he knew it wasn't just because Wiley had told him about the dagger that might be hidden in his walking stick.

After a dessert of bananas Foster, served flaming at their table, the blood brothers sat back and smiled at each other as they sipped wine.

"Are you enjoying your first steamboat trip?"

"Hell, yes!"

Jake clapped his hand over his mouth. Seeing no one glaring at him, he relaxed. "Guess I got too excited." He looked around freely and grinned. "I ain't never seen nothin' like this, or ate nothin' like what we just ate."

"I think they're preparing us for New Orleans. I've never eaten eggplant soufflé or bananas Foster anywhere but there."

As Wiley enjoyed a cigarette, he suddenly sat forward in his chair and kicked Jake's boot. "Fainsworth is looking around again."

Turning to his left, Jake saw Fainsworth staring at him, then the women drew his attention back to them.

Jake shuddered. He remembered the look on Billingsly's face in the Silver Heels Bar the night he'd met Wiley. But Fainsworth was different. He hadn't looked at him with bed-longing like Billingsly had. Fainsworth made him think of a fox watching chickens.

Turning to Wiley, Jake said, "That Fainsworth don't like me. What'd I do?"

"Fainsworth doesn't like *me*. He doesn't like you because you're with me." Wiley stubbed his cigarette in the silver ashtray. "Let's walk the promenade deck. It's chilly outside, but you'll like the foggy night on the river."

Following Wiley to the side door, Jake kept his eyes on Fainsworth's back. He thought of the black spiders that lived in the corners of his barn back home in Kentucky.

When Jake caught up, Wiley slid his hand across his back, then swiped his butt. Wiley's spirit soared into the night sky. Jake was the most beautiful person he'd ever known. He felt glad to be Jake's blood brother and Pinkerton partner. He shuddered. Was it the chilly air?

As they stood at the railing, peering into the mist lit yellow by deck lamps, Wiley marveled that Mort Benchly could maneuver the steamboat through this thick fog. He allowed the cold damp breeze to caress him. He loved fog. Hearing people approach and not knowing when they would suddenly appear was wonderful training for his profession. No matter where he was, he always took to the streets during fog.

Wiley gripped Jake's arm. "Let's walk."

They turned and threaded through the gangway. Arriving at the stern, Jake grabbed the brass railing and stared into yellow spirals of fog from the passage of the riverboat.

"Wiley? Can we sometime get us a dog? My only dog's name was Puck. Ma named him that after he ate two'a her dresses." Jake lowered his head. "Puck died when I was fifteen, an' I never knew what Puck meant."

Wiley chuckled, slid his hand over Jake's far shoulder and drew him close. "Puck was an imp in Mythology. An expert at being mischievous. A brat. Your mother probably named your dog that because he ate her dresses." Wiley squeezed Jake. "That reminds me. What did you get out of Rodney?"

Jake twitched as though bitten. He looked away from Wiley. "Thought you didn't want to know about him."

Wiley grabbed Jake's arm and jerked him close. "That was how I felt then. I know you like Rodney, but you can't let your feelings keep you from telling me what he's up to. Is he a runaway?" When Jake didn't answer, Wiley gently shook his arm. "Jake, you're a Pinkerton! I'm your partner! Tell me!"

Jake stiffened, then slowly relaxed. He shrugged. "Guess you're right. After doin' lots'a lyin', Rodney told me he hops trains an' riverboats all'a time." Jake hung his head. "His ma died three years ago, an' his pa tossed him out cuz he's like us." Jake glanced pleadingly at Wiley. "We gotta help him."

"We can ask the kitchen to give us a meal for him." Wiley looked sternly at Jake. "He's breaking the law, Jake. He has to get off the boat at the next stop."

"I know that, an' told him that. When I was talkin' to him I was tryin' to think like you...an' about bein' a Pinkerton an' stuff. It weren't easy."

Jake blinked into the swirling fog. "He ain't got nobody, Wiley, an' he's only a boy."

Searching Jake's profile, Wiley knew he had teary eyes. He squeezed Jake's shoulder. "Let's go see how he's doing."

* * *

Wiley knocked at Jake's cabin door.

No answer.

Wiley knocked again and tried the knob. Locked. Wiley growled, "Rodney, unlock this door!"

The latch clicked and the door cracked. Seeing a single eye peering at him, Wiley shoved open the door, flinging Rodney back. Wiley and Jake slipped into the dark room, lit only by the light from the Grand Saloon through the round, frosted window.

The instant Jake shut the door, Wiley asked, "Are you hungry?"

Unable to face Wiley, Rodney looked at the floor. "Guess so. Ain't et nothin' for two days."

"I'll be back." Wiley grabbed the knob, then turned and looked into Jake's eyes. "Lock the door behind me. I'll knock two times, twice, when I return." He slipped through the door and firmly shut it.

Jake locked it at once, then turned to Rodney. "Wiley's gettin' you somethin' to eat." He motioned for Rodney to sit on the bed. Sliding into the armchair, Jake stared at his hands, then raised his eyes to Rodney. "Wiley said you was breakin' the law an' you gotta get off the boat at the next stop. Like I told you."

Rodney cringed. "I...I *can't* get off there! I'll be knifed in the back!" He rubbed his face. He shouldn't have mentioned it. Peeking through his fingers at Jake's handsome, loving face, he couldn't help but tell the truth. "A bunch'a boys in Memphis found out about me. They'll kill me if I go there again."

Someone outside tried the knob.

Jake rushed to open the door.

"Wait!" Rodney whispered. "Wiley said he'd knock four times."

"That you, Wiley?" Jake asked through the door.

No one answered. He heard a hard tapping on the deck as the person walked away.

Jake spun to Rodney. "Think that was the captain?"

"No. The captain on this boat's beat up, but he don't use a cane."

A cane? Jake shuddered. Fainsworth? Why would Fainsworth try this door? Was Fainsworth after Wiley?

"Damn!" Jake shouted. "Wiley's in danger!" He spun to Rodney. "Lock this door when I'm gone! I gotta help Wiley!"

Jake slid back the bolt, rushed out to the deck and pulled the door shut.

Not knowing where the kitchen was, Jake ran toward the dining room. He stood in the side door and looked around. Wiley wasn't in there. Back outside, he dodged people walking the Promenade as he made his way toward the entrance to the Gentlemen's Social Hall. After searching that area and realizing Wiley wasn't in there, he elbowed his way outside and pushed his way along the foggy deck.

CHAPTER 10

"Put another half rack of lamb, one more helping of soufflé and three more potatoes on the plate," Wiley suggested to the cook.

After serving the portions, the chef grinned. "Collard greens?" He winked at Wiley. "Tender and spicy tonight."

Wiley squinted and rubbed his beard. "Probably not. But I liked them."

With a knife, fork and napkin stuffed into the outside pocket of his suit coat, Wiley grabbed the plate, a large glass of milk and headed toward the stairwell.

"Tell your partner I hope his leg's better," the cook shouted after him.

Cringing from the lie he'd told, Wiley turned, smiled and nodded. As he headed up the stairs to the Promenade Deck, he heard the cook slam and bolt the kitchen door.

Reaching Jake's room, Wiley knocked twice, two times.

Rodney unlocked the door, opened it a crack and peeked out. Seeing Wiley, he flung open the door. The instant Wiley slipped inside, he slammed the door and turned the lock.

"Where's Jake?" Wiley asked.

"Lookin' for you. He said you was in danger."

Wiley spun to Rodney. "Danger? From what?"

"Don't know. Somebody usin' a cane tried the door after you was gone."

"A cane? And he tried the door? This is Jake's room. Good God! Fainsworth is after Jake!"

Wiley shoved the plate and glass of milk into Rodney's hands, saw the boy's face brighten when he saw the food, then barked, "Lock the door after I'm gone!"

After Wiley slammed the door, he waited until the lock clicked, then shoved his way along the crowded deck. After scanning the dining room and Gentlemen's Quarters and not seeing Jake, Wiley rushed out to the deck and plowed through passengers. Some turned and frowned at his rudeness.

* * *

Not finding Wiley anywhere, Jake spotted the boat's ticket-taker leaning against the wall enclosing the starboard paddle wheel. One hand rested on the rail as he smoked a stogie and stared into the fog. Jake rushed to him and grabbed his arm. "Where's the kitchen? Wiley went there an' somebody's gonna kill him!"

His serenity broken, the head clerk jerked his arm away from the grasp, then realized Jake's agitation. "Who's going to get killed?"

"Wiley! Wiley Deluce! Him an' me're Pinkerton partners, an' some man wants t'kill him. I gotta find the kitchen!"

A tall, thin man with a black walking stick strolled by, smiled, kept walking a few more steps, stopped, spun on his walking stick and turned toward the river.

The clerk gave Jake the once-over. "I remember you." He looked into Jake's eyes. "You're William Deluce's partner? What about a killing?"

"Where's the kitchen! Wiley went there t'get Rodney some food. I gotta find him!"

"Rodney! Rodney's on this boat? *Again*?" The clerk cursed, hurled his half-smoked cigar far into the river, then grabbed the rail so hard his knuckles turned white. "He slipped by me *again*!" Trying to shake the solid brass railing, he growled, "I'll find that rascal or my name isn't Edgar Breen!" He spun around and headed into the crowd.

Jake grabbed Edgar's arm, jerked him back and shouted, "Where's the damn *kitchen*!"

Edgar waved at a side staircase leading to the main deck. "Down there. First door in front of you at the bottom. Now, let go of me! I have to find that conniving little bastard!"

Jake released the clerk and rushed to the dark stairwell. He descended the staircase two steps at a time. When Jake reached the inner hall of the main deck, lit by a single gas lamp turned to it's lowest flame, he saw only closed doors down the long hallway that faded into darkness. No one was around. He tried the door in front of him. Locked.

"Wiley?" Jake asked softly. He peered into the deepening shadows. "You down here, Wiley?"

Jake heard footsteps descending a staircase at the far end of the hallway. He walked toward them. Whoever it was must know the boat if he was walking in the dark. Maybe he knew which door led to the kitchen. In the growing darkness, Jake heard the footsteps stop, then retreat. A door opened and shut.

Quickening his steps, Jake walked to the door he thought had closed. Feeling a knob, he turned it and opened the door. Blackness in the room made him stop.

"Anybody in here?" Jake asked. "I gotta find the kitchen."

No one answered. He heard muffled sounds from the Grand Saloon above him.

"Anybody here?"

A hand grasped Jake's left shoulder from behind, and he spun around. Against the dull glow on the walls from the dim light at the far end of the hallway, he saw the silhouette of a tall thin man. Jake shoved the man's hand from his shoulder.

"You know where the kitchen is?"

"Who are you?" the man asked.

"Jake Brady. I'm lookin' for the kitchen."

The man moved into an assured stance, allowing Jake a glimpse of a walking stick. Fainsworth!

"Why're you down here, Mr. Fainsworth? An' why're you wantin' t'kill Wiley?"

"So. You know who I am. But, of course. Deluce told you." Fainsworth grabbed his walking stick with both hands and held it against his body.

"You have it wrong, Jake Brady. I'm not here to kill William Deluce. I'm here to kill you."

Fainsworth silently drew the thin, six-inch dagger from the top of his walking stick, aimed the point at Jake's chest and lunged.

* * *

Half-running around the Texas deck, Wiley bounded down the stairs and shoved his way through the milling people. In the gangway, he slammed into a man running the opposite direction. Wiley grabbed the man to keep him from falling backwards.

"Sorry," Wiley said. "I'm in a hurry."

"Well, so am I!" Edgar Breen snapped. He suddenly recognized Wiley. "You! William Deluce! I...er, just saw your partner. He said Rodney is aboard! Where is he?"

Wiley yanked him forward. "You saw Jake? Where?"

Edgar squinted. "I'll tell you *after* you tell me where Rodney is!"

Unconcerned that he blocked traffic in the narrow hallway, Wiley gripped Edgar's upper arms and lifted him off his feet. "You tell me where Jake is or I'll toss you overboard!" Holding Edgar in mid-air, Wiley plowed through the gangway and headed to the railing.

From stories he'd heard about William Deluce, Edgar realized he'd be in the river in seconds. "Wait! I saw him right here a few minutes ago. He wanted to know where the kitchen was."

Wiley dropped Edgar and charged back through the gangway toward the staircase.

"What about Rodney?" Edgar shouted.

Wiley flew down the steps, stopped at the bottom and turned up the gaslight. He tried the kitchen door. Locked. He knew it would be. Wiley headed down the long hallway. Even with brighter light, he entered growing darkness.

Wiley spotted the shape of a man lying prone on the floor forty feet away. Another man crouched beside him. As Wiley ran toward them, he saw a glint of light from the blade of a long knife in the crouched man's hand.

Knowing he'd left his gun in the room, but had forgotten to give Rodney his eating utensils, Wiley slid the knife from his suit pocket and positioned it to throw. He'd nearly reached the shadowed pair.

"Get your hands up!" Wiley demanded. "And drop that knife! If I throw the knife I'm holding, you're dead!"

The man with the dagger dropped the weapon and struggled to his feet.

"Wiley?"

"Jake! Are you all right?"

"I'm fine, but Mr. Fainsworth ain't. Wiley, I might'a broke his neck. I gived him a mule-kick punch when he stuck me with that knife from his walkin' stick."

"He stabbed you?" Wiley grabbed Jake's arm and pulled him toward the light. Under the gas lamp, Wiley jerked Jake toward him. He saw a tiny hole in his shirt in the center of his chest. Buttons flew as he ripped open Jake's shirt.

They both gasped. The rawhide bag had threads from Jake's shirt stuck to it, but no hole could be seen.

"The rawhide bag stopped the dagger from killing you."

Jake examined the bag, then looked at Wiley with wide eyes. "Hell, it was dark. I just figgered he didn't know which end the point was on."

* * *

Hands tied behind the chair, Fainsworth stopped trying to free himself. Every movement he made tightened the rawhide strap binding his wrists. Not only did his hands throb, he saw his own agonizing death in the eyes of William Deluce as the man leaned over and glared at him.

"For the *fourth* time," Wiley demanded, "who paid you to kill Jake?"

Fainsworth looked at the floor. "No one. I just wanted to kill him."

Jake shoved Wiley aside, grabbed Fainsworth's pointed beard with one hand and his hair with the other. He jerked the hired killer's face toward him. "I'll make him talk, Wiley." With a spit-covered tongue, he slowly licked the middle of Fainsworth's face from his chin to his hairline.

Fainsworth swore and spat, nearly upsetting the chair, but Jake held him in place.

"Dammit!" Fainsworth screamed. "Don't do that again!" He spat again and tried to lower his head to wipe Jake's saliva on his lapel. He couldn't. Jake held him too tight.

Jake pulled back and grinned. "I'm gonna keep doin' this 'til you tell us who paid you t'kill me."

"Leave me alone!" Fainsworth shrieked, squirming in the chair.

Standing behind Fainsworth, Captain Finn clasped his hands behind his back, rocked on his heels and grinned.

Jake tightened his grip on Fainsworth's hair, leaned forward, slathered his tongue over Fainsworth's eyes, then sucked on his nose.

Fainsworth thrashed violently. "Stop! I was paid by a woman named Betty Gringold! Stop licking me!"

Wiley gasped. "Betty! Good God! Betty?"

Jake released Fainsworth's head, then spat. "You taste like a damn hog!" He spat again, wiped his tongue on his sleeve, then looked at Wiley. "We gonna arrest Betty, too?"

"Absolutely! Behind bars, she can't try anything like this again. When we get to Memphis, I'll wire Mike to have her arrested." Wiley eyed Captain Finn. "Do you have a jail aboard?"

"Certainly." Finn chuckled. "It's a cage on the main deck...in the middle of the chickens. Put it there myself." He grinned and hooked his belt with this thumbs. "Hate for prisoners to be lonely." Smiling at Jake, he said, "That was the worst way of getting a man to confess I've ever seen. I might try it myself someday, *after* I've smoked a stogie."

* * *

In Jake's cabin, Wiley folded his arms and eyed Rodney. "I've already paid for this cabin to New Orleans. Jake told me what would happen to you in Memphis, so I'm letting you use it. I'm also going to give you forty dollars. I suggest you find a place to live and a job, and stop stealing rides to all parts of the country." He handed Rodney two gold double eagles.

Rodney stared at the coins, then briefly glanced at Wiley. "I'll try an' find a job in N'Awlins. I know some folks there."

As Jake left Rodney's cabin, lagging a few steps behind Wiley, he slipped two more double eagles into Rodney's hand, then put his finger to his lips. They grinned at each other.

When the riverboat stopped at Memphis, Wiley went ashore and wired Mike McGelvy about the attempt on Jake's life, of Fainsworth's capture and for Betty's immediate arrest. He didn't wait for a reply.

CHAPTER 11

As the sun dipped low on the horizon, Jake stepped off the gangplank at the New Orleans dock. He stopped and breathed deeply, loving the smell of the river and the warm humidity cloaking him. He grinned at the wharf, lined with dirty-gray, wooden buildings and gas lamps perched on rusting metal posts.

"Wiley, this here town smells like the river back home. An' it feels good here."

Wiley grabbed Jake's arm and ushered him away from the gangplank so others could depart. "Wait until you taste the food. I can hardly wait to eat...*anything*. Food tastes better here than anywhere I've ever been. And the people here are extremely genteel." Wiley breathed deeply. "This is my favorite city."

They made their way along the dock. After walking a block, Wiley turned down a street lined with cypress buildings. At the corner of Decatur and St. Philip, he stopped, set his bag on the ground, pulled out a slip of paper and read his own writing.

"620 Burgundy," Wiley muttered to himself. He picked up his bag and turned to Jake. "It's about eight blocks to Senator Faubourg's house. That's where Mike arranged for us to stay."

Soon, the streets became crowded. Wiley wanted to point out an especially beautiful courtyard, but realized Jake was no longer beside him. He spun around and saw Jake shuffling a dozen steps behind, looking cautiously down every passageway and into each courtyard, all the while dodging people and buggies. Wiley watched him turn completely around and walk backwards a few steps, then continue toward him at a faster pace.

When Jake caught up, Wiley asked, "I know I told you to always be watchful, but what are you looking for?"

"Hell, Wiley. I don't want one'a them gators to take a bite outta me."

Wiley chuckled. "Jake, I told you alligators don't live in town. They only live in swamps, and the swamps are a long way from here."

As they walked up St. Philip Street, Jake gawked at the ornate buildings that lined both sides. Many were three-stories with balconies on the second and third levels held up by iron posts. Some railings displayed cast-iron filigree.

"This here town's sure somethin', Wiley. If they put a roof over these here streets, it'd look like that mall we went to in nineteen-ninety-three." Jake glanced both ways down a side street. "'Course, this here town's better lookin' than that only-white mall."

A short time later, they arrived at Senator Faubourg's three-story brick home near the corner of Burgundy and Toulouse. A second and third-story balcony stretched the entire length of the house and upwards to its own roof nearly as high as the eaves and decorated with cast-iron lacework. Wisteria wove its woody vines throughout the trim and draped grape-like fuchsia blossoms to the top. Green shutters flanked high windows extending to floor level that opened up from the bottom. Wiley had heard the residents of New Orleans were taxed on windows but not on doors, so they used what he called door-windows.

Jake pointed to an iron gate to the right of the house that closed off a shadowed passageway. "They must keep their horses an' buggies in the back. Lookit all them tracks goin' in there."

"Good deduction. Most of these homes have central courtyards."

Wiley rapped the brass knocker.

Moments later, a handsome black woman answered the door. She wore a floor-length yellow dress, overlaid with a gathered white cotton shawl belted at the waist that became a wrap-around apron. A yellow bandanna, tied in front, covered her hair.

"Yes, suh?"

Wiley swept off his hat, smiled and bowed. "Ma'am. I'm Wiley Deluce and this is my partner, Jake Brady. We've been informed by our Pinkerton agency that we are to be guests in this home for a few days."

The woman beamed. "Yes, suh! Mista Faubourg's been expectin' you. Please come in."

They entered the house and quietly set down their bags. The woman carefully shut the door and turned to them. "I'll get Mista Faubourg." She glided across the room and through a far door.

The partners stood in the parlor in silence.

Jake stared at the twin love-seats. Slender rosewood arms poked out from billowy, cotton covers in a bright yellow-and-pink floral pattern. He thought of the summer Pa had gone to Lexington for three weeks. It was the only time he'd seen his mother so radiant. One of those days, she'd looked cool and fresh in that yellow-and-pink dress, the one she wore on Sundays when she'd felt well enough to go to church. Sitting at the table outside, she'd poured them glasses of lemonade. Jake remembered thinking her arms, extending past the ends of her sleeves, had looked too thin to lift the pitcher.

Wiley folded his arms. He was in New Orleans. And he was here with Jake. He carefully observed the room. A woven reed mat covered much of the cypress plank floor. Large lavender urns sat in two corners. One held stems of pink azaleas and the other spilled with peach camellias and tall white swamp lilies with long curling tips of each petal. Artfully grouped paintings and tintype photographs graced the walls. The fireplace mantle displayed a bronze bust of Henry Clay, a Seth Thomas balloon clock and a cut crystal vase contained a single stem of rare white azalea.

Wiley wondered if it had been an exceptionally warm winter. If he remembered correctly, these flowers were blooming nearly a month early.

Jake whispered, "Wiley, this here room's like summertime. Does Mr. Fogberg have lots'a money?"

"It's pronounced Faw-berg, Jake. He's a state senator."

They heard heavy footsteps in the hall, and a portly man hurried into the room. His gray vested suit matched his frizzy hair and bushy mutton chops. He adjusted his royal purple cravat as he crossed the room and smiled when he stopped in front of the partners.

"Gentlemen, welcome. I'm Senator Maurice Faubourg. Mike McGelvy holds you two in high regard. My house is open to you." He shrugged and glanced at the ceiling. "Except the upper two floors, of course. Those are the family quarters. Which of you is William Deluce?"

"I am." Wiley extended his hand, then nodded toward Jake. "This is my partner, Jake Brady."

Maurice Faubourg shook Wiley's hand with both of his. "Your stature matches your reputation, Mr. Deluce." He turned to Jake and grasped his hand in the same manner. "Am I right in saying, Mr. Brady, that you are Mr. Deluce's first partner?"

Jake beamed. "Sure am, Mr. Senator."

"Please, call me Maurice. Here in New Orleans we're quite informal." He chuckled. "Except during Mardi Gras."

Maurice smiled. "Please, excuse me a moment. I'll get Seek and August to take your bags to your quarters." He spun on his heels, headed toward the hall, then stopped at the door and turned back to face them. "You men need to keep your wits about you while you're in this house." He raised an eyebrow. "My two daughters are of marrying age." Stepping into the hall, he shouted, "Seek!"

Jake cringed at the remark about the daughters, but grinned when he saw a black boy of about six years rush into the room.

Maurice smiled, patted the boy's shoulder and gently led him to the partners. "Gentlemen, this is Seek. He's been waiting since Christmas to meet you. His father and mother are our live-in servants. August is his father, and Chida his mother. You met Chida at the door." He looked down at the boy and smiled. "Seek's real name is Bartholomew. I'm the only one who calls him Seek. We've always had such fun playing hide-and-seek together." He squinted at the boy. "It seems I'm always seeking him. He hides in the most astonishing places, and I can *never* find him." He winked at Jake and Wiley.

Seek giggled, then smiled. His two front teeth were missing. "Are you them Pinkerton men?"

"Sure are," Jake said at once. "Think we could play hide'n seek, sometime?" His grin faded and he looked at Senator Faubourg. "Uh...only if it's okay in this here house."

Maurice noticed the way Wiley smiled at Jake and relaxed about having these two dashing men staying so close to his daughters. He nodded at Jake. "Only if you let Seek tell you where you can and cannot go." He eyed Jake's formidable stature. "But I have to warn you. You'll have a difficult time hiding from Seek." Laughingly, he patted his paunch. "I'm easy to find also, but for a totally different reason."

After Maurice whisked Seek off to find his father, he took Jake and Wiley on a tour of the house. The building that faced the street housed the parlor, dining room and servants' quarters on the main level.

"I don't mean to be rude, Senator..."

"Please, call me Maurice."

Wiley grinned and nodded.

"You were worrying about being rude?"

"Er, yes. Just curious. Everyone I've met in New Orleans houses their servants in the back buildings."

"Quite right. However, we've come to love August and his family like...family. They stay over here with us. And we pay for them to go wherever they want for two weeks out of every year. Last year they traveled to Africa. We gave them an extra two weeks travel time."

Wiley smiled. "I'm impressed."

Entering the courtyard through one of many arches that lined the porch, Maurice pointed to the back building, a three-story, brick structure enclosing the rear of the courtyard. It contained the male guest lodgings. He explained if he had had any sons over twelve, they would have rooms there. "Purely custom," Maurice informed them.

He led the partners down a walkway lined with long, sharp tipped leaves of mother-in-law tongue. The large courtyard, enclosed on both ends with ten-foot brick walls, had horse stalls along the entire left side. Four corrals housed six horses. A spirited, bay gelding lunged toward the rail and seemed to enjoy Jake and Wiley's caresses of his ears, nose and neck. By herself, a gray mare with black legs, mane and tail, turned her rump toward their greetings. Two other mares, an older black with a white splotch on the left shoulder and a much younger paint, shared the third stall. Both allowed the men to pet them. Two white geldings in the last pen quietly eyed the partners.

A black lacquered buggy sat between the corrals and a tack room that housed saddles and buggy parts.

Surrounded by eight-foot azalea bushes in new bloom, a spotless, open-front enclosure containing two wood cookstoves dominated the center of the courtyard. Steaming pots puffed delicious aromas as the partners followed the senator past the hut. Maurice explained that all meals were prepared there in enormous quantity. Whatever wasn't eaten by the family, August and Chida dished out to the poor or those living in the street.

Wiley closed his eyes and smiled as he slowly inhaled the evening's cuisine, glad they'd arrived today.

When they reached the far corner of the courtyard, Jake turned and looked back at the stables. He could barely see them through the vegetation. He looked at the benches on greenish, brick walkways and hiding in groupings of azaleas. He gasped at a moss-covered urn containing...a tree! The tree's roots grew down the outside of the urn and into the ground, and Jake figured it was trying to climb out of the pot. He liked the looks of the worn track used by the buggies, lined with fat-budded, flower bushes.

"Damn, Wiley! It's like a little countryside in here!"

The partners' ground-floor suite, one of six stacked three stories high and connected by wrought iron stairs and walkways, sat secluded under an oak that provided day-long shade. As Maurice opened double curtained doors, the partners looked into a large room containing an iron-filigree double bed. They followed the senator inside and saw two chairs and a lamp table in front of the door-window beside the door.

As Maurice opened a closet, he said, "I hope these quarters will be adequate."

Jake said nothing as he stared at paintings of horses on each wall. A grouping of three hung beside the bed.

"This is more than adequate. Thank you for letting us stay here." Wiley grasp the man's hand and shook it. "We will respect all your wishes."

Catching Jake's interest in the etchings, Maurice took hold of Jake's elbow, gently led him toward the largest one and began relating the artist's name, that he came from France, and his skill in drawing horses had yet to be surpassed.

Wiley quietly slipped away and inspected the two rooms on his right. One contained a tub, a pull-chain toilet and a basin with a faucet below an oval mirror. The front sitting room had two love seats facing each other. An arm chair and a table with an oil lamp took up the wall opposite the door. Wiley didn't see a single book. He shrugged and walked to another door-window that opened into the courtyard. He swept back the curtains and peered outside. The backside of the oak tree, flanked by azalea bushes as tall as himself, formed a triangular area beside the stone wall. It appeared completely hidden from the main house. He figured the sitting room must also be hidden from the second and third floors. Wiley smiled. He and Jake might use this room...even if it did lack books.

As Wiley started to turn his gaze back into the room, he caught sight of a greenish, high-backed wrought-iron bench nestled in the azalea wall in total obscurity. Wiley knew that bench would be his and Jake's hideaway.

"Unfortunately, you will have to share that bed," Wiley heard Maurice say. "All the larger rooms on this side are being refurbished in preparation for my wife's brothers. They'll be arriving from France next month."

Back in the main room, Wiley asked, "How many brothers does your wife have?"

Maurice chuckled. "Four."

Jake approached Wiley, grabbed his arm and pointed at a framed etching. "Wiley, these here pitchers were done by..."

A handsome, muscular black man suddenly appeared at the door with Wiley and Jake's bags.

Maurice smiled, waved the man in, then turned to the partners. "Gentlemen, this is August. I don't know what we would do without him. August, this is Wiley Deluce and Jake Brady. They are the Pinkertons I told you about."

As the men shook hands, August bowed slightly and smiled. Stunned by his masculine stature and extreme good looks, the partners could only grin.

"I sure can see why Seek's so good lookin'," Jake said. "He's got him some fine lookin' folks."

August flashed a smile at Jake, then turned to Maurice. "The suh's might like a washin' b'fore dinner. I'll fill the tub."

Maurice nodded and turned to the partners. "Dinner is at six sharp." He pointed across the courtyard to the center arched door of the main house. "In case you get turned around, the dining room is through that middle arch and straight ahead. Proper dining attire is expected." He smiled, spun on his heel and departed.

The moment August finished filling the tub with heated water and left their apartment, Wiley stripped naked and slid into it.

"Jake, quit looking around in there and get in this tub."

"Wiley, these pitchers'a horses in here cost lots'a money. An' Mister...uh, Senator Fogburg told me the man that drawed 'em is the best drawer in the world. He's from France." Jake ambled to the bathroom, leaned against the open door and stared down at Wiley's soaped, hairy chest. He grinned at it, then looked Wiley in the eyes.

"Wiley, if that man's the best drawer in the world, them horses in France must look like they're made outta wood."

"Get your clothes off, and get in this tub."

CHAPTER 12

Standing with one foot on a chair, Wiley finished buffing his left boot. He lowered his foot to the floor and inspected both boots side-by-side.

The dinner bell rang.

Wiley straightened his cravat, then slipped into his suit jacket.

Frowning at himself in the standing oval mirror, Jake growled, "Wiley, why we gotta be dressin' up like this to eat? We ain't on the boat no more. Ain't we gonna get food all over?"

Wiley looked into the mirror at Jake. "The Faubourgs are French. We have to respect their customs."

"What's that mean?"

"They dress formally for dinner and expect their guests to do the same." Wiley touched Jake's arm. "They'll expect us to eat with the knife and fork. We can't eat with our fingers like we do at home."

Jake frowned into the mirror at Wiley. "Hell, they sound kinda spoiled."

Wiley chuckled. "One other thing. The food here is different than we're used to. We can't insult them. We have to eat what they serve. They'll probably serve seafood."

"Sea food?" Jake spun around and looked at Wiley. "Damn! Are we gonna be eatin' stuff *fish* eat...like worms an' stuff?"

Wiley clenched his teeth and flexed his muscles, successfully suppressing a chuckle. "Jake, seafood is fish, oysters and crayfish, just to name a few. If you don't like something, gently push it to the side of your plate and leave it." He straightened Jake's cravat and squeezed his shoulder. "Let's go. Guests don't keep their hosts waiting."

Entering the dining room, they found the senator standing at the far end of the table, facing them. To his right fidgeted a pretty, young woman with short brown hair wearing a pink cotton, billowy dress with three-quarter-length puffy sleeves. Already quite shapely, she grinned when the men entered the room.

Next to her stood a beauty with long, auburn hair gracefully curled about her shoulders. Taller than her sister, she wore a simple, flowing peach gown tied at the waist with an orange sash. The woman flickered her lashes and half-smiled at Wiley and Jake as they entered the room. Tidying her dress, she exposed cleavage.

Jake noticed the fussing and wondered she'd just gotten out of bed and still wore her nightgown.

Wiley cringed when he saw the look on the older sister's face, glad Jake followed him to the chairs Maurice indicated. Wiley stood closest to Maurice and rested his hands on the back of his chair.

Watching Wiley's every move so he wouldn't do anything wrong, and already feeling sweat under his shirt, Jake quickly grabbed the back of his chair. He looked across the table into the face of the tallest daughter. She smiled at him. He grinned, then lowered his eyes.

"Lucille will be along shortly," Maurice said to Wiley. "Chida spilled a bowl of gumbo, and she's helping clean up."

"Mamma acts like a servant herself, Daddy," the tallest of the two girls said. "You've got to talk to her. It's disgraceful."

"Never mind, Margarite," Maurice said. "You know your mother. Right now, I want you to meet the two Pinkerton agents who will stay with us a few days." He motioned to Wiley. "This is William Deluce, the Pinkerton's top man."

"The gunfighter?" the younger daughter asked. She squinted at Wiley. "Some boys at school brag about shooting you when they get older."

"They better not try," Jake said. "Wiley'd hafta shoot 'em."

"What if they're faster?"

"Ain't nobody faster'n Wiley!"

Maurice tapped his glass with a spoon. After the sudden silence, he gestured toward Jake. "And this is Jake Brady, Wiley's top partner."

Top partner? Jake beamed and nodded to the women. He grinned broader when he thought their smiles reflected his being Wiley's top partner.

Wiley flickered a smile at both women. He cringed when Margarite smiled at Jake.

"Gentlemen, these lovely young ladies are my pride and joy. My youngest is Bess. She's fifteen."

"Daddy, I'm your *younger* daughter!"

"You're right, my dear, younger daughter." Senator Faubourg swept his arm toward the other woman. "My oldest daughter, across from you, Jake, is Margarite. She's nineteen."

Margarite curtsied and flitted her eyelashes at Jake.

Jake stared at her without smiling and nodded. Margarite dismissed him and moved her gaze to Wiley, smiled and slinked her shoulders, opening the top of her dress even more.

Wiley jerked a bow from the hip. "Nice to meet you ladies."

A gracefully beautiful woman glided into the room. Her long, black hair, loosely tied and adorned with a pink camellia, spilled over her left shoulder. Her flowing yellow and lavender linen dress with yellow neck and sleeve frills, swished as she stopped at the end of the table opposite Maurice. Her smile turned everyone toward her. Even Wiley recognized her loveliness.

"Ah, Lucille!" Maurice said. "You must meet our celebrated guests." As he introduced Wiley and Jake, Lucille left her spot at the table and went to each man. Wiley bowed as he took her extended hand. He noticed a large amethyst ring on one of her fingers.

Jake blushed and lowered his head when Lucille squeezed his hand and smiled. He thought of the time he'd met Rachael Harrington. Feeling little-boylike and not sure why he did it, the moment Lucille Faubourg returned to her place, Jake pulled out his chair and slid into it.

Maurice raised an eyebrow. Horrified, Wiley and Margarite glared at Jake. Bess snickered.

Controlling her amusement, Lucille leaned toward Jake. "We must let Maurice thank the Good Lord for our meal before we sit down. It's a custom we have in this family."

Jake noticed Wiley's glare and scrambled to his feet. As he shoved in his chair, it bonked against the table.

Bess snickered.

Squelching a smile, Maurice lowered his eyes and said, "May the Good Lord bless this family, our guests and our food."

Everyone bowed their head.

"May our guests also feel welcome and become acquainted with our customs and our city."

Bess snickered. Margarite frowned at her sister, then scrutinized every inch of Wiley. Lucille pressed her lips together, trying not to smile at Jake's flushed face. Wiley glanced at Jake and ached to comfort his uneasiness.

"And may the Good Lord protect Wiley and Jake in whatever confrontation they have ahead." Maurice noticed Margarite undressing Wiley with her eyes. He closed his eyes and raised his voice. "And also protect them from *other* dangers they might not be prepared for. Especially in this house."

Lucille frowned at him. "Maurice!"

Bess snickered.

"Amen," Maurice concluded with a grin. He pulled out his chair and seated himself, then motioned the others to follow. Jake waited until everyone else sat.

Chida, followed by August and Seek, entered the dining room. Chida set a large tureen of rich, brown broth at one end. Circular slices of green onions floated on the surface.

August set a heaping bowl of rice near the shrimp gumbo.

Maneuvering between Jake and Wiley, Seek set a large silver platter, piled with oysters on the half shell, in the center of the table. He nudged Jake and grinned as he turned to leave.

Jake's spirits rose. He grinned back.

As the servants left the room, Bess reached across the table and grabbed three oyster shells.

"Bess, you should let our guests serve themselves first," Lucille said. "Where are your manners? And you should be ashamed for snickering at the table."

Not hearing a word, Jake stared at the pile of shell-things filled with gray snot. "What're them things?"

"They're raw oysters," Maurice said. "Bess and I love the tasty morsels, but some people don't care for them. You might want to try one. If you don't like it everyone will understand."

Margarite frowned at the platter. "I *hate* those nasty things!"

Jake looked at her and grinned. Margarite smiled back.

Wiley took two oysters. "I'll show you how to eat them, Jake." He grabbed the tiny fork farthest from his plate and picked up a shell. After carefully dislodging the oyster, he dipped it in a creamy mixture of mustard, horseradish and whipped egg that filled a small bowl near the top of his plate. He popped the oyster into his mouth, chewed a few times and swallowed. He smiled at Maurice. "These are very fresh."

"Dredged this morning." Maurice smiled. "I get the best. It's...er, a favor from the oystermen."

"After all you've done for them, they *should* give us the freshest ones," Lucille said. She looked at Wiley. "Maurice fights for their rights for dock space. Cotton and sugar cane luggers but mostly the riverboats try to control the entire waterfront."

The senator sighed. "It's an on going battle, and may never be settled in my lifetime. It's the age-old story of the common man fighting for his rights from the greedy rich."

Wiley smiled at the senator. "I'd vote for you."

Maurice laughed. "Why, thank you, Wiley."

Jake gingerly took an oyster shell and set it in the middle of his white china plate trimmed with hand-painted violets. He stared at it, then shook it. The oyster shuddered. He turned to Wiley. "What's an oyster?"

"They live in the water. They're like clams. You've heard of clams, haven't you?"

"Don't them clams bite off your toes? That's what Billy John told me. He'd been to Mass'chuser an' back."

Bess snickered, caught Jake's eye, held up a shell and scooped the oyster into her mouth.

"Bess, that's a disgusting way of eating those ghastly things," Margarite snapped.

"I *like* eating them that way! And I can crunch on the pieces of shell." Bess picked up another, loudly slurped the oyster into her mouth and smirked at Margarite.

"Girls!" Lucille said. "We have guests!"

Margarite leered at Wiley and Jake. "Very handsome ones."

"Margarite!" Lucille scolded.

Wiley ignored the comment. He watched Jake scrape the oyster free with his tiny fork, jab it for a good hold, dip it into the sauce, then stare at it.

"Chew it a few times, then let it slide down your throat," Wiley said.

All eyes were on Jake as he slowly brought the fork to his mouth. He stared at the yellow-coated gray thing, hanging down on both sides of the fork. Shutting his eyes, he shoved it into his mouth. Not hearing the chuckles in the room, Jake felt the slimy, rubbery thing settle onto his tongue. The oyster slid toward his teeth. Biting it, Jake felt a squirt inside his mouth.

"Do you like it?" Wiley asked him.

Everyone stared at Jake, sitting statue-like, with his eyes closed.

Jake chewed a few times, then swallowed. His eyes snapped open and a smile flooded his pinched face.

"Damn, Wiley, I like this here fish-food stuff! Even if it does look like snot."

Wiley cringed. "It's called seafood, Jake."

Bess laughed before the others. Margarite tried frowning at Jake but failed.

A plate of corn pone cut into three-inch squares, bowls of collard greens garnished with bacon bits, sausage jambalaya and a platter piled with fried chicken swiftly appeared before them. Seek poked Jake in the back before he left the room.

Ignoring everything, Jake grabbed two oyster shells with each hand and plunked them into the middle of his plate. He grinned at Bess, picked up a shell and scooped the oyster into his mouth with the tiny fork.

Wiley slowly surveyed the display of food and sighed. He loved New Orleans and couldn't believe Jake liked raw oysters. He glanced at Jake's plate. Five empty oyster shells already sat to one side. He watched Jake grab four more from the platter.

Serving himself two pieces of fried chicken, Senator Faubourg said, "Wiley, what business brings you here? Or are we allowed to know?"

Wiley hesitated while he spooned jambalaya onto his plate, then speared a chicken thigh. "All I can tell you is we're on the trail of a hired assassin."

"It's Santa-man," Jake said, clunking the eighth empty oyster shell into his plate.

"Jake!" Wiley snapped.

Lucille dropped her fork into her plate. "Santivan! He's in town?" She looked at Maurice. "You've got to notify the police!" Turning her gaze to Wiley, she said, "We read he killed two Pinkertons, then decapitated them. You need protection!"

Irate that Jake blurted out that information, Wiley frowned at him, but realized his partner didn't notice. With his eyes closed and a grin on his face, Jake scooped another oyster into his mouth.

"Jake, there's other food," Wiley said. He looked apologetically at Maurice. "We can't talk about Santivan, and we already have help in capturing him."

Jake grinned at Wiley. "I know there's other food, Wiley, but these here oysters're good. I ain't never had nothin' like 'em before."

Bess giggled. "It's a fight to the finish, Jake." She grabbed four more oysters.

"You two are disgusting!" Margarite snapped.

Bess slurped down another oyster and frowned at her sister. "Well, at least I don't have a snooty horse and keep opening the top of my dress!"

"Girls!" Lucille said. She looked at Margarite. "Cover your bodice, dear. We're at the table."

Margarite flicked back her hair, glanced at Wiley, who refused to look at her, then closed her dress somewhat.

Oblivious, Senator Faubourg looked at Wiley. "Where do you gentlemen live in Colorado?"

"In the mountains. A place called South Park."

"It's on Miss Cast...uh, Mrs. Ratchett's ranch," Jake said. His plate of empty shells resembled a boneyard, but his eyes strayed to the remaining two oysters.

Jake grinned at Bess. "You take the fattest one."

"No, you take it."

Marguerite frowned, grabbed an oyster shell and plunked it on Bess's plate. "There! Jake, that last one is yours! Now, stop this! You're making me *sick*!"

Ignoring Jake, Wiley turned to Maurice. "I haven't been in New Orleans for almost two years. What's happening in town?"

Jake watched Bess slide the shells on her plate onto the empty silver platter. He did the same. They grinned at each other.

"The big concern in town is to move the statue of Henry Clay out of the middle of Canal Street," Lucille said. "It's been there twenty-six years, and it's causing traffic congestion."

"Hell, I know Henry Clay," Jake said. "He was from Kentucky, like me. Ma said he tried to stop the Civil War."

"That he did, Jake," Maurice said. "He also said, 'I would rather be right than be president,' when his views of reconciliation of the slave and free states were rejected. The people of New Orleans respect him. We erected a statue in his honor in eighteen-sixty, eight years after his death."

"And now it's in the way," Lucille said. She looked at Maurice. "Will it be moved?"

"Probably not for years, if ever. It's too popular where it is. Besides, buggies and riders can still get around it. Canal Street is quite wide, you know."

"Is there an alternative site to move it to, if comes to that?" Wiley asked.

"Some want it moved to Lafayette Square," Lucille said.

Following Beth's lead, Jake scooped rice into his side bowl, then covered it with shrimp gumbo. Before Jake plunked his plate down, he'd heaped it with some of everything on the table. He grinned with each bite as he wolfed-down two helpings.

* * *

Later, in their quarters with the drapes closed and removing their suits, Wiley said, "Jake, I was surprised you liked raw oysters."

"Hell, them things was like you squirtin' your juice in my mouth. My dick kinda got hard eatin' 'em an' thinkin'a you."

Wiley nestled against Jake's back. He slid one hand across Jake's chest and the other inside his unbuttoned pants. He grabbed Jake's crotch rested his chin on his shoulder. "The next time we eat raw oysters I hope we're naked."

"Me too." Jake leaned against Wiley. "I liked funnin' with Beth. Is it wrong to fun with a girl bein' how I am?" He shoved his crotch into

Wiley's hand. "I like your hand holdin' my dick an' nuts an' don't want no girl doin' that to me."

Wiley squeezed Jake's balls. "There's nothing wrong with joking around with Beth. I wouldn't want a woman to do this to me, either."

Wiley pulled his hand out of Jake's pants and turned Jake to face him. "Let's get into our Levis and walk the streets. There's things I want to show you. You'll love New Orleans."

"I don't wanna see no gators!"

Wiley kissed Jake's worried face. "I won't take you where we'll see one. I would never venture near the swamps at this time of night."

* * *

After walking through the French Quarter, Wiley took Jake into the dimly lit St. Louis Cemetery. Jake held Wiley's arm as they ventured a short distance along a dark walkway lined with ornately-carved stone crypts.

"Let's get outta here, Wiley. This place gives me the willies."

On bustling Canal Street, the partners stood against a building and watched people hurrying across the wide street, dodging buggies and trolly cars.

Looking above the lamp light, Jake saw a few drops of rain streak at a slant. "Looks like it's gonna be rainin' soon."

"I hope so," Wiley murmured. "I love rain in New Orleans. Thunder sounds like it's in a closet. Let's buy umbrellas, then go and watch the river."

Huddled together under their umbrellas in the sudden downpour, they watched the lamp lights of freighters and fishing boats traversing the wide river.

Jake turned to Wiley. "I could live here. But we couldn't ride naked nowhere."

"Maybe we could talk Mike into letting us stay here for a couple months each winter. I'd love to take you all over the city. Especially to the restaurants."

"Talkin' about restaurants makes me hungry. Can we eat?"

"Again?"

"I wanna eat more'a them oysters."

They each had two dozen raw oysters and bowls of soup garnished with shrimp at Maylie's Restaurant. Jake was horrified that the meal, including a ten-year-old bottle of wine, cost four dollars. Wiley shrugged. The food and being in New Orleans with Jake made it worth every penny.

The rain had stopped, and they leisurely walked back to the Faubourgs. Wiley noticed Jake scrutinizing every dark passageway.

"Still looking for alligators?"

Jake snickered. "I was practicin' bein' a Pinkerton this time."

As they walked through Jackson Square, a man lunged from the shadows and shoved a gun in Wiley's back. "Give me your wallets and watches! Now!"

Jake stopped and glanced over his right shoulder. "I ain't got me no watch. All I got is four dollars. It's in my boot under my sock, an' it's gonna stink like hell."

The thief looked over at Jake. "Take your boot off and give it to me!"

The instant Jake bent over, Wiley swung his left arm around and whacked his fist against the thief's wrist, breaking it. The man's pistol sailed into the grass. Wiley's right uppercut slammed into the robber's jaw, knocking him cold.

"Damn, Wiley! I ain't never seen nobody move so fast as you just did!"

Leaving the thief lying in the middle of Jackson Square, Wiley walked over and picked up his gun.

"Jake, we have to report this to the police."

Wiley started toward the Canal Street police station. At the edge of the square, he noticed Jake shuffling a few paces behind him with his head down. He allowed Jake to catch up to him.

"What's wrong?"

"Hell, I was tryin' to be a Pinkerton an' watch for crooks, but that man snuck up on us."

"He caught me off guard, also. We both have to be more aware of our surroundings." Wiley slid his hand across Jake's butt. "The thing you did right was distract him so I could get the drop on him. I'd say we make the perfect Pinkerton partners."

As they turned in the gun to the police, Wiley pinpointed the location of the unconscious man.

"You said you broke his wrist?" the portly officer at the front desk asked.

"I felt bones crack when I hit him," Wiley said.

"If that's the case, we'll leave him where he is."

"You're gonna leave him there?" Jake asked. "He needs him a doctor."

The officer squinted at Jake. "If we pick him up, the city pays for medical attention. Let him pay for a doctor himself. He's probably stolen more money than all three of us ever earned."

Wiley grinned. "You have a point. I'll remember that."

As the partners headed for the door, the officer said, "Nice to meet you, Mr. Deluce." He nodded when Wiley turned and smiled.

As the door shut behind them, Jake frowned at Wiley. "That poor man needs him a doctor an' somebody could rob him."

Wiley stopped and turned to Jake. "Think about what you just said. I believe in helping anyone as much as I can, just like you. But that police officer was right. Letting that thief wake up in the park, even if he has been robbed, might help him realize the consequences of what he's done to others...how it feels to get injured and robbed. Like the officer said, if the city pays to get his wrist mended, they're paying for him to go back out and rob other people." Wiley shrugged. "This way, he might think twice before doing it again. It's a hope, anyway, and we may actually be helping him change his ways."

In the gas light, Wiley saw understanding in Jake's eyes. As they walked to the Faubourg's house, he kept silent but more watchful, letting Jake mull things over.

Back in their suite, they stripped naked and slid into bed. Lying on his back, Jake remained silent even after Wiley draped his right arm and leg over him.

"Ask your friend Jesus to explain what happened tonight," Wiley whispered. "But it may take Jesus time to tell you. He's probably sitting in the grass next to the thief."

Jake snickered.

"What's funny about that?"

"Jesus is prob'ly glad I ain't there so He don't haft'a hear me sayin' dummer'n hog...uh, I mean...talkin' all the time."

"You'd certainly make Jesus laugh."

Jake snickered in the darkness long after Wiley fell asleep.

CHAPTER 13

The next evening after dinner, Jake and Wiley walked toward the Levee Pub, a two-story bar on the corner of Chartres and Barracks. The tavern, a shabby, eighty-year-old structure, had a narrow balcony around the second floor and four arched doors on the street level, all open.

A half block from the bar, Wiley grabbed Jake's arm and pointed at the building. "Just so you know, later tonight, we'll meet Jamie Chapman there. Jamie may be one of the top agents, but he and I have never seen eye-to-eye. I feel he's too eager to kill, and he refuses to tell Mike where he disappears to for days at a time."

Jake frowned at Wiley. "Why don't Mike *make* Jamie tell him where he's goin'?"

"Mike's afraid Jamie will get angry and quit. Jamie's moody, but he's been with the agency five years. He's been responsible for the capture of more criminals than any other Pinkerton. And Jake, he's thin. Very thin. You may be shocked by his appearance."

When they approached the open doors of the Levee Pub, Wiley said, "Be careful in here. This can be a rough bar."

"Hell, I just don't wanna see no gaters."

The blood brothers found the Levee Pub lit by low gas lamps and a brick fireplace, struggling to burn damp logs.

When his eyes adjusted to the smokey gloom, Wiley scanned the room. Two groups of men and a few stragglers stood in front of the cyprus-plank bar. Three tables, lit by shaded oil lamps, held card games. Other tables sat in semi-darkness. Many patrons wore rough, filthy clothes, and Wiley knew they were oystermen, fishermen or freight luggers. He zeroed in on four men arguing at the end of the bar. One raised his voice about dock space. Wiley realized Senator Faubourg had his work cut out for him.

Jake looked around the bar, then grabbed Wiley's arm and whispered, "Wiley, I don't wanna end up in no stewpot."

"Stewpot?"

"Tully, he's Stinky's older brother. Tully told me they hit you on the head in places like this, an' you wake up on some island in a pirate's stewpot."

Wiley hid his grin. "I suppose that could happen, but not while I'm with you."

Standing at the bar, they each had two surprisingly-chilled beers, which refreshed them in the heavy humidity that hung in the early evening air. Jake wondered why they even had a fire going in the fireplace. It wasn't one bit chilly.

They talked to no one, but Wiley listened to all the bits and pieces of conversation that he could distinguish. Jake crowded next to Wiley and scanned the bar, hoping no one would notice him. No one did.

Later, walking the streets of the French Quarter at twilight, Wiley nudged Jake's arm. "Let's keep our wits about us. Someone may leap from a dark courtyard and jump us like last night."

As they ate a snack of oysters on the half shell and shrimp cardinal at Antoine's on St. Louis Street, Wiley tried desperately to contain his amusement at Jake slurping down two dozen oysters, grinning at him between each one.

* * *

When the partners returned to the Levee Pub at eight that evening, Wiley spied a man sitting alone at a table in deep shadows.

Wiley headed toward him and held out his hand when he approached. "Jamie, good to see you," he said with forced cordiality.

The thin, skeletal man squinted a half-smile, set down his beer and got to his feet. The top of his head barely met Wiley's shoulders, and his thinning, sandy hair had been finger-combed across his skull. He smelled of sweat and alcohol.

"Wiley, how are you?" Jamie scowled at Jake, who appeared stunned by his ghastly appearance. "Who's this country bumpkin? Is he the new partner Mike said you had?"

Always before, Wiley had been able to restrain his distaste for Jamie, knowing the man was like himself. He'd snubbed Jamie's advances the first week he'd been on the job as a Pinkerton, which had caused strained relations between them ever since. He also distrusted Jamie for his close relationship with Betty. After Jamie's remark about Jake being a country bumpkin, Wiley lost any control he cared to have.

"Yes, Jake is my new partner. But he's hardly a country bumpkin. Unlike you, Jake is not out to make a name for himself. Nor does he look like he's already dead."

Shocked by Jamie's appearance and what he'd heard Jamie and Wiley say to each other, Jake figured he didn't understand what they were talking about. He grinned and extended his hand to the Pinkerton agent who was suppose to help them capture Santivan. "I'm Jake, an' glad to meet you."

Though Jamie barely touched Jake's hand in his limp shake, he was shocked that Jake had completely overlooked the nasty remarks. Suddenly filled with envy that Wiley had this gorgeous partner, Jamie snapped, "Where did you find him, Wiley, in a whore house?"

"Jamie, we have to work together," Wiley growled. "Why Mike decided to send you I'll never understand, but stop making insulting remarks to Jake. He's more of a man and a Pinkerton than you will *ever* be. On the riverboat to here, Jake captured Fainsworth single-handed. Now, let's get down to business. What information do you have about Santivan?"

Jamie glared at Wiley, but kept silent. Wiley had never talked to him that way, and his savage expression made him shudder. He looked at Jake. That's the man who'd captured Fainsworth? He doubted it and assumed Wiley lied, trying to justify his relationship with this...*gerkin.*

Ignoring Wiley's ire, Jamie said, "Santivan arrived tonight. I know where he is right now. I also know he'll be taking a train out later tonight. If we're going to catch him, it has to be now."

"Lead the way." As Jamie headed for the door, Wiley shuddered at the atrocities Santivan was capable of and turned to Jake. "You don't have to come with us."

Jake bristled. "Hell, I'm your Pinkerton partner! I gotta come!"

After the three men left the bar, Jamie headed toward the river. He led them down deserted and poorly lit streets. A half-block from the docks, he turned his head and looked back at the partners. "We have to be careful from here on." As he turned to keep going, he tripped on something and fell headlong into the street.

As Jake and Wiley stooped to help Jamie to his feet, two men slipped from shadows and level shotguns at their backs.

"Hands up!" one man shouted. He shoved his sawed-off Greener against Wiley's back and grabbed the gun out of his holster. "Go in that open door down the block with the light inside."

The other man deftly lifted Jake's pistol. With the barrel of his shotgun, he shoved Jake toward the door.

As they entered, the partners found themselves at the head of a long hallway. After being escorted halfway down the hall, Jake and Wiley became separated from Jamie when they were forced into a room on their right and shoved into chairs, side-by-side.

"Who are you an' what're you tyin' us up for?" Jake asked.

Holding a small pistol in one hand, a bald-headed man with a black handlebar moustache and bushy eyebrows snapped his riding crop against his leg. "Never mind who we are. Tying you up is necessary."

A small spectacled man finished tying the partner's hands and feet to the chairs. He stood up straight and said, "They're tied tight, Mjorg. I'll go tell Santivan." He left the room and slammed the door.

"I'm not surprised you tied us up," Wiley said calmly. "We're dangerous." He tried to ignore the dread he felt that it was Santivan's men who had captured them. How had they known they were in town? What had happened to Jamie? Were they slicing off Jamie's privates? Would they all end up like the other two Pinkertons?

Mjorg laughed. "You're both tied to chairs, and my gun is pointed at you. How dangerous can you be?"

A double rap on the door caused Mjorg to turn his head. He walked toward it, then turned back and sneered at Jake and Wiley. "There's someone waiting outside who wants to see you." He opened the door and motioned the person into the room.

Jake gasped when Jamie Chapman stepped through the door.

Jamie walked up to the two men, smiled, then frowned when Wiley's face remained impassive.

"You don't seem surprised to see me free as a bird, Wiley." Jamie raised his skinny arms and spun around.

"Should I be?" Wiley said flatly. "You always seemed like a sewer rat...out of place in broad daylight."

Jamie sneered, grabbed a few black hairs peeking over the top of Wiley's shirt and yanked them out. Wiley kept his stony expression.

Jake thrashed and nearly upset his chair. "Don't you hurt Wiley!"

"It didn't hurt, Jake," Wiley said. He looked up at Jamie. "I am surprised you had the courage to show yourself."

Jamie laughed. "I wanted to see the mighty William Deluce tied up and totally at my mercy."

"*Your* mercy? Since when did *you* take over this gang of--"

"He's not in charge of anything but getting rid of you!" Mjorg shouted.

"I'm not surprised at that, either," Wiley said. "Santivan may be a murderer, but he's no fool."

Jamie slugged Wiley in the face, and Jake squirmed in his chair. The door opened and the man wearing glasses stuck his head into the room. "Boss wants to see you both. He said tie them to each other and come now."

Jamie leaned close to Wiley. "I'll be back!" He turned and left the room.

Mjorg scooted Jake and Wiley's chairs back-to-back and tied the men together. As the ropes were wound across their shoulders and around their chests, Wiley wondered why Jake didn't protest.

Once the ropes were secured, Mjorg walked around the partners and laughed. "Next time you see Jamie will be the last time you see anyone." As he left the room, he slammed and locked the door.

Alone in the room with Jake, Wiley turned his head to the side and whispered, "Jake, are you all right?"

Jake gasped out air. "Damn, Wiley! Thought I was gonna bust holdin' my breath that long!"

"Why did you do that?"

"I think I can get loose."

Wiley strained to look around. "What are you talking about?"

Dipping his body to the right, Jake said, "Clem an' me tied each other up alla time when we was little. We tried seein' who could get loose the fastest." Jake twisted in his chair. "I'd hold in air when he'd be tyin' me, an' when I let it out them ropes was looser." He turned his head and tried to look at Wiley. "When that man was tyin' us together, I did that an' flexed my muscles, too. I think I can squeeze outta these here ropes."

"Jake, you're a true genius. What can I do?"

"Blow out all your air."

When Wiley exhaled, Jake did also. He squirmed his right shoulder and slid it under the rope strands that went back to Wiley. After a few contortions that nearly tipped over both chairs, Jake finally got his left shoulder free. Two lengths of rope fell slack on both sides.

"Do what I'm doin', Wiley." Jake began moving his body in a circular motion in the opposite direction the ropes had been wound around them. Slowly, some of the slack was taken up and the rope loosened around their chests so they could move their arms behind their backs.

"Try an' get your hands to me, Wiley an' I'll untie 'em."

Wiley shoved his hands through back rungs of the chair as far as he could. Jake grabbed them and squeezed, then picked at the knots.

When the rope loosened around Wiley's right hand, he'd almost yanked it free when the lock in the door clicked. "Jake, don't move or say anything," he whispered.

The door opened and Jamie, holding Wiley's Navy Colt, entered the room alone. He'd slipped Jake's gun into his belt. Jamie kicked the door shut and grinned at Wiley. "Have you made peace with your Maker before I kill you with your own gun?"

Since Jamie hadn't seen Mjorg tie them to each other, Wiley hoped he wouldn't notice the slack ropes on either side of them. "So this isn't just a plan to infiltrate Santivan's ranks," he asked quickly. "You really *are* a traitor? Why? Did Betty put you up to this?" He slowly worked his right hand against the ropes.

"Betty?" Jamie laughed. "Betty does her own things, and I do mine." He glared at Wiley. "Fortunately, I was in Mike's office when he received the wire from you about Fainsworth's capture and your demand for Betty's arrest. I barely had time to warn her before I hopped the train here." Jamie smiled at Wiley's angry face. "I'm not doing this for Betty. Not even for money. It's for the extreme pleasure of seeing you dead."

Jamie cocked the pistol. "For the past two years, you've been the darling of the agency." His face turned hateful. "I'm sick of hearing Mike expound on how you're the best Pinkerton he's ever had working for him!" Jamie pressed the barrel of the gun to Wiley's forehead. His eyes became slits. "But the main reason I want you dead is...you brushed me off as though I were a gnat. You think you're to good to sleep with me, then pick a country bumpkin?"

"Jamie, it's not that I think I'm too good. I knew I wouldn't enjoy doing *anything* with a skeleton."

"You ain't like Wiley'n me!" Jake shouted. "You don't got no love in you!"

Jamie moved the gun away from Wiley's head and pointed it at Jake's. "Shut up, bumpkin!" He turned back to Wiley. "Want to know something else? Betty is still after you." He pulled back and laughed. "The crazy bitch will *hate* me when she finds out I killed you."

Wiley wondered how he would ever be fast enough to get his hand free, grab the knife and throw it. Jamie had already cocked the gun he now pointed at Jake. Knowing Jamie loved talking about himself, he asked, "Just tell me two things before you kill me. How and when did you hook up with Santivan?" Pretending to shift in his chair, Wiley yanked his hand free. He felt a line of blood run down his thumb.

Jamie grinned wickedly and flicked Wiley's nose with the barrel of the gun. "Trying to stall me? I should think so! Where I met Santivan isn't important. I've been with him for *years*." He laughed. "I took the Pinkerton job to find out information for him. He gave me information on where some of his enemies were. Why do you think I captured so many criminals? And who do you think tortured John and Art. Remember them? They had to fill in for you when Santivan was in Philadelphia. You were supposedly detained on Cape Cod. I wanted to kill you then, and when I saw John and Art arrive instead of you, I flew into a rage and sliced them up."

"So it wasn't Santivan who's been the butcher. It was you?"

"Surprised?" Jamie laughed. "You may be a good marksman and tracker, but you don't know anything about me."

"Wiley's the best Pinkerton there ever was!" Jake shouted.

Ignoring Jake, Jamie squinted into Wiley's eyes. "We're on our way to New York. He...or rather, *we've* been paid to kill a wealthy businessman who got wind of our smuggling operation. He's been in hiding ever since he wrote to Washington about it. I got his whereabouts from Mike's files."

Jamie puffed up and smiled. "Santivan stopped here only long enough to lure you to me. It's to repay me for a favor."

The door opened and the spectacled man stuck his head into the room. "Boss says to hurry it up. We got a train to catch."

Jamie turned toward him and growled, "I'm getting to it! I'm savoring this for a few minutes longer!"

"Just hurry it up." The man pulled his head back and slammed the door.

When Jamie glanced at the door, Wiley slipped his right hand from between the chairs and reached for the knife hidden in the moccasin design. The instant Jamie turned back to him, Wiley threw the knife. The five-inch blade buried itself to the hilt in Jamie's neck.

Eyes wide in shock, Jamie staggered backward against the wall. The pistol he held discharged into the floor. Making gurgling sounds, Jamie dropped Wiley's gun and clutched his throat as he slid to a sitting position.

Wiley finally freed his left hand.

"Damn!" Jake yelled as he stared at Jamie.

"Jake, get out of these ropes!" Wiley said in a hushed command as he bent to work on the knots at his ankles.

Jake gaped open-mouthed as Jamie fell on his side in front of the door. The man still clutched his neck, and blood leaked from his mouth. Jamie shook violently and his eyes opened wider. He relaxed, turned his eyes to Jake, then stared blankly into eternity.

"Jake!" Wiley almost yelled. "We have to get out of these ropes before the others come back!"

Finally untying his feet, Wiley tossed the ropes to the floor. He elbowed Jake's arm before he got to his feet.

Jake shuddered and began struggling in his chair.

Wiley untied Jake's hands, then rushed to Jamie. He stooped next to the dead Pinkerton traitor, picked up his own Colt, holstered it, then shoved Jake's gun into his own belt.

Leaning forward, Wiley muttered, "I want Grandpa's knife." Blocking Jake's view with his body, Wiley grabbed the bone handle, jerked the knife out of Jamie's neck, wiped the blade on the dead man's shirt and slipped it into the hidden slot in his moccasin. He gently closed Jamie's eyelids.

Jake threw off the remaining ropes, jumped up, felt faint and plopped back into the chair. He put his head in his hands.

Wiley rushed to him and grabbed his shoulders. "Jake, I wouldn't have killed Jamie if he wasn't planning to kill us." He shook Jake gently. "Let's go. We have to stop Santivan from getting on that train."

Jake raised his head and looked into Wiley's eyes. "I ain't never seen nothin' like that my whole life. Kind'a makes me sick seein' Jamie die like that. An' I'm the last thing Jamie seen in this world." He pressed his cheek against Wiley's hand, still squeezing his left shoulder.

Wiley shook him. "Jake! Snap out of it! We're Pinkertons. We can grieve later. We've *got* to get out of here and stop Santivan!"

The latch clicked. Wiley motioned to Jake to stay put. He rushed to Jamie's body, dragged it out of the way, and crouched behind the backside of the door.

Mjorg stuck his head into the room. When he saw Jake sitting back-to-back with an empty chair, he shoved his body against the door, opened it wider and crept into the room, waving his pistol from side to side as he peered around.

Wiley leaped from behind the door, grabbed Mjorg around the neck with his left arm and grasped the man's gun with his right hand. He pulled Mjorg completely into the room, kicked the door shut, then shoved his left leg in front of Mjorg's and forced the man to the floor. Mjorg's pistol fired into the wall when Wiley flattened him.

Kneeling on the man's back, Wiley stripped Mjorg's gun out of his hand and slugged him across the back of the head with it, knocking him cold. He slid the gun toward Jake. The palm-sized Forehand & Wadsworth revolver hit the side of Jake's foot.

"There's a boot gun for you," Wiley whispered. He slipped a rawhide cord out of his pocket and began tying Mjorg's hands.

As Wiley stooped over Mjorg, Jake noticed the door silently open. He panicked, bent down and scooped up the small pistol Wiley had slid to him.

A man with shaggy black hair and a full black beard stuck his head into the room. The man frowned at Wiley's back, moved farther into the room and drew his gun.

That man was going to shoot Wiley in the back! Jake pointed the gun at the big man's head and pulled the trigger.

The far wall splattered with blood. The bearded man dropped to the floor.

Gun in hand, Wiley spun around. Jake sat in the chair with an outstretched arm, holding a smoking pistol and staring at the floor. Wiley gasped when he saw the dead man.

Santivan! Jake killed Santivan!

The spectacled man appeared in the doorway. He screamed at the sight, then turned and ran toward the street.

Wiley heard a deep voice yell, "Halt! Police!" A whistle blew. He heard running, then a gun blast. A body hit the floor. Several sets of heavy boots rushed toward the room.

* * *

Much later, walking down an empty street toward Senator Faubourg's house, side by side and in silence, Jake looked at Wiley. "I know I ain't smart like you an' can't read nothin' yet, but...Wiley, you did somethin' wrong back there."

Wiley bristled. "I'm sorry I killed Jamie. I didn't want to, but I didn't want us to be killed either. Besides, you killed Santivan."

"Hell, I ain't talkin' about that. I'm talkin' about when you was tyin' up that there bald-headed man." Jake hesitated. "You had your back to the door, Wiley. You could'a been shot in the back."

Wiley grinned at Jake. "You're absolutely right. That was foolish." He shook his head. "I guess since I've known you I've let down some of my guard." Wiley slid his hand over Jake's shoulders. "I love you, Jake, and I've been so taken with you that...I admit...lately, I haven't been as good a Pinkerton as I should."

Jake jerked away from Wiley's grasp and moved in front of him. He grabbed Wiley's shirt with both hands and yanked him forward. "I love you, too, but you gotta start bein' the best Pinkerton there is. Again!" He shook Wiley. "I'm your Pinkerton partner an' your real partner an' your blood brother. But, Wiley, when we're bein' Pinkertons...I don't want neither of us dead."

Wiley placed his hands on Jake's shoulders. "Thanks for saying that." He looked into Jake's eyes. "We're like one together. Hearing you say it makes me want to be who I am...a good Pinkerton." He kissed Jake on the nose. "And you are a damn good Pinkerton, mister. Don't forget it."

A grin took control of Jake's serious face. "Don't you be cussin', *Willy*."

Wiley laughed. He pulled Jake into a dark passageway and into his arms.

* * *

In the dead of night, as Jake snored softly, Wiley stared into darkness, glad Jake had handled the killing of Santivan so rationally. Jake had only said Jesus didn't want Santivan to kill him.

Wiley slid his hand over Jake's massive chest, knowing Jake's friendship with Jesus was real, as real as their own. Wiley thought of Betty. Why Betty? Why now? Jamie said he'd warned Betty of her pending arrest. Had she escaped? If so, would Mike send anyone to look for her? Wiley shuddered. Jake's life was in danger as long as Betty ran loose. He knew he'd have to concentrate more on protecting Jake. Somehow, he'd have to temper being totally enamored by Jake's presence in his life.

Jake murmured in his sleep and snuggled closer. He grabbed Wiley's crotch.

Wiley's cock sprang to life. He sighed. Keeping his mind on work with Jake at his side might be the most difficult thing he'd ever done.

CHAPTER 14

Senator Faubourg shook each partner's hand. "I'm leaving for an appointment with the mayor. I hope you gentlemen have a nice day here in New Orleans." He smiled. "And I must say, I'm impressed at what a thorough job you did ending Santivan's reign of terror. This country can breathe much easier. You can stay with us as long as you like."

The moment the senator's buggy disappeared down the long corridor to the street, Seek ran to Jake. "Mama's got yo' breakfast cookin'." He grabbed Jake's hand, then looked up at Wiley. In awe of this huge and dangerous man he'd heard so much about, he dropped his gaze, slowly looked up again and broke into a grin when he saw Wiley's broad smile. "She's got yo' breakfast, too."

"Let's all go together." Wiley grabbed Seek's other hand and they tried skipping in unison toward the house. The three were still laughing when they reached the kitchen door.

Holding both men's hands, Seek looked up at his mother. "Mama, kin I help 'em eat?"

"You ain't sittin' with 'em, child," Chida said as she handed Jake and Wiley their plates piled with bacon, eggs and grits. "They need their peace, an' you gots chores b'fore you can play." She smiled at Jake and Wiley as she shoved a small platter piled with fresh oysters toward Jake. "Bench outside yo' door's a fine place t'eat in the mornin'."

Sitting together under the oak, after sharing the oysters with Wiley, Jake mashed his runny eggs into his grits and grinned. "I missed havin' grits. Ain't no grits in Col'rado." Stopping his fork, Jake looked over at Wiley. "I sometimes can't believe we're really blood brothers'n partners, bein' I'm dum--."

"Don't say it! You do, and I'll upset your plate!"

Jake snickered. "Promise you'll teach me to read?"

"We'll start as soon as we get home."

After eating the last specks of food on his plate, Jake inspected each shady cranny and under every bush, making sure no one was around. Looking deep in thought, Wiley seemed busy scooping up remaining egg yolk with his fork. Satisfied no one was watching, Jake licked his plate.

While they sat listening to the birds and breathing in scents of New Orleans, gumbo cooking and the river, Jake asked, "What're we gonna do now?"

Wiley watched a yellow bird hop along the ground, then fly into the oak tree. He turned to Jake. "I've been thinking. Let's take a vacation as they say in nineteen-ninety-three. We can ride the riverboat back to St. Louis, then take the train to Philadelphia. I know Mike wants to meet you. On the way back to Colorado, we can visit your brother, Shed. I'm sure he and Louise would be pleased to see you."

"Damn, Wiley! That's a good idea."

"That isn't fair, Jake. You cuss all the time, but when I do, you tell me not to. Like last night."

"Hell, I..." Jake clamped his mouth shut and snickered. "I don't know when I'm cussin', Wiley. It just comes out."

"I know that. I usually don't notice until you correct me for cussing. Why do you cuss so much?"

"Hell..." Jake shut his eyes and blushed.

Wiley laughed. "It must be as much a part of you as your blue eyes, just like Pike said before we left. I'll let it go, but why do you always correct me when I cuss?"

Jake hung his head. "I like callin' you Willy. Like Tubs did that night we met. An' you callin' me Jack. It makes me feel closer to you." He shrugged. "I don't remember no other time to call you Willy 'cept when you're cussin'."

* * *

Jake played hide-and-seek with Seek most of the day. They loved each other and laughed until they cried after Jake, convinced Seek had sneaked up to the second floor, had opened Margarite's door while she was changing clothes. Behind hands shielding amusement, Lucille and Chida scolded them both.

Wiley busied himself cleaning his gun and scrubbing every speck of Jamie's blood off his knife. He walked to Canal Street and sent a telegram to Mike McGelvy about Jamie and Santivan. He also mentioned their visit to Philadelphia. Wiley didn't wait for an answer. He knew Mike would approve of Jake. As for their being blood brothers...?

After dinner, Margarite boldly asked Wiley to walk with her through the French Quarter. Wanting to be diplomatic for the Agency, Wiley agreed, then spent several minutes in private reassuring Jake nothing would happen.

A half-block from the Faubourg home, Margarite grabbed Wiley's arm and held it to her side while they walked.

Wanting to pull his arm away, Wiley clenched his teeth but said nothing. Thoughts of his dating in college and how those women had tried to force him to love them made him want to rush back to Jake.

After walking several blocks and explaining the history of the French Quarter, Margarite suddenly asked, "Are you married, Wiley?"

Wiley stiffened. "No."

Margarite pulled Wiley to a stop and looked up at him. "Why not? A handsome man like you should be married. Do you have a fiancee?"

Wiley pulled his arm from her grasp. He felt savagery taking control and calmed himself. "I'm a Pinkerton. I don't have time to be courting women." Wanting to put her off completely, he added, "When Jake and I are not on a case, we work on Jake's training, and Jake works on mine. Shall we go back? Jake and I are leaving tomorrow. We need to go over our travel plans."

Margarite stuck up her nose, spun around and marched down the street.

Realizing he'd been too curt, Wiley caught up to her. "Margarite, I apologize for being rude. Please, let me explain." He gently grabbed her arm and stopped her. When she turned to him, he saw her hurt expression. In a soft tone, he said, "The level of danger

Jake and I face doesn't permit us to think of anything else." He folded his arms. "Jake and I protect people from criminals. For either of us to marry would be a disaster. It would take our mind off our work. To do that means one of us could get killed. It would also be a tragedy for the woman. She would be alone for weeks at a time."

As they returned home, Margarite held Wiley's arm in a sisterly manner and resumed pointing out dwellings and explaining the history of the area.

In the low-lit parlor, Margarite turned to Wiley. "I apologize for being so forward tonight, Wiley. You are an extremely handsome man, and I had to try my hand for you. What you said about being a Pinkerton makes sense. Rose, one of my college friends, married a U.S. Marshal. She rarely sees him, and she's very unhappy." Margarite stood on her tiptoes and kissed Wiley's cheek. "Thank you for a lovely time. And thank you for what you said." She turned and left the room.

The main floor became silent. In his mind, Wiley looked beyond the ceiling. He assumed the family had congregated in the second floor parlor, waiting impatiently to hear news of the walk. He sighed and left the house.

Wiley crossed the dark court yard, dimly lit by a single oil lamp in the cooking hut. As he approached the door to his and Jake's quarters, he felt someone in the shadows of the oak tree.

Gun drawn, Wiley spun toward the alcove.

"You back, Wiley?" Jake asked.

Holstering his pistol, Wiley sighed. "I'm back. What are you doing out here?" He gently grasped Jake's arm, pulled him through the azalea bushes and into their room. After closing the door and turning up the lamp, he looked into Jake's worried eyes.

"What's wrong, Jake?"

"Wiley...? Wiley, did she see your scar?"

"Of course she saw my scar." Wiley touched his face. "Everyone sees it."

"Not that scar, Wiley. The scar on your leg from when Winder shot you."

Wiley squinted at Jake. "I told you, we just went for a walk. I didn't take my pants off in the street."

"I know, Wiley, but what happened *after* your walk?"

"We were only gone an hour." Not putting up with Jake's attitude, Wiley said, "Sit next to me on the bed, and I'll tell you everything that happened."

After Wiley finished explaining the events of the walk, he told Jake that Margarite had kissed him on the cheek, then left him standing alone in the parlor. "All I could think of during the walk was rushing back here to you."

Wiley firmly grabbed Jake's slouched shoulders and turned him toward himself. "Jake, I want you to promise you'll believe me from now on. I don't want to make love to a woman. I know I lied to you before, but I'm trying not to lie anymore. And, Jake...the more you don't believe I'm telling the truth, the harder it is for me to tell the truth. We have to completely trust each other. If we don't, we'll never make it as partners, and one of us might get killed."

Stunned that Wiley said they wouldn't make it as partners, Jake's mind raced. Before Wiley had left on the walk, he'd grabbed his shoulders, kissed him and said that Margarite meant nothing to him. Jake remembered how he'd paced the room the whole time Wiley had been gone. When he'd heard someone walking across the courtyard, he'd rushed outside into the deepest shadows, terrified he'd see Wiley bringing Margarite to their room. He'd made up his mind to hide outside until they were in bed, then open the door. But that didn't happen.

Jake wondered if he still mistrusted Wiley for not telling him he was a Pinkerton when they'd first met. Wiley didn't tell him about Betty, either. But that was a long time ago. He shuddered at what Wiley had said about one of them getting killed. Jake looked into Wiley's brown eyes.

"Wiley...I." Jake grabbed Wiley around the neck, buried his face into his shirt and sobbed, "I'm sorry, Wiley. I ain't never had nobody like you love me before, an' I'm scared you sometime won't love me no more."

Wiley's eyes teared. He encompassed Jake and thought of how Jake had been tormented all his life by his father and the Harrises. He squeezed Jake tighter.

"I understand, Jake. Don't worry. I've never loved anyone as much as you, either. That's why I snapped at Margarite when she asked me if I was married. Can't a man and a woman be friends without this marriage obsession? Margarite's a very intelligent person. I enjoyed what she told me about this area. But there's always entrapment! It makes me angry. And why do so many people frown on two men together? Don't they realize we don't *want* a woman?"

Jake pulled back, wiped his eyes with the back of his thumbs and his face brightened into a grin. "Hell, Wiley, maybe they're scared Jesus an' his Pa made 'em kinda like us, an' they're makin' sure nobody calls 'em sissies."

Drinking in Jake's handsome, innocent face, Wiley smiled. "I think you're absolutely right."

CHAPTER 15

Wiley and Jake left the Faubourgs early the next morning. Since they didn't have horses, they left by the street door.

Maurice stood on the front walk and said his farewell. "You gentlemen are welcome to stay here whenever you come to New Orleans." He winked at Wiley, glanced at the partly open door and lowered his voice. "And many thanks for handling Margarite so firmly but gently last night. Bess chides her on becoming an old maid with a snooty horse." Maurice chuckled. "The ingenious ways Bess brings it up makes me laugh, but Margarite is becoming desperately forward because of it. I think you helped her realize that."

"Glad to be of help." Wiley raised an eyebrow. "Margarite is not a woman to worry about being an old maid. She's...very lovely."

As they walked toward Canal Street and a telegraph office, Jake glanced at Wiley. "Sorry about last night an' thinkin' you'd do somethin' with Margarite. I'm glad you helped her."

Wiley shrugged. "I didn't realize I did. During the walk, all I wanted was to be with you. I felt nervous being alone with her."

"Hell, I ain't scared of women. I just don't like 'em huggin' me. But you an' Dave don't like 'em at all."

Wiley sighed and shook his head. "It's not that I don't like women. After the women I dated in college, and then *Betty*, I have a difficult time being around them. I always feel they're trying to get their clutches in me and drag me away from who I really am." His frown softened. "Besides, I love you."

"Does Dave in nineteen-ninety-three feel that way about women, too?"

"Dave tries to get a laugh by being a smart ass. Like Harry, but more cynical. Listening to Dave makes you wonder if he likes anyone or anything."

"I miss Dave'n Jim. Wish we could see 'em again."

"I miss them, also. But I hope we don't find ourselves in a situation where they have to rescue us. They may have helped us when we found ourselves in their Time, but they know only a little about eighteen-eighty-seven."

Wiley sent a wire to Belinda and Jimmy about their plans and how to get in touch with them in Philadelphia. At ten o'clock, they boarded the riverboat to St. Louis. The trip proved uneventful. They ordered room service three days in a row and left their cabin only to use the comfort station and bathe.

During the journey in the larger cabin that Wiley had secured, defying the Pinkerton regulation of paying for two separate rooms, he asked Jake to show him the exercises he'd learned from Sergeant Moss when he'd been eighteen. They did push-ups, sit-ups and other drills together. Wiley taught Jake wrestling and boxing maneuvers which Jake learned quickly. Since Wiley insisted on training naked, they took frequent breaks locked in each other's sweaty arms.

During one of their breaks, Wiley pulled away from a kiss. "Jake, I've never spunked so many times in four days in my life. Training like we've been doing makes me want to experience your body in every possible way." He slid his hands along Jake's arms to his wrists, pinned him to the bed and whispered, "Jake, I want to feel your cock up my butt. Dave said it feels wonderful."

Jake thrashed, but Wiley held him.

Calmly, Wiley said, "I know we both experienced pain from having that done to us in a violent way, but I want to put that behind us." Wiley grinned. "Dave said it can be a wonderful experience...if we do it out of love, and if we're relaxed."

"Damn, Wiley! I don't want us to hurt each other like Abe Harris done when we was tied up!"

"I don't either. But, I want to try it. With you. Since we love each other, maybe we can do it without pain."

"You really want me to put my dick up your butt?"

"Yes. But slowly. I want to sit on it."

"My dick'll get all smelly!"

"We can wash up afterward. We have a pitcher of water, a basin and soap."

"What if my dick gets stuck in there? How'll you shit?"

Wiley chuckled. "It won't. I'll use butter."

He reached toward the room-service tray, grabbed three fingers of butter, and smeared it on Jake's stiff cock. Wiley gouged the butter again and forced his fingers up his own anus, surprised how good it felt.

"Jake, hold still and let me sit on your cock."

Holding Jake's stiff cock, Wiley slowly lowered himself so just the head penetrated. It hurt, but he didn't let on, knowing Jake wouldn't let him continue if he showed any pain. Wiley let the head of Jake's cock stay there for a moment while he forced himself to relax. Slowly, he lowered his body down the shaft. The pain only lasted a few seconds, then a feeling of extreme pleasure and oneness with Jake flooded his entire body.

Wiley shuddered. "Jake, this feels wonderful! Grab my cock and stroke it!" With Jake's tight stroking of his cock and Jake's cock inside him, Wiley began raising and lowering his body. He and Jake were one. Jake began caressing his chest, then pinched his right nipple. The sensuous feeling in his butt became overwhelming. He couldn't help himself!

"Oh, God, Jake!"

Seeing no trace of pain on Wiley's face, Jake relaxed. He felt his dick sliding in and out of Wiley's butt. It felt glorious in that tight, slick space. He and Wiley were one...like when he and Wiley had been struck by lightning on the cliff. Jake looked at Wiley's hard dick and worked it slowly. He slid his free hand over Wiley's hairy chest, felt his rock-hard muscles, then squeezed his nipple. He'd never felt closer to Wiley, or anybody. The sensation of being inside Wiley surged through his body and he reached a climax.

Hearing Wiley cry out, Jake grabbed him around the neck and pulled him down into an open kiss.

Their muffled groans filled the room.

With Jake's cock still inside him, Wiley collapsed onto him. When his breathing slowed, he whispered into Jake's ear, "I've...never experienced...*anything* like that. Someday...you'll have to try it."

Finally catching his breath, Wiley whispered, "Dave was right. But only after I relaxed."

"I liked it too, Wiley. It feels like you're holdin' my dick with your whole body. An' it's like when we was on the cliff and was turned into one person."

"You're so right," Wiley barely whispered.

Tightly wrapped in each other's arms, they slept long past the final dinner bell.

* * *

In St. Louis, the partners boarded a train east to Philadelphia. Jake noticed Wiley acted dreamy-like after he'd sat on his dick, and it worried him. Wiley had to be at top performance. At all times. Wiley was the best Pinkerton ever, and he couldn't let down his guard. Maybe sitting on his dick wasn't such a good thing after all. Jake resolved to keep Wiley in top shape and awareness.

Jake gawked in Philadelphia. This had to be the biggest city in the world, and with the tallest buildings. He thought of Denver in Dave and Jim's Time. Those buildings had been a lot taller than any of these, but that was over a hundred years from now. He wondered how big Philadelphia's buildings might become.

As they climbed the steps of the former mansion where the Pinkerton Agency housed their headquarters, Wiley touched Jake's arm. "Don't be nervous about meeting Mike. He'll approve of you. After all, you captured Fainsworth and killed Santivan."

Jake stopped. "I ain't worried about Mike." He grabbed Wiley's arm and looked him in the eyes. "You ain't been yourself since we did that on the riverboat with that butter. You gotta stop bein' dreamy-like. Since we done that, you ain't been Wiley, the top Pinkerton. I ain't never gonna let you do that again."

Jake turned and charged up the final steps and through the main door.

Stunned, Wiley rushed after him. He knew Jake was right. The relaxed feeling he'd felt after Jake's cock had been inside him had made him feel different...in his entire body. Maybe it was dangerous for his prowess? Definitely wanting to do it again with Jake, he mentally got a hold of himself.

"Mike's office is this way," Wiley said as he passed his gawking partner and headed up the curved, marble staircase to the second floor. When he reached the door to Mike's office, he turned and waited until Jake caught up to him. "Be prepared for a dingy, smokey office. And Mike is the opposite of Jamie in stature."

Wiley knocked on the heavy oak door.

"Come in!" a deep voice shouted.

Opening the door, the stale smell of cigar smoke made Wiley shudder. He remembered the last time he'd entered this office when he'd received orders to go west.

Mike saw Wiley and labored his huge body out of his chair. "Wiley, my boy! How good to see you! Come in! Come in!"

Wiley entered, and Jake followed at his heels. They shed their dusters and hung them on the coat tree.

After a warm greeting, Mike looked at each man and smiled. "Wiley, I see Jake is as strapping as you. That does my heart good. You can look out for each other equally well." He motioned to the chairs in front of his desk. "Sit down, lads. Would you like a cigar or a spot of scotch?"

Jake slid into a chair. "I don't want me no cigar, an' what the hell's a scotch spot?" Jake shifted in the chair and grimaced. "Why don't you open one'a them windows? It stinks like hell in here!"

Mike threw his head back and laughed. "Wiley, you found yourself a partner that speaks his mind. No one, not even you, ever had the gumption to tell me that."

Shoving back his chair, Mike lumbered to two windows and strained to open them as high as he could. A blast of cold air assaulted the room.

When Mike sat at his desk, he motioned behind him and winked at Jake. "Those windows haven't been opened for years. I did it as a tribute to the man who killed Santivan and captured that despicable Fainsworth." He poured two fingers of scotch into a glass and slid it across his desk toward Jake. He poured a second one for Wiley.

Jake sipped the scotch, frowned at it, then looked at Mike. "You *never* open them windows? You gotta come where Wiley'n me live. You gotta have fresh air. Fat like you are, ridin' in Col'rado air'll do you good."

"Jake!" Wiley snapped. "Mike is chief of the Pinkertons. You can't talk to him that way."

"Nonsense! Jake can talk to me any way he wants." Mike looked down at his obese body, frowned, then smiled at Wiley. "For the past two years, I've considered you to be the top Pinkerton in this agency. I knew Jamie hated you, and Betty was obsessed with you. Well, some of that's changed. Jamie is dead." He shrugged. "And to think he'd been working with Santivan all this time." Sitting back in his chair, he added, "From now on, I'm going to start an investigation into the past of every new agent." He raised an eyebrow at Wiley. "As for Betty...well, she escaped."

"Escaped!" Wiley banged his fist on the top of Mike's desk. "Jamie's the one who warned her!"

Mike frowned and shook his head. "We haven't found a trace of her." Mike slid a few papers around on his desk, grabbed one and glanced at it, then tossed it back to the pile. "That's a telegram from New Orleans. At least, Fainsworth is in custody for attempted murder."

Shaking his head and squinting at Wiley, Mike said, "Forget about Betty. We'll get her. With all her money, she's bound to surface. Right now, I'd like to say that you and Jake did a wonderful job in New Orleans." He leaned forward and clasped his hands. "Tell me about Ben Harrington. Did you catch the killers of the men on the Castille Ranch?"

Still angry about Betty's escape, Wiley muttered, "Ben's fine. I'm afraid I wasn't the one who..."

"Sheriff Cline killed Bingsly," Jake interrupted. "Wiley had the sheriff get him cuz Wiley come after me. Winder's dead, too. Winder was the real killer, an' Bingsly made him do it." Jake's face fell and he looked at his knees. "Seth, Aaron an' Abe're dead, too. An' Sergeant Moss."

Relieved Jake had saved him from embarrassment, Wiley went to Jake's rescue. "First of all, the lawyer's name was Billingsly. He'd hired a gunman named Winder, or Sidewinder. They were responsible for the murders on the Castille Ranch. Billingsly wanted the ranch. The Harrises Jake mentioned were his neighbors in Kentucky, and Sergeant Moss was a friend from his youth. They all turned outlaw, and Jake feels their loss."

Mike observed the way the partners covered for each other, but especially how they looked at each other. He recalled how he and Ben Harrington had always done the same on both counts. But that had been a long time ago. After the war, Ben had moved to Colorado and had taken a wife. They were a thousand miles apart. Mike suddenly felt a great loss for the closeness he and Ben had shared. It had been a bond he'd never experienced with his own wife or any of his mistresses, and he longed for it. Two men couldn't get that close now, here in the East. Maybe he needed to check on the Pinkerton office in Denver...and Ben.

"How are partnerships...er, such as yours, accepted in the West?" Mike asked.

Jake perked up. "Hell, nobody says nothin'. There's lots'a partners out there like us. An' Wiley'n me are even bl..."

"It's more accepted than here," Wiley interrupted. "We...fit in."

Mike nodded slightly. "I grant you permission to stay in Colorado. You'll be under Jim McParland in Denver." He eyed Wiley. "I should put you in charge of the Denver office, but I know you'd hate it. Besides, I need you both in the field. How's Jake's training coming along?"

Wiley grinned. "Jake is learning more than I'm teaching him. In fact, he's teaching me things."

"What the hell am I teachin' you?"

Wiley winked at Jake, then turned his eyes to Mike. "Jake keeps me at top performance."

Jake glanced around the office and grabbed himself. "Hell, it's freezin' in here! You gotta shut them damn windows."

* * *

After lunch with Mike McGelvy, who paid for everything but ate little, saying he needed to trim down for his trip west, the partners left the cafe with him.

In the street, Mike pulled two telegrams from his pocket and handed them to Wiley. "Expect me in Colorado when you see me." He nodded, then hailed a buggy.

Wiley read the first telegram out loud.

"'Soaring Raven left without notice. Belinda in shock. Pike hired three men. Ranch running smoothly. We read about you both. Come back soon. Jimmy.'"

"Wonder why Soaring Raven left? Thought she liked it better with Pike there."

Folding the paper and pocketing it, Wiley shrugged. "She must have had a good reason. Maybe she didn't like the men Pike hired." Not believing what he'd just said, he wondered what was really going on there.

The second wire was from Shed, Jake's half brother and his wife, Louise. They had received the money from Wiley and preparations were in the making for Jake's surprise birthday party. Wiley remembered Jake had accidentally told him about his own party and he squelched a chuckle. And the truss! He turned away from Jake and tried to fake a cough.

"Why you laughin'? It ain't funny Soaring Raven bein' gone."

"You're right, Jake. I was thinking of...when Pike and Soaring Raven were yelling at each other the night we left."

Jake eyed Wiley, wondering if he believed him. But Wiley said they had to trust each other.

"Who's the other telegram from?"

"Shed and Louise. They're expecting us."

"It'll be good to see my very own brother, again an' see my ol' farm. I'll be glad to see Zeke an' Hank...an' my friend, Stinky."

* * *

As they walked Philadelphia's streets, Wiley pointed out things he knew about the city. At a residential intersection, he looked around, grinned, then led Jake up a narrow side street. Nearing the middle of the block, he stopped in front of a white, two-story house.

"Jake, I want you to meet someone. I know you'll like her."

"Her? Hell, is she gonna be like Betty?"

"She's nothing like Betty. She dislikes Betty intensely. Mrs. Gunther's an old lady. I rented a room from her before I left for Colorado. I'd like to see how she's getting along."

"I like ol' ladies, Wiley. They know ever'thin'."

Wiley chuckled, climbed the steps to the porch and pulled the cord for the inside chimes.

Moments later, the lock clicked and the door opened a crack. Wiley heard a gasp, then the door flung wide. A spry, white-haired woman stepped out to the stoop.

"Wiley!" Mrs. Gunther threw her arms around him. "I've prayed to see you again."

Wiley gathered the woman to himself, gently squeezed her, then pulled back. "It's good to see you, Mrs. Gunther. I'm sure your prayers kept me from being killed."

Mrs. Gunther pulled back and looked up into Wiley's eyes. "Killed? You? Nonsense! I've heard it's impossible to kill a male grizzly."

Wiley laughed and turned toward Jake. "Mrs. Gunther, I'd like you to meet my partner, Jake Brady."

Still observing Wiley's radiant face, she asked, "You're working with a partner? He must be a very speci..." Seeing Jake, she let go of Wiley and put her hands to her cheeks. "Oh, my!" Mrs. Gunther stepped toward Jake and grabbed his huge calloused hand. After taking in Jake's massive stature from top to bottom, she looked into his sparkling blue eyes. "My name is Martha Gunther. No wonder Wiley looks so--."

"You're Martha, too? That was Ma's name!"

Martha Gunther smiled, squeezed Jake's hand, then let loose of it. "I'm sure we've much more in common than that." She observed Jake's arms bulging under the heavy duster, then looked up at him. "I've prayed Wiley would find someone like you to back him up. You do back him up, don't you?"

"Yes, ma'am! Wiley'n me're the best partners there ever was. Wiley'n me're blood brothers, too."

"Jake, I'm sure Mrs. Gunther doesn't know about that."

Grabbing Wiley's closest hand, Martha patted the back of it. "You have always been so secretive about yourself, Wiley, but I always suspected if you ever went west, you would find a partner exactly like Jake. And I do know about blood brothers."

Jake grinned. "See, Wiley. I told you ol' ladies know ever'thin'."

With a laugh Wiley had never heard before, Mrs. Gunther ushered the men inside, closed the door, hung up their dusters and led them to the parlor.

When the partners seemed comfortable, she said, "Excuse me for a moment, and I'll put on some tea."

"Tea? Hell, ain't tea only for ol' ladi...?" Blushing and hanging his head, Jake added, "Sorry, Ma'am."

Martha pushed three fingers against her lips and rushed from the room.

Wiley saw Jake's beet-red face. No harm had been done. He'd lived with Mrs. Gunther for two years, knew she liked Jake, and was greatly amused by what he'd said.

"Don't worry about saying that, Jake. I'm sure Mrs. Gunther's in the kitchen laug...er, she's not angry."

Not responding and trying to forget what he'd said, Jake leaped to his feet and walked around the spartan parlor. He silently inspected framed tin-types of people he didn't know on two walls, then discovered a large, leather-bound book with thick pages lying on the top of a buffet beside the hallway door. He touched the book with one finger. Would Wiley really teach him to read?

Turning away, Jake walked to the other side of the room, sliding his hand across Wiley's shoulders on his way. In the middle of a table next to the divan, he saw an ornately carved and shiny wooden box. He touched the top of it but didn't open the lid. Ma had a music box once. Pa'd smashed it against the bedroom wall when Ma'd got so sick she couldn't work the garden.

After plopping onto the divan, Jake looked at Wiley, sitting in a chair next to him. He hoped the sight of Wiley would block the music box scene from his mind. It worked.

Jake grinned, then gestured around the room. "She ain't got much stuff in here, Wiley. Is she poor?"

"Mrs. Gunther is far from poor. Her late husband left her quite a bit of money and railroad stock. She told me she doesn't like nicknacks. After her husband died, she even sold his animal trophies."

"What the hell're animal trophies?"

"They're stuffed heads of the animals George shot in hunting trips out west and in Africa. Some hunters hang them on their walls."

"Animal heads? Hangin' on walls? Why?"

"Because George was a pompous ass," Martha Gunther said as she entered the room. She walked up to Jake and handed him a glass filled with amber liquid. "I thought you might like whiskey rather than old-lady tea."

Jake's eyes brightened. "Thanks, Ma'am!" He grabbed the glass and took a swig.

Martha laughed, bent down and kissed Jake's forehead. "You're just the partner Wiley needs." She straightened up, flashed a mischievous grin to Wiley, then looked seriously at Jake and folded her arms. "Wiley can be somewhat pompous himself, at times."

Jake took another swig of the whiskey, then looked up at Martha Gunther. "Hell, Wiley ain't pompous. He don't hang no animal heads in our cabin in Col'rado. We let the ravens have 'em an' bury what's left."

Martha sighed. "That seems much more civilized than anything George would have thought of." She rested her hand on Jake's shoulder. "I need Wiley's help. Will you be all right here by yourself for a few moments?"

Jake glanced at Wiley, saw his smile, then nodded.

Martha went to the buffet, picked up the leather-bound book and placed it on the low table in front of Jake. "These are photographs of George's hunts in Africa. He always took his photographer with him. You might like to see them. Wiley will be away only a few minutes."

As Mrs. Gunther and Wiley left the parlor, Jake looked at the very book he'd touched. His finger-smudge marred the rich leather surface and he rubbed it off with his elbow. Jake opened the book and leaned closer. He could read photographs.

In the kitchen, Martha asked Wiley to fill the wood bin next to the stove. Since it reminded him of when he'd lived here, Wiley filled the bin to overflowing, then pulled out a chair, sat at the table and looked around, smiling.

Martha added three wrist-sized logs to the fire in the cook stove and placed the kettle over the open hole. After checking something in the warming oven, she turned to Wiley and smiled.

"I'm not your mother, Wiley, but if I were, I'd tell you to hold onto Jake for dear life. Not many women would defend you on a simple matter of animal trophies. And with your Iroquois heritage, the only woman you would be happy with would be an Iroquois." Seeing

Wiley flinch, she added, "But how silly of me to say anything like that. You're the most manly man I've ever known, and you need to stay that way. Most women would destroy it in you. I know about that all too well."

Martha sat at the table across from Wiley. "I've never told you this, but for years, I tried to destroy all the manliness in George. I felt he got along much better with men than with me...and I wanted to rid him of that. It took fifty years of marriage to find out I was right." She sighed. "My nagging about his hunting safaris and the men he always took with him ruined what little we shared together. He became pompous just to spite me, knowing how much I hated it in him."

"What did you want him to be?"

Shocked Wiley confronted her with that, she clasped her hands and shook her head. "I don't know. Maybe...just to love me as a woman. George's male friends were everything to him. He should have married a...rather, he should have never married me and found himself a male partner. We both would have been much happier."

Martha stood and waved Wiley toward the parlor. "You get back to Jake. I'll be there shortly."

Wiley sat on the divan next to Jake and began looking at the album open on Jake's lap.

Pointing at one particular photograph, Jake said, "Look, Wiley! That there's a dead elerphant! Look how big he is by that man standin' there with his foot on his leg. They must'a been feedin' a whole town to hafta shoot him."

Wiley slipped his hand on Jake's shoulder. "I doubt anyone ate it. They just wanted it's head as a trophy."

Staring in silence at the photograph, Jake suddenly yelled, "How could somebody kill that elerphant just for his *head*?" He looked at Wiley. "That elerphant didn't get to feed nobody?"

Squeezing Jake's shoulder, in a low voice, Wiley said, "It's like the buffalo out west. Some hunters don't care about the meat. They just want the hides of the animals they've killed for the money they bring. Some men hang the heads on their walls to prove they're brave hunters." He shrugged. "The animals they kill don't even know they're around, so it isn't bravery."

"It's being a pompous ass," Martha said.

The two men looked up and saw Mrs. Gunther standing in the parlor doorway holding a silver tray with a steaming teapot, cups and saucers, a glass of bourbon and plate of scones. She walked into the room and set the tray on the low table in front of them.

Wiley leaped to his feet and scooted the armchair closer to the table, seated her, then took his place on the couch beside Jake. In silence, Martha handed Jake the glass of bourbon, then poured tea for Wiley and herself.

Jake took a swig of his fresh glass of whiskey, looked at the photograph of the dead elephant and pointed to the grinning man standing beside it. "Is that your husband?"

"Yes. George always posed by the animals he supposedly killed." Martha picked up the plate of scones and held it toward the blood brothers. Watching them both take one, she said, "I said 'supposedly killed,' because I think Ronald, George's photographer, actually killed it. George always took Ronald on his hunts. George had bad eyesight and rarely hit anything he shot at." She looked at Wiley. "Ronald is the one George should have been with. They should have gone West together and lived off the land."

"Hell, that's what Ma told Pa alla time."

CHAPTER 16

Jake and Wiley visited with Martha Gunther well into late afternoon. The moment Wiley reminisced about her breaded pork chops, she excused herself and began preparing them for dinner. They ate in the kitchen. After the two men washed the dishes, Martha gave Jake another whiskey and made another pot of tea. They retired to the parlor and laughed as they traded stories. Martha shuddered when the partners told about Betty.

It was late when Jake and Wiley left Mrs. Gunther's. As they walked down a dark street, five blocks from their hotel, Jake broke their long silence.

"I was right, Wiley."

"Right about what?"

"Ol' ladies do know ever'thin'."

Wiley laughed. "You were right about Mrs. Gunther."

They walked in silence for a block before Jake said, "Wiley, I ain't seen no skunks around our cabin."

"I haven't either. Maybe it's too high there." Wiley looked over at Jake. "Why?"

"Mrs. Gunther said tomato juice gets skunk stink off. I never heard that an' wanna see if it works."

Wiley bit his lip and shook his head. "If you decide to try it, please let me know ahead of time. And I think you should already have the tomato juice on hand."

Within seconds, ten men slipped from the shadows and surrounded the partners. Wiley noticed three holding knives. Others carried iron pipes or clubs. Two men approached head-on and pointed pistols at them.

Taken completely by surprise, Wiley cursed himself for being distracted from his surrounding. As a result of the city's gun laws, he had no time to dig for his Navy Colt concealed under his jacket. He remembered Jake had decided not to carry his gun.

"Be ready for anything," Wiley whispered.

Glaring at the two men approaching, Wiley shouted, "What do you want?" Knowing they were outnumbered ten to two, he didn't want the thugs to think they were going to be pushovers.

"Maybe we want'a rob you or just kill you," the largest man with a gun said in a clipped accent.

From his speech, Wiley knew the man was a transplant from the docks or bowery of New York City. He wondered if the entire group came from there since he didn't recognize any of them.

Frozen in his tracks, Jake looked around at the circle of men. He'd gotten into fights, but never with anyone who'd carried knives or clubs. Hoping Wiley would know what to do, he did a complete turn to see where every man had positioned himself. He didn't like what he saw. They inched closer.

Wiley knew the two holding guns were the leaders. The biggest man, as large as Jake or himself, wore a dark, seaman's sweater and wool knit cap. He had black stubble on his handsome face, and his barrel-shaped chest showed great power. The other man, short and knife-edge thin, wearing a shabby black suit, had a skeletal face like Jamie. Wiley realized the guns the two men carried were old single-shot pistols, but at this close range neither would miss.

As the two approached, Wiley tensed his muscles. He'd been in this situation more than once and had learned tactics from the derelicts he'd taught wrestling and boxing to right here in Philadelphia. He was ready, but was Jake? He glanced at his partner. Jake looked terrified.

"That's far enough!" Wiley shouted at the two men when they were ten feet away. "What are you doing so far from New York?"

Both men stopped.

"Know where we're from, eh?" the big man said in his clipped manner. "Pickin's 're no good there. Too many immigrants. Nobody's got money." He grinned and leveled his gun at Wiley's chest. "You look like you got money."

Jake remembered New Orleans. "We ain't got no money! I only got me five dollars. It's in my boot, an it's all smelly."

"Jake, that won't work here," Wiley whispered.

"Well, now," the big man said. He eyed Jake up and down and closed the gap between them to three feet. His partner followed. "Lads, we got us a hillbilly. Easy pickin's in my book."

"I'm from Kentucky!" Jake yelled. He balled his fists. "Don't you go callin' me no damn hillbilly!"

"Jake, now is not the..."

"I'll call you a hillbilly if I want," the big man said. "You talk like a bloody hillbilly. And *smell* like one." He glanced at his men and grinned when some of them laughed.

Furious, Jake dove at the two men in front of him. Their guns discharged into the air as they fell backward from Jake's tackle.

Instantly, Wiley found his gun, spun in a circle and shot the knives out of the hands of three men, all poised to throw them. He plowed through the dwindling circle and held his gun on the remaining men. "Drop you weapons and get your hands up, or I'll shoot the rest of you!"

Five men dropped their clubs or pipes and shoved their hands into the air. Except for the men groaning from their shot-up hands, all watched the tussle on the ground. The thin man had been knocked unconscious when his head hit the street, but Jake and the larger man rolled on the ground, growling and slugging each other.

Wiley heard clapping from the darkness behind him. He spun around and saw a man approach from the shadows followed by twelve others.

"Welcome back, Wiley," the man said.

"Burt!" Wiley holstered his gun, ran to the man and embraced him. They spun around in the middle of the street. The others swarmed the area, seized the New York thugs and helped Jake to his feet.

Shoving Burt away, Wiley said, "I have to see how Jake is." Wiley rushed to Jake and found him being escorted to him by Burt's men.

"What's happenin'?" Jake asked. He briefly inspected his bloody right fist.

"Jake, I want you to meet a good friend of mine." Wiley turned toward Burt and grabbed his shoulder. "Jake, this is Burt Peterson. He's my...Zeke."

Jake looked at Burt, but couldn't see any resemblance to Zeke, his neighbor in Kentucky. Burt made his body tingle the way it always did when he saw a handsome man. It wasn't just Burt's square-jawed face and curly brown hair that made his knees weak. Burt's tight-fitting, multi-patched pants exposed areas of muscled, hairy legs. And the man wore his dick on the right. Jake could see why Wiley would fool around with Burt. Like he used to with...Zeke!

* * *

Sitting on a wooden crate across from Wiley, Jake looked around the room in the vacant, partly burned-out warehouse in the middle of Philadelphia's Little Russia district. The men had built a small fire in a cut-off drum that everyone sat around, but the room remained cold. In silence, he watched Wiley and Burt, sitting side-by-side, talk and laugh about old times. He felt sorry Wiley could barely get in a few words. Though liking Burt's looks, Jake wanted to hit the man when he joked about Wiley's tracking ability. Jake knew he wasn't jealous of Burt. He vaguely reminded him of Sergeant Moss, his childhood idol. Was it Burt's deep, musical voice? He thought of Burt and Wiley fooling around with each other. He would like to see Burt naked. Maybe even lie on top of him naked. Getting an erection, Jake diverted his eyes to the flames peeking over the rim of the drum.

Staring into the fire, Jake felt glad Wiley had gotten to fool around with another man before they'd become blood brothers. He shuddered when he thought of Betty, or any woman, touching Wiley while he was naked.

Lost in thoughts of Betty wanting him dead, Jake didn't hear a door open and three men enter.

The first man in the group, clutching a cloth satchel, stopped beside Burt but said nothing.

Burt ignored him, touched Wiley's shoulder and nodded toward Jake, staring into the flames. "He's your new partner, eh? Heard you'd got one. He gets downright nasty when he's riled. Either that, or he's crazy taking on Al and Skell." Burt grinned. "We've been after Al Smitz and his men ever since they moved here and invaded our territory." He shook his head. "Al killed Cookie and Runt in an ambush like they tried on you." Burt slid his hand over Wiley's back.

"Cookie and Runt are dead?" Wiley lowered his head. "I didn't care much for Cookie. He wanted your position. But Runt?" Closing his eyes and shaking his head, Wiley said, "Runt always made me laugh. He called me Big Chief."

Burt shrugged and slid his hand to Wiley's butt. "You're right about Cookie, but damn it, Runt called me Bossie."

Wiley laughed. "I remember."

"Er, a...Boss, we got the whiskey like you asked," the man holding the cloth satchel said. "An' I'm glad Runt's dead 'cause he called you that."

Burt glanced up at the man and pulled the bag out of his grasp. "Get lost, Slide!" He turned to Wiley. "Now, we can celebrate."

After setting the satchel at his feet, Burt opened it and pulled out three bottles. He uncorked the whiskey and held it high. "Boys, it's time to celebrate Wiley's return." In an flat voice, he added, "And his new partner."

As Burt's men gathered around, they greeted Wiley and slapped him on the back. Only one man shook Jake's hand. As the bottles passed around, Wiley took a small sip once in a while. Jake glanced around the room, inspected each man, and wished he were in their cabin in Colorado. He took a swig every turn.

"We miss the wrestling lessons you gave us," Mory Serat whispered into Wiley's ear from behind.

Wiley turned toward the man who made him think of a riverboat gambler. His sharp, handsome features set him apart from the others despite his shabby clothes.

"You're good enough, Mory. Why don't you give the lessons."

"Oh, no! That's Burt's job." Mory half grinned at Wiley. "I take care of the...books."

After talking to several more men, Wiley touched Burt's arm. "Let me pay for this whiskey. It must have drained your funds."

"Don't worry about that." Burt looked at his hands. "I...recently made a deal with someone that set us right for several months. Maybe longer."

"I hope it doesn't involve anything against the law."

Burt glanced at Wiley, but couldn't hold his gaze. "Er...it's payment for information. Street information."

Wiley nudged Burt. "That can get you killed if the person you're collecting on finds out."

"I'll take my chances." Burt grabbed Wiley's arm. "What are your plans? Are you staying around for awhile so we can...get together?" He searched Wiley's body, leaned close and whispered, "God, Wiley, I've missed you! Can we find time to wrestle naked?"

The familiar come-on Burt used had always aroused Wiley before. He looked into Burt's eyes and saw longing and even a little caring. He felt his cock tingle slightly from the man's sensuousness, and from remembering their times together. He gave Jake a quick glance.

Jake grinned at him with one eye shut.

Good God! Jake was drunk!

Distracted by a circulating bottle, Wiley passed on it, then felt dizzy. He closed his eyes briefly and shook his head, realizing he was a little drunk himself.

"Sorry, Burt. I have to get Jake back to the hotel. We're leaving in the morning." Wiley stumbled slightly while getting to he feet.

As Wiley stood up to leave, Burt grabbed his arm and pulled him back into his seat. "Can't you...uh, we can put Jake to bed in the other room. He looks too drunk to walk. We've got blankets." Lowering his voice to a whisper, he said, "It's been so long since I've held you."

Wiley smiled crookedly and grasped Burt's arm. "Sorry, Burt, Jake and I don't share each other."

Forcing himself to his feet, Wiley walked unsteadily around the barrel, grabbed Jake's arm. He looked into half-closed eyes that barely recognized him. "Let's go, Jake."

Shocked and angered Jake was more than just Wiley's Pinkerton partner, Burt glared at Jake, then took in Wiley's massive frame. He leaped to his feet.

Wiley shook Jake. "Jake, let's go! We have a train to catch tomorrow."

"Leaving town so soon?" Burt asked Wiley. "Another job catching crooks?"

"No. Back to Colorado." Wiley tensed his muscles to stabilize himself, then yanked Jake to his feet and steadied him. "Jake, we have to go. We have to leave early in the morning."

"I hate to see you go, Wiley, but hope we see each other again," Burt said as he clung to Wiley's shoulder. "Keep in touch. Who knows, I may show up in Colorado."

Jake squint-eyed Burt. "Gotta see my farm, first." He began falling to one side.

Burt caught him. "God, you're heavy. Where's your farm?"

"Wilmore, 'Tucky."

Wiley grabbed Jake away from Burt. "Let's go!" He manhandled Jake toward the door.

"We goin' t'see Shed'n Loozie, ain't we, Wiley? An' my farm in 'Tucky."

"Just keep walking, Jake."

Burt hung onto Wiley's shoulder the entire way. At the door, he whispered, "I loved seeing you, Wiley. If anything happens, I'll be there."

Wiley turned toward him. "It was good to see you, Burt. We'll be back next year. Mike'll see to that."

Holding onto Jake, Wiley occasionally double-stepped as he helped his staggering partner to their hotel and up a flight of stairs. As he closed the door to their room and locked it, Jake stumbled to the bed and fell across it.

"Jake, are you going to be able to travel tomorrow?"

Jake didn't answer.

Wiley sighed. He removed his duster and holster and hung them on a chair next to the bed, occasionally grabbing the back to steady himself. After stripping naked, he plopped onto the bed and drank in Jake's person. He ran his hand over Jake's back, sorry he still had on his duster.

After rolling Jake on his back, Wiley struggled with Jake's coat, clothes and boots, then sat back and looked at Jake's naked body, caressed it, kissed it. Even though Jake had passed out, he felt lucky they were partners and blood brothers. Jake was the most beautiful man he'd ever known.

Wiley struggled with Jake's limp body and got him under the blankets next to himself. After turning the lamp low, he slid into bed, stared at the dim ceiling and thought of the times he and Burt had wrestled naked. Though handsome and sensuous, Burt would never measure up to Jake. He knew Burt missed him, but that was...so long ago. Wiley hoped Burt understood. Why had Burt asked where Jake's farm was?

He sighed when he remembered Jake tackling the two thugs after they'd called him a hillbilly. He needed to remind Jake to keep a level head in danger. Jake could have gotten himself shot, and at that close range, he would have been...

Wiley shuddered, rolled over, draped his arm across Jake's chest, kissed his cheek, then nestled his face against Jake's shoulder and fell asleep.

CHAPTER 17

The moment Wiley and Jake left the warehouse, Burt grabbed his coat and gloves and rushed into the street. He watched Wiley help Jake until they turned the corner, then spun on his heel and ran in the opposite direction.

On a main street, Burt hailed a buggy-for-hire, barked a location and ordered the driver to hurry. Settling back in the closed compartment, he smiled and lit up his last stogie.

After leaving the buggy and paying the driver, Burt held his hand toward the street lamp and counted a double eagle, a dime and two pennies. His life savings. Vacantly watching the buggy disappear around the corner, he thought of the better times coming. With the information he'd obtained, he'd be richer than he'd ever been in his life. Selling the information, tonight, was critical. And he'd never be implicated in the murder, a murder he now wanted to happen. With his share of the three thousand, he'd head to Colorado and try to win back Wiley. Maybe he'd take all the money. What ties did he have here? Mory? Spud? They'd get along. Mory'd become Boss. So what? He wanted Wiley.

Two blocks from where the buggy let him off, Burt climbed the steps of a two-story row house. He squinted at the numbers a second time. The entire block looked the same, and he didn't dare try the wrong door.

His coded knock was met with such a long silence, he knocked again.

"Who is it!" a high-pitched, disguised voice shouted from within.

"Burt"

"Burt who?"

"Burt Peterson."

The lock clicked, and the door opened a crack. A single eye peered out along with the barrel of a gun.

"What's my password?"

Burt whispered, "Naked in bed with me."

The gun disappeared. A few moments later, the door opened wider and a hand reached out, grasped Burt's arm and yanked him inside. The door shut softly behind him and the lock clicked.

Burt found himself in total darkness.

"Dillard, light a candle," ordered the person gripping Burt's arm, still using the disguised voice.

Across the room a match was struck. It's fading burst lit the wick of a candle. The soft light enabled Burt to recognize the person still clutching his arm. Betty Gringold.

* * *

Squinting at the bright sunlight in the compartment, Jake watched the western part of Philadelphia slide by the window. As the train picked up speed, the rocking motion made Jake's head pound and his stomach queasy.

"I don't feel so good, Wiley." Jake turned his head and saw Wiley studying a paper.

Wiley looked up from the train schedule in his lap. "I'm sure you don't. You kept grabbing the bottles out of the hands of Burt's men last night. They didn't care because you knocked over Al Smitz and his partner, but under normal circumstances, they would have been angry you drank so much of their whiskey."

"Are Burt an' them crooks?"

"They can be." Wiley folded the schedule and slipped it into his jacket pocket. "They're what Jim and Dave in nineteen-ninety-three call street people. Men like that band together to help each other survive. They steal food and whiskey if they can't find odd..."

Jake clasped his hand over his mouth, lurched out of the compartment and headed for the comfort station, leaving the door wide open.

Wiley shook his head and got to his feet. He knew all too well how Jake felt and remembered puking in the bushes after drinking too much in his college days. Before he shut the door, he glanced toward the comfort station, thankful Jake had closed that door.

Ten minutes later, Jake stumbled into the compartment and held onto the door as he closed it. "Damn, Wiley, I ain't gonna do no drinkin' like that again."

"Why did you drink so much last night?"

Jake slumped into the seat across from Wiley and leaned his head against the window. "Guess I thought you was riled at me for jumpin' them two men. An'..." He closed his eyes.

"And what?"

Looking at Wiley with red-rimmed, blue eyes, Jake shrugged. "Somma them men gave me the willies an'...guess I thought you might wanna do somethin' with Burt like you used to." He looked at his knees. "I'd like to fool around with him, too."

Wiley chuckled. He leaned forward, slid his hand up Jake's leg and gently grabbed him in the crotch. "I told you Burt was my Zeke. I don't want to do anything with him, now. Just like you don't want to do anything with Zeke. We have each other." He released his grasp on Jake sat back and sighed. "God knows, you're enough to handle."

"You mean it?"

"I mean it on both counts. But we have to talk about you jumping those two men." Wiley leaned toward Jake. "We're partners. We have to let each other know what we're doing. If I'd been any slower getting my gun into play, we'd be dead. The three with knives had them ready to throw at us."

Jake hung his head. "Sorry, Wiley. I got riled at them men callin' me a hillbilly." He glared at Wiley. "An' I don't smell like no damn hillbilly, neither!"

"Those men were just taunting you. Promise me you won't do anything like that again without warning me first."

Jake shrugged. "I'll try, Wiley."

CHAPTER 18

A day later, as the train pulled into Lexington, Jake grinned as he peered out the window. He turned to Wiley. "I'm excited to be visitin' Shed. Wonder what he's done to the farm?"

"We'll soon find out. I've already booked tickets for the stage to Wilmore. We'll have to hurry to catch it once we leave the train."

Wide-eyed, Jake asked, "When'd you do that?"

"Just before we left Philadelphia. You were in here asleep, or rather still drunk. I got off the train before it left and wired ahead."

The moment the train came to a complete stop, Wiley ushered Jake from the car, and they rushed to the street in front of the station. Seeing two stage coaches, Wiley ran to the first one.

"Is this the coach to Wilmore?"

The driver shook his head and motioned to the one behind him just pulling into the street.

"Wait!" Wiley yelled as he ran toward it. "We have to get to Wilmore."

The young blond driver wearing a huge handlebar moustache and a battered straw hat hauled back on the reins. "Get on aboard. There's plenty room inside fer yer bags. Yer can pay when we arrive."

The partners climbed in and found the coach empty except for an elderly woman in the seat opposite the one they took. The stage lurched to a start, then stopped again as a man outside ran toward it yelling. The door opened and a middle-aged, balding man wearing a brown pin-striped suit climbed aboard. He glanced at Jake, then Wiley, nodded curtly, tipped his hat to the woman and sat next to her, then plopped his satchel at his feet and stared out the window.

Wiley instantly recognized the man's face, but couldn't recall from where. He searched his memory.

The woman across from Jake stared open-mouthed at him as he shoved his bag under the seat. "Land sakes! Are you Martha Brady's son?"

Jake smiled at her. "Yes Ma'am. You knew Ma?"

"Of course. I'm Daisy Coddlestone. Your mother and I went to the same church." She bowed her head. "That is, until she got so ill she couldn't attend."

"Now I remember! You come to the farm years ago an' brought Ma chicken soup." Jake shrugged. "Sorry I didn't recognize you, Ma'am. It's been a long time." He grinned at Wiley, then looked back at Mrs. Coddlestone. "This here's Wiley. We're Pinkerton partners."

Wiley nudged Jake with his elbow, then nodded to the woman. He noticed the man next to her glance at them and shift in his seat. Wiley wondered if he was trying to hide his face when he nearly stuck his head out the open window of the coach. Where did he know him from?

"Your a Pinkerton?" Daisy asked. "Land sakes! Your mother would be proud if she were still alive." She smiled at Wiley. "Very glad to make your acquaintance."

Wiley smiled. "Ma'am. Did you know Jake's father?"

"*Yes!*" Daisy said icily. "He didn't think much of me, and I thought even less of him. He told me once my chicken soup tasted like I'd left the feathers on the chicken. I never spoke to him again after that."

"He didn't think much'a me, neither." Jake motioned toward Wiley. "An' it's a good thing Wiley didn't know him. Wiley would'a strung him upside-down from my old tree house."

They all laughed, except for the man sitting across from Wiley.

By the end of the two-hour stage ride, filled with talk of past times and acquaintances remembered by Jake and Daisy, Wiley had recalled the male passenger's name. Alfred Swift. He'd met the man only once in Philadelphia. Burt had introduced them and had mentioned later that Alfred had gotten himself into sordid affairs.

As they got off the coach in Wilmore, Wiley grabbed Alfred Swift's arm and led him away from the others.

"I know who you are. What are you doing in Wilmore, Kentucky?"

Alfred tried to pull away from Wiley's grasp, but failed. He glared at Wiley. "I'm here visiting my mother."

"Is that so." Wiley yanked Alfred over to Jake and Daisy. "Do either of you know this man? His name is Alfred Swift. He said he's in Wilmore visiting his mother."

"I ain't never seen him before," Jake said.

"Swift?" Daisy looked Alfred over carefully. "I have never heard of a Swift in this town. And he doesn't look at all familiar."

Wiley grinned menacingly at Swift. "I thought so. Jake, we have to make a visit to Sheriff Tyborn's office." After saying the sheriff's name, Wiley cringed remembering his first encounter with the obese lawman. The gunfight at Jake's farm left five men dead. Wiley had thought often about the sheriff who had inspected the scene, then fled when he found out nearly everyone in the yard was "gay" like Jake. Hanging Sheriff Tyborn upside-down from Jake's tree house was a comforting thought, but Wiley didn't think he was strong enough to haul him up there.

They took leave of Daisy Coddlestone and marched Alfred Swift down the main street to the sheriff's office. Wiley opened the door and shoved Swift into the building.

Sitting at his desk, Sheriff Tyborn looked up and frowned at Alfred being manhandled into his office. When he saw Wiley, then Jake, he struggled his huge body to his feet and yelled, "What're you two doin' here? Thought you'd gone west?"

"We're back." Wiley shoved Alfred toward the sheriff. "This man is Alfred Swift. I know him from Philadelphia. He told me he's here to visit his mother. Have you ever seen him before?"

Tyborn tried to pull up his slipping pants. "Can't say I have. People move in an' outta town all'a time. What of it?"

"This man is a thief and who knows what else," Wiley snapped. "I expect you to watch his every move. If he gets into any trouble while he's here, I will hold you personally responsible. Jake and I will come after *both* of you!"

"I ain't gonna do no sech thing," Tyborn said. "This man's free to go as he pleases. I ain't takin' the word of no sissie as fact."

Wiley walked over to Sheriff Tyborn, whipped out his Navy Colt and stuck it into the folds of Tyborn's neck. "You sorry excuse for a man! You forced Curtis to leave town just because he was decent enough to help us bury the five bodies on Jake's farm. Now, you won't watch a possible criminal in your town. What kind of lawman are you?" Shifting his pistol to the sheriff's cheek, Wiley shouted, "I'll tell you what you are. You're a fat, slovenly pig, more on the side of criminals than the law. I was told you stole money from a dead man at Jake's farm. Do you remember that?"

Holstering his gun, Wiley shoved the huge, sweating man into his chair. "You watch this man, Sheriff, or so help me God, I'll dig up enough charges against you to put *you* behind bars!" He turned toward Jake. "Let's go. He has his orders."

Out in the street, Jake turned to Wiley. "Damn, I ain't never heard nobody talk to Sheriff Tyborn like that. We'd best watch out. He's most likely gonna arrest us."

Wiley winked at Jake. "I'm sure he'll try. Is there a place we can rent horses?"

"Mr. Tollifson'll rent us some. He's a Quaker an' owns the town livery."

Following Jake down the main street of Wilmore, Wiley watched the expressions of the townspeople as they recognized Jake. Many turned up their noses and passed as if he wasn't there. Being with Jake, Wiley also received haughty glances. Already annoyed with Sheriff Tyborn, these people riled Wiley even more, but he forced himself to keep his mouth shut. He remembered what Dave had said about people like these: "Blind to love but convinced they see the truth." For an instant, Wiley wanted to be back in nineteen-ninety-three with Jim and Dave. The inventions of that Time enthralled him. Then he remembered the people and changed his mind.

A man in a black suit grabbed Jake's arm and stopped him. "Well! What are *you* doing back in town? I thought we'd seen the last of your kind."

Jake grinned. "Glad to see you, Reverend Fall. I'm visitin' my brother, Shed. I gived him my farm."

"I know," the reverend snapped. "Why don't you let Shed and his wife live in peace. We don't want your kind in this town."

Wiley grabbed the reverend's arms and shoved him against a store front. "What do you mean, his kind?"

"Let go of me!" screeched Reverend Fall. "I'm the Methodist minister in this town! How *dare* you pin me against this building!"

Women screamed and pointed. People ran to the scene as Wiley lifted the reverend so their faces were level. "What do you mean, *his kind*?"

"Let go of me!" Reverend Fall screamed. "Someone get the sheriff!"

Jake grabbed at Wiley's shoulder. "Wiley, that's Reverend Fall. He ain't no criminal."

Ignoring Jake and the growing crowd, Wiley shook the reverend. "I asked you what you meant by *his kind*?"

Reverend Fall looked into Wiley's savage eyes and shuddered. "Er...you know, a sissy." He stiffened. "An abomination in the eyes of the Lord!"

"Sissy?" Wiley bellowed. "*You're* the sissy! And the abomination!" He shook the reverend again. "I'll have you know Jake is one of the top Pinkertons in this country. He's not a sissy!" Wiley shook the reverend one last time, dropped him to the boardwalk, then turned and glared at the angry people crowding closer.

"I'm William Deluce! Why are you standing there?" He pointed to the reverend. "This man insulted Jake!"

Several people in front stopped their advance.

"Jake is my Pinkerton partner! He saved my life twice in one month! And he single-handedly dealt with two dangerous assassins and the leaders of a mob in Philadelphia. Jake is a hero!"

The silent crowd parted as Sheriff Tyborn shoved his body toward Wiley and stopped ten feet from him.

"What're you doin' now?" Tyborn shouted.

Wiley stepped down from the boardwalk, approached the sheriff and looked around. "Where's Alfred Swift? I told you to watch him." In a much louder voice, he said, "Alfred Swift is capable of robbing and killing every resident in this town before he leaves!"

Murmurs rose from the onlookers. A woman shouted, "Is that true, Sheriff? Are we gonna get killed?"

"Nobody's gonna get killed!" Sheriff Tyborn tried to hike his pants. "This man's one'a them damn sissies like Jake. Sissies don't tell the truth. Y'all know that."

"Speaking of the truth, Sheriff," Wiley snapped. "Did you or did you not steal money from a dead man?"

Some in the street gasped.

A boy pulled two others to the front of the still growing crowd. The boy said loudly to his friends, "That's my friend Jake, and t'other man's William Deluce, the gunny. Said so, hisself. An' he said Jake's his partner!"

"See here, Deluce," Sheriff Tyborn said as he dabbed his face and neck with his kerchief. "You can't be accusin' me of things in *my* town. I might juss toss you in jail for tryin' to scare ever'body, back talk, an' roughin' up the good reverend."

Wiley grinned. "And I might wire Philadelphia for permission to lock you up for stealing that money." He spun to the gathering of people. "Did you know the sheriff forced Deputy Curtis to resign because he stayed at Jake's farm to help bury bodies."

"Is that the truth, Sheriff?" a man yelled. "Curtis was the best deputy this town's ever had. We all wondered why he up an' left."

"Hell yes, it's true," Jake said. "Just cuz all'a you called me a sissy all my life, Sheriff Tyborn called Curtis a sissy after he helped us with them bodies."

"That's outrageous!" the same man shouted. "Deputy Curtis weren't no sissy!" He shoved through the people and frowned at the sheriff, then held out his hand to Wiley. "Can I shake the hand of the famous William Deluce?"

Wiley folded his arms. "If you shake the hand of Jake Brady, first."

The man shrugged, flickered a glance at Jake, then looked at the ground and shoved through the crowd.

The boy who'd gathered his friends ran to Jake. "I missed seein' you, Jake." He held out his hand.

Jake grinned and shook the boy's hand. "Missed seein' you, too, Timmy. How's your ma?"

"Ma's fine. Uh..." Timmy grinned at his friends, then motioned Jake closer. When Jake bent down, the boy whispered, "You think I can shake William Deluce's hand?"

"You shook my hand," Jake whispered back. "He'll likely shake yours, too."

As Jake straightened up, Timmy stuck out his hand to Wiley.

Wiley's fierce expression suddenly disappeared. He smiled as he shook Timmy's hand.

Looking into Wiley's eyes, Timmy asked, "Will you show my two friends'n me how fast you can draw your gun?"

"It's not polite to do that in the middle of a crowd," Wiley said as he lightly tapped Timmy's cheek with the butt of his lightning-drawn Colt, barrel pointed at the ground and fingers closed over the trigger guard.

"Wow!" Timmy yelled. "I didn't even see you do it!"

Timmy's two friends, and a few others in the crowd clapped and cheered, but most stared at the partners with scorn.

Looking around at the haughty faces, Wiley holstered his gun. "Let's go, Jake." He winked at the three boys, then pushed his way through the onlookers.

As Jake followed, he smiled and nodded at people he knew, though some frowned at him.

"You be outta this county tomorrow or I'll arrest you!" Sheriff Tyborn yelled after them.

Wiley stopped and slowly turned around. "We'll be here three days, Sheriff. Long enough for us to find out what other crooked dealing you've been up to."

* * *

As the partners walked their horses into the Brady farm, Jake glanced around. "Hell, it looks the same."

"It's still winter, Jake. Shed and Louise wouldn't have been able to make many changes."

The moment they dismounted, the front door opened and Louise ran out to greet them. Throwing her arms around Jake, she buried her face into his chest. "Jake. I'm so glad to see you. I love this farm, and want to thank you for giving it to us."

She let go of Jake, looked up into his startled face and smiled impishly. "If I hadn't done it quickly, you wouldn't have let me give you the hug you deserve." Turning to Wiley, she grabbed his hand and squeezed it, then kissed his cheek. "It's good to see you, Wiley." She spun around, ran to the porch, grabbed an iron bar and rang the dinner triangle.

"Shed's in the fields. That will get him back. Please, bring your things inside. I'm in the middle of baking pies." She opened the front door and disappeared into the house.

Frozen in his tracks from Louise's exuberant hug, Jake didn't move.

Wiley walked to Jake's side, slid his hand around his back and squeezed. "Louise is your sister-in-law. You don't have to worry about her hugging you. After all, you did deserve it. You gave them your farm."

Feeling Wiley's arm around him, Jake looked into his eyes. "Guess you're right. But I don't like them big tits pushin' against me."

Wiley laughed. "Just be thankful it lasted only a few seconds."

Jake snickered and lifted his saddlebags from the horse.

Entering the house, Jake stopped and stared. His saddlebags dropped to the floor. "Damn! What's *happened* in here? This don't look like the house I lived in!"

Hands buried in pie dough, Louise smiled. "I hope you like what we've done in here. Mamma sent us some money and we used it to fix up the house."

Jake gawked around. "Wiley, they took off Ma's pink roses wallpaper! It's all yellow in here!"

Louise shot a terrified glance at Wiley. "Er...Shed and I thought yellow brightened up the house. It was so...dark."

"What happened to the damn floor?" Jake asked.

"We put down a new floor." Louise smiled at it. "Shed and I did it ourselves."

"It's beautiful," Wiley said as he draped his arm over Jake's shoulders.

"Granma an' Granpa's rockers're still in front of the fireplace, but where'd *that* chair come from?" Jake pointed to a carved, hickory settee sitting in front of a curtained window, then waved his hand toward the kitchen area. "An' what happened to the old table an' chairs?"

Still mixing dough, Louise smiled. "Your friend, Morgan made the settee and our new table and chairs before he and Curtis moved to Lexington. He also made our new sideboard and my work counter. Everything is hickory. We love every piece."

"Morgan made 'em?" Jake glanced at Wiley, then looked around the room. "Hell Wiley, it seems happy in here now. Not like when Pa was always yellin' at Ma an' me."

Wiley and Louise looked at each other and sighed.

"You did a fine job of making this house a home, and I agree, your new furniture is beautiful. I'm impressed at Morgan's skill."

"Jake!" Shed rushed in the back door, ran through the house and grabbed Jake.

"Shed!" Jake lifted his brother, spun him around, then gently lowered him to the floor.

After trying to heft his younger brother off the floor, and failing, Shed laughed. Releasing his hold on Jake, he stepped back and looked up at him. "You're the biggest little brother in the world. It's good seein' you again." He grabbed Wiley in a brief hug, then headed toward the sideboard in the kitchen.

Shed brought out a bottle of whiskey and three glasses. While Louise rolled out pie crust, the partners sat with Shed at the table and told of their adventures since they were last here.

"My little brother's a Pinkerton! An' William Deluce's partner!" Shed threw his head back and laughed. "Jake, if your pa knew that, he'd most likely faint face-down in pig shit!"

"It's so dangerous being a Pinkerton," Louise said. "What if either of you get shot, or killed?"

Shed turned to her. "Don't you see? Two big strappin' men as partners? They cover each other an' pertect each other. What could be more perfect?" He looked at Jake and Wiley. "Wish I could see you two in action."

"If Sheriff Tyborn comes to arrest us, you'll most likely see Wiley get riled."

Shed's eyes got big as he looked at both men. "Sheriff Tyborn? Why would he arrest you?"

Wiley shrugged. "We haven't had time to tell you what happened in Wilmore before we arrived here."

"What happened?" Louise asked as she froze and looked at them past the pie pan she held up while trimming dough from the edges.

After Jake told of Wiley grabbing Reverend Fall, Shed pounded the table and laughed. "That'll teach those snooty jackasses t'mind their business." He leaped to his feet, reached across the table and extended his hand to Wiley. When Wiley grabbed it, Shed said, "Thank you for standin' up for my little brother. Except for Ma, it don't sound like he's ever had anybody stand up for him his whole life."

Louise began trimming her third pie pan. "What will happen if Sheriff Tyborn comes out here tomorrow during the party?"

Shed glared at her. "Louise!"

Realizing she'd given away Jake's surprise birthday party, Louise set down the pan and looked at the three men. Jake's puzzled look and Wiley's controlled laughter gave her confidence.

Louise smiled. "It's a welcome home gathering."

CHAPTER 19

The next morning, as Jake walked sleepy-eyed into the house from the barn where he and Wiley had slept, he saw Shed standing on a chair, attaching a long streamer of red-white-and-blue festooning to the corner of the ceiling. Across the room, on another chair, Wiley held the other end. Louise turned toward him from stirring a large pot on the stove. She wiped several strands of hair from her face and smiled at him.

"What's happenin'?" Jake asked. "Why's ever'body fussin' so much?" He pointed to the festooning. "What the hell's that doin' in here? Ain't that stuff for town partyin'?"

Wiley looked over his upheld arm at Jake. "Why don't you go back to bed, Jake. It's too early for you to be up."

Instantly pouty-faced, Jake looked at the floor. "It ain't early. Why don't you want me in here? What'd I do?"

Finally fastening the streamer, Shed turned toward Jake and grinned. "You didn't do anythin', Jake. We're havin' a...a doin's here today."

"Hell, I can help. Why don't you want me helpin'?"

Louise pointed to the nearly empty wood bin. "You can fill that. I have a lot more cooking to do today."

Jake crossed the room, grabbed the rope handles of the box, yanked it off the floor and glared at everyone. He let the back door slam as he shoved his way outside.

Wiley and Shed snickered.

"You're both mean," Louise said. "It's obvious Jake doesn't remember today is his birthday."

"Does Jake always pout so easy?" Shed asked Wiley as he stepped down from the chair.

"Unfortunately, yes. It's the result of his father treating him so badly while he was growing up."

"I hated John," Shed growled. "Sometimes durin' the fightin' in the war, I wished the enemy I was shootin' at was Jake's father instead'a somebody's brother." He shuddered and forced away the thought of killing so many fine men. One of them might have been Jake, or Wiley.

Louise put her hands on her hips. "You have to tell Jake the party is for him. I know you sent us money for it, Wiley, and told us to keep it a secret, but I hate seeing him upset."

Still standing on the chair, Wiley fastened his end of the fuzzy festooning, then turned toward her. "I know we shouldn't string him along, but to see his surprise when he finds out the party is for him will be worth..."

The back door banged open. Jake wrestled and bumped the wood bin into the house. He dropped it beside the stove. Hurriedly gathered, the wood was in jumbled disarray.

"There's the damn wood. Guess y'all want me outta here, now."

"You can stay an' help if you want." Shed turned away and bit his lip to keep from laughing.

"We thought you would have other things to do, Jake," Wiley said. "We didn't want to bother you with this."

"Hell, you wanted me to go back to bed. That ain't somethin' I wanna do. You don't want me in here. What'd I do?"

"You turned twenty-five today, Jake." Louise frowned at Shed and Wiley.

"I did? Today's my birthday? Damn, I forgot." Jake looked around the room at the streamers and already set table. "Is this here party for me?"

Wiley stepped down from the chair, crossed the room and gently placed his hands on Jake's shoulders. "Yes, this party is for you. It's a surprise party, like the one you gave me. We don't want you to help. But you have to act surprised when the guests arrive. Like you told me to."

Teary-eyed, Jake stammered, "I...I ain't never had me no birthday party my whole life." He wiped his eyes and grinned at Wiley. "Guess

I'll go see how Smiley an' the pigs're doin'." He turned and rushed out the front door.

Seeing that interaction, years of worry about his younger brother disappeared from Shed in an instant.

* * *

Zeke and Annie Harris and Hank Foxton arrived first, three hours early. Seeing Jake leaving the barn, Zeke leaped from the buggy and ran to him. They threw their arms around each other and spun in the dirt. Their laughing quickly turned to sobs of happiness.

Pulling back and searching Jake's face with his tear-filled, gray-blue eyes, Zeke whispered, "It's good seein' you again, Jake."

"An' me seein' you, Zeke."

The life-long friends hugged again, harder.

"Hey, you two!" Hank teased, running to them. He threw his arms around the two men and kissed each on the cheek.

Wiley burst out the front door and ran to them. The four men hugged and laughed in a tight group.

When Shed stepped out to the porch, he saw Annie Harris still sitting in the buggy and rushed to her side. He helped her out of the carriage and walked with her to the porch where Louise stood. They looked at the four men, laughing and all talking at once.

"They truly love each other," Shed whispered.

Annie Harris grasped Shed's arm. "Yes. An' I never knew what love was 'til Zeke brought Hank home. There ain't been laughin' like there is now on the farm since we bought the place thirty-two years ago."

Smiling broadly at the four men, Louise turned to Annie. "Mirabella, our Cajun housekeeper while I was growing up in Louisiana, told me once in secret that men and women like those four are the ones who teach us all how to love one another. I never knew what she meant, until now. Mirabella was always right."

Everyone gathered inside, except Jake. He felt more excited than he'd ever been and couldn't sit still. After wandering around the yard, he went inside the barn and re-inspected every new thing Shed had done. He liked where the ropes hung now. The sun wouldn't rot them, and the way Shed had wound them didn't look at all like nooses. He breathed deeply at the fresh sweet smell of the hay and remembered how rotten it had been the last time he was here.

Jake noticed Shed had fixed the third and fifth rung of the ladder to the loft and had moved the bull to the middle pen. Jake wondered why he'd done that. It would be harder to dump hay into his bin. The trap door in the loft was over the stall where the bull had been.

Jake shrugged and left the barn by the back door, threaded the bushes and crossed the bridge. Standing in front of his grandfather's leaning barn, he wondered when it would fall over. After slipping through the door, his boots sunk into the spongy soil as he walked to the wall leaning toward the barn's eventual fall. He touched the wall. The structure groaned and shuddered. Jake rushed outside and stood behind the bushes to watch if it fell.

Annie barely took off her coat before helping Louise with the food. Shed asked Hank's help with seating fourteen people near the fireplace. He willingly agreed.

Wiley pulled Zeke aside. "Can you keep Jake out of here? We had to tell him about the party because he started pouting when we didn't want his help. Maybe you two can go get Stinky."

Looking deep into Wiley's eyes, Zeke grinned. "Sure will." He grabbed Wiley's hand and squeezed it, then ran out the front door.

Zeke searched the yard and entire barn and found Jake outside the rear door, staring at the old leaning barn.

"Jake, Wiley wants us to find Stinky."

"He does? You know where Stinky is?"

"Saw him hidin' in the bushes on the way here. He always hides where I can see him. We can take our buggy."

Jake took one last look at the leaning structure and followed Zeke into the barn.

As the men hitched the horse to the wagon, Jake slid his hands over the animal. "Where'd you get this horse? He's purty bein' white with brown spots."

"Morgan an' Curtis gave him to us b'fore they left to Lexington. Said where they was goin' they could only keep two horses. His name's Cutter." Zeke patted the horse's neck. "Cutter's old, but he likes pullin' the wagon."

As they turned onto the road, they noticed the weather had become cold and windy. Jake looked back at the ominous fingers of dark-gray clouds reaching across the afternoon sky from the northwest. Occasional wind gusts whipped long-nestled leaves into frenzied swirls and steered them along the road in front of them.

Jake raised the collar of his jacket and pulled down his hat. "Looks like a storm's comin'. We gotta find Stinky so he don't freeze."

"We'll find him. I reckon he knows you're here."

Loosely holding the reins, Zeke let the horse amble along the road toward the spot he'd seen Stinky peering out from the leafless tangle of brush. Everyone in the area knew Zeke and Jake were Stinky's only friends. When Jim and Dave were here, Jim had mentioned that Stinky wasn't deformed, but had Downs Syndrome. Since he'd had his thumb cut off by Zeke's older brothers and had been continually terrorized by them his entire life, Stinky hid from everyone.

Jake slid his arm across Zeke's back. "How's it been with Hank?"

Zeke grinned, searched the bushes on both sides of the road, then snuggled toward Jake. "After y'all left, Hank got scared'a all the work on the farm. But after a couple'a weeks he settled down an' told Ma an' me he kinda liked workin' outside in the fields an' not robbin' people." Zeke snickered. "After the first good frost, he quit complainin' about the bugs."

Jake laughed. "Ain't no bugs in Col'rado. Not that you'd notice, anyway. But there ain't much rain, neither, an' I like rain." He glanced behind his shoulder. "I don't like the snow an' cold much, but won't live nowhere else but with Wiley in our cabin."

Chuckling, Zeke grabbed Jake's leg and squeezed. "How's Soarin' Raven? She still riled at me for holdin' a gun on her? An' what happened to Jim an' Dave? Hank's been wonderin' about 'em, too."

Jake told of the telegram he and Wiley had received about Soaring Raven leaving the Castille Ranch, and how Dave and Jim had disappeared back to their own Time in a lightning storm. He also filled Zeke in on the riverboat trip down the Mississippi, the happenings in New Orleans and Philadelphia...and that Betty had escaped.

A cold blast whipped dust past them and obscured what lay ahead.

Jake shuddered. He turned all the way around and squinted into the wind at the thickening clouds, then looked at Zeke. "Wiley said Betty'll most likely try havin' me killed again."

Zeke stopped the buggy. He peered over the collar of his jacket at Jake. "Wiley'll pertect you. Ain't nobody loves you more'n Wiley." Zeke glanced around. "This is where I saw Stinky hidin' when we was goin' to your farm."

Not seeing the short, rotund man, Zeke stood up in the wagon. "Stinky! Jake's here an' you're invited to his birthday party!"

"Stinky! This is Jake! We gotta get you outta this here wind!"

Zeke plopped to the seat. They heard nothing except the raging wind that bent leafless trees toward the east and flung leaves and twigs at their backs.

"Stinky!" Jake yelled. "Get your butt in this here wagon!"

"Let's wait a bit," Zeke said. "Stinky might'a stayed, but might'a gone to your farm." He searched Jake's face. "Why's that Betty wantin' you dead?"

Jake shuddered from the icy wind that seemed to chill his blood. He pulled down the back of his hat and fastened the top button of his coat. "Wiley said she's touched an' wants him all to herself. He said we gotta watch ever'where for somebody else she might send to kill me. He said Alfred Swift, the man in our coach from Lexington, might be after me."

A hand grabbed Jake's shoulder from behind.

Jake gasped and spun around with his hand on his gun.

Wrapped in a horse blanket, Stinky grinned at him from the wagon bed, then shoved his fist over his mouth and snickered. "I hidin' here from your barn."

* * *

When the three Quaker couples arrived, the only others invited to the party, the wind had become stronger and a few flakes of snow could be seen in the overcast light of late afternoon. Zeke and Hank took care of the guests' horses and buggies, then crowded near the warmth of the fireplace the moment they came inside.

As soon as brief introductions were made and everyone had been seated, they gave Jake his presents. He received a handmade shirt from Ronson and Bessie Holt. The instant he saw it, he stripped to the waist and slipped into the light blue, soft muslin shirt with a snow-covered mountain embroidered on the pocket.

"Damn, this shirt's the best one I ever got!" Jake strutted the room. When he got to the rocker where Bessie Holt sat, he bent down and kissed the elderly woman on the forehead. "Thanks, Ma'am."

Bessie grabbed Jake's head and kissed him back. "Thou art a beautiful man, Jake. And God loves thee."

Jake walked to thinning-gray and spectacled Ronson Holt, sitting in the other rocking chair. He shook the man's hand. "Thanks, too, Mr. Holt."

John Tomwell and his wife Hanna gave Jake two pair of wool socks. Jake's eyes teared slightly when he thanked them.

Huge Jeramiah Meehan handed Jake a package wrapped in brown paper. He stood up, towering over Jake, and smiled. "Lucy and I made this for thee. We like the way thou befriended Stinky." He gripped Jake's waist with his big hands. "This present's the same size I wear."

Seeing muscular Jeramiah standing in front of him with his huge chest and arms, then touching his body, Jake's heart lurched. While growing up, he'd always tingled whenever he'd seen Jeramiah, and had thanked Jesus for the time Jeramiah had scolded Pa, right on Main Street in Wilmore. Jeramiah had shouted to everyone that John Brady treated his son like a slave.

Jake ripped open the package and uncoiled a leather belt and a hammered-copper buckle with a raised J in the center.

"Lucy and I hope thou like it."

Partly because he'd wanted to his whole life and now he had an excuse, and partly out of thanks for the gift, Jake slid his arms under Jeramiah's and hugged the man's massive body. "Thanks for the belt. An' thanks for scoldin' Pa in town that time."

Jeramiah chuckled, wrapped his huge arms around Jake and lifted him off the floor. "Thou art welcome, Jake." As he lowered Jake to his feet, he whispered softly, "Thou have a blessed and dangerous partner. Protect him."

Watching closely, Wiley felt glad for Jake getting the belt, but envious when Jeramiah hugged Jake and lifted him off the floor.

Louise also made Jake a shirt, and he immediately put it on, after gently laying aside the Holt's shirt.

"Hell, this shirt's the best one I ever got, too!" He pulled at the draw-strings of its V-neck and looked at Wiley. "Now I got me one like your rawhide one."

Shed had made Jake a new holster for his Colt pistol, which Jake put on immediately, then tried drawing his gun. Hard to do each time, he frowned at it.

Snickering, Shed approached Jake. "You gotta oil it until it's soft. Wiley'll show you how. Then, he'll show you how to make it fit your gun for a faster draw." He leaned closer and whispered, "You make Wiley teach you shootin'."

Overhearing that, Wiley smiled at the floor.

Jake shoved his pistol into the new holster and threw his arms around Shed. "I got me the bestest brother in the whole world."

Zeke made Jake a fishing pole from seasoned willow. It came complete with green cork bobbers, hooks and handmade lead sinkers. Annie knitted Jake a sweater that was much too large. She scolded Zeke for the measurements. He defended himself saying Jake had always seemed so big.

"Hell. It don't matter. With all the stuff we gotta wear in Col'rado tryin' to keep warm, this'll be just right over two shirts."

Hank shoved a brown-wrapped bundle into Jake's lap. "I hope I made this big enough."

After ripping open the package, Jake held up a cowhide vest. Intricately burned patterns lined the edges and blackened rawhide laces crisscrossed the sides.

"Damn! You made this?"

Hank blushed. "Ma-Annie helped."

Jake scrambled into the vest. It fit perfectly. He tugged on it and grinned. "Hell, this here vest'll make Frank, back in Alma, chase me down the street wantin' it."

Wiley waited until last. He gave Jake a book of Grimm's Household Fairy Tales with illustrations by R. Andre and a copy of Arabian Nights, arranged for the young by Helen Marion Burnside. Out loud, he promised to teach Jake to read using those books.

Crushing the books to his chest, Jake tried to hold back tears, but couldn't. He grinned and blinked at everyone. "When I come back to visit, I'm gonna read somma these here books to you."

Shed's eyes teared, also.

Jake gently laid the books on the kitchen table, then charged out of the house by the front door. Zeke took out after him.

After watching Zeke chase after Jake, Wiley approached a Quaker couple about his own age, who sat timidly amid the loud gathering.

"I haven't had a chance to talk to you. My name is William Deluce. I'm Jake's partner." He extended his hand to the man.

The thin, bearded man stood, smiled and grasped Wiley's hand. "John Tomwell." He turned to a petite woman with a sweet face. "This is my wife, Hanna. Good to meet thee." John looked toward the front door, then eyed Wiley. "Maybe thou can tell us why Jake ran out the front door. Is not this his party?"

"Jake's never had a birthday party before. He's quite emotional about it."

"Why did thou not run after him?" Hanna asked. "Are not thou his partner?"

"Zeke went after him. They've been friends all their lives. I'm sure Zeke can calm Jake down much better than I could."

"Thou art a wise man," John said. "Jake and Zeke are looked up to by the Quaker community. They truly are men of peace and love." He shrugged. "I must tell thee...most of the townsfolk think badly of them."

Wiley shrugged. "I'm well aware of that."

The front door burst open with a blast of cold air and swirling snowflakes. Sheriff Tyborn shoved his huge body into the house. Behind him, Deputy Foster, three men and three women, all bundled from the cold, filed through the door. Their forced entrance met silence in the entire house and the invited guests all stood.

Sheriff Tyborn pulled his gun, pointed it at Wiley's back, then approached him. "Mr. Deluce, you're under arrest for roughin' up Reverend Fall." He motioned to the people crowding behind him, all with frowning faces. "These are good Methodist folk from Wilmore who..."

"John and I are Catholic," Lily Burkhardt shouted.

"Er, and two Catholics," Sheriff Tyborn said, turning his head and glaring at Lily. "They come with Deputy Foster an' me to make sure we haul you back t'jail."

With his arms folded and his back straight, Wiley turned toward the sheriff and slowly approached him.

"Sheriff, I did not harm the Reverend in the least." Wiley frowned. "Not even his hate for Jake was damaged, and hate like that is very unbecoming for a minister."

Stopping in front of the obese sheriff, Wiley asked loudly, "You brought women to arrest me? How brave!"

"We're here to protect our husbands from people like Jake!" Lily Burkhardt snapped. "And to make sure you are brought to jail!"

Ignoring the woman, Wiley stared at Sheriff Tyborn. "I told you in town to keep track of Alfred Swift! I'm sure, by now, he's robbed half the citizens of Wilmore."

Gasps escaped the lips of the Quaker guests.

"You can't tell me what to do in my own county!" Tyborn shouted. "I come here to arrest you an' that's what I'm gonna do! Now come along. You're gonna spend the next three days in jail!"

"Three days? That's interesting." Wiley calmly turned toward the invited guests. "When I was in town, I told the sheriff Jake and I would be here three days." He spun back to the sheriff and smiled. "Like I said, three days is plenty of time to dig up more of your sordid affairs. How many people here know you caused Deputy Curtis to move to Lexington because of how you treated him?"

Murmurs spread through the house.

"Deputy Curtis *should* be gone from our town," Methodist Simon Bently shouted. "He come out here an' spent time with Jake."

Wiley's eyes turned deadly. "Yes, he did. He helped us bury five bodies. Something your sheriff and his deputy here wouldn't do." Wiley squint-eyed the sheriff. "What did you do with the money you stole from one of the dead bodies? Buy yourself a dozen pork dinners?"

Amid snickers in the room, Sheriff Tyborn shoved the barrel of his gun into Wiley's gut and grabbed his arm. "You come with me now, or I'll shoot you!"

"You would never be fast enough!" Wiley snapped.

The front door opened. Jake and Zeke rushed into the house. Zeke slammed the door behind him.

"Damn! It's snowin' so hard, Zeke an' me could hardly find the house from the barn!" Grinning, Jake stomped his boots on the floor. Seeing everyone standing silent, then realizing Sheriff Tyborn was there pointing his gun at Wiley, Jake's eyes became slits. "What the hell's goin' on in here?" He looked at Shed. "Why's the sheriff here an' why's he pointin' his gun at Wiley? An' what're all these other people doin' at my party?"

Shed pushed through the stunned guests and grabbed Jake's arm. "Sheriff Tyborn's arrestin' Wiley for roughin' up Reverend Fall. The others come to see it's done."

"Roughin' up Reverend Fall?" Jake balled his fists. "Wiley only lifted him off the boardwalk. I was there."

"I saw him slam the good reverend against Jenny's dress shop," John Burkhardt shouted. "He deserves to be arrested, even if Reverend Fall *is* only a Methodist. The sheriff is only doing his duty. And we're here to see that he does it. We can't have men like you and Wiley in Wilmore! That's why we're here. We want *both* of you arrested and jailed."

Louise rushed to John Burkhardt. "You devil! How dare you burst into my house and accuse Shed's brother and his partner of being unworthy of this town! I want you to leave this farm at once! You have ruined our party!"

"They can't leave. Nobody can leave."

Everyone turned toward Zeke, still standing by the front door.

"It's too blindin' outside," Zeke said. "Y'all are gonna have to stay here 'til it's done snowin'."

Wiley rolled his eyes. "This certainly will be a day to remember."

CHAPTER 20

As darkness thickened outside, snow swirled so densely it blotted out the glowing windows of the house four feet from the front porch. Drifts already climbed two sides of Shed and Louise's snug home, trapping twenty-two people inside.

Louise, Annie Harris and the three Quaker women took turns peeking out the front door and gasping at the blizzard, then began working as a unit in the kitchen area, fixing extra food for the uninvited people. It didn't matter who they were or why they had come, they needed to eat and there was plenty of food.

While Shed and Jake conferred on how to bed down so many persons, Sheriff Tyborn, spurred by the townsfolk who insisted on Wiley's immediate arrest, took Wiley's pistol and marched him to the door at gunpoint.

Hands held high, Wiley reached the door and stopped. "You're not even going to let me wear a coat?"

Jake rushed to the front door, blocking any exit. "You ain't takin' Wiley nowhere, Sheriff! Ain't nobody leavin'. Zeke an' me could hardly find the house from the barn."

"Get outta my way, you sissy, or I'll arrest you, too," Tyborn growled. "I'm arrestin' this man an' you ain't gonna stop me."

"I will," Shed said softly as he walked to the sheriff. Snapping his shotgun closed, he shoved the double barrels into Tyborn's gut. "I'll cut your fat body in half if you take one more step to that there door. An' I'll have your gun an' everybody else's gun. Now! Put 'em on the table. You'll get 'em back when it's safe to travel, but not one moment b'fore."

"Now see here," Tyborn shouted. "You can't point a gun at me. I'm the sheriff'a this county."

Jake pulled his own gun. "You heard my big brother. Ain't nobody goin' nowhere, an' nobody's gettin' their guns back 'til you leave. Zeke, you an' Hank get all their guns."

Tyborn scowled. "It ain't right for me to not be wearin' my piece."

Tall, thin and graying Branch Carson snapped, "I have a right to protect myself."

"I agree," Simon Bently said. "God knows what vileness lurks in this house."

"The only vileness here is you and people like you," Wiley countered. He slowly turned and faced the sheriff and his entourage. "You hate anyone who doesn't think like you, and that's a danger to every person alive. We're taking your guns to protect the good people who were invited to this party that you so rudely interrupted."

"How dare you say that!" Mildred Carson said as she put her hands on her broad hips, which made her large breasts stick out even more. "We Methodists are better than these...these Quaker persons who can't even speak proper English. Thee and thou? Who do you people think you are?" She glanced around the room. "I don't like being in this house. What will people say?"

"Tell the gossips the truth," petite Hanna Tomwell said from the kitchen. She smiled sweetly as Mildred glared at her.

The sheriff and townsfolk shouted protests as Zeke and Hank collected the guns. White-headed and spectacled Ronson Holt, John Tomwell and Jeramiah Meehan all quietly placed their guns on the table. As a precaution, Wiley placed every weapon, which included his own, into a flour sack. He secured it with a rawhide strip and hung it from a nail high on the wall.

In the confusion, Shed secretly stowed his shotgun out of sight.

Realizing they were actually stranded in Shed's house, the Catholic and Methodist women quickly shoved the two rocking chairs and the settee near the fireplace, claiming the most comfortable seating as their own. Sheriff Tyborn, his deputy and the men with him seated themselves around the kitchen table, leaving the straight-backed chairs Annie had brought, a few rustic outside chairs and a barn bench for the original guests of the party.

Jake frowned as he watched the uninvited people take over Shed's house, but suddenly scanned the room in panic. "Where the hell's Stinky?"

"Don't tell me that smelly, deformed dwarf is here!" Lily Burkhardt hissed, her obese body taking up the entire settee. She shook her head and loudly whispered to the thin woman with brown hair tied in a bun sitting in a rocker next to her. "Mabel, this is going to be a night in hell!"

Jake, Shed and Zeke frantically searched behind every piece of furniture in the main L-shaped room. Stinky was nowhere to be found.

Returning from his search of the bedroom, Wiley tapped Jake on the shoulder and whispered, "He's hiding under the bed."

Jake started toward his parent's bedroom but stopped at the door. Memories of his late father kept him from going in the room. He motioned for Zeke to get Stinky.

Everyone heard Stinky protest as Zeke tried coaxing him out from under the bed. After a few minutes, Zeke appeared. "Stinky don't want to come in here. Says somma these people call him bad names."

"I wonder who that could be?" Wiley asked, glaring at Lily Burkhardt.

Lily pointed her pudgy nose to the ceiling and closed her eyes.

"We have plenty of food if anyone is hungry," Louise said.

"Simon and I are not eating *anything* in this house," Mabel Bently snapped.

"Speak for yourself, Mabel. I'm starved."

Louise smiled. "That's up to each of you, but in this house we value everyone equally, no matter who they think they are. Or why they're here."

"That's quite obvious," Mildred Carson said as she turned in her rocker and frowned as she watched Hank, Zeke and Jake crowd the stove to fill their plates. "You don't seem to care *who* you invite into your house."

Folding his arms, Wiley turned to her and said, "Just so you remember, you were *not* invited, but Louise will feed you anyway, like the Jesus would you claim to follow."

Jeramiah Meehan laughed in his deep voice.

"You Quakers *would* laugh at a blasphemous statement like that," potbellied John Burkhardt said. "What would you know about Jesus?"

"Not much, according to thee," Jeramiah said. "But Wiley's right. Jesus would have fed everyone here...even thee. Wiley said nothing blasphemous. Thou art blind because thou doest not listen."

"I've heard enough!" Mildred Carson yelled. "I'm leaving this sinful place. Branch, take me home this instant!" She hefted her overweight body out of the rocker, grabbed her coat and stomped to the door. Glancing over her shoulder at her tall, graying husband sitting at the table, she snapped, "I'll be waiting on the porch." Mildred flung open the door and saw a two-foot wall of snow blocking her way. The fierce wind blasted her with stinging flakes. She screamed and forced the door shut.

Chuckles could be heard from several people, including her husband.

Above the howling wind, everyone heard a distant groaning, loud screechings, then a hideous roar.

Mildred screamed again and rushed to her rocker. "For heavens sake! The Devil must be here!"

Jake glared at her. "That ain't no devil." He looked at Shed with sadness. "Granpa's ol' barn just fell over."

* * *

Jake and Wiley sat on the floor next to Zeke and Hank, balancing their plates over crossed legs. None of them spoke as they wolfed down roast turkey with oyster stuffing, candied sweet potatoes and dark-colored rice. Louise also served steamed beets with bacon since the town market didn't have any greens. And pie. She'd made apple, mince meat and pecan pies, three of each.

The men who had interrupted the party, sitting around the kitchen table, also ate ravenously. The three women who had accompanied their husbands and Sheriff Tyborn glared at everyone from the rockers and settee, eating nothing.

Louise, Annie and the three Quaker women ate from plates they'd fixed, but had to put them aside often to dish up food for the others. Occasionally, they sat on the barn bench to rest their feet.

Ronson Holt, uncomfortable because of a painful back injury a year ago but saying nothing about it, sat in a wooden, outside chair. Bessie had set her plate on the wide arm of the chair next to him.

Ronson held up his hand. "Louise, pray tell what is in this rice that makes it so tasty?"

"Chicken livers. My mother taught me to make it when I was six years old. We call it dirty rice."

"What a horrible name," Lily snapped as she tried to maneuver her obese body into a more comfortable position on the settee.

"Please don't have any," Hank said, "so the rest of us can have seconds."

"Thou hast made us a feast," Ronson continued. "I have not tasted such wonderful cooking." He glanced at his wife who had just sat beside him. "Except for thy cooking, of course."

Bessie frowned a smile at him. "Bread and water for thee...for a month!"

Amid a few chuckles, Wiley waved his fork in the air toward the fireplace. "You women sitting in the *comfortable* chairs don't know what you're missing by refusing to eat. However, it would do two of you good to miss a few dozen meals." He gestured to the men sitting on the floor, which included Jeramiah Meehan and John Tomwell. "Jake, I have a feeling your Jesus would be sitting with us on the floor." He winked at Jake, then speared a chunk of turkey.

"Jesus would *never* eat with sissies!" John Burkhardt yelled from the kitchen table. "He hated sissies! He said so!"

Jake glanced at Wiley, set his nearly empty plate on the floor and got to his feet. He clomped heavily the few feet to the kitchen table, put his hands on his hips and leaned over John Burkhardt. "Jim told me men who yell all'a time how bad sissies are gotta be sissies, too. They yell like that cuz they don't want nobody knowin' they're sissies. Listenin' to you, I know Jim's right."

Jake walked completely around the table with six stunned men sitting at it, Shed included, all following his every move. Stopping again behind John Burkhardt, Jake rested his hand on the man's shoulder, then forcefully turned him in the chair to face him.

"John, hit him!" Lily shouted from the settee. "Don't let that sissy touch you!"

Ignoring the woman, Jake squinted into John's eyes. "Y'all come to Shed's house wantin' to arrest Wiley for pickin' up Reverend Fall an tryin' to shake some good into him! An' you had to bring your damn wives with you. Now, you can't leave. Louise feeds you an' you still complain about ever'thin' an' call us sissies. My friend Jesus never acted like you. You ain't got no damn manners." He turned to Shed. "Get your shotgun and make these damn people leave. They ain't got no right bein' in your house."

Mildred maneuvered her rocker to better face Jake and shook her finger at him. "You can't make us leave! We'll freeze to death out there! There's *never* been a storm like this around here."

Jake banged his fist on the table and glared at the woman. "You're damn right, you'll freeze! You *gotta* stay here cuz we don't want any'a you freezin'. But you're gonna keep your damn mouth shut!" He motioned to Lily. "An' get your fat butt off'a that couch an' let Ronson an' Bessie have it. Can't you see he's hurtin' in that outside chair!"

"How dare you talk to my wife that way!" John Burkhardt shouted. He tried to stand, but Jake shoved him back to his seat.

As Sheriff Tyborn yelled a protest at Jake's words, Wiley jumped to his feet, walked over to Lily and waved his hand. "Off the settee! Like Jake said, you're no Christian. You're a selfish fraud trying to buy your way to heaven by condemning others, like so many Christians I've met in this country."

Seeing Wiley's vicious expression, Lily lowered her feet to the floor and tried to raise her nearly prone body. She couldn't. She raised her hand toward Wiley for help.

Arms folded, Wiley glared down at her. "You told your husband not let Jake touch him. I won't let *you* touch me! You got in that position yourself! Get your fat body off that settee!"

The house remained silent as everyone watched Lily struggle to her feet. Finally standing, she snapped, "Where am I going to sit?"

Wiley pointed to the rustic chair where Ronson sat. "You sit there. And keep your mouth shut!" He waited until Ronson and Bessie meekly moved to the settee. Hank snickered when Lily forced her body into the too-narrow chair. The wide arms pushed her fat into a mound in her lap.

Lucy Meehan glanced across the room at Jeramiah. They both turned away from the scene and tried desperately not to smile.

Shed stood up from the table. He grinned at Jake, then at Wiley.

"Thanks for what you said in Louise an' my house. When I was fightin' in the war, I asked Jesus t'keep me from bein' killed so I could come back here an' kill Jake's pa." He lowered his head. "I moved to

Al'bama to keep from doin' it." Shed frowned at the gasps of the Methodists and two Catholics, then looked at them. "Jake's pa was just like you people. He treated us terrible, an' you most likely treat your families terrible if they ain't like you want them to be!"

In a ragged group, Jeramiah, followed by Zeke, then Hank, stood up and started clapping. Annie, Louise and the Quaker women joined. To everyone's amazement, Branch Carson got up from his chair at the table and began clapping. He glared at Mildred's protest.

Branch raised his hand and silenced everyone. He nodded at Shed, then turned toward Jake. "I've heard the best sermons in my life, tonight. And they came from Shed, and William Deluce, a Pinkerton-killer and even you, Jake, a..." He shrugged. In a softer voice, he added, "A sissy." He lowered his eyes and mumbled, "Couldn't think of what else to call you."

"I'm a Pinkerton, like Wiley." Jake grinned at Wiley.

Relieved Jake wasn't angry, Branch scanned each shocked face in the room, then smiled at everyone. Looking at his slovenly wife, frowning at him from a rocking chair, a scowl darkened his face.

"Mildred! You look disgusting, stuffed in that rocker! Either you start cleaning the house and tending the garden in summer and helping with the pigs or you can go live with your mother! And I'm through with your Christianity! I thank these people for feeding us and keeping us safe in this terrible storm, no matter how bad you say they are. *We* would have let them freeze to death, and you would have called it *God's will*!"

Jake grabbed Branch Carson's arm and looked him in the eye. "You can give up Christianity if you want. But don't give up talkin' to my friend Jesus an' his Pa, or Wiley's Great White Father."

Carson's eyes misted. He grabbed Jake's arm. "I won't. I swear, I won't. Thanks to you." Branch pulled back and grinned. "You big, strapping...sissy."

Jake laughed and hugged him.

After Mildred spat a curse at her husband, Wiley turned toward her and smiled. "You may be visiting your mother sooner than you think."

* * *

At three in the morning, the wind outside still howled. No one knew if snow still raged. Curled up on the floor or trying to sleep in chairs, covered with blankets and coats, the twenty-two people had become increasingly cold. Hours ago, the pots ceased hissing on the cook stove. White ash in the fireplace winked red in only a few places, and both wood boxes sat empty.

Shed, in bed next to Louise, felt cold seep through the walls. Stinky slept on the floor underneath them and Shed worried about him. He could freeze to death. Everyone could freeze to death. Assuming there was no more wood in the house, he thought of breaking up the furniture to feed the coals. No! He and Louise loved Morgan's dining room table and chairs, and the settee. He had to bring in more wood.

Slipping out of bed, Shed dressed, donned his heavy coat, hat and gloves and tiptoed into the main room. He stepped over sleeping bodies, and just as he unlatched the back door, Jake sat up from where he slept.

"Where you goin'?"

"Shhh. I gotta get more wood."

"I'll help." Wiley tossed back his duster, got to his feet, then shoved his arms into the sleeves. "If it's still snowing, you shouldn't do it alone."

Jake, Zeke and Hank silently got ready to help, as did Jeramiah. They quietly crept to the back door.

Shed grabbed the softly lit Cold Blast Buggy lamp, guaranteed not to blow out, and shook it to see how much oil it contained. It had enough. He turned up the wick and quickly opened the door.

The howling wind sucked the remainder of the warmth from the house and caused sparks from the fireplace embers to blow on Mabel Bently. She screamed and scooted her rocker into Mildred Carson's.

"Get off me, you skinny bitch!" Mildred yelled.

Everyone in the house sprang awake.

"Now, what?" Sheriff Tyborn yelled. "What're you sissies sneakin' off to do?"

Shed marched to the corner where the sheriff lay, covered with two blankets and his heavy coat. He bent over him and shouted, "We're gettin' wood, so your fat body won't freeze an' stick to the floor!" Shed stomped back to the door and nodded to Wiley, who had purposefully held the door wide open.

"Don't lose anyone," Lucy Meehan said. She nodded to Jeramiah when he glanced back at her as the group headed out the kitchen door.

Stepping outside, the wind sucked Shed's hat off his head and sent it sailing into swirling snow.

"Guess I won't be seein' that 'til spring," he growled. He shined the light on the swollen impression of a shovel handle leaning against the back of the house. After wiping away the snow, he pulled the scoop shovel from its frozen tomb and began making a path between two four-foot high snow drifts, both curving to the left.

"Wood pile's outta ways," Shed said as he tossed a shovel of snow to his right.

"I know where it is," Jake shouted. "I got wood twice, today." He charged forward, tripped on Zeke's boot and plunged headlong into a wind-carved drift, which collapsed on him. Jake disappeared completely.

"Jake!" Wiley lunged into the snow and grabbed Jake's body. More of the drift slid to fill the depression, covering all but Wiley's legs.

Jeramiah scooped away snow. When he felt Wiley's back, he reached deeper and grabbed him. With a groan, he lifted Wiley from the snow and set him on his feet.

Jeramiah started to lunge back into the drift. "Now for Jake."

"Hell, you got me out, too!" Jake yelled over the wind. "Wiley was holdin' onto me."

"Is ever'body all right?" Shed asked.

"Everyone's fine," Jeramiah said. He pushed his huge body to the front and grabbed the shovel out of Shed's hands. In the light, the others saw he didn't wear a coat. "Where's the wood pile?" he asked.

"In front of you," Shed said.

Globs of snow flew as Jeramiah dug a path to their left. When the shovel clanked something solid, he cleaned away four feet of snow from the side of the stacked wood. Shortly, he began handing split logs to the man behind him. The others quickly formed a chain. Inside, Branch Carson piled the wood where Louise indicated.

"Can't you hurry?" Mildred demanded. "It's so cold in here."

Branch turned to her. "As soon as we get home, you're leaving for Charleston!"

CHAPTER 21

Dawn broke to a cloudless sky. The rising sun lit a dazzling landscape of total silence broken only by hissing snow slipping from branches in the slight breeze. Drifts, some as high as the eves of the house, fantastic in shape and sparkling like diamonds, transformed the yard, the road, the entire countryside into a motionless, frothy sea of white.

"Damn!" Jake yelled from the front door. He gawked at the snow-covered everything, turned to Wiley and whispered, "I ain't never seen nothin' like this my whole life."

Sliding his hand up Jake's back and resting it on his shoulder, Wiley whispered back, "It truly is beautiful."

"See there?" Sheriff Tyborn shouted. "Him feelin' on Jake? What'd I tell y'all! This here ain't no place no God-fearin' man should be."

Annie Harris stomped across the room and stood in front of Sheriff Tyborn. She swiped a strand of hair from her face. "You fat hog! You don't know anythin'!" She eyed his bulging gut. "Except eatin'! If you spent as much time tryin' to be human as you do sloppin' down grease, you'd know a thing or two." Annie gave him the once-over, then sighed and shook her head. "But it ain't possible for a hog to be human."

"Get outta my way, woman!" The sheriff shoved Annie aside and charged toward Jake and Wiley, now looking his way. He stuck his face into Wiley's. "You get my gun, or I'll...!"

Wiley shoved Tyborn away from him. "Or you'll what? Kill me? Men kill pigs, Sheriff. Pigs rarely kill men." Wiley folded his arms. "I'll give back your gun if you leave now, and take everyone who came with you." He glared at Sheriff Tyborn. "Do you understand what I'm saying to you?"

"No sissie Pinkerton's gonna tell me what t'do!"

Jake shoved a palm-sized gun into Sheriff Tyborn's gut. "If I pull this here trigger, ain't no way the bullet'll see the outside again. You'd best do like Wiley said."

"Where'd you get that gun?" Tyborn said. "Thought all the guns was in that bag on the wall?"

"This here baby-gun was in my boot."

Wiley grinned. "The same gun, I might add, that Jake used to kill Santivan."

"Santivan?" The color drained from Tyborn's fat cheeks. "That sissy killed Santivan?"

"If you'd stop stuffin' your face with grease an' read the town paper, you'd know that!" Annie shouted.

"Good heavens," Lily Burkhardt said from the settee she'd again absconded. "Jake is also a murderer?" She struggled her feet to the floor. "John, take me home, at once!"

Lucy Meehan, tired of the bickering that had gone on in spurts all night long, shoved her way through the room and grabbed Jeramiah's arm. "My husband, we need to put this to rest."

Smiling at his lovely wife, Jeramiah nodded. Holding hands, they approached the front door where Jake and Wiley stood, then turned to face everyone.

"This arguing must stop," Lucy said. "There is no meeting of minds, and we must go to our homes. But first, we must thank Shed and Louise, and all thee who helped us get through this storm." She smiled at Shed and Louise. "Thou hast saved our lives."

Jeramiah beamed as he watched every face turn toward his wife, then held up his hand.

"*And*," he boomed, "remember one thing. The only law that remains after Jesus graced this earth, is the law of *love*. Jesus told us that many times." Letting go of his wife's hand, Jeramiah nodded to Jake and Wiley. "Thou practice the Law of Love." He spun to Shed standing beside Louise. "Thou practice that Law. And I've seen Zeke and Hank in town." He grinned at the partners standing together but not touching each other. "Thou also practice that Law." Shoving his huge fists to his hips, Jeramiah turned and glared at the Catholics and

Methodists, grouped together with shock on their faces. "But *thou* do not!" He paused and squinted at them for a moment. "Christ said love thy neighbor as *thyself*! Do it!" He walked closer and leaned toward the group. "*Thou* are the man standing upright before the altar of God, pointing in scorn at the humble man in back and calling *him* a sinner! Remember this! The humble man received salvation. The upright man did *not*!"

Lucy grabbed Jeramiah's arm and smiled up at him. "Enough, my husband. Thou must now lead us all home."

* * *

Jake sat in a rocker staring at the flames in the fireplace. He suddenly shoved his body forward, covered his face with his hands and snickered.

"Jake, stop laughing at Lily falling in the snow," Louise said as she poured heated water into the dish basin.

Shed and Wiley burst into laughter, as did Jake, then Louise.

"Seein' them fat, naked legs stickin' in the air was the awfulest thing I ever seen my whole life," Jake said. "But I'm glad she weren't hurt none." He bent over farther and tried not to snicker, but failed.

* * *

The tracks of the horses and buggies that had left the farm many hours earlier made it easy for the lone rider to get though from town. Laughter in the small house masked the muffled sound of his horse entering the yard. The man dismounted and tied the reins of his horse to the porch railing. He quietly stepped onto the porch, waded through the deep snow and flattened himself against the house, then slid toward the front window until just one eye peered through the glass. He saw Jake bending over in a rocker in front of the fireplace. Wiley sat at the table, facing the front window, grinning as he cleaned his pistol. The other man and the woman, at the sink, had their backs to him. It would be a clear shot at Jake, and he'd kill Wiley for a clean getaway.

Slowly, the man pulled his pistol, gently rested the barrel against the glass and cocked it.

* * *

"I feel bad we're laughing at Lily's fall," Louise said as she handed Shed a pot from the evening meal to dry. "The poor woman can hardly get around she's so large."

"Fat!" Shed stated, then ducked the wet dish rag Louise swung at him.

That sound! Wiley tensed. He knew the sound of a gun being cocked through any distraction. He'd listened to it every evening for weeks, sometimes blindfolded, in Bristol Campion's home in Boston. Bristol, Wiley's Criminology instructor at Boston University, owned over a hundred pistols and had insisted on training Wiley to memorize the sound from each make of gun as it was being cocked, saying it was important to know what firepower an enemy had. He'd made Wiley listen over the screams of children playing, lightning storms, social gatherings and any other distractions he could come up with.

The sound Wiley had just heard came from a Hopkins and Allen .38 double action revolver. And it had been magnified by the front window glass!

He slid the last bullet into his Navy Colt, pointed it toward the window and fired three shots. The first slug plowed through the center of the pane. The other two ripped along the edges of the molding on either side.

The deafening blasts of Wiley's gun jolted the others. Shed pulled Louise to the floor. Jake dived toward the front door, upsetting the rocker. He drew his Colt on the way. Wiley disappeared out the back into darkness and deep snow.

"Shed, get your shotgun!" Jake yelled as he reached the front door.

Louise struggled to her feet, ran to the sideboard and blew into the chimney of her green glass lamp, then dropped back to the floor behind the cabinet work space in front of the stove. In a crouch, Shed rushed behind the cook stove, slid back a wooden panel in the wall and yanked out his shotgun. Pointing it at the front window, he rushed to the fireplace, grabbed the lamp off the mantle and blew it out. Silhouetted by the fire, he ran to Louise, slid between her and the front window, placed the shotgun on the top of the cabinet and pointed it at the shattered hole in the window.

Jake silently opened the door a crack, put his ear to it and listened for any noise outside. Hearing nothing, he tried to think what Wiley would do. To see down the porch, he'd have to stick his head all the way out, and he could get shot. Was there another way out of the house besides the front door? Trying to get to the back door would put him in the line of fire, but he knew the window in his parents bedroom opened easily. Shed mentioned he'd fixed it since he and Louise liked fresh air when they slept. But he couldn't go in there! That room brought back thoughts of his father. Jake gently closed the front door, stared into the darkness of the bedroom and shuddered. Somehow he had to get outside and help Wiley.

Dampness and cold hit Wiley full force when he slipped out the back door. Little snow had melted during the day and he hesitated before trudging through the three-foot drifts. Positive Jake's life was in danger, he forced himself into the deep snow. Halfway to the front of the house, he stopped to listen. He'd heard Jake yell to Shed about the shotgun, then the house went dark. There was no sound except the gentle breeze that still loosened globs of snow from branches. A stronger gust dislodged snow from the roof. It fell on his head and slid down the back of his shirt.

Almost cursing out loud from the sudden cold next to his skin, Wiley yanked his shirt from his pants to let the snow fall. He shivered, then carefully trudged forward. Snow had crept up both pant legs, and he wished he'd charged the front door from inside.

Still no sound from the porch. Approaching the corner of the house, Wiley heard a noise and stopped to listen. Someone was breathing hard from the porch or beyond it. He crept closer, his gun held in front of him. He reached the corner of the house and stopped to listen. The heavy breathing had slowed, but seemed to come from the opposite corner of the house. Had the man moved to the front door? Was he going to shove his way in, shooting? Wiley poised like a puma, then grabbed the railing and leaped it. The ice on the top let go, and Wiley fell face down into the deep snow on the porch.

A gun blasted. The bullet shattered the railing where Wiley's hand had just been.

Raising his Colt, Wiley shouted, "Put your gun down, or I'll kill you!"

"Wiley?"

"Jake?"

"I just shot at you, Wiley. Thought you was that man. Did I hit you?"

Wiley sighed. "You missed. Where is he? I can hear his horse."

"Don't know, Wiley. You could'a hit him when you first shot."

Wiley slid a hand through the snow. He felt something. An arm? He grasped it. The arm didn't move.

"Jake, get a lamp."

* * *

They left the body of Alfred Swift where it lay. Wiley's second bullet, fired from the table inside, had blown away the right side of his face.

"Was he after me, Wiley?" Jake asked, wide-eyed with shock. He scooted his chair closer to the table, grabbed his mug of whiskey with both hands and took a sip.

"I think he might have been. We'll never know for sure. Burt told me Al had become a dangerous man."

"How'd he know where I was gonna be?"

"That's a good question. One I think I can answer, but hope I'm wrong. Burt must have told him where we were going." Wiley banged his fist on the table. "How could I have been so blind. The information he was selling was about *us*. And he must have sold it to Betty!"

"Betty? Damn!"

Sitting opposite Wiley at the table, Shed frowned at him. "Is that the Betty you said got shot in Alma?"

"The very same. She escaped capture after Fainsworth was arrested on the riverboat."

Louise reached from the end of the table and grabbed Wiley's arm. "What can be done about her? We don't want Jake killed. What will happen next time?"

Wiley smiled slightly at Louise and patted her hand as she pulled it away. He stared at the center of the table a moment, then turned his head toward Jake. "Do you think you could squeeze into the rawhide bag Chief Eagle Rising gave you? It might protect you from all sides."

Pulling the bag from his shirt, Jake held it up in front of his face. "Hell, I can't even get my big toe in there." He shifted his eyes to

Wiley and grinned. "I ain't worried. You're my blood brother, Wiley. You'll pertect me."

"I'll certainly try."

Louise noticed Shed sigh, close his eyes and smile.

"By the way, Jake," Wiley said, "how did you get outside? Using the front door was very risky since someone was on the porch."

Jake lowered his head and shrugged. "Knowin' you was outside an' could get shot, I went out the bedroom window."

* * *

By morning, Alfred Swift's body had frozen solid. The partners loaded it into Shed's wagon, tied Swift's rented horse to the back and made their way to town.

Even at nine o'clock, the sheriff's office was locked. Wiley wrote Tyborn a note and slipped it under the door, then they headed to the mortician, whose primary job was a cabinet maker.

"Who you got there, Jake?" Trent Watkins asked as the men pulled up in front. He shut the door to his store, pulled a jacket over his lean frame and trudged through the snow.

"Alfred Swift. He tried killin' me last night. Wiley shot him through Shed's front window."

"Ain't he the gent you warned the sheriff about?"

"The very same," Wiley said as he tossed back the blanket from the body.

"Glad he's frozen. Can't bury him 'till the ground thaws." Watkins raised one eyebrow. "You go through his pockets?"

Jake looked at the body. "Ain't never thought of that."

Trent reached down and emptied the pockets of the dead man. He whistled when he held up a wad of bank notes.

"Whatever you found, it's yours to bury him." Wiley grabbed the body under the arms. "Where do you want him?"

Trent Watkins pointed to the barn beside the building. "Jess toss 'im in there on the floor somewhere. He'll keep 'til the weather warms up." As the partners hefted the frozen body to the barn, Watkins counted the notes. "I'll be go to hell," he whispered to himself. "There's over a thousan' dollars here." He opened the message that had been wrapped around the notes, read it and said, "Well, I'll be dammed. Guess he had family after all."

After depositing the body, Jake led Wiley to the telegraph office where he sent a telegram to Mike McGelvy telling of the event and to arrest Burt for conspiracy to commit murder. He asked Mike to keep searching for Betty.

* * *

After a long good bye to Shed and Louise, the partners left that same afternoon. They took the stage to Lexington and, the next morning, started the four-day journey by train back to Colorado. Jake loved the train trip this time. The Harrises weren't chasing him nor was he tied to the seat. He mostly stayed in their compartment, in Wiley's arms.

In Denver, they checked in with James McParland, head of the Denver Pinkerton office, who had no assignments for them at the present time. Jake looked up Dorsey Coburn and Elliot Ramsey, the partners he'd worked with building houses before he'd left for Alma, and the four men had a night on the town.

On the third day in Denver, anxious to get back to their cabin, Jake talked Wiley into leaving. They wired the Castille Ranch of their arrival and boarded the Denver and South Park train two days later at seven in the morning.

CHAPTER 22

On one of his weekly errands, Pike Lacy slowly rode Bucko down the main street in Como. Unusually sunny and warm for the second week of March, he grinned and nodded at the townspeople crowding the boardwalks, all taking advantage of the brief respite of winter's frigid grip.

Approaching the train depot and scanning the passengers leaving the station, he caught sight of a beautiful woman. The beaver Mackintosh coat made her appear more stately than any woman he'd seen in a long time. A few strands of hair peeking out the sides of her hood almost matched the leopard fur that framed her lovely face. Pike stared at her, then nudged Bucko forward. Not caring he was merely a dusty cowboy, the woman had captured his heart. She reminded him of his wife, Constance, and he had to get closer.

When the woman looked directly at him, Pike gasped and reined Bucko to a stop. He touched the brim of his hat and said, "How do, ma'am. I'm Pike Lacy, at your service."

The woman smiled. "Pleased to make your acquaintance, Mr. Lacy. I'm Mary Williams."

Pike dismounted at once. He felt flushed and awkward as he tied Bucko to the rail. He approached her, whipped off his hat and curled the brim with nervous fingers. "Er, what's a purty lady like you doin' in Como?"

"Traveling across the country."

"Alone?"

Mary batted her eyes at Pike. "Mostly."

"Can I buy you a drink...er, I mean, supper?"

"Why, yes. If you like. The train's fare was only roast beef sandwiches."

"I'll take you to the Como Hotel. They got good eats, an' I'm payin'."

Mary took in Pike's superb body as he picked up her two leather bags. She walked with him up the street to the hotel.

After removing their heavy coats, they were seated in the dining room large enough to comfortably place twenty tables. A silver vase in the center of their cloth-covered table held a leafless, chartreuse sprig of aromatic rabbit bush and a single red rose.

When the waitress appeared, Pike said, "Ma'am an' me'd like supper."

The woman smiled at Mary. "Anything to drink while you wait? We import the best brands of wine and sherry."

"I'll have sherry, thank you."

"An' I'll have a whiskey," Pike said.

Once the waitress left, Pike looked deep into Mary's blue eyes that seemed to be searching the room. He loved the way she'd piled her blond hair up in so many folds, just the way his wife had before she'd left him. Mary's face and even her sensuous figure reminded him of Constance. He suddenly realized he hungered for the touch of a beautiful woman.

"Uh, how long you stayin' in Como, ma'am?"

Mary looked at Pike. "I don't know. I'm running low on money and would like to take a job in the area for awhile. Do you know of any that a woman can do?"

"Can you cook, er, ma'am?"

"Of course I can cook. Any woman can cook. But I'd prefer not doing that for work."

Pike grinned. "Just wonderin'. The ranch I'm workin' at needs a cook. Soarin' Raven just took off, not tellin' nobody where she was goin'." He glanced around the room, then lowered his voice. "Belinda ain't much of a cook. Soarin' Raven cooked since Belinda was little. 'Sides, she's got too much else to do."

"What else did this Soaring Raven do? Is she an Indian?"

"Yes ma'am. She's Ute. We used'ta do the huntin'." He shrugged. "Jimmy does that, now." Pike sighed. "Soarin' Raven's gone an' Jake an' Wiley're back east. The ranch don't seem like it used to."

The waitress appeared with their drinks. As she set them lightly on the table she said, "Tonight's fare is timothy hay fed beef tips."

Mary looked up at her. "That will be fine."

"Fine with me, too," Pike said. When the woman left, he leaned over the table. "Timothy hay's the best feed for cows. Makes 'em fat and tasty. They're so tasty, they..." Pike stopped, deciding not to bore this woman with his many stories, but be on best behavior.

Mary sipped her sherry and chose not to ask what Pike was going to say. She searched his face and liked his strong, handsome features. "What does the job of cook pay on your ranch?"

"Don't rightly know. Ain't been talked about. Belinda an' Jimmy're fine people. An' Jake an' Wiley're due home anytime." He grinned. "Them two boys're real nice. You'd like 'em." Chuckling, he said, "That Jake's a real sweet man. Wiley got himself a dang good partner in that one."

During the leisurely meal, Mary examined Pike from the top of his head to his broad shoulders and huge chest, down to where the table blocked the rest. She smiled. "Maybe I can cook well enough to help on your ranch."

After picking up supplies and a telegraph message to Jimmy and Belinda, Pike talked constantly as he and Mary walked to the livery. Shortly, he was snapping the reins of a rented horse and buggy. Tied behind the wagon, Bucko tossed his head and reared. Realizing Pike didn't notice, being caught up with Mary, he settled down and trotted stiff-legged the rest of the way to the ranch.

* * *

Two days later, Jake and Wiley, accompanied by Pike, who'd met them in Como and brought their horses, arrived at the Castille Ranch at twilight. Pike yelled for his hands, and three men scrambled out of the main barn to care for the horses. Pike ushered the partners into the warmth of the kitchen.

Jake stamped his frozen feet and stood in front of the cookstove. Wiley crowded beside him and held his hands over a puffing jet of steam from the covered pot simmering on the cast-iron top.

Jake sniffed the air and wrinkled his nose. "What's that smell?"

Pike punched him in the back and whispered, "Keep yer voice down. We got us a new cook an' that's yer supper cookin'."

"I ain't eatin' nothin' smellin' like that!"

"Wiley! Jake! You're home!" Belinda rushed into the kitchen, grabbed each man and hugged him. She stood back and took in the two men. "You both look exhausted. I hope you can stay around the ranch for awhile and rest up."

"Well, the famous Pinkertons are home," Jimmy said as he sauntered through the door. "You've made the local papers the entire time you've been gone." He shook Jake and Wiley's hands.

"We don't have a new assignment." Wiley shrugged. "As of yesterday, anyway. James McParland in Denver said he'd try to let us rest for awhile, but wouldn't promise."

Jake eyed the cook pot and nudged Wiley. "We gotta be gettin' back to our cabin."

"It's too late, Jake," Belinda said. "You should stay here tonight. It's turned cold again, and you don't have any food there."

Jake sniffed the air and frowned. "We got elk meat frozen under the cabin."

Grimacing, Belinda said, "I'm sure it's spoiled by now. It turned warm for a few days."

Jake nodded at the stove. "Hell, even if it's rotten it'll taste better'n that stuff cookin' here."

Pike waved his arms. "Shhh! Mary'll hear you!"

Agreeing with Jake about the food but not letting on, Wiley didn't want to ride another hour in the frigid wind. Where had he smelled a strange aroma like that before?

"I'd like to stay here tonight, Jake. We need to catch up on what's been happening." Wiley looked at Belinda. "You have no idea where Soaring Raven went, or why?"

Biting her lip, Belinda merely shook her head.

"One morning, she was gone," Jimmy filled in. "She didn't leave any note, and she took all her traveling gear and her shotgun. That was a month ago. We haven't heard a word since."

Pike grinned. "We got us a new cook, though. I found her in Como jest gettin' off the train."

"She ain't no cook!" Jake snapped. "I wouldn't feed Mac nothin' smellin' like that!" He turned to Wiley. "Wonder if tomato juice'll kill the smell?"

"I told you to keep it down," Pike threatened. "Mary might hear an' she'd be sorely rankled."

Belinda half grinned at Jake. "She's only been here a few days. I promised her I'd try her out for a week. Pike is quite taken with her." She looked at Pike. "A few minutes ago, Mary said she wasn't feeling well and went upstairs to lie down."

"Prob'ly got sick eatin' her own food," Jake grumbled. "You got anythin' to eat she ain't cooked?"

"I'll get you fer that!" Pike yelled.

"You try, an' I'll make you eat that whole pot'a stinkin' stuff!"

* * *

After eating two cans of peaches apiece and a mound of elk jerky while telling Belinda, Jimmy and Pike of their adventures, Jake and Wiley retired to the upstairs room at the far end of the hall. Since Belinda had said Mary was staying in the first room at the top of the stairs, Wiley wanted to be as far away from her as possible. Pike had said she was a single woman, and he didn't want her anywhere near either of them.

Sprawled on the bed on his back, head raised by crossed arms, Jake grinned as he watched Wiley prop a chair under the door knob. "I won't let no woman get at you, Wiley."

Wiley kicked the chair secure and smiled at Jake. "Thank you. An unmarried woman has no right being near you, either."

As they nestled together in the featherbed, Jake whispered. "I don't wanna do nothin' tonight but hold you, Wiley. This here room's the one Zeke an' Hank first made love, an' I could hear ever'thin'."

"That's fine with me. I'm exhausted from the train trip and the long time we've been away from South Park. Let's just hold each other, like the first time we slept together in Bill's barn."

"Damn, Wiley. I loved it when you kissed me that night. Guess I was still drunk, cuz I thought I heard people watchin' over us."

"You did. It was Grandpa Gray Feather and his friends."

Jake sighed and snuggled closer to Wiley.

CHAPTER 23

The next morning, without waking Jake, Wiley rose at five and rode to Como, leading a pack horse. He wanted to stock up on supplies for their cabin and send a wire to Shed and Louise that they had arrived home safely. The frigid cold of the two-hour ride made Wiley think of Jake, still in the featherbed. He smiled, glad Jake was cozy.

Reaching town at seven, Wiley headed straight for the Como Hotel to get warm and eat breakfast. In the dining room, sitting at a table next to the wall so he could see the entire room, he ate steak, eggs and potatoes as he scanned the patrons. He wondered why Judge Parker was in Como. The Gilsons, who attended Belinda's wedding and also came for his birthday party, waved at him. As he waved back, he spotted Ted Hoover, the bank teller from Fairplay. Ted looked at him, and Wiley nodded.

Ted flew out of his chair, threaded through the room to Wiley's table and plopped into the chair across from him.

"What are you doing in Como?" Wiley asked.

Blushing, Ted stammered, "Er, I visited a good friend of mine last night." He composed himself and leaned over the table and whispered excitedly, "Remember the woman that was shot in Alma last year and stayed in Doc Coulter's office for three weeks?"

"Betty? What about her?"

"Randy, er, my friend here in Como, was there when she got shot, and..."

"What about Betty?"

"Well, she's back. Randy saw her in here with Pike Lacy from your ranch a few days ago. Pike rented a buggy and took her back with him."

"Good God!" Wiley leaped out of his chair, tossed two quarters on the table and rushed from the hotel. Without getting supplies, he stabled the pack horse and galloped out of town toward the ranch. He suddenly remembered the strange smell from the kitchen last night. Betty's cooking! She had ruined a Pinkerton Christmas party from the smell of what she'd brought.

* * *

When Jake woke at six, he went looking for Wiley, or anyone since the house seemed deserted. Finding Jimmy in the barn shoeing his horse, he asked, "Where's ever'body?"

Jimmy looked up from nailing a horseshoe. "Belinda's ill and still in bed." He winked at Jake. "She thinks she's with child."

Those words brought back memories of Sara Jean and the Harrises. Jake forced a grin and said, "Damn!"

Jimmy picked up another nail. "Wiley went to Como to get supplies and send a wire. He left at five and said he'd be back after noon."

Jake kicked a dried horse apple. "Hell, I would'a gone with him. Wonder why he didn't wake me?"

"He mentioned he wanted you to catch up on your sleep since you were going back to your cabin today."

Pouting, Jake headed for the kitchen, hoping to scrounge something to eat the new cook hadn't touched. When he opened the door, a woman with blond hair stood at the stove with her back to him. Jake slammed the door and said nothing to her as he stomped to the pantry. While searching for a couple cans of salmon or peaches, he felt someone close behind and spun around to find a gun pointed at him.

"What the hell...?" Jake recognized her. "Betty! What the hell're you doin' here? How'd you know where I was?"

"How do you think? I made Alfred Swift carry a note saying I was his sister. The mortician in Kentucky wired me of his death. I'm here because all my other attempts to kill you failed, so I'm going to do it myself."

"Why you wantin' to kill me? I ain't never done nothin' to you."

"You took Wiley away from me! I want him back!"

Jake shook his head. "Hell, killin' me ain't gonna get Wiley back. You never had him. Wiley ain't never liked you."

"We were *engaged* before he met you!" Betty screamed. She waved the gun at Jake. "Get out of the pantry and sit in that chair beside the door. I want to shoot you out in the open and leave your body for Wiley to see. He'll run to me for comfort!"

Jake moved into the kitchen and sat in the chair. "You weren't never engaged with Wiley. That's a damn lie. Wiley don't like most women, 'specially not one that lies an' tries to kill people. An' how're you gonna keep from gettin' shot by Wiley if you kill me?"

Betty leaned toward Jake. "Wiley would *never* shoot me."

Jake shrugged. "Guess you're right. Wiley don't shoot women. He'd most likely bury you up to your neck in a road and drive a buggy over your head. Wiley's mean when he gets riled, an' killin' me'll rile him somethin' terrible."

Betty scoffed. "That's ridiculous. Wiley would never do that to me. We love each other."

Beginning to get angry, Jake snapped, "Hell, ma'am, you don't know nothin' about love. You ain't nothin' but spoiled an' selfish, an' you don't care nothin' about Wiley. Wiley can love who he wants. An' he *don't* love you!"

Betty levered her pistol at Jake's head. "How dare you talk to me like that! I'm one of the wealthiest women on the east coast! I can have what I want! I want Wiley, and *no one* is going to stop me from getting him!"

"Me stop you!"

Jake leaped out of his chair. "Soaring Raven!"

Betty spun around and saw the huge Ute woman pointing a shotgun at her.

"Me shoot you in half! Put down gun! Wiley no belong to you. Wiley belong to Jake. Like Rising Moon belong to me."

With Betty distracted, Jake scrambled out the back door and ran to tell Jimmy that Soaring Raven had returned.

"So! You're the filthy savage who's job I filled!" Betty pointed her pistol at Soaring Raven. "I'll kill..."

Both barrels of the shotgun blasted. Bloody bits of Betty splattered the kitchen wall and shattered the window.

* * *

When Wiley reached the ranch, he leaped off Buddy, rushed through the gate and ran to the porch. Jerking open the front door and storming into the parlor, he stopped when he saw Jake sitting alone on the divan.

"Jake! Betty's the new cook! You have to get out of here!"

Jake looked up from staring at his knees. "Hell, Wiley, Betty's dead. Soaring Raven shot her." Jake's eyes teared. "Guess nothin' else could'a been done with her." He jerked his head toward the kitchen. "Soaring Raven an' Rising Moon're helpin' Belinda clean up the kitchen."

Wiley slid next to Jake and wrapped his arms around him. "Betty's dead? Thank God!" After a moment, he pulled away. "Soaring Raven is back? Who's Rising Moon? What's been going on here?"

"Hell, Wiley, Betty was gonna kill me cuz she wanted you, but Soaring Raven shot her with her shotgun. Rising Moon's the woman Soaring Raven went to get. They're like us, Wiley. They love each other like we do."

Wiley rested his head on Jake's shoulder. "God, I'm so glad you're alive! I got here as fast as I could. And I'm thankful I didn't have to empty my gun into Betty if she'd killed you." He squeezed Jake.

Jake bear-hugged Wiley. "I'm glad, too, Wiley."

* * *

Jake and Wiley rode to Como, picked up the pack horse and purchased their supplies. Wiley sent a wire to Mike McGelvy about Betty's demise, then they accompanied Marshal Eliott and Robert Mason, the mortician, back to the ranch.

Mason promised Wiley he would ship what was left of Betty's body back to Philadelphia in a sealed casket. Wiley gave Mike McGelvy's name as someone who would contact any possible relatives. He was glad the casket would be shipped east, not wanting to be within a thousand miles of Betty, dead or alive.

After Marshal Eliott and Mason left for Como, while adding logs to the parlor stove, Jimmy said, "I'll have Pike re-paint the kitchen and fix the window. He's the one who brought Betty here." He returned to his chair and stretched an arm to the rocker next to him and grabbed Belinda's hand. "I'm sorry you had to see the gory scene in the kitchen. It's bad enough to see a dead body, but only half of one has got to be hard on you in your condition."

Belinda squeezed Jimmy's hand and smiled weakly at him. "She had it coming." She looked across the parlor at Jake and Wiley, sitting together on the divan. "Betty caused you both much distress, and for a long time. I'm just glad Sa-Ra returned in time."

"Where's Soaring Raven?" Jake asked. "I ain't even got to talk to Rising Moon."

Belinda smiled. "I'm afraid you'll have to wait. Sa-Ra carried the oval washtub and several buckets of heated water into her bedroom. She told me she would fix breakfast tomorrow, then gently ushered Rising Moon into the room and slammed the door."

"Why didn't Soaring Raven tell you where she was going before she left?" Wiley asked.

"I asked her. She said it wasn't my business." Belinda smiled. "She did tell me she'd recently found out Rising Moon was living in Santa Fe, teaching English at the Indian School. I think Sa-Ra left in a hurry to make sure she found Rising Moon before she left there for any reason."

A knock on the front door startled them.

"Who is it?" Jimmy yelled.

"Pike Lacy."

"Come on in, Pike."

The door opened and Pike slowly shoved his head into the room. He looked at Wiley, Jake, then Belinda and Jimmy.

"Pike, what's this knocking on the door about?" Jimmy asked.

Relieved no one had a gun pointed at him, he entered the house, closed the door and whipped off his hat, then looked at his feet. "I...er..." He peered at Jake and shrugged. "Sorry about bringin' Mary, er, Betty here. Didn't know who she was. Got taken with her is all.

Got t'missin' my wife after Soarin' Raven left, an' looks-wise, Mary kinda took after my Constance."

"Hell, it don't matter." Jake rose from the divan, walked over to Pike and put his hand on the foreman's shoulder. "Ever'body here's got a partner 'cept you. Hope you find somebody that loves you back." He grinned. "An' I hope it ain't nobody wantin' to kill *me*."

Laughing with the others, Belinda pushed herself out of the rocker and headed toward the kitchen. "Since Soaring Raven is...busy, I'd better start dinner."

Wiley caught the pained expression on Pike's face and said, "Why don't you let Jake and me fix it."

Spinning around, Jake yelled, "*Us* fix supper?"

With an even more pained expression, Pike said, "Er, hold on. Either'a you gents ever fixed grub for a cattle drive?" When both men shook their heads, Pike looked pleadingly at Belinda. "Ma'am, I'd be 'bliged if you'd fix the grub."

"I intend to, whether you like my cooking, or not." Belinda opened the door to the stairwell, turned to the men, curtly nodded her head, then smiled. She closed the door behind her to keep the warmth in the room from escaping up the stairs.

CHAPTER 24

Gun drawn, Wiley opened the door to their cabin at Chipmunk Rock and peered into the gloom. He entered and stood for a moment to let his eyes adjust to the shuttered sunlight. Even if Pike hadn't told them he'd stayed in the cabin a couple nights while herding cattle, and had left it spotless with a ready-for-lighting fire built on the rock ledge, Wiley would have known someone had been there.

Jake entered the room, looked around and sighed. "We're home." He grabbed Wiley in a bear hug. "An' I wanna hold you naked."

Wiley laughed and kissed Jake's neck. "Don't you think we need to light the fire first? It's freezing in here."

"You light it, Wiley. I'm gonna warm the bed up." Jake stripped off his clothes. Naked, he crawled between the covers and began thrashing his arms and legs.

Once the kindling blazed, Wiley carefully placed three different sized aspen logs over the center, the thinnest on the bottom and at the back. He knew when that log burned away, the largest log on top would roll in its coals and keep the fire burning for an hour or more. As he stared briefly into the flames, hearing Jake's teeth chattering as he tried to warm the bed, his spirit rose to the foot of the Great White Father, and to the foot of Jake's friend Jesus, thanking them for the grand experience of knowing and loving Jake. And for keeping him safe.

The Great White Father and Jesus seemed to smile at Wiley. Grandpa Gray Feather appeared before Wiley's eyes, nudged him and pointed to the bed. "Your brother cold. Go to him."

Seeing Wiley staring into the fire, Jake asked, "You gonna get naked?" After a long silence, Jake stopped moving. "Wiley? You okay?"

A log popped. Glowing sparks sailed into the room. Two hit the wood floor, and a third landed in the seat of an armchair. It began smoking.

Trance broken, Wiley wheeled around, shook the ember from the chair, crushed it with his boot and doused the seat with nearly-frozen water from the metal pitcher sitting on the table. He splashed water on the other sparks. Knowing it was unusual for aspen logs to pop like that, Wiley thought of his grandfather and chuckled.

"We gonna burn up, Wiley?"

Wiley laughed. "Not yet. I have to get undressed first."

* * *

The third day back at their cabin, bundled in his duster and thinking of Grandpa Gray Feather, Wiley sat on the bench outside the door. Resting his hands on his knees, he watched the line of the morning sun slowly travel up his fingers.

A rustle in the brush on his right caught his attention. He looked up the hill and spotted glimpses of Jake half-running down the leafless, wooded slope. When Jake got to a small clearing, Wiley saw he carried a large, flat rock with a pile of dirt heaped on top. A moment later, Jake approached him and grinned.

"Jake, why are you carrying dirt?"

After dumping the pile of dirt in the snow beside the cabin wall, Jake tossed the rock to the ground. "I'm makin' us a flower garden for next summer." He grinned. "Them orange wallflowers Miss Castille has growin' by her kitchen door made me want some by our home. An' I'm gonna plant red gilia, them baby yellow daises an' that Indian paintbrush Soaring Raven likes."

"But it's winter. Where are you getting dirt? I thought the ground was still frozen."

"It ain't frozen by that big rock up the hill. Ain't no snow there neither, an' the rock feels warm even in cold weather."

Jake slid onto the bench beside Wiley so their shoulders touched. He rubbed his cold hands, shoved them between his legs, glanced briefly at Wiley and smiled, then looked off into the distance. "Ma said somebody's rich if they can spend time plantin' flowers." Jake brushed Wiley's leg with the back of his fingers. "We're rich, Wiley, cuz we got each other. We can plant flowers."

Wiley leaped to his feet, walked to the flat rock Jake had discarded and hefted it. "Show me where you got that dirt."

* * *

"I hope Soaring Raven lets us talk to Rising Moon," Jake said as he dismounted and tied Mac's reins to the rail outside the Castille Ranch gate. "She's a pretty lady, an' I like the way she only has one braid instead'a two." Opening the gate for Wiley, Jake grinned. "An' she smiled at me."

Wiley slid his arm over Jake's shoulder as they walked to the porch. "Soaring Raven seems very protective of Rising Moon, and from what Belinda said, they haven't seen each other for twenty years. I hope they haven't changed so much they don't get along anymore."

"Hell, they're Indians, Wiley. Indians love ever'body. It's us white people that hate people."

"That's not quite true, but I understand what you mean."

As they climbed the porch steps, the parlor door opened and Rising Moon rushed outside. "Jake! Wiley! I knew you would come today!" She hugged Jake first. "Soarie told me about you. We four are like family."

"Soarie?" Jake asked. "Who the hell's that?"

Rising Moon laughed. "Soaring Raven. She hates me calling her that, or so she says." The heavy-set woman, almost as tall as the two men, but not nearly as big as Soaring Raven, winked at them. "I love her more now than in our youth. She was bossy then."

"Hell, I ain't never met nobody bossier'n her, *now*!"

Wiley looked at Rising Moon. "You don't think she's bossy?"

"Now? It's an act." Rising Moon ushered them in from the cold. As she shut the door she chuckled, then turned toward the partners. "It's good to see her happy. She loves it here, and Belinda has treated her well." She smiled. "When I saw her outside my classroom, I knew she finally came for me."

"It must have taken a long time making arrangements to leave the school," Wiley said. "Soaring Raven was gone over a month."

"It took two seconds. I walked out of class and the building. We went to my home and packed. Only my mother knows I left." Rising Moon smiled. "She was happy for me. She will tell the school...and the town." Her eyes turned mischievous. "We played in frozen streams on the way back."

Jake gasped. "*Soaring Raven* played in streams?"

The kitchen door opened and Soaring Raven walked toward them. She zeroed in on Jake. "Why you yell my name?"

"I...uh..."

Rising Moon touched Soaring Raven's elbow. "He can't believe we played in streams on the way here."

Hands on hips, Soaring Raven gave Jake a piercing look. "Naked!" When Jake's face flushed, she smiled at him. "You red-face man, too."

Later, as they sat at the table for supper, Jimmy noticed Belinda listening carefully to every word Rising Moon said about their adventures on the way back from Santa Fe. He knew Belinda was making sure Soaring Raven was truly happy having Rising Moon here, and also making sure Rising Moon cared for Soaring Raven. He chuckled when he spotted Pike silently glaring at Rising Moon. There hadn't been a single evening since he'd been here that Pike had been so silent at the table.

Jake watched Pike and understood the man's loneliness. He remembered how he'd punched the wall of the train when he'd thought Wiley was naked in the arms of Betty. Wanting to help Pike from that blackness, he asked, "Rising Moon, do you hunt?"

"She no hunt!" Soaring Raven said. "She teach. She help cook."

Rising Moon laughed. "Even after all these years, Soarie knows me well."

Jake caught Pike's eye and grinned at him. "Soaring Raven's most likely gonna do the huntin' again, an' you can go with her."

"Him no hunter!" Soaring Raven said. "Him shoot off ears!"

Pike cackled and grinned at Jake.

Looking at Rising Moon, Jake asked, "Can you help Wiley teach me to read?"

"No. *I* will teach you to read." Rising Moon secretly winked at Wiley, then looked into Jake's pleading blue eyes. "Wiley is a Pinkerton. I am a teacher."

"I got Pinkerton things t'do, too."

"Reading and writing are Pinkerton things. I will teach you."

Jake looked at Wiley. "Will you be riled if Rising Moon teaches me instead'a you?"

"It's training, Jake. She'll teach you to read much better than I could."

Jake grinned, then turned to Rising Moon. His countenance fell. "You gonna laugh at me when I say dummer'n hog shit stuff?"

Frowning at Jake, Rising Moon said, "Why do you say that about yourself? Hog shit is not dumb. It's not smart. It only stinks. Why do you call yourself hog shit?"

"Jake's father always told him he was dumber than hog shit," Wiley remarked.

Jake lowered his eyes and shuddered.

"Your father is like hog shit, not you," Rising Moon said. "You will never learn to read or write if you keep being hog shit. You're a human, a spirit being and Wiley's partner. Wiley could not love hog shit."

Rising Moon shoved back her chair and got to her feet. "You must bathe. Now! I will prepare it." She left the table and headed toward the kitchen, then stopped and turned. "Wiley. You must help."

As he rose out of his chair, Wiley winked at Jake, then followed Rising Moon into the kitchen.

Jake looked pleadingly at Soaring Raven. "Why's Rising Moon gonna give me a bath? An' why's Wiley gotta help?"

"Wash away hog shit. Rising Moon then teach. Wiley part Indian. He know."

"Do what them Indian women say, Jake," Pike said. "Ain't nobody smarter'n Indian women. I should'a married one 'stead'a Constance. They know life ain't always purty as gold aspens."

Carefully observing Soaring Raven, Belinda said, "Sa-ra, since Rising Moon came here, I've...well, we've all seen a side of you we've never seen before. Especially me, and I've known you since I was a little girl. Why did you go get Rising Moon, now?"

"Me stay here 'til time right," Soaring Raven muttered. "Rising Moon not come when I leave village. Many tears. She must teach, me must run ranch. When time right, me find and get."

* * *

Wiley alone attended Jake in his bath. Shirtless, he poured herb-water over Jake's head, then kissed him and spread the water over his body with both hands.

"Jake, this bath is to wash away every thought of you being...like your father. You are like your mother." He grabbed Jake's rawhide bag and flung it to his back. "This scented water will help you acquire the beauty of your mother's soul. She will help you learn from Rising Moon." Wiley scooped cupped hands into the water and poured it over Jake's head, then kissed him. "This water washes away your father and all thoughts of you being dumber than hog shit."

Jake looked into Wiley's eyes and grinned. "I like doin' this, Wiley, an' I wanna read. Wash me off ever'where. My nuts, too."

* * *

"You two have an urgent message from Denver," Benton Riley announced the moment Jake and Wiley entered the Fairplay telegraph office. "If you hadn't come in today, I would have had someone take it to you."

Jake grabbed Wiley's arm. "Maybe we gotta job to do."

"I have a feeling you're right," Wiley muttered.

The telegram was from James McParland in the Denver Pinkerton office. Wiley read it out loud. "Go at once to Gunnison. Moras brothers fleeing Denver murder. Dangerous."

Wiley crumpled the message and tossed it into the brass trash bucket. He could barely contain his anger. A new assignment only a week after arriving home! While in Denver, he'd had a feeling James McParland wouldn't leave them alone. McParland was known for making his agents work as hard as he did. Wiley clenched his teeth. Didn't McParland have any other life?

After a deep breath, Wiley growled, "I don't care what McParland wants, we're going to Alma and visit Bill and Harry like we'd planned. Hopefully Matt and Frank will be in town."

They rode the five miles up to Alma, entered Bill Chasteen's livery and found him huddled by his potbelly stove carving whistles.

"Howdy, gents!" Bill shouted as he leaped out of his hand carved, form-fitted chair. "What brings you up here?"

"Came to see you an' Harry an' them," Jake said. "Wiley'n me's got us a Pinkerton job to do."

"Here?"

"No!" Wiley snapped. "Wish it were. It's in Gunnison. Where is that?"

"Dang! It's south an' west'a here. A hundred miles'r more. Best way in winter is take the train. Snow's too deep over them passes fer horses. Train tracks're cleared after every storm, an' I heard the train's still runnin' regular this winter."

"Does a train go there from Fairplay?" Wiley asked, hoping they wouldn't have to go clear back to Denver.

"Sure does. Train goin' south takes you right there. 'Course you gotta switch in Nathrop." Harry grabbed his coat. "Let's go get Harry."

As they walked up the boardwalk, Jake turned to Bill. "You an' Harry partners yet?"

"Dang-it, Jake! Told you b'fore not to bring that up! Harry'n me're just fine the way we are!"

"Harry don't think so."

"You leave Harry outta this!"

"Then, why we goin' to get Harry?"

Wiley forced himself not to chuckle.

"Because I..." Bill stopped in his tracks. "Jake, you got the brain of a dang hawk!"

Stopping, Jake put his fists on his hips and leaned toward Bill. "I ain't got me no hawk brain! You an' Harry're like Wiley an' me! An' your first partner's prob'ly wonderin' when you're gonna let him do what he wants up there!"

Wiley turned away and bit his lip.

"How am I keepin' Chuck from doin what he wants?" Bill shouted.

Turning slightly, Wiley made sure he could hear what was coming.

"My friend, Jesus, said stuff is better up there. If it's better there, why would Chuck want to come here every time you want him back? He prob'ly thinks you're too old now, anyway!"

Wiley clamped his hand over his mouth.

"Dang, you two! I never should'a let you hide in my barn that first night!" Bill turned to Wiley. "Stop you're dang laughin', you...*gunfighter*!"

Wiley turned toward him and grinned. "Even Jake thinks you're *old*.

Passers-by stared at the three laughing men.

When they reached the barber shop, Bill stopped them. "Let's go around back, peek in the window an' see if Harry's busy. Maybe he's doin' some miner."

"It should be you he's doing," Wiley quipped.

"It's his job!" Bill snapped, then shrugged. "Even if I don't like it much."

"Hell, it wouldn't hafta be his job if he could fool around with you. Even if you are old, you still gotta a dick."

"Dang you, Jake!"

* * *

While the three men sat at their corner table in the Regal Cafe, Harry arrived and slid into a chair.

Bill glared at him. "You said you'd only be a few minutes!"

Harry smirked. "I couldn't rush Casey's bath. He'd shoot me." Harry grinned at Jake and Wiley. "Lordy, what have we done to have the pleasure of your company?" He frowned at Bill. "It certainly isn't a wedding!"

"Dang it!" Bill pointed at Jake. "You put him up to this!"

Wiley held up his hand. "Before you accuse anyone, Bill, Jake already told you Harry doesn't like your present situation."

Harry rolled his eyes. "What can I do? I'm mad about Bill, but all he thinks about is Chuck." He turned to Bill. "It isn't fair! If you'd never met Chuck, we'd be partners right now. You like me as much as I like you!"

"Chuck an' me was partners for--"

"I'm tired of this arguing about Chuck!" Wiley growled. He pulled his knife and slammed it on the table. "Jake's right, you have to become blood brothers. Now! Then you can fight all you want, but you'll be together!" He reached across the table, grabbed Bill's wrist in an iron grip and yanked his arm across the table. "Jake, get Harry's hand over here."

Bill's resistance was no match for Wiley's grasp. Harry allowed Jake to grab his arm and he even shoved his hand toward Wiley. Wiley made a lightning-quick cut on both men's hand, then forced them together, mixing the blood.

After pressing Bill and Harry's palms together for a few moments, Wiley released them. "Now you can do what you want, but you're both bound to each other. For life." He looked at Bill with squinty eyes. "Let Chuck rest in peace." He sheathed his knife and flagged the waitress.

Bill frowned at Wiley, shoved back his chair, got to his feet and headed for the door. He slammed it behind him.

"He'll be back," Wiley said. "He didn't like being forced into this, but he'll realize it's what he wanted all along."

Crestfallen, Harry mumbled, "I hope you're right." He grimaced at the sting from the cut on his palm.

"Wiley's part Indian," Jake said. "He knows stuff like that."

A short time later, the cafe door opened, then slammed.

"Bill's back," Wiley whispered. "Let's ignore him. Jake, tell something that happened on the riverboat."

"...an' Wiley gave Rodney two gold double eagles when he left." Jake grinned. "I gave him two more when Wiley weren't lookin'."

Wiley laughed. "So that's why you were short money when we arrived in St. Louis."

Bill listened for a moment, then pulled out a chair and plopped into it. No one looked his way.

Laughing, Jake yelled, "Hell, Wiley!" He clapped his hand over his mouth and looked around the room. No one but the men at his table looked his way for cussing so loud. He grinned as he relaxed. "That was damn close. Er...I didn't get to buy that candy I wanted cuz I gived that money to Rodney." He shrugged. "Hope he got him a job like he said he was goin' to."

Bill scooted his chair closer to the table. "He most likely gambled that money away that same night. You got scal'wagged."

"You been off poutin', Bill?" Jake asked.

Wiley kicked Jake's boot.

"Dang it!" Bill shouted. "Had to pee!"

Ignoring Wiley's kick, Jake asked, "You been peein' in the street? No wonder Harry don't want to be your partner."

"I weren't peein' in the dang street! An' it ain't Harry not wantin' to be *my* partner, it's *me* not wantin'... Oh, hell!" He looked at smiling Harry, then shrugged. "Guess it is time to let Chuck be gone, seein' I feel the same way about you as I did him."

Harry leaped to his feet. "Hallelujah! Dinner and drinks are on me!"

Matt slid his hand over Harry's shoulder. "What's this all about?"

"Where'd you two come from?" Bill asked the two miners standing by their table.

Frank grabbed a chair from an empty table, shoved it next to Bill, plopped into it and leaned toward him. "This have anythin' to do with us seein' you pacin' the street out front like a bear I seen at Elitch Gardens in Denver?"

"Wiley just made Bill and me blood brothers," Harry said as he sat down and scooted his chair nearer Jake to make room for Matt. "And Bill just admitted we were partners." He pounded the table. "Hallelujah!"

Still standing beside Harry, Matt grinned, placed his hands on Harry's shoulders, then sat between him and Frank.

Jake leaned toward Wiley and whispered, "Why're all them people starin' at Harry sayin' a good word, an' they didn't look at me when I was cussin' so loud?"

"Good words aren't said as often. People aren't used to hearing them." Wiley slid his hand over Jake's leg and looked into his eyes. "I wish we could become blood brothers all over again."

"Can't we? I liked doin' it."

Wiley laughed. "I don't see why not." He pulled out his knife again and placed it on the table.

"What's this about?" Matt asked.

"Wiley'n me're gonna become blood brothers again."

Matt squinted. "Why do it again?"

"Cuz we love each other." Jake grinned at each man. "Let's all become blood brothers. We all love each other. Dave an' Jim become blood brothers with us before they went back to nineteen-ninety-three. We gotta be a family. Ain't many people care about us like we all do."

"Even less so, in Dave and Jim's Time," Wiley muttered.

"I'm in!" Frank shoved his right hand to the center of the table. "I've wanted t'be blood brothers with every man I've ever met, an' mostly with Matt." He winked at Matt.

"Jake's right," Wiley said. "We love each other, and each one of you. We defied a Pinkerton order to be with you today. I'm glad we're all here."

One by one, the five men stretched their arms toward Wiley's knife. Wiley deftly made a small, painless cut on six palms, his own included. In turn, starting with Jake, the men shook hands with each other. Bill punched Harry's arm when he refused to let go of Wiley's hand.

Things settled down when the food arrived. The six blood brothers loaded their plates with steaks and potatoes and doused them with rich brown gravy. Before leaving, they clinked their glasses together three times in a final toast for the evening together, for becoming blood brothers...and a family.

CHAPTER 25

The next morning in Fairplay, Jake and Wiley boarded the Denver and South Park train heading south to Buena Vista. As the train slowly descended the steep canyon into the Arkansas River basin, the partners stared out the window of the train. The snowcapped Collegiate Range enthralled them. Gleaming white teeth so foreboding in their majestic immensity...and so near.

"Damn, Wiley! I didn't see them mountains like that when we came here buyin' clothes in Dave an' Jim's Time! They didn't have much snow on 'em."

"They're beautiful!" Wiley wished Grandpa Gray Feather could see the mountains, and knew instantly why the town, far below, had been named Buena Vista.

At Nathrop, south of Buena Vista and on the Arkansas River, they changed trains and headed west into the steep canyon between Mounts Princeton and Antero. During the layover in St. Elmo, a rip roaring town of three hundred miners, merchants and dance hall girls, the partners dodged their way down the crowded boardwalk. Wiley was amazed at the activity. Light snow, floating from the dull gray sky, made him remember the bustle of the streets of Philadelphia the day before Christmas.

They left the raucous Pat Hurley Saloon behind them, dodged their way passed the Miners Exchange building and the Mongrain Grocery Store and approached the Home Comfort Hotel. A large group of people had gathered outside the main entrance.

Wiley nudged Jake. "Let's walk slow and listen to what that group is talking about. We might learn something about this town. A few of the people are on the train, and they seem excited."

Jake suddenly realized he hadn't even noticed anyone on the train. He'd been captivated by the steep mountain sides and white-rock pinnacles while traveling up Chalk Creek Canyon.

As they reached the crowd of people, Wiley saw a man point up the canyon and say, "It's been snowin' up there fer a day an' a half. Yours might be the last train that gets over this winter. It's cursed up there, y'know. Utes cursed the railroad, an' I don't blame 'em one damn bit. Huntin' was ruined up there fer layin' the tracks to Gunnison an' the noise'a the engines."

A few gasps from the crowd gave the man the attention he'd hoped. "Three years ago," he yelled, "just this side'a Alpine Tunnel at the top, thirteen railroad workers was buried alive in a snow slide. It covered their boardin' house called Woodstock. Thirteen men killed an' on Friday the Thirteenth, to boot." He'd thrown in Friday the Thirteenth to further scare his audience.

Ute Indians cursed this railroad? Wiley stopped abruptly at the edge of the group.

Jake ran into him. "Hell, Wiley, why'd you--?"

"Jake, listen to this man!"

"'Nother time," the man said, "a snow slide took the whole damn train down the side'a the mountain hundreds'a feet. Them preachers said it was a miracle nobody was killed."

Pinkerton duty called, but Wiley balked. It had been snowing up there for all that time! How deep would it be? Would Jake be killed in a snow slide? Just because he was part Iroquois did not free either of them from a Ute curse.

Jake felt a spark from Wiley...or something. He saw worry on his face. Why? He'd heard the word miracle from the man but nothing else. He grabbed Wiley's arm. "What's wrong, Wiley?"

Turning to Jake, Wiley's face seemed ashen. "Jake, it's been snowing farther up the canyon for a day and a half. The train might get stranded up there...or a snow slide. The railroad has been cursed by the Utes."

"Damn, somethin' bad must'a made 'em rankled."

"The railroad ruined their hunting."

"Hell, we ain't doin' no huntin'. We're just goin' by."

"Jake, it's the *railroad* that's cursed."

"Hell, you're part Indian. Them Utes'll let you go." Jake grinned. "An' I'm with you. B'sides, that man said somethin' about a miracle."

Wiley shrugged. "I know, I heard him." He looked deep into Jake's eyes. "Promise me you'll stay by my side at all times going over the pass."

"Hell, I promise. Bein' with you's the only way I feel safe." Jake silently asked his friend Jesus to help Wiley feel safe, too.

* * *

As the train chugged up Alpine Pass, Wiley could see the enormity of the task of laying this track. On the mountain side, the men had constructed a rock wall, sometimes six feet high, to contain the sloping soil. It seemed miles long. When they reached Romley, the snow deepened and covered every trace of the wall. By the time they reached the Mary Murphy mine, the train traveled in a slot carved out of five-foot snow drifts, and the profusion of flakes began obliterating everything. The train chugged ever upwards and around bends so tight the wheels screamed against the rails.

"After we go by Hancock, we'll get to what's left'a Woodstock," a man one seat behind the partners said to the woman next to him. "Then, the train gets to the snow shed leadin' to the Alpine Tunnel. That's a wooden tunnel a hundred'n fifty feet long. On this side, that is. The snow tunnel's almost seven hundred feet long on the Gunnison side. An', mind you, the Alpine Tunnel's eighteen-hundred feet long. The whole length inside the tunnel is lined with California redwood to hold up the roof. But you gotta breathe through wet kerchiefs goin' through there, an' try not to breathe a'tall. People been suffocated in there just sittin' in these seats."

Wiley cringed and nudged Jake. "Did you hear what the man behind us said?"

Jake looked away from the window. "What?"

"You didn't hear a word that man said. Jake, you have to start listening to everything around you."

"Hell, Wiley, I couldn't listen to nothin' an' watch the snow, too."

"You have to learn how." Wiley leaned past Jake and looked out the window. God! The snow was almost six feet deep! And the train crept along at five miles an hour, if that. He wondered if this train bit through the snow, or a plow train had gone by shortly before. He sat back, watched Jake stare out the window and thought of the snow tunnel the man had mentioned. He'd said it was a hundred and fifty feet long. It must be completely covered with snow. Doing simple math in his head, Wiley realized the train would be traveling through the two wooden tunnels and the main one for a half mile! They could be in the tunnel over six minutes...breathing *coal gas*!

Wiley spun around to the man behind him. "Where are we now?"

Startled from his conversation, the man glared at Wiley, glanced out the window for a moment, then snapped, "We just passed Hancock."

"How long before we get to the first snow tunnel?"

Frowning, the man peered out the window again and said, "At the rate we're goin'...five, ten minutes. Why?"

Wiley leaped to his feet, ran to the head of the car and began forcing his way between people in seats and opening windows.

"What are you doing!" a portly man yelled. "It's freezing in here with you doing that!"

Wiley stood between two seats. "Listen to me! We are going to be in tunnels for over six minutes, breathing coal gas! Don't think six minutes is a short time! Try holding your breath for that long. Cold or not, we have to get fresh air in here, then shut the windows tight just before we enter the tunnels to keep the coal gas from killing us as we breathe." He pointed to the potbelly stove. "Close that tight so it doesn't draw."

The man sitting behind Jake and Wiley leaped to his feet and shouted, "He's right! Get these windows open!"

The passengers frantically donned their coats and wraps and struggled with the frozen-shut windows. Excited murmurs filled the frigid air with puffs of steamy breath.

Jake rushed to Wiley. "We gonna die, Wiley?"

"No, Jake." He pointed at two women struggling with a frozen window. "Go open that window for them."

Jake rushed to the women and said, "Allow me, ma'ams." As they giggled and moved aside, Jake yanked up on the window. Ice crackled as it slid up the metal casing, and huge snowflakes swirled inside the car.

"We're gettin' close to the snow tunnel," a man in front of the car yelled. He stuck his head out into the blizzard, then pulled it inside. "Close them windows! We're enterin' the first snow tunnel!"

Windows slammed the entire length of the car. Wiley forced three shut that no one else could budge.

"Sit down, and be quiet!" Wiley yelled. "Breathe as *little as possible*! Think of nothing but how cold you are!" He slid into the seat next to Jake and tightly clutched his arm. "Let's try not to breathe."

Complete darkness engulfed the train. Everyone in the car huddled forward and together. No one spoke. The train lumbered and swayed along the tracks. The smell of coal gas seeped into the car from under the doors. A woman in the back whimpered. Somewhere a small girl only said, "Mamma?" before a hand was clasped over her mouth.

Six minutes and thirty-four seconds seemed to last forever.

* * *

When gray light finally brightened the inside of the car, Jake leaped to his feet. "Ever'body all right?"

One by one, the passengers raised their heads and turned toward Jake. One woman said, "It seems like everyone is fine, but I smell coal gas."

"Open the windows!" Wiley and the man behind him yelled in unison.

As the people closest to the windows raised them, the train suddenly screeched to a stop, tossing some passengers down the aisle.

"What's that all about!" a tall thin man shouted as he struggled to raise himself over the back of a seat.

Shortly, the forward door of the car opened and the conductor rushed in and shouted, "Any sick or dead in this car?"

"Ain't nobody sick," Jake said. "Why?"

"There's one old woman dead in the first car and many are sick."

Amid gasps and women whimpering, Wiley shouted, "Why didn't you warn the passengers of the coal gas?" He shoved his way down the aisle and stood before the conductor. "I'll report this to the Pinkerton Agency and Washington!"

The burly conductor glared at Wiley and whispered softly, "You do, and you'll be dead in a week. Railroad won't stand for it."

"I'll take my chances. This is an outrage, and it has to be stopped. The passengers have to be warned."

With a smirk, the conductor said in a low voice, "Word gets out, nobody'll ride this train." His countenance darkened. "We can't have that. Put too much money into building it to let something like this stop it. Besides, people in Gunnison and Crested Butte need this train. The woman was old. She might'a died anyway. Just mind your business!"

"Don't threaten me!" Wiley snapped. "As soon as I get to Gunnison, I'm wiring the Pinkerton office in Philadelphia. They'll contact Washington on my orders."

"And just who do you think you are?" the conductor demanded.

Wiley folded his arms and leaned toward the conductor. "I'm William Deluce. And if anyone from the railroad comes after me, my partner and I will dispatch him at once."

The man's face turned white. "You're William Deluce?" He turned on his heel and walked toward the end of the car.

Standing behind Wiley, Jake asked, "What does dispatch mean?"

Still watching the conductor, Wiley said, "It means send."

"Where we gonna send them railroad men if they come lookin' for us?"

As the conductor slammed the car door, Wiley thought of hell. He shrugged and smiled at Jake. "Er...nowhere, Jake. I just wanted to scare him."

As the curious, chatty passengers surrounded the blood brothers, the train began descending the long western side of the pass toward Gunnison.

CHAPTER 26

As the train neared Gunnison, patches of blue sky peeked between dispersing clouds and the only snow on the ground hugged deep shade.

Wiley politely asked the conductor to be let off the train two miles from town and to unload their horses. After his and Wiley's confrontation, the conductor wouldn't hear of it.

Already irate about this railroad's attitude regarding the woman who had died, plus wanting to enter the town secretly, Wiley grabbed the conductor by the shirt, pulled his knife and stuck the point to the man's neck. "Stop this train *now*, or I'll carve you up like a Christmas goose!"

When the train stopped, Wiley asked the passengers in the car to keep his and Jake's identity a secret. Knowing Wiley's quick action saved all their lives, everyone wholeheartedly agreed, but Wiley knew some would tell of the exciting train ride and that they had met him and Jake in person.

* * *

As the partners rode Mac and Buddy down the side of a treeless hill in a region of flatish-topped mesas peppered only with sage brush, Gunnison, a town of 5,000, appeared as a haphazard scattering of houses spread out from the six-block-long main street. They stopped and looked down at the sprawling town.

Wiley grasped the pommel of his saddle with both hands and glanced at Jake. "Are you ready for this? The Moras brothers are killers, and there's three of them. Rugger's the oldest...and the worst.

Iram and Garrod try their best to keep up with him, but they're only punks. Dangerous punks. Rugger is a crazed murderer. He's raided farms in the Mid-West, raped and murdered the women, beheaded children and strung men upside-down in barns with their throats slit and their cock and balls cut off. He's killed five lawmen the same way."

Jake shuddered at the thought of having his dick and nuts cut off. He stared at the town far below. That wouldn't happen to him, he was Wiley's Pinkerton partner. He remembered when they were in the Fairplay telegraph office, and Benton Riley had said they were scary. He grinned at Wiley. "Hell, them brothers ain't met us yet."

"Don't get overconfident. They aren't greenhorns. They know how to provoke an argument to make the other person draw first. We have to keep our wits about us and somehow catch them off guard."

Wiley nudged Buddy down the slope and Jake followed. Scanning the town, Wiley wondered if he should be more concerned about Jake or himself. Jake had the rawhide bag and the golden feather to protect him. But how would it protect him? And from what? He remembered Fainsworth's dagger hadn't penetrated the bag and marveled at it. The leather of the bag seemed tough. Maybe that was all that had stopped the knife?

Thoughts of Grandpa Gray Feather flashed into Wiley's mind. He wished Grandpa were riding with them now. Grandpa would be instilling courage with every word he spoke.

Wiley suddenly missed his grandfather. He'd been the ultimate source of any love, bravery or self reliance he'd experienced while growing up. Why had it been so long since he'd had a vision from him?

"Grandpa, where are you?" Wiley whispered under his breath.

Looking at him, Jake asked. "Wiley, what'd you just say?"

Wiley smiled at his pommel, then shook his head. "I was just thinking out loud. I miss Grandpa Gray Feather."

Jake bowed his head. "Wish I could'a met your granpa. Then I'd have somethin' to smile about, too, when I think'a when I was a boy."

"Grandpa would have loved you, Jake. He *never* would have called you...."

"I ain't dumb no more, Wiley." Jake grinned. "You an' Rising Moon washed me clean." He shrugged and lowered his head. "But I still can't read none."

"As soon as this is over, Rising Moon will teach you."

Descending the slope in silence, Wiley turned toward Jake. "Sometimes I think you're more aware of what's happening than I am...even with all my schooling and training." He grinned. "I hope you'll protect both of us down there."

Jake stopped Mac. When Wiley reined Buddy and looked around, Jake yelled. "Don't you be sayin' that stuff! Your granpa'd scold you for sayin' what you just did! We gotta pertect each other! You're the best Pinkerton there ever was!" Jake glared at Wiley, then nudged Mac alongside him. His frown brightened into a grin. "Hell, don't worry about me. I got me the rawhide bag. An' someday I'm gonna be a Pinkerton as good as you."

Wiley raised an eyebrow. "I'll accept that. But I don't want either of us getting shot. Just be careful. We got off the train early on purpose. I don't want anyone to know we're coming. I'm sure someone from the train will let it slip that we're on our way, and it may filter to the Moras brothers, if they're there. We have to scout the town and memorize everyone. If people look at us with terror, that's fine, but if they glance in terror somewhere else, search out who they're looking at. We have to check every alley, doorway and window and each horse brand."

When the blood brothers reached Gunnison, hats pulled down in front, they rode straight to the telegraph office. Wiley sent a telegram to Mike McGelvy about the death on the train and demanded an investigation. He also mentioned they were on assignment and who they were sent to capture.

Later, as the partners walked their horses down Main Street, Wiley scrutinized each building. Most were two-story structures with ornate false fronts and built of pre-cut lumber brought in by train. Only a few buildings had been painted. Some homes, scattered in large lots, had been decorated with bright colors and contrasting trim.

With the brim of his hat raised slightly, Wiley glanced at all the windows. Not a curtain moved. His eyes searched every shadowed space between the buildings and each doorway. He noted the colors of the horses tied to rails and read their brand.

As they passed the Lucky Miner bar, Wiley tensed, then relaxed in his saddle. In the next block, he asked, "Jake, what have you noticed so far, like I told you?"

Jake quickly looked away from the front of Webster's Dry Goods and shrugged. "Uh...Wiley, I was..." His voice trailed to silence.

Wiley tried faking a frown. "You were staring at that cowboy with the muscles and the bulge in his pants, weren't you?"

Jake's face flushed.

Still sweeping the town with his eyes, Wiley glanced at the cowboy, arms folded as he leaned against a porch post. His brown hair stuck out around his flat-crowned hat. A hand-rolled cigarette hung from his mouth, and its smoke curled about his handlebar moustache, stinging his squinted right eye. A half-buttoned coat and shirt exposed a fuzzy chest as large as Jake's or his own. Tight, well-worn trousers stretched over his huge legs and covered the tops of scuffed brown boots. He wore his cock on the right and it seemed semi-hard.

"I'd say he's better looking than either of us." Wiley nodded and smiled at the cowboy.

The man jerked a nod.

"He ain't better lookin' than you, Wiley." Jake took another full-length scan of the man and stared at his dick pushing out his pants. When the stern-faced cowboy nodded at him, Jake's entire body tingled and his mind flooded with things he'd like to do to him, naked. He cut his eyes to Wiley. "He sure is fine lookin'. An' he nodded at me."

Wiley tipped his hat at the cowboy and felt a surge of lust for the man. He quickly turned to Jake. "Have you been searching for three horses with a M-bar-S brand? They belong to the Moras brothers."

Jake shoved his hat back on his head. "Hell, Wiley, we passed 'em a block back."

"You *have* been observing." Wiley smiled. "I'm proud of you. I knew you'd be good at this." He glanced back at the cowboy once more. The man still watched them. Wiley would love to get him naked, but even if he could, he assumed Jake would never go along with it.

The partners rode another block and stopped in front of Delmonico's Restaurant. Many horses and buggies crowded the front.

After riding to the side of the building, the partners tied Mac and Buddy to the only space at the last rail. Jake balked when he entered the large room filled with people.

Entering behind Jake and resting his hand on his shoulder, Wiley noticed a group of dusty cowboys in back, wolfing down their food in silence. Closer to the stove, a drummer in a black suit and derby with his sample case held tightly between his legs, sat by himself reading a newspaper. Wiley thought of a parson. At the next table, three grizzled mountain men in rawhide talked and laughed raucously as they ate. Their antics seduced the scowls of a heavy-set man with a handle-bar moustache and slicked-back hair. A silver star studded his homespun shirt. The lawman also scowled at Jake and him.

Closer to the front, Wiley saw three black prospectors huddled forward. They had shoved their empty plates aside and whispered as they pointed at a map spread out in the center of the table.

In front of the window, two ranchers sat sedately with their wives, trying to ignore the painted ladies at the table next to them. Wiley suspected the ranchers knew the four chatting women intimately.

"Welcome, gents!" an obese, bald man yelled to the blood brothers from across the room. He stood in the kitchen door and wiped his pudgy hands on a filthy apron that barely covered half his frame. "Best eats in town in here. Don't be shy. Find yourselves a seat and I'll send Alison out with your plates. Tonight's fare is beef chunks in gravy over taters." He turned and struggled into the kitchen.

Eyeing the cook, Wiley assumed the food was good in this restaurant. He squeezed Jake's shoulder and nodded his head. "There's two places on the end of that long table in the center."

After they wove through the room, Wiley sat next to a thin man with a pointed face and dressed in a brown tweed business suit. So intent in poking at his food, the man didn't look up when Wiley slid onto the bench. Jake plopped down across from Wiley beside a brawny man with bushy brown hair and matching beard.

The bearded man looked them over, grabbed one of the pitchers along the center of the table and poured two beers. He clunked them down in front of the newcomers and said, "Howdy, gents, I'm Charley Covill, the town blacksmith. You two drifters?"

Wiley smiled and nodded. He noticed a long drip of gravy imbedded in Charley's beard.

"I'm Jake Brady." Jake motioned to Wiley and said, "This here's my partner, Wiley Deluce."

"Glad to meet you gents."

The man next to Wiley snapped his head up and glanced at Jake, then stared at Wiley. He gasped, slid his skinny legs over the bench, got up from the table, leaving his nearly full plate, and rushed out the door.

Charley watched the man leave then looked at Wiley. "Don't bother about him. That's Raymond Black. He's a squirrely sort. Owns the gambling parlor down the street called Lucky Miner." Charley leaned toward Jake but looked at Wiley as he whispered, "You gents look like decent folk. If I was you, I'd stay away from the Lucky Miner. Bad goin's on down there. Always gunslicks in there." He jerked his head toward the man wearing the badge. "Marshal Payton leaves that bar alone except when there's been a shootin' inside. Some say he's in cahoots with Black, but don't tell nobody I said that."

A young woman with a perky, freckled face, wearing a blue calico dress protected by a frilly, white apron, approached the table and placed heaping plates of steaming-hot food in front of Jake and Wiley. She batted her eyes at Jake. "My! You're handsome. My name is Alison. What's yours?"

Jake tore his eyes away from the meat and potatoes and gave her a forced grin. "Jake, an' all I wanna do is eat." He grabbed his fork, bent over his plate and stuffed food into his mouth.

Alison put her hands on her hips. "Well, I hope you *choke*!" She turned her back on the men and stomped back to the kitchen.

"Jake, you didn't have to be rude," Wiley said in a low voice.

With his mouth full, Jake frowned at him.

Charley chuckled. "You don't know Alison, Wiley. Jake handled it best. Once you take any notice a'that woman, you'd best leave town or she'll follow you everywhere makin' weddin' plans."

Jake washed down his food with a swig of beer and peered across the table at Wiley. "Hell, I thought there was only one like Betty."

Wiley shuddered. "I take back what I said. I guess you handled it perfectly."

Despite Charley's warning, after eating, the blood brothers mounted their horses and rode the three blocks to the Lucky Miner saloon.

* * *

Rugger Moras sat across from Iram at a darkly lit table near the bar in the Lucky Miner. They both watched Garrod, their youngest brother, leaning on the bar talking to the heavy-set bartender with a patch over his right eye. Iram tried to hear what they were talking about, but couldn't. Rugger stared at Garrod's firm, rounded butt. Someday he'd plow that ass like a woman.

"What're we gonna do 'bout the law bein' after us?" Iram asked Rugger. "That man you killed in Denver was on the city council. Somebody might be tailin' us."

"Will you shut up!" Rugger snapped. "I should kill *you*. All you do is whine! Ain't nobody tailin' us clear up here. B'sides, that man I killed knew us an' said he was gonna tell the city police we was in town."

Iram sipped his beer. "When we was in Bailey, I heard somebody sayin' William Deluce, that Pinkerton gunny, was gonna be tailin' us. He's got him a partner an' people're talkin' about 'em bein' dangerous. His partner killed Santivan."

"Well, you heard wrong!" Rugger leaned over the table. "Randy said Deluce is back East. Kentucky. Relax. Randy knows everythin' goin' on out here."

"Don't know why you listen to Randy," Iram said. "He don't like you. I can tell."

"Shut up! Randy an' I bin friends fer years!"

"Yeah, but you killed his brother."

"I out drew him. So what? Randy knows Smitty started it by accusin' me a cheatin' at cards."

"You was cheat--."

"Shut up!"

Glancing at his youngest brother's butt, Rugger swore someday he'd screw Garrod's ass and jerk him off at the same time. That is, if his brother was alive to be jerked off. If Garrod squirmed and fought while he plowed his butt, he might just put a bullet through his head.

Raymond Black came out a door behind the bar, approached the bartender and whispered into his ear, then turned abruptly and returned to his office.

Stunned by the news, the bartender related it to Garrod.

A man entered the bar and Iram grabbed for his gun.

"Put that thing away!" Rugger snapped as he eyed the newcomer. The man looked like a gambler. "You'd shoot Ma if she flipped eggs the wrong way!" He turned his chair toward Iram. "You skinny asshole! You're the one that kilt the man outside Bailey while he was peein' in the bushes. Prob'ly killed him 'cause you couldn't see his whanger!"

"How'd you know I killed him?" Iram snapped.

"'Cause I followed you, that's how I know. Seen you roll his body over an' grab his whanger an' pull on it. You damn sissy! A man's whanger don't get stiff if he's dead!"

Iram grabbed for his gun. "I'm tired'a you always callin' me a damn sissy! I'm gonna plug you!"

Already pointing his gun at Iram, Rugger cocked it. "You'd never make it. I'd kill you faster'n a bolt'a lightnin'."

Garrod Moras left the bar, pulled out a chair at the table and sat with his brothers. Ignoring the drawn gun, he leaned over the table and whispered, "This here bartender knows how we can get our hands on a shipment'a gold."

"What kind'a gold is it?" Rugger asked, holstering his pistol.

"Coins. That's what he said."

"What's he get outta it?" Iram asked.

"Ten percent is all."

Rugger squinted. "When and where does this happen?"

"I ain't got that far."

"Well, get back to him and find out, jackass!"

"Oh," Garrod said. "Bartender said the owner told him he thinks he saw William Deluce in town. I'll get the rest'a the news about the gold fast." He headed toward the bar.

"Shit!" Rugger shouted. "Deluce is here? How could he be? Randy said he's still in Kentucky! An' he's the fastest draw alive!"

"Told you Randy don't like you."

"Shut up an' let me think!"

The moment Garrod arrived at the bar, a man walked through the batwings, hesitated for a moment to observe, then moved on into the room. A second man, just as big, followed after him. All three Moras brothers, and the bartender, eyed the newcomers.

* * *

Wiley slipped off the rawhide cord securing his Navy Colt before he entered the batwings of the Lucky Miner. He stopped and quickly scanned the smoky, dimly lit room.

Five shaded lamps that hung from the rafters pinpointed the gambling tables. Two were in use with four men at one table and five at another. A few of the poker players glanced at Wiley, then back at their cards. Other tables in the shadows were occupied by cowboys or ranchers. A couple prospectors sat at a table by the main stove.

Two men, sitting erect at a table in a dark corner near the far end of the bar, caught Wiley's eye. Both men looked his way, and their faces resembled bloodhounds. Wiley knew at once they were Rugger and Iram Moras. He spotted Garrod a few feet from his brothers' table, standing at the bar across from the bartender. All four men stared at him.

Jake walked through the doors a moment later and followed Wiley to the bar. He glanced around the gloom and stood at Wiley's left, closest to the door.

The burly bartender leaned across the bar and muttered something to Garrod. He adjusted his eye patch, then grabbed a glass and towel and began wiping the glass as he started toward the partners. Wiley spotted Raymond Black's skeletal face peering out from a half-open door behind the far end of the bar.

"What'll it be?" the bartender asked bruskly as he clunked down the glass and tossed the rag into a battered metal tub, never once looking Wiley in the eye.

"Two whiskeys," Wiley said.

The bartender slid two shot glasses onto the bar, grabbed a bottle and poured each man a drink. "Driftin' through?" He set the bottle down and shoved each glass toward the partners.

"Staying awhile," Wiley said.

A single eye searched Wiley, then Jake. The bartender's eyebrow raised. He hesitated, then silently walked to the opposite end of the bar and whispered to Garrod without moving his lips. Both men stared at Wiley and Jake.

"This here bar gives me the willies," Jake whispered. "Are them brothers here?"

Wiley turned his head toward Jake and said in a low voice, "Garrod Moras, the youngest, is talking to the bartender. Rugger and Iram are sitting at the table closest to him.

Jake grabbed his drink, took a swig, then slowly turned his body and glanced around the room. He shoved himself away from the bar and ambled toward the two occupied game tables. Raising his eyebrows at the pile of money in the center of each table, he sipped his drink, then wandered back to the bar and took up position on Wiley's right. Jake figured if he stood on that side, when Wiley looked at him, he could also keep track of the Moras brothers.

Wiley shifted his left foot to the floor rail. "If you just did what I think you did, Jake, you're a natural Pinkerton. And I'm glad I wore my right-hand holster."

"What're you two whisperin' about?" Garrod yelled. "It ain't po-lite comin' in here an' whisperin' like that!"

To Wiley's horror, Jake spun around to face Garrod. "I just asked Wiley if them More-butt brothers're in here."

Garrod flinched as if he'd been shot. Two chairs slightly turned from the table closest to him.

"What'd you call me?" Garrod hollered. He stood away from the bar, his hand hovering near his gun.

The poker players jerked toward the scene and froze into pale statues of terror.

Jake grinned, picked up his drink and walked toward Garrod.

"Jake, be careful," Wiley whispered. He swept back the right side of his duster.

Ignoring Wiley, when Jake got two feet from Garrod he placed his drink on the bar and shoved his hand toward the man. "You talk like you're from Kentucky'er Tennessee. I'm Jake Brady. I'm from Kentucky an' pleased to meet you."

Garrod's surprised look turned to hatred. "You called me More-butt! It ain't More-butt, it's More-*ass*!"

One of the poker players came to life and snickered.

Garrod turned toward the man and grabbed for his gun. "Who's laughin'?"

Positive Garrod was going to shoot the gambler who laughed, Jake used all the force of his muscled body and bashed Garrod in the jaw with his mule-kick punch. Garrod lifted an inch off the floor, then fell flat on his back.

A chair by the wall scooted. Iram Moras leaped to his feet and grabbed for his gun.

Jake saw him and gasped.

Iram's gun had barely cleared leather when a white-hot pain shot through his head, then he felt nothing. His body, with a hole between the eyes, dropped to the floor.

Jake spun around, saw Wiley's smoking gun in his hand and yelled, "Damn, Wiley! I thought I was gonna be dead!"

Wiley tore his eyes away from the back door where Rugger Moras had fled. He sighed. "Hopefully, you won't get killed while I'm around. Why did you do that?"

"Hell, I thought he was gonna kill somebody."

Wiley heard a horse gallop beside the building toward the main street and head west. Raymond Black appeared from his office and ran out the front door.

Wiley glanced at Iram's body on the floor, then raised his eyes to Jake who looked at Iram with horror. Not wanting to, but compelled to, Wiley said, "Jake, he might not be dead if you hadn't slugged his brother. Why did you go over to him?"

"Hell, back on the hill, you said we gotta catch 'em off guard. I was catchin' 'em."

Raymond Black charged through the batwings with Marshal Payton following. Wiley raised an eyebrow. Black must know where the marshal is at all times.

Marshal Payton walked over to the two men on the floor, then spun around and faced Jake and Wiley. "Which one of you did this?"

Wiley folded his arms. "Do you know who those men are?"

"Can't say as I do. Who are you? Are you responsible for this?" Payton jerked his head to the dead man. "It's a good thing his gun is out of his holster or I'd run you in for murder."

Whipping out his Pinkerton badge, Wiley flashed it in front of Marshal Payton's face. "I'm William Deluce." He motioned to Jake. "This is my partner, Jake Brady. The men on the floor are two of the Moras brothers. Rugger Moras escaped. Posters have been sent out across the country about them. It's hard to believe you've never received one."

Recovering quickly from astonishment of seeing William Deluce face-to-face, Marshal Payton asked, "Er, just what is it you're saying?"

"What I'm saying, Marshal, is you must jail Garrod when he comes to. I'll wire the Pinkerton office in Denver about his capture. If he's not still in jail when the authorities arrive, it will be *your* neck in the noose." Wiley glared at Black, then at the bartender. "And yours too for harboring criminals."

The three men glanced at each other, but remained silent as Wiley, followed by Jake, left the bar.

Out in the street, Wiley grabbed Jake's arm. "Jake, you have to let me in on your plans before you do anything like that again."

"But, I didn't have no plan. It just come to me all sudden-like."

"Please promise me you won't do that again. If Rugger had pulled his gun instead of running out the back door, one of us might be dead right now."

Jake pouted the entire way to the telegraph office.

Using code, Wiley sent a message to James McParland in Denver about the capture of Garrod Moras, the death of Iram and the escape of Rugger, and that he and Jake would pursue him. Wiley waited until the agent sent the complete message.

By the time they reached the general store, Jake had forgotten about pouting since Wiley had ignored it. In Webster's Dry Goods, they stocked up on provisions and ammunition, then headed west and out of town.

CHAPTER 27

As the Pinkerton partners followed the faint tracks of Rugger Moras' horse twenty miles due west of Gunnison, Wiley gazed at the treeless mesas with flat tops that soared skyward around every bend. He wished Hector, his friend majoring in geology at Boston Univesity, could see this. He had no idea what Hector would say caused this landscape, but he couldn't help thinking that an enormous volume of water, ages past, scoured this area allowing only sage and rabbit brush to flourish. The land was carpeted with it.

Wind whipped down the long valley of the Gunnison River, causing the ancient shrubs to jostle.

"Damn, Wiley! I ain't never seen nothin' like this here land my whole life." Jake pointed to the distant horizon. "Lookit out there. Them mountains with flat heads're blue like the lace Ma had on that dress she always wore."

Wiley gazed around and breathed deeply. How could a man exist without an occasional soul-cleansing from the beauty of nature? Still taking in the scene, Wiley half smiled when he saw the tracks of Rugger Moras' horse stretch across the dry expanse. It was easy to follow Rugger here. Wiley wondered if the outlaw assumed he wasn't being hunted since he'd made no attempt to cover his tracks. Or was that what he wanted them to think?

Jake looked around. "Where's he goin', Wiley? What town's that way?"

"The old hostler I talked to in Gunnison said Grand Junction is west and a bit north. Rugger may be heading there." Wiley glanced around. "Jake, I think we're in the area the hostler warned me not to gallop our horses. He mentioned a deep canyon here somewhere that can't be seen until we're right at the edge. He called it the Black Canyon of the Gunnison."

They lost Rugger's tracks through an area of broken rocks and scattered boulders. Traveling fifty feet in front of Jake, the canyon suddenly yawned in front Wiley. At the point where he stopped his horse, the land dropped a thousand feet, straight down. The Gunnison River, a frothy blue-green ribbon far below in the two hundred foot wide chasm, roared with foreboding power.

Wiley steered Buddy away from the edge, up a slight rise then down the back slope to meet Jake.

"I found the canyon." Wiley quickly dismounted, tied Buddy to a sturdy sagebrush, then approached the rim on foot. The canyon's depth staggered him, and for some reason he felt it wanted to suck him into it.

After tying Mac to a bush near Buddy, Jake ran toward Wiley.

Wiley spun around and grabbed him. "Stop, Jake! You'll fall off the edge!"

Jake looked into Wiley's horrified face and smiled, then glanced down at the river far below. His face froze. "Damn!"

A horse galloped toward them from behind.

Wiley spun around and saw Rugger Moras charging, gun drawn and pointed at them. He fired.

Jake cried out, grabbed his chest and fell backward into the chasm.

Seeing Jake disappear off the edge, Wiley yelled in horror, then from rage.

Rugger shot again and Wiley felt a blow to the top of his head. He reeled and nearly passed out.

As Rugger rode by him, Wiley shouted the Iroquois war cry, lunged at the horse, yanked Rugger out of the saddle and heaved him over the side of the canyon. Rugger's long trailing scream was lost in the roar of the river.

Wiley felt blood stream down his face and into his left eye, then blackness overtook him. He dropped to the ground.

* * *

"Grandpa, Jake is dead!" Wiley sobbed. "What will I do without him?" He slid against the bark of a tree, fell against Grandpa Gray Feather's shoulder and wept.

Gray Feather caressed Wiley's hair and his hand came away bloody. As he looked at it, the blood disappeared. He reached up and touched Wiley's scalp wound, healing it completely.

"Great Running Bear," Gray Feather said. "Your wound healed. Do not leave this place. Ancients dwell here. They guide you."

* * *

A pinpoint of light found its way through Wiley's shut eyelid. It startled him. Where was he? What had happened?

He snapped his eyes open and realized he was lying face down on a smooth, lichen-covered rock. Tall, dried grass surrounded it and blocked his view of anything else.

Wiley suddenly knew where he was. How long had he been unconscious? He shoved himself to this hands and knees.

Oh, God! *Jake had fallen off the cliff!*

Ignoring his pounding head and groaning through gritted teeth, Wiley crawled to the spot where Jake had fallen. He looked over the edge. Pine branches beneath a slightly protruding rock eight feet below blocked his view of the bottom of the canyon. Scrambling to a different vantage point, Wiley looked over again. The boiling river at the bottom of the gorge flowed uncaringly to the distant Pacific Ocean.

Wiley's heart skipped a beat when he saw a tiny body on the rocks beside the river. The man was dressed in black, and he knew instantly it was Rugger Moras. Leaning farther out revealed no other clue of Jake's whereabouts.

"Jake!" Wiley shouted into the canyon. Jake's name echoed distinctly, then faded into overlapping murmurs. Wiley bowed his head. His body jerked from sobs.

Slowly, Wiley got to his feet and staggered toward the horses. He tripped a few times from his watery eyes but finally made it to the top of the small rise that paralleled the chasm. Mac and Buddy, tied down the slope, both had their heads up, looking at him.

When Wiley reached the horses, he hugged Mac around the neck. "God, Mac, Jake is gone. Somehow, we have to go on."

Mac pulled away from Wiley's grasp. He bit through the branch he was tied to, snorted and walked up the slope toward the canyon.

Wiley lurched up the rise after Mac. He couldn't leave him here. When Mac stopped near the edge, Wiley grabbed the reins and tried to lead him back to Buddy.

Mac refused to budge.

Wiley knew the horse was waiting for Jake and he let his emotions take control. "God, Jake!" he shouted, then fell to his knees. Holding his pounding head, he slumped to the ground and sobbed. He should have quit the Pinkertons and talked Jake into living a quiet life with him at Chipmunk Rock. That's all Jake had wanted to do. He'd loved that life. Why hadn't he been insistent they stay there?

"Wiley?"

Wiley pounded the ground with his fist. He'd killed Jake by involving him in his job. They were happy together just rounding up Belinda and Jimmy's cattle. And they had their waterfall. God! He could never go there again!

"Are you up there, Wiley? Are you shot?"

Wiley held his breath. Had he just heard Jake? How could that be? "Wiley are you dead?"

"Jake?" Wiley raised his head. "Jake, is that you?"

"Wiley, you're not dead!" Jake yelled from a short distance below.

Wiley scrambled to the edge. "Jake, where are you?" He looked over and saw the same rock jutting out and the pine branches.

"I'm down here, Wiley. This here pine tree caught me when I fell an' tossed me back on the ledge where it's growin'. I'm caught an' can't move none. My chest is hurtin', too."

"Jake, are you bleeding where you got shot?" Wiley struggled to his feet and scrambled to a different area, hoping to see Jake.

"I ain't bleedin' where I got shot, Wiley. My head's bleedin' where I hit this cliff when the tree tossed me."

"Don't move, Jake," Wiley said as he ran along the cliff to a point that jutted out into the chasm. He crawled out onto a protruding rock and could finally see Jake wedged sideways. He faced the cliff between the rock and the massive trunk of the pine that had anchored itself into the rock and grew out into space a thousand feet above the river. Jake was ten feet down from the top.

Wiley scrambled back to the spot where Jake had fallen. "Jake, I'll be right back. I'm going to get the rope we got from Jimmy and Belinda." He ran over the small ridge and down the slope to Buddy, untied the horse and led him to the edge of the cliff beside Mac.

"Jake, will Mac stay where he is?" Wiley yelled. "I'm not sure if Buddy will."

"Mac, you be stayin' there," Jake shouted. "What you gonna do, Wiley?"

"I'm going to tie the rope to Mac's saddle and lower it down to you. Jake, you have to tie it around yourself and I'll pull you up."

"I ain't gonna be tyin' that rope around me. I can't move none."

Wiley thought a moment. "Jake, I'm going to tie the rope around myself and climb down to you. I just hope Mac stays here in case I slip."

After tying Mac securely to a thick, wizened juniper growing ten feet from the edge, Wiley tied Buddy to the same tree. He uncoiled the fifty-foot rope, looped it twice around the saddle horns of both horses and tied two square knots. Wrapping the rope around his waist twice with one pass through his crotch, he tied a double knot. Wiley wound the remaining rope under his arms, hoping he could loosen it a loop at a time as he climbed lower. If he fell, he wanted his arms to keep the rope from uncoiling too fast.

At the edge, Wiley studied possible hand and footholds, then steeled himself. He grabbed the thick stem of a sagebrush and slowly inched over the side. At first he couldn't locate any places for his feet, but finally found one for his left foot. It seemed solid, but when he put his full weight on it, it gave way and he slid. The sagebrush he'd grasped held him. Flailing his feet, he found another protruding rock and it held his weight. As he put his face against the cliff trying to calm himself, far below, he heard the faint crashes of the rocks he'd dislodged. Frantically, he tried finding handholds since the sagebrush began pulling out of the ground.

After lowering himself two feet, the rope became taut, but Wiley couldn't release his handholds since only his right foot was anchored and it felt unstable. Searching with his left boot, he finally found a toehold higher up. He raised his body, balanced on his left foot and unlooped the rope twice, then continued his descent.

The next few feet went easier since the rocks stuck out farther and were more stable. Again, Wiley had to unwind the rope around his body.

He heard a scream of a mountain lion somewhere near. Both horses shifted positions and Buddy whinnied. The slack Wiley had just unwound tightened. He lost his footholds and a rock gouged his cheek as he was pulled two feet up the cliff.

"Mac! Buddy! Stay still!" Wiley shouted as he scrambled with his hands and feet to keep from falling or being pulled to the top of the cliff.

The horses quieted. Not trusting them, Wiley quickly found footholds, unwraped the rope several more times and tried to descend as quickly as possible. He hoped he could reach Jake before the horses bolted. But what if they bolted after he got down to Jake? The horses would take the rope. He and Jake would be stranded on the ledge...possibly to die there!

Wiley lowered himself as fast as he could. He didn't dare look down. Sheer drop-offs made him dizzy, and that's the last thing he wanted right now.

When his left foot hit a solid shelf, Wiley looked down and saw Jake ten feet to his right. He sighed with relief. The rock ledge where he stood was four feet wide and thirty feet long. Some sections had eroded and fallen. At those places it narrowed to two feet, but he knew he could make it to where Jake was trapped.

Wiley's head pounded as he untied himself from the rope and scrambled to the tree. He tied the rope securely to the ancient pine, hoping to keep the horses from bolting.

"I'm here, Jake," Wiley said. He touched Jake's back.

Jake started, then groaned. He tried to turn his head, but couldn't. "Wiley, how'd you get here?"

"I climbed down with our new rope, but I haven't any idea how I'm going to get you back up with you hurting."

"I'm hurtin' all over, Wiley. An' my chest hurts worser'n anything."

Carefully, Wiley surveyed how Jake had gotten stuck. When the tree caught Jake, it must have bent down from his weight, then snapped back, tossing Jake into the wedge between the cliff and the trunk. A second sway of the tree must have pinned Jake in a tight squeeze. He realized the only way to free Jake was to climb out onto the tree so it would bend and relax the pressure against Jake's body.

"Jake, can you free yourself if I bend the tree down?"

"I think so. My legs don't hurt none."

"I'm going to climb out onto the tree. As soon as it releases you, get up as fast as you can."

"I'll try, Wiley. You climbin' out now?"

"Yes. As soon as you can, struggle out. I don't want to climb out too far."

Wiley inched himself out the main trunk. He could feel the tree groaning as his two-hundred-twenty pounds bent it toward the river. The roar below made him tremble. As he inched farther out over the thousand-foot drop, he heard a loud snap in the trunk. He froze.

"Jake! Can you get out?"

Jake groaned. Wiley gripped the trunk tighter, turned his head and saw Jake slowly struggle to his feet. At once, Wiley backed along the trunk until he was on the rock ledge. He knelt on the shelf and closed his eyes for a moment, then got to his feet, grabbed Jake and kissed him.

"God, Jake, I thought you were dead."

"You're hurtin' my chest huggin' me so hard."

Wiley pulled back. "Let me see your chest where it hurts."

As he unbuttoned Jake's shirt, both men gasped. The bullet Rugger had shot at Jake had flattened to a puffed-out disk against the rawhide bag. When Wiley touched it, the compacted bullet fell to the ground and rolled into the canyon.

Jake looked up at Wiley. "My bag stopped the bullet from killin' me!" He felt his chest. "But I think it broke somethin'. My chest hurts like hell."

Above, the puma's scream sounded yards away. Both horses bolted and ran to safety. The rawhide rope snapped near the tie at the tree. Wiley grabbed for the end, but it disappeared up the cliff.

They were trapped!

CHAPTER 28

The horses broke free from the juniper, whinnied and reared. Together, they fled the crouching puma.

Wiley watched the end of the rope disappear. He knew Mac wouldn't go far and he'd tied Buddy to him. But even if the horses came back to the edge, use of the rope was lost.

"Jake, we're trapped on this ledge."

"Hell, maybe I can use the rawhide bag an' get Dave an' Jim t'come help us." Jake lifted the bag, opened it and peered inside at darkness. He stuck in two fingers to feel for the golden feather. Something pricked him! He yelled, jerked his hand away and held it up for inspection. A tiny drop of blood swelled on the tip of his middle finger.

"Damn, Wiley! We can't be usin' this bag t'get us outta here." Jake looked up at Wiley. "What're we gonna do?"

Wiley placed his hands on Jake's shoulder. "I don't know, but if we can't use the bag and the feather, we must be able to get out of here on our own. Let's study the rocks and see if there's a way I can climb up to get the horses and the rope." Wiley tightened his grip on Jake's shoulder and looked him in the eye. "Jake, are you all right?"

Trying to grin, Jake nodded.

Not convinced, Wiley hesitated, then pointed to the west end of the shelf. "Maybe you can start over there and work your way back to the middle. See if there's any place I can climb up. But do it slowly. I don't want you hurting yourself."

Ignoring the pain in the middle of his chest, Jake climbed over the tree trunk. He held onto protruding rocks and gnarled stems of dwarf sagebrush that clung to cracks in the cliff as he shuffled along the shelf that dwindled to eighteen inches wide. Ten feet from the tree, the ledge ended abruptly.

Still grasping the rock face, Jake peered over the edge. The depth of the canyon and rushing ribbon of water made him dizzy. He closed his eyes and leaned against the cliff, pushing himself into a wide depression in the rocks that sheltered a gnarled sage barely clinging to life.

Searching the cliff upwards from the horizontal trunk, Wiley realized the protruding rock above made ascent at that spot impossible. He stepped carefully the few yards to the opposite end of the ledge that widened to four feet but stopped when it met a smooth, convex rock sweeping to the top of the cliff. The position of the sun cast oval shadows on the face of the boulder, and Wiley realized they were depressions in the rock, worn smooth from ages, and extended upwards beyond where he could see. Were they hand and foot holes? They looked hand cut, and ancient.

Ancient? Wiley vaguely remembered leaning against a tree next to Grandpa Gray Feather. He'd been sobbing...about the loss of Jake, and Grandpa had caressed his head. Wiley sighed, closed his eyes and relished his grandfather's gentle touch. He suddenly remembered his grandfather had said ancients lived here and they would guide him! Were these handholds what Grandpa was talking about?

Wiley grasped one of the depressions. It fit his hand perfectly, and he reached for the next one. The spacing seemed meant for the best use of strength. He found a foothold and stuck the toe of his left boot into it. Worn smooth, his foot slipped out on his first try. Wedging his toe differently and feeling it solid, he swung away from the ledge and clung to the rock. He looked down. The ledge ended at his right. Directly below him was...nothing! He heard the river's roar a thousand feet below.

The depressions felt smooth, almost slippery, but more secure than he would have guessed. Wiley continued climbing. He found the next handhold right where it should be. Finding a higher foothold, he inched higher. Two more sets put him five feet above the ledge, halfway to the top. He reached for the next handhold. It wasn't there!

Wiley searched the rock face. He saw nothing but a wide convex surface above him that seemed smoother than the rest of the boulder. The top of the rock had broken off long ago and slid into the canyon.

"You found a way up!" Jake yelled. "I'm comin' up, too!"

"Jake, wait!"

Not listening, Jake grabbed two handholds, swung his body away from the ledge and began climbing. When he reached Wiley's boot, Jake groaned from the pain in his chest, made worse by stretching his arms. His eyes teared as he groped for the next handhold. Where was it? His foot slipped from the shallow depression and he grabbed Wiley's boot. He slid away from the rock. His legs flayed the air.

Wiley gripped the handholds tighter, but his fingers began slipping. "Jake, you're pulling me away from the rock!"

Dizzy from pain, Jake floundered in mid-air. Holding onto Wiley's boot, he tightened his grip, groaning in agony.

"Jake! I know you're hurting, but find a foothold! I'm losing my grip! We'll both fall!"

Jake opened his eyes, wiped them on his arm, then groped for a handhold. Barely seeing one, he gritted his teeth, grabbed for it and got it. Holding onto Wiley's boot and the depression, he groaned as he stretched his body and managed to touch the rock shelf. He put his weight on it, but the edge let go, and Jake swung back into space.

"Jake, I'm losing my grip!"

Trying to ignore the pain, Jake again tried reaching the ledge. He swung his leg and missed.

"Jake! We're going to die! I can't hold on any longer!"

Wiley die? Jake's head cleared. Using all his strength, he jammed his boot against the rock and shoved his body toward the ledge. He landed on it, collapsed into a ball and whimpered in pain.

Wiley hugged the rock until he'd calmed, then slowly lowered himself back to the shelf. He sighed with relief, then slid his arms around Jake.

"Are you all right?"

"Sorry, Wiley," Jake whimpered. "My chest hurts like hell. I could'a got you killed."

"We're safe now. You may have some broken ribs from the impact of the bullet. Lie down. I'll figure out a way off this cliff." Wiley glanced over his shoulder. "We can't go the way I was climbing. The handholds above aren't there any longer."

As he leaned against the rock wall, Jake mumbled softly, "I found a cave, Wiley."

Wiley caressed Jake's hair, then gently helped him lie prone.

"You found a cave? Where?"

Jake jerked his arm toward the tree trunk. "Behind that bush on the other side'a that tree. I didn't go in 'cause I saw you climbin'."

Wiley sat back on his boots. Handholds to this ledge? A cave?

"Jake, do you have any matches? I only have five."

Groaning as he searched his pockets, Jake produced a packet with eight matches. It had gotten wet and Wiley doubted they would strike, but the phosphorus tips might keep a tiny fire going. He could use the match sticks to build it up until he found more wood.

Wiley caressed Jake's face. "You stay here. I'll be back." He scrambled to the horizontal trunk of the pine, slid over it, then gingerly stepped along the narrowing ledge to the gnarled sagebrush. Breaking away dead branches, he saw a jagged hole over two feet in diameter that opened into the rock wall.

"You're right," Wiley called back. "It *is* a cave."

Wiley picked up a dead sage branch, struck one of his matches, lit the end and crouched over it until it burned steadily. He held the burning branch in front of the hole. Seeing the smoke being sucked into the blackness, he knew there must be another opening somewhere inside...hopefully a way off this ledge.

When the branch burned strongly, Wiley held it in front of him and slid into the hole. He crawled on his stomach down a passageway. After five feet, the cave opened into a room the size of their cabin at Chipmunk Rock. When he got all the way in, he sat cross-legged and held up the burning branch.

The room was somewhat dome-shaped and the ceiling, high enough for a man to stand, had been blackened by fires built ages past. In the center of the room a three-inch hole had been cut into the rock floor. He saw another dark tunnel on the far side of the room leading away. Kindling and firewood had been stacked beside that opening, and two clay bowls of dried corn sat next to the wood.

Wiley leaned toward the passageway to the cliff and yelled, "Jake, if you can, come in here and see this!"

Wiley busied himself with building a small fire, and quickly had one going in the blackened pit in front of the second tunnel. He smiled as he watched the smoke being sucked into it, leaving the air in the cave fresh.

"Damn, Wiley!" Jake said softly as he looked around. "This here's like a house in the rock." Jake crawled all the way into the room, leaned against the wall, held his chest and closed his eyes. "Wiley, I don't feel so good. My chest hurts like hell."

Jake fell over on his side.

Wiley rushed to Jake and cradled him in his arms. After a few moments, convinced by his breathing that Jake wasn't dead, Wiley carefully stretched him out and covered him with his own jacket. He lightly caressed Jake's face, glad he'd passed out and no longer felt the pain.

Kneeling beside Jake's prone body, Wiley remembered the scared man he'd met for the first time in the Silver Heels Bar. He kissed Jake's dirt-streaked face, then gathered him into his arms and whispered, "I love you, Jake. My life started when I finally met you. Grandpa was right. I've known and loved you since I was born."

Wiley heard a sigh behind him. Pretending to ignore it, he gently lowered Jake, then spun around with his gun already drawn.

"Great Running Bear, I not want you to learn pistols."

"Grandpa!" Wiley quickly holstered his Colt.

"Your brother hurt. I heal." Gray Feather seemed to glide across the cave. He brushed passed Wiley, knelt down, touched Jake's chest and caressed his hair, then looked up at Wiley. "I protect your blood brother. I not like you being gunman. You use gun for good...but beware. Killed men haunt your soul. Haunt your blood brother's soul. Many hauntings destroy love. We watch you." Gray Feather stood and swept his arm around the cave.

Wiley turned and gasped. Ten Indians sat in a circle around the hole in the floor. The fire at the entrance of the other cave burned brightly but cast no shadow except his and Jake's. Every man in the room looked at him with a solemn face. Wiley recognized Chief Eagle Rising, astonished his garb was dusty-brown rawhide and not the glistening robe of rainbow light he'd worn in their cabin the night he and Jake had become one person for an instant.

Chief Eagle Rising smiled at Wiley and held out a long, pipe decorated with carvings and wrapped with a strip of rawhide holding blue and red feathers. "Smoke this in peace, for you and your blood brother."

Wiley looked at the pipe. A thin filament of smoke curled from the bowl, scenting the air with a sweetness Wiley had never smelled before. The odor entranced him. He filled his lungs with it and held it there. It made him dizzy. He glanced at Jake, at Grandpa Gray Feather smiling at him, then around the room at the seated Indians. All of them appeared to be filled with great wisdom. Was this a dream?

"No dream, Great Running Bear," Gray Feather said softly. "Take pipe and smoke. This your cleansing."

Wiley walked to Chief Eagle Rising, took the pipe, drew in deeply, then handed it to the man seated at Eagle Rising's left.

Wiley blew the smoke toward the fire and suddenly found himself sitting cross-legged inside the circle of men. He felt the river at his back, a thousand feet below, still pulling at him.

Each in the circle took a puff and passed the pipe to the man on his left.

When it reached Gray Feather, he drew in a little smoke, then placed the pipe on the floor and turned to Wiley. "We here to help purify you and your brother of killing spirits. You go from here with clean souls." Gray Feather raised his arm toward the hole in the floor. "Great Running Bear, sit with legs crossed around hole. Ancients cleanse you."

Wiley scooted his crossed legs over the hole in the floor, then looked into it. The hole's blackness seemed to draw him into it. As he bent down, a sudden burst of smoke engulfed Wiley's face. Dizziness overtook him. He seemed to fall into an infinite void as deep, musical whisperings encircled him. Chanting, distant drums, then louder chanting.

A blast of white light! A bloodcurdling scream! Cade Bently stood before him. The first man he'd ever killed. Cade suddenly shot through the tunnel behind him and fell screaming into the canyon outside. Then, silence.

Another flash. Another scream. Another face. Jude Brundig. Wiley's blood froze. He'd killed Jude in a shootout on Cape Cod. Jude filled Wiley's mind and the killer's screams swirled the room, then fell into the raging river far below. Many other chilling visions, each the face of a man he'd killed. Then, Blackwood. Ray Moss. Iram Moras. They each appeared, flew from the cave screaming and dropped into the river. Wiley grabbed his head and bowed to the ground. "God! I've killed so many!" He raised and gritted his teeth. "But I'll kill *any* man, woman or child who tries to kill Jake!"

A flash. Another face appeared. Rugger Moras screamed again as he fell to the rocks below.

After a time of silence, Wiley heard a distant scream and saw Santivan's fleeing face. Jake had also been cleansed. They could start over.

In the flickering firelight, Wiley looked passed the circle of men at Jake's prone form, then blackness overtook him and he collapsed to the floor of the cave.

* * *

"Wiley?"

Had he slept for ten years? Wiley snapped open his eyes and realized he was lying face down on the cold floor of...?

"Wiley, are you here?" Jake asked. "It's dark in here."

The blackness startled Wiley. Where was he? Was Jake in trouble?

Wiley scrambled into a sitting position and looked around. A vague glimmer of light from the cliff passageway dimly lit the room.

"Jake?"

"Wiley, you're here! What happened?"

Wiley shook his head. "Where are we?"

"Wiley, what's wrong? We're in this here cave I found. The fire you made went out an' it's dark in here. Are you okay?"

Cave? Wiley touched himself, then the rock floor. He felt the hole he'd been straddling and suddenly remembered Grandpa Gray Feather, Chief Eagle Rising, the circle of Indians, a pipe. The cleansing!

"Jake, I think we're in a holy place."

"Wiley, this here cave's only got one hole an' we can't get outta here that way. You know that!"

Wiley chuckled. His eyes had gotten used to the dim light in the cave, and he finally knew where he was. He crawled to Jake, slid his arms around him and drew him to himself.

Jake snuggled into Wiley's arms. "You smell good, Wiley. I ain't never smelled you like that b'fore. An' somethin's gone from you, too."

"There's no more haunting spirit in you either, Jake. We've been cleansed from any killings we've done in the past. We can start over. Just you and me."

Jake moved his head up from Wiley's chest, kissed Wiley on the lips, then buried his face in the side of Wiley's neck. "My chest don't hurt no more."

"I'm glad. Grandpa touched your chest and healed it. Chief Eagle Rising gave me a peace pipe to smoke and...we were cleansed from all the killings we've done. You were cleansed from killing Santivan." Wiley closed his eyes and shook his head. "I was cleansed from a few more than that."

"Was I cleaned up from killin' Nance?"

"Nance? You didn't kill Nance. You shot him in the shoulder. He fell off the cliff."

"But he died!"

"He died from the fall, not your bullet."

Jake pulled away. "Damn! Why didn't I get to see your granpa an' Chief Eagle Rising? What was I doin'?"

"You dozed..." Wiley shook his head. No more lying. "Jake, you passed out from the pain in your chest."

CHAPTER 29

"How we gonna get outta here, Wiley?" Jake asked in the darkness.

Wiley couldn't help it. He slid his hand over Jake's body. "I found another cave, my big, handsome blood brother. I'm so thankful you're still alive." He pulled Jake to himself and kissed him on the mouth.

Jake snuggled into Wiley's embrace. Wiley smelled wonderful! Jake's body jerked as intense love from Wiley sparked through him. Why hadn't he ever felt that before? Jake suddenly realized Wiley really *did* love him. He'd always believed it, except when he'd thought Wiley was going to marry Betty, but the love he felt now from Wiley seemed like...like swimming naked in the cold, fresh pool at their waterfall. And Wiley smelled smoky fresh.

Wiley pulled back from the kiss. "We have to get out of here and find Mac and Buddy. I'm going to see where that other cave goes." He pecked Jake on the nose, then struggled to his feet.

Jake watched the coals from a dying fire across the cave wink as Wiley walked toward it. Jake grinned in the darkness, squeezed himself and thanked his friend Jesus for him and Wiley being blood brothers, and loving each other.

Wiley stooped over the glowing embers and added a few twigs. When they caught, he dropped on a few larger sticks. In the growing light, he looked at Jake and smiled when he saw him still sitting against the wall, eyes closed and holding himself, grinning. Knowing Jake was talking to Jesus, he kept silent and quietly reached for a stick the thickness of a broom handle and shoved one end into the flames until it blazed. Holding the burning limb, he turned to Jake. "Keep this fire tiny. I don't want too much smoke in my face when I'm in that tunnel."

Jake's eyes snapped open. Before he could say anything, Wiley slid on his stomach and disappeared into the cave. Jake scrambled to the entrance and looked inside. He saw the silhouette of Wiley's body inching forward as he held the burning branch in front of him. Wiley barely had enough room to keep going, and he watched as Wiley struggled through an especially tight place. Soon, the tunnel veered sharply to the left. After Wiley's boots disappeared around the bend, Jake could only see an orange glow, and that soon faded into total darkness.

"Wiley?" Jake yelled into the tunnel. No answer. His voice seemed to die out completely a few feet from the entrance. Cupping his hands around his mouth, Jake yelled Wiley's name as loud as he could. Still no answer, and still his voice seemed to mute into silence. He clutched his stooped legs and whimpered, "Wiley?"

"Damn! Wiley might be stuck! I gotta get him." Jake leaped toward the wood pile, grabbed a stout piece of kindling and buried one end into the dying fire. The moment it flamed strongly, Jake dove into the entrance of the cave and wormed his body through the passageway. He could feel dirt being scooped into his pants, and he scraped both shoulders in the tight space that Wiley had struggled through. Jake asked Jesus for help, then gouged his hip on a rock and shouted cuss words. The tunnel veered to the left. After a few yards, it turned to the right. Still, he couldn't see any light from Wiley's burning branch, and he couldn't hear anything. The air smelled moldy and stagnant, and his stick burned fast. He was glad the smoke swirled toward the darkness in front of him.

A sudden rush of air through the tunnel snuffed out Jake's torch. The total darkness shocked him.

"Damn!" Jake shouted. "Wiley, I can't see nothin'!"

He heard no sound. The blackness seemed to crush him until he couldn't breathe.

"Jesus, help me," Jake whimpered. "I don't wanna die in here." He buried his face in his folded arms.

"You no die here, my second grandson."

"Who's that?" Jake jerked up his head and bumped it on a low rock. "Damn!" He opened his eyes and gasped.

"You no die," Gray Feather said. He smiled at Jake as he lay in the tunnel facing him. A silver light seemed to encompass the Iroquois brave.

"Wiley's granpa! Damn! Now I can smile when Wiley talks'a you!" Jake felt captured by Gray Feather's face. "You're more beaut'ful than I ever thought."

Gray Feather's silver hair turned black and his ancient face became young and strong before Jake's eyes. "This how I was, my second grandson. And how I will be again."

Jake's eyes became saucers. "Damn! It's a good thing Wiley'n me didn't know you when you was young!"

Gray Feather laughed and instantly turned ancient. "You make hearts good, Golden One. Keep forward in darkness. You find light. When Great Running Bear found light, wind put out your fire. Go to him."

Gray Feather vanished.

Jake could see nothing. He held his breath in the blackness. The wind rushing through the tunnel made him shudder.

Golden One? Jake finally breathed. Wiley's grandfather called him Golden One! What did that mean? Jake looked toward his arm. He couldn't even see it. Golden One?

The sound of Mac's whinny somewhere far down the tunnel snapped Jake out of his thoughts. Or did he hear it?

"Mac?" he whispered. "Wiley?"

"Jake, keep coming!" Jake heard Wiley yell, somewhere, far away. Or was it just the rushing air? He scrambled deeper into the tunnel, bumping his head, scraping his shoulders and cursing each time.

Eyes shut from falling dirt, Jake's probing hand hit a solid wall of rock. He felt around. The tunnel ended!

"Damn!"

"Don't cuss, *Jack*."

Jake wiped his face and looked out a hole to his right.

Outside, Wiley held back the flat rock that had partially covered the opening. "You're in the light now, Golden One."

* * *

Sitting together on the bed in their room in the La Veta Hotel in Gunnison, Jake leaned into Wiley and slid his arm around him. "Somethin' happened to you in that cave, Wiley. You look an' smell different."

Grabbing Jake, Wiley snuggled his face into the side of his neck. "You too Jake. I told you, we were cleansed by the Ancients."

Jake pulled away. "Why didn't I get to see 'em?"

"You were hurting. You'd passed out from the pain in your chest. Grandpa healed you." Wiley snuggled against Jake and smiled when Jake relaxed into his arms.

Jake pulled away, again. "Wiley, why'd your granpa call me Golden One? An' how'd you know?"

"He called you Golden One because you are. You glow with goodness. I've never known anyone as beautiful as you are, inside and out." Wiley kissed Jake's cheek. "I knew he named you Golden One because Grandpa let me see him talking to you in the cave." Wiley smiled. "He *was* beautiful when he was young. No wonder my grandmother fell in love with him."

"Hell, Wiley, I looked at myself in the dark but couldn't see no glowin'."

Wiley grabbed Jake and pulled him back on the bed with himself. "You glow, Jake. Even in the dark. You can't see it because you won't believe it." He began unbuttoning Jake's shirt. "See how your chest glistens with sweat?"

* * *

As they snuggled together under the covers, Jake scrambled out of Wiley's embrace and got on all fours.

"What are you doing?"

"Wiley, I been thinkin'. I wanna sit on your dick like you did me. I stole some butter in a napkin from supper an' wanna try it."

Remembering the instant of pain he felt as Jake's cock entered his rectum, Wiley said, "I don't want to hurt you, but if you relax, you'll only feel pain for a second."

"Hell, nothin' could hurt worser'n my chest after I got shot. An' you was all dreamy-like after I did it to you. I wanna feel like that, too."

"I'd be honored, Golden One."

Jake snickered, punched Wiley, then leaped out of bed to retrieve the butter. Back in bed, Jake climbed over Wiley and sat on his stomach. He gouged the butter with his fingers, reached behind him and greased Wiley's hard dick, then his own butthole and dick.

"You ever do this before?"

"No," Wiley whispered. "But I've wanted to."

Jake tossed the napkin to the floor and tensed his body. "Once, Zeke wanted me to stick my dick up his butt. I tried, but he started yellin' an' I quit. I liked it, but it didn't feel nothin' like it did when my dick was up your butt, Wiley."

Wiley grabbed Jake's shoulders firmly. "Jake, you're talking too much. You need to relax. Lie on top of me."

Sinking onto Wiley, Jake snickered as Wiley traced his spine with strong fingers. He snuggled into Wiley's hairy chest and warm crotch and nestled closer when Wiley kneaded his butt.

"You feel good next t'me, Wiley. I like you touchin' me all over."

"Shhhh. Just relax."

* * *

The front door of the La Veta Hotel opened. A big man in a leather duster and a flat-crowned, black hat stepped into the room and flung the door shut behind him. He walked to the counter and banged the bell, then scanned the lobby and adjoining dining room, dark at this late hour.

A skinny, thin-haired man pushed through the curtain from the back room, yawned and adjusted his spectacles. He frowned as he held his robe closed. "What do you want?"

"Who's on the second floor?"

"Only the two Pinkertons."

"Which room?"

"Twelve. The one next to yours, just like you told me."

"Who's below 'em?"

"We only have five guests. No one's on that side of the hotel, except them." The clerk shrugged. "And you."

The big man grabbed the clerk's robe and yanked him halfway across the counter. "Keep it that way!" He released the clerk and headed for the stairs.

* * *

Squirming his body against Wiley's, Jake said, "Wiley, I love bein' next to you like this."

Wiley hoped he wouldn't spunk too soon. With Jake's body rubbing against his own, he was close. "Jake, you're suppose to be relaxing. I don't want to hurt you when I slide my cock up your ass. If I make it that far."

"Hell, Wiley, I...."

The door to their room opened, then slammed.

Wiley tossed Jake to the side and tried reaching for his gun on the chair. He froze. A man had just entered their room with his drawn gun leveled at them.

"Thought you gents was like that," the man said as he walked toward the bed. "Saw you ride into town last week. Then you left. Now you're back." He stopped beside the bed.

Jake sat up and gasped. "You're the cowboy we seen in the street!"

"That's right. You both looked long at me."

"I wanted to see how you was naked. You gonna shoot us?"

The cowboy grabbed the blankets and ripped them away from Wiley's legs. As he scanned their bodies, his free hand grabbed his own dick, swelling in his pants. "I won't shoot unless you put up a fight about me joinin' you."

Wiley looked at the cowboy, then at Jake. He had no problems with the request, but wondered what Jake would do since he was always talking about Jesus.

"What do you think about that, Jake?" Wiley asked.

"Hell, Wiley. My dick started gettin' hard just lookin' at him standin' by that post." Jake saw the cowboy had gotten fully hard and his dick pushed against his Levis. "An' I still wanna see him naked." Jake spun to Wiley. "But only if you want to."

Wiley smiled at the cowboy. "Put that gun away. Let's see what you look like."

Stripping out of his clothes and tossing them on the floor, the cowboy said, "I'm Cal Estrada. I already know who you gents are."

Naked with a full erection, Cal lunged at Wiley's dick, shoved his mouth on it down to Wiley's balls and held it there.

Wiley groaned and fell back to the bed.

"Damn!" Jake yelled. "You got you a fine body an' a big dick!" Jake climbed off the bed, plopped to his knees, grabbed Cal and pulled him close. He slid his hand over the cowboy's balls, then turned and grinned at Wiley. "Damn! I ain't never done nothin' with *two* men before. This is gonna be *somethin'*!"

Wiley sighed. Cal was beyond description. The bulging muscles of his chest and arms, flexed from his bent-over position and covered with brown fuzz, drew him like a magnet. He ran his hands over Cal's arms, chest, neck, then leaned forward and sucked on his ear. Wiley groaned as the cowboy slid his mouth up to the head of his cock. He barely noticed Jake nearly devouring Cal.

Jake's body exploded into desire seeing the husky, naked cowboy. Now, he could do all the things he'd wanted to do when he'd first seen him. He grabbed Cal's legs and buried his face into his crotch, licked his balls and the shaft of his dick. Jake nearly spunked when he slid the cowboy's dick into his mouth. He grabbed Cal's balls and his butt, and shoved the cowboy's dick so far down his throat his nose flattened against Cal's body. Jake held Cal's dick there, feeling the man inside his mouth.

Sucking on Wiley's dick, Cal sighed with relief that his plan had worked. He knew of Wiley's reputation with his gun, but it paled compared to his body. He ran his hands over Wiley's chest. When he'd seen the two men for the first time as they rode by, he'd nearly spunked in his pants. Two huge men, both handsome, and both noticed him immediately. His dick had stayed semi-hard the rest of the day, and for the past week he'd jerked off whenever he'd thought of them.

Feeling Jake's mouth working his dick and Wiley's dick in his own mouth made Cal explode. He spunked as he drank Wiley's spurts. When Cal pushed himself closer and squirted down his throat, Jake touched his own hard dick and shot halfway across the room.

* * *

Crowded naked in the bed, with Cal in the middle, the three men dozed. When Cal awakened, he discovered Jake's hand holding his crotch and Wiley sliding his hand over his chest. He got an instant erection and they all went at it again. After several times that night and again in the morning, they'd shot quarts of spunk.

Lying in bed, exhausted, Wiley asked, "Who do you work for?"

Cal turned his head. "I own the C-Bar-P ranch south of town."

"I assume the 'C' stands for Cal. What does the 'P' stand for?"

"Pancho Sanchez. He's my partner and half-owner. He's from Mexico. I grew up in New Mexico and met him there. We've been partners for ten years and run two thousand head of cattle on twice that many acres."

"Were's Pancho, now?" Jake asked.

"Mindin' the ranch. We give each other time in town now an' again. He'll sure be sore when he finds out he didn't get to partake'a you two.

Jake couldn't help himself. "What's Pancho look like?"

"Bigger'n me. Hairy like Wiley. He's a mighty fine lookin' man. Sticks his dick up my ass and carries me 'round the room."

Wiley ran his hand over Cal's chest. "Your last name is Estrada? Forgive me, but you don't look or talk like a Mexican."

"Father's Mexican. Mother's English. She schooled me, but I can speak fluent Spanish. Pancho teases me 'bout my gringo accent an' Mother scolds me on how I talk."

"Do you have ranch hands?" Wiley asked. "What do they say about you and Pancho being together?"

Cal laughed. "Come and visit. We have fifteen men, hand picked from men Pancho and I bedded at one time or 'nother. Some're partners like us. Once a month, we have fiesta in the main house. Every hand's invited. First rule is, they have to come naked."

Jake sat up straight. "Damn! What happens?"

"You name it, it happens. Helps morale. The men love it. Haven't had anyone quit in five years." Cal shrugged. "Had to fire two men last year. They were partners, an' got jealous'a each other in another man's arms. Got into a fist fight. Can't have that. Only other rule is, it's share and share alike on that night. If they don't want to share, they don't come."

Jake grinned at Wiley. "Maybe we can visit there sometime."

Wiley laughed. "You're full of surprises. Here I thought you didn't want to share me with anyone."

"Hell, Wiley, one night foolin' around with other men sounds like fun! Besides, we ain't gonna build cabins with any of 'em."

Cal laughed. "How long you boys been partners?"

"We been partners an' blood brothers since last May."

"Blood Brothers?" Cal shook his head. "My men'll eat you two alive all night long."

"Can we go, Wiley?"

Wiley fell back to the pillow and laughed. When he raised up, he turned to Jake. "Why don't we wait until next summer. I'm sure Matt and Frank would want to come with us." He cut his eyes to Cal. "When are your fiestas?"

"First day of every month. Bring anybody you like. But like I said, anybody starts fightin' over who their partner's with, they're out."

* * *

Sitting by themselves in the half-empty rail car heading for Fairplay, Wiley slid his hand over Jake's leg. "I didn't know how you would react to Cal coming into our room and making love with us. I was surprised at your acceptance. I thought you would get angry."

"Hell, Wiley. Foolin' around with Cal was fun. An' it ain't cuz I don't love you."

"I understand. I felt the same way seeing Cal in the street." Wiley squinted out the train window at the snow covered mountains in the distance. What was it that made him and Jake, and other men like them, so attracted to other men, especially when they're naked? Why hadn't he ever felt that way about a woman? He'd never wanted to even see a woman naked.

"Wiley?"

"What?"

"Wiley, I'm glad Jesus an' his Pa made us like we are."

CHAPTER 30

The Silver Heels bar in Alma was quiet for a Tuesday night. A few miners stood at the bar and three groups sat at tables. Only one poker table in the next room was active with six men who had just begun a game.

Jake stared at the three poker-playing cards dealt to him. The first two lay face down and the third, face up. He grinned at Wiley, sitting next to him. "What do I do with 'em?"

Wiley glanced at the other men at the table. "Jake has never played seven card stud before. Let's go easy on him."

"Dang!" Bill shouted. "Everybody's played poker! Jake's just bluffin'."

Harry slugged Bill on the arm. "People in the East don't play that much poker."

Frank winked at Wiley. "Fine with Matt'n me to play that way. We'll get all your money anyway." He laughed and winked at Matt.

"I'll be glad to teach you, Jake," Matt offered.

"I'll bet you would," Wiley teased. "You'd teach him how to lose."

"Now, now," Harry said. "Let's not have rivalry." He smiled sweetly at Matt. "Even though Wiley's right."

Bill flagged Tubs, who nodded at him from behind the bar in the front room. "Whiskey!" Bill shouted at him.

All six men fell silent as they examined the cards they'd been dealt. Wiley quickly placed his hand on Jake's before he'd turned over his face-down cards.

"Jake, leave those cards the way they were dealt. No one but you is supposed to see them."

"I open for two bits," Matt announced. He slapped a quarter on the table.

"What?" Jake said.

Wiley leaned toward Jake. "He's starting the game."

"Oh!" Jake grinned, shoved his hand into his pocket and pulled out a handful of coins. He dumped them in a pile on the table. When his turn came to bet, he picked out a quarter and tossed it toward the center of the table. It rolled across the table and dropped into Frank's lap.

Frank grabbed for it, then tossed it on the pile. His turn came next, and he winked at Jake. "That quarter landed on my whanger, so I'll match your bet and raise you two bits." He plopped another coin on top of Jake's.

"Jake, did you look at your other two cards before you bet?" Wiley asked.

Jake shrugged and peeked at his two face-down cards. Two eights, with a nine showing. He didn't know what it meant, but an eight and a nine looked fine to him.

"Jake, are you going to stay in the game?" Matt asked. "Everyone has folded except Frank and me."

"Sure am."

"Well, you have to add another quarter to match Frank's bid. Or raise it."

Jake grinned. "I'll raise it." He added two more quarters.

"Jake, what are you doing?" Wiley asked.

"I'm playin' poker."

Jake was dealt a four, face up. The four seemed good, so he raised the bid a quarter and grinned at Wiley's horrified expression. Matt and Frank chuckled.

During the next hands, Jake was dealt a three, a five and the last card, face down. He peeked at it. Another three. Liking the two threes, he raised the bid a quarter, now only playing with Matt.

"Call," Matt said, matching Jake's raise.

"What?"

"Jake, you have to show all your cards," Wiley said testily.

Grinning, Jake turned over the remaining three cards.

Matt slapped down his cards and shouted, "You have two pair!"

"Two pears?" Jake looked at Wiley. "What's that mean?"

Harry laughed. "Keep playing like that, Jake, and you'll give Matt and Frank sore pockets."

As the next hand was dealt, Jake grinned at everyone. "We all been invited to Cal's feasta."

"It's fiesta, Jake," Wiley corrected.

"Who's Cal?" Bill asked as he peeked at his two face-down cards.

Wiley shrugged. "Cal is a rancher we met in Gunnison. He and his partner hold a fiesta for his hands on the first day of every month."

"Cal come in our room an' we all fooled around naked." Jake grinned at Wiley, who squinted at him.

Harry choked on his drink. "What room?"

"Our hotel room in Gunnison."

Wiley kicked Jake's foot.

Frank perked up. "You all fooled around?" He winked at Matt, then raised his eyebrows at Jake. "We'll go to this fiesta with you!"

"I'm danged surprised you two're still partners after doin' that!" Bill growled.

Glaring at him, Harry said, "Well, at least they do it with *someone.*"

"Wiley'n me didn't get riled at each other. Can't anyhow at the feasta, or Cal'll toss you out. Neither of us wanted to build a cabin with Cal'r nothin'. Both Wiley'n me wanted to see Cal naked when we seen him in the street. Never thought we'd be doin' it."

Frank leaned over the table. "What's he look like?"

"He's like Wiley'n me. I liked suckin' on his dick, an' he liked suckin' on Wil--"

"Jake, never mind!" Wiley snapped.

"Now, wait just a minute!" Harry shouted. "Wiley, you're not getting away with telling Jake to keep his mouth shut. We have a right to know!"

"What right?" Matt asked. "I'd never tell you what Frank and I do. It would be all over town in five minutes."

"I don't gossip!"

"The heck you don't," Frank said. "Next mornin', everybody in town knew Matt an' me took home Jesse Green. You an' Bill was the only ones seein' us. An' Bill don't hardly say nothin' to nobody."

Harry shifted in his chair. "Well, I only mentioned it to..."

Tubs bumped his egg-shaped body against the table. "Here's yer bottle, gents." He clunked the whiskey down and grinned. "I don't often listen to whatcher talkin' 'bout." He rested his hands on the slope of his stomach and raised an eyebrow at Harry. "But! Matt an' Frankie didn't get Jesse home b'fore it was bein' talked about in here." He jabbed a fat finger toward Harry. "I seen you talkin' to Miller from the Alma Hotel. That's the same as usin' a fog horn." Tubs chuckled and left the room.

"Miller!" Matt shouted to Harry. "No wonder everybody knew. Why did you tell Miller, of all people?"

Harry shrugged. "Miller and I are friends. I made him swear not to say anything to anyone else. He gave his word."

"He have a drink in his hand when you asked him that?" Frank asked.

"Of course."

"I'm s'prised he remembered the gossip."

* * *

Ten poker hands later, Matt shoved back his chair and pushed himself to his feet. "Jake, I will *never* play poker with you again! You've won every hand! When I thought you were bluffing, you beat me fair and square! And when I thought you had good hands, you were bluffing!" He stormed out of the room. A few moments later the batwing doors rattled shut.

Shocked, Jake asked, "Hell, why'd I make Matt so riled? I didn't do nothin'."

Frank laughed. "Matt'n me think we're the best poker players in Alma. You skunked us."

Harry leaned back in his chair. "The best part is, Jake, I don't think you knew you were doing it." He laughed and pounded the table.

Roughly counting Jake's winnings, Wiley said, "Jake, I think you won over twenty dollars."

* * *

"What're you gonna be teachin' me readin' from?"

"Maud's Reader." Rising Moon held the book in front of Jake's face. "I used it at the Indian School."

"Is it a baby book?"

"No. A beginners reading book. I used it for people older than you."

"Older'n me?" Jake leaned forward in his chair. "Older'n me people can't read, neither?"

"Many people can't read. Others can, but don't."

"Hell! I thought it was just Donny'n me that couldn't read nothin'."

* * *

Six weeks later, snug in their cabin as rain pounded the roof, Wiley sat at the table reading by the oil lamp. A thumping noise in the room distracted him, and he looked at Jake, slumped over in the corner by the door with his back to him.

"Jake, are you all right?"

Still messing with his saddle bags, Jake froze, then jerked his head to the side and crouched over even more so Wiley couldn't see what he was doing.

"I'm fine, Wiley."

Wiley shrugged, watched Jake for a moment, and went back to his book.

So engrossed, Wiley didn't notice when Jake shoved a chair close and plopped into it. Jake watched Wiley read silently for a few minutes, then asked, "Wiley, how can you read when you don't say it?"

Wiley looked at him. "Say what?"

"Say what you're readin'."

Wiley saw the book in Jake's hand and his face brightened. "Are you going to read to me?"

Jake blushed. "Only if you want."

"After a month and a half of lessons with Rising Moon and you not wanting to talk about it, of course, I want to hear you read!"

Beaming, Jake opened the book where he'd stuck his finger to keep his place.

Wiley knew the book. He'd bought it for Jake's birthday present, but asked, "What book is that?"

"Grime's Fairy Tales."

"It's *Grimm's* Fairy Tales. They were brothers. Their names were Jakob and Wilhelm. Jake is a shortened form of Jakob."

Jake's eyes got big and he looked at the book. "Damn, maybe we're kin!"

Closing his own book and shoving it aside, Wiley smiled. "Maybe, eons ago. They were German. You're Irish." He pointed at Jake's book. "What are you going to read?"

Jake looked down at the title page of the tale and read, "The Boating Wolf. I picked that cuz we went on the riverboat."

Reading upside down, Wiley clenched his jaws and calmed himself. "It's Boasting Wolf, Jake."

Jake stared at the title. "Bh...o...ay...sss...." He shrugged. "You're right, Wiley." He raised his head and squinted. "I wondered why he never got on no damn boat. An' he got hisself stabbed an' shot by a hunter."

Wiley smiled. "Yes, he did. Because he was boasting that he could capture a man." He grabbed Jake's hand and squeezed. "Will you read to me?"

Jake's face blossomed into a radiant smile that nearly made Wiley's eyes tear. "I'm gonna be readin' the book you gived me for my birthday!"

With full attention on the words, Jake read slowly, "'A fox was one day...uh, spe...speaking to a wolf of...of the great stench of human beings, uh, 'specially men. No animal can stand...'"

"Jake." Wiley smiled apologetically. "Stench is not the right word. The word is strength."

Jake snickered. "Hell, Rising Moon was teachin' me words that mean stink, an' them two words kinda look like each other."

Wiley sniffed himself. "Sometimes they even mean the same thing." He grinned at Jake's puzzled look. "Please, Jake. Read some more. I'm sorry I corrected you. I'm impressed at how well you're doing."

"Hell, Wiley. Rising Moon said it's good you're correctin' me. She said older'n me people can't read, neither, an' they need correctin', too."

So thankful Jake didn't pout and call himself "dummer'n hog shit," Wiley swore he'd give Rising Moon a kiss the next time he'd see her. But only on the cheek.

Jake read even more slowly, pronouncing every long word, sometimes several times. He read, "Then a little child passed who was goin' to school. 'Is that a man?' asked the wolf. 'No, not yet,' said the fox. But he will be one by-and-by.'"

Jake stopped reading and looked at Wiley. "That makes me think'a Rodney. I hope he's okay. He was only a boy, but he weren't goin' to no school."

"He'll make out just fine. He's more cunning than either of us." Wiley slid his hand over Jake's arm and held it. "That's one of the wonders of reading. You can live another lifetime with each book. You can be reminded of people you know and learn about people you don't know." He squeezed Jake's arm. "Let's take turns reading this book out loud."

* * *

Snuggled together in the featherbed in the dancing firelight, Jake snickered.

"What's funny?"

Jake snickered again. "Wiley, you said we gotta each read outta that Grimes' book."

"Yes. But what's funny about that?"

"I'm only gonna know what's happenin' when you read. I'm gonna be messin' with words when I read."

Wiley snuggled closer. "That will only happen for a short time. You'll soon master the words. After that, you'll begin to understand what the books are saying. I'm sure when you reach that point, you'll become an avid reader. Knowing your inquisitive mind, you'll..."

"Wiley?"

"What?"

"Wiley, bein' so close to you made my dick hard."

Book Five does not yet exist, but I'm hearing whispers. A chrome toaster keeps popping up, and it'll be interesting to find out what that's about. I'll keep you posted of the book's progress on the web site: goldenfeatherpress.com.

Dave Brown

Also look for:

Dave Brown's first, second and third books of the

LEGEND OF THE GOLDEN FEATHER SERIES

BRISTLECONE PEAK

THE PROTECTORS

and

HOME TO KENTUCKY

DAVE BROWN